GONE

JONATHAN KELLERMAN

GONE

AN ALEX DELAWARE NOVEL

DOUBLEDAY LARGE PRINT HOME LIBRARY EDITION

Ballantine Books
New York

This Large Print Edition, prepared especially for Doubleday Large Print Home Library, contains the complete, unabridged text of the original Publisher's Edition.

Gone is a work of fiction. Names, characters, places, and incidents are the products of the author's imagination or are used fictitiously. Any resemblance to actual events, locales, or persons, living or dead, is entirely coincidental.

Copyright © 2006 by Jonathan Kellerman

All rights reserved.

Published in the United States by Ballantine Books, an imprint of The Random House Publishing Group, a division of Random House, Inc., New York.

ISBN-13: 978-0-7394-6673-5
ISBN-10: 0-7394-6673-9

BALLANTINE and colophon are registered trademarks of Random House, Inc.

Printed in the United States of America

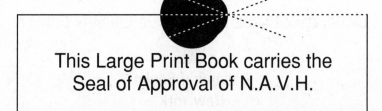

This Large Print Book carries the
Seal of Approval of N.A.V.H.

This one's for Linda Marrow.

Special thanks to Captain David Campbell (Ret.)
Los Angeles Coroner's Office

GONE

CHAPTER

1

She nearly killed an innocent man.

Creighton "Charley" Bondurant drove carefully because his life depended on it. Latigo Canyon was mile after mile of neck-wrenching, hairpin twists. Charley had no use for government meddlers but the 15 mph signs posted along the road were smart.

He lived ten miles up from Kanan Dume Road, on a four-acre remnant of the ranch his grandfather had owned during Coolidge's time. All those Arabians and Tennessee walkers and the mules Grandpa kept around because he liked the creatures' spirit. Charley had grown up with families like his. No-non-sense ranchers, a few rich folk who were still okay when they came up to ride on week-ends. Now all you had were rich pretenders.

Diabetic and rheumatoid and depressed, Charley lived in a two-room cabin with a view of oak-covered crests and the ocean beyond. Sixty-eight, never married. Poor excuse for a man, he'd scold himself on nights when the medicines mixed with the beer and his mood sank low.

On happier days, he pretended to be an old cowboy.

This morning, he was somewhere be-tween those extremes. His bunions hurt like hell. Two horses had died last winter and he was down to three skinny white mares and a half-blind sheepdog. Feed and hay bills ate up most of his Social Security. But the nights had been warm for October, and he hadn't dreamed bad and his bones felt okay.

It was hay that got him up at seven that morning, rolling out of bed, gulping coffee, chewing on a stale sweet roll, to hell with his blood sugar. A little time-out to get the inter-nal plumbing going and by eight he was dressed and starting up the pickup.

Coasting in neutral down the dirt road

that fed to Latigo, he looked both ways a couple of times, cleared the crust from his eyes, shifted into first, and rolled down. The Topanga Feed Bin was a twenty-minute ride south and he figured to stop along the way at the Malibu Stop & Shop for a few six-packs, a tin of Skoal, and some Pringles.

Nice morning, a big old blue sky with just a few clouds from the east, sweet air blowing up from the Pacific. Switching on his eight-track, he listened to Ray Price and drove slow enough to stop for deer. Not too many of the pests before dark but you never knew what to expect up in the mountains.

The naked girl jumped out at him a lot faster than any deer.

Eyes full of terror, mouth stretched so wide Charley swore he could see her tonsils.

She ran across the road, straight in the path of his truck, hair blowing wild, waving her arms.

Stomping the brake pedal hard, Charley felt the pickup lurch, wobble, and sway. Then the sharp skid to the left, straight at the battered guardrail that separated him from a thousand foot of nothing.

Hurtling toward blue sky.

He kept hitting the brake. Kept flying. Said his prayers and opened the door and prepared to bail.

His damn shirt stuck on the door handle. Eternity looked real close. What a stupid way to go!

Hands ripping at his shirt fabric, mouth working in a combination of curses and benedictions, Charley's gnarled body tightened, his legs turned to iron bars, and his sore foot pressed that brake pedal down to the damn floorboard.

The truck kept going, fishtailed, slid, spattered gravel.

Shuddered. Rolled. Bumped the guard.

Charley could hear the rail groan.

The truck stopped.

Charley freed his shirt and got out. His chest was tight and he couldn't suck any breath into his lungs. Wouldn't that be the shits: spared a free fall to oblivion only to drop dead of a damned heart attack.

He gasped and swallowed air, felt his field of vision grow black and braced himself against the truck. The chassis creaked and Charley jumped back, felt himself going down again.

A scream pierced the morning. Charley

opened his eyes and straightened and saw the girl. Red marks around her wrists and ankles. Bruises around her neck.

Beautiful young body, those healthy knockers bobbing as she came running toward him—sinful to think like that, she was scared, but with knockers like that what else was there to notice?

She kept coming, arms wide, like she wanted Charley to hold her.

But screaming, those wild eyes, he wasn't sure what to do.

First time in a long time he'd been this close to bare female flesh.

He forgot about the knockers, nothing sexy about this. She was a kid, young enough to be his daughter. Granddaughter.

Those marks on her wrists and ankles, around her neck.

She screamed again.

"Ohgodohgoohgod."

She was right up to him, now, yellow hair whipping his face. He could smell the fear on her. See the goose bumps on her pretty tan shoulders.

"Help me!"

Poor kid was shivering.

Charley held her.

CHAPTER

2

L.A.'s where you end up when you have nowhere else to go.

A long time ago I'd driven west from Missouri, a sixteen-year-old high school graduate armed with a head full of desperation and a partial academic scholarship to the U.

Only son of a moody, hard drinker and a chronic depressive. Nothing to keep me in the flatlands.

Living like a pauper on work-study and occasional guitar gigs in wedding bands, I managed to get educated. Made some money as a psychologist, and a lot more from lucky investments. Got The House In The Hills.

Relationships were another story, but that would've been true no matter where I lived.

Back when I treated children, I routinely took histories from parents and learned what family life could be like in L.A. People packing up and moving every year or two, the surrender to impulse, the death of domestic ritual.

Many of the patients I saw lived in sun-baked tracts with no other kids nearby and spent hours each day being bused to and from beige corrals that claimed to be schools. Long, electronic nights were bleached by cathode and thump-thumped by the current angry music. Bedroom windows looked out to hazy miles of neighborhoods that couldn't really be called that.

Lots of imaginary friends in L.A. That, I supposed, was inevitable. It's a company town and the product is fantasy.

The city kills grass with red carpets, worships fame for its own sake, demolishes landmarks with glee because the high-stakes game is *reinvention.* Show up at your favorite restaurant and you're likely to find a sign trumpeting failure and the windows covered with brown paper. Phone a friend and get a disconnected number.

No Forwarding. It could be the municipal motto.

You can be gone in L.A. for a long time before anyone considers it a problem.

When Michaela Brand and Dylan Meserve went missing, no one seemed to notice.

Michaela's mother was a former truck-stop cashier living with an oxygen tank in Phoenix. Her father was unknown, probably one of the teamsters Maureen Brand had entertained over the years. Michaela had left Arizona to get away from the smothering heat, gray shrubs, air that never moved, no one caring about The Dream.

She rarely called her mother. The hiss of Maureen's tank, Maureen's sagging body, ragged cough, and emphysemic eyes drove her nuts. No room for any of that in Michaela's L.A. head.

Dylan Meserve's mother was long dead from an undiagnosed degenerative neuro-muscular disease. His father was a Brook-lyn-based alto sax player who'd never wanted a rug rat in the first place and had died of an overdose five years ago.

Michaela and Dylan were gorgeous and

young and thin and had come to L.A. for the obvious reason.

By day, he sold shoes at a Foot Locker in Brentwood. She was a lunch waitress at a pseudo-trattoria on the east end of Beverly Hills.

They'd met at the PlayHouse, taking an Inner Drama seminar from Nora Dowd.

The last time anyone had seen them was on a Monday night, just after ten p.m., leaving the acting workshop together. They'd worked their butts off on a scene from *Simpatico.* Neither really got what Sam Shepard was aiming for but the play had plenty of juicy parts, all that screaming. Nora Dowd had urged them to *inject* themselves in the scene, *smell* the horseshit, open themselves up to the pain and the hopelessness.

Both of them felt they'd delivered. Dylan's Vinnie had been perfectly wild and crazy and dangerous, and Michaela's Rosie was a classy woman of mystery.

Nora Dowd had seemed okay with the performance, especially Dylan's contribution.

That frosted Michaela a bit but she wasn't surprised.

Watching Nora go off on one of those

speeches about right brain–left brain. Talking more to herself than to anyone else.

The PlayHouse's front room was set up like a theater, with a stage and folding chairs. The only time it got used was for seminars.

Lots of seminars, no shortage of students. One of Nora's alumni, a former exotic dancer named April Lange, had scored a role on a sitcom on the WB. An autographed picture of April used to hang in the entry before someone took it down. Blond, shiny-eyed, vaguely predatory. Michaela used to think: Why her?

Then again, maybe it was a good sign. If it could happen to April, it could happen to anyone.

Dylan and Michaela lived in single-room studio apartments, his on Overland, in Culver City, hers on Holt Avenue, south of Pico. Both their cribs were tiny, dark, ground-floor units, pretty much dumps. This was L.A., where rent could crush you and day jobs barely covered the basics and it was hard, sometimes, not to get depressed.

After they didn't show up at work for two days running, their respective employers fired them.

And that was the extent of it.

CHAPTER

3

I heard about it the way most everyone else did: third story on the evening news, right after the trial of a hip-hop star accused of assault and floods in Indonesia.

I was eating a solitary dinner and half listening to the broadcast. This one caught my attention because I gravitate toward local crime stories.

Couple abducted at gunpoint, found naked and dehydrated in the hills of Malibu. I played with the remote but no other broadcast added details.

The following morning, the *Times* filled in a bit more: a pair of acting students had left a nighttime class in West L.A. and driven east in her car to the young woman's apartment in the Pico-Robertson district. Waiting at a red light at Sherbourne and Pico, they'd been carjacked by a masked gunman who stashed them both in the trunk and drove for more than an hour.

When the car stopped and the trunk popped, the couple found themselves in pitch darkness, somewhere "out in the country." The spot was later identified as "Latigo Canyon, in the hills of Malibu."

The carjacker forced them to stumble down a steep hillside to a densely wooded area, where the young woman tied up the young man at gunpoint and was subsequently bound herself. Sexual assault was implied but not specified. The assailant was described as "white, medium height, and stocky, thirty to forty, with a Southern accent."

Malibu was county territory, sheriff's jurisdiction. The crime had taken place fifty miles from LASD headquarters, but violent whodunits were handled by major crimes detectives and anyone with information was requested to phone downtown.

A few years back, when Robin and I were

rebuilding the house in the hills, we'd rented a place on the beach in western Malibu. The two of us had explored the sinuous canyons and silent gullies on the land side of Pacific Coast Highway, hiked the oak-bearded crests that peaked above the ocean.

I remembered Latigo Canyon as cork-screw roads and snakes and red-tailed hawks. Though it took a while to get above civilization, the reward was worth the effort: a wonderful, warm nothingness.

If I'd been curious enough, I could've called Milo, maybe learned more about the abduction. I was busy with three custody cases, two of them involving film-biz parents, the third starring a pair of frighteningly ambitious Brentwood plastic surgeons whose marriage had shattered when their infomercial for Facelift-in-a-Jar tanked. Somehow they'd found time to produce an eight-year-old daughter, whom they now seemed intent on destroying emotionally.

Quiet, chubby girl, big eyes, a slight stammer. Recently, she'd taken to long bouts of silence.

Custody evaluations are the ugliest side of child psychology and from time to time I think about quitting. I've never sat down and calculated my success rate but the ones that work out keep me going, like a slot machine's intermittent payoff.

I put the newspaper aside, happy the case was someone else's problem. But as I showered and dressed, I kept imagining the crime scene. Glorious golden hills, the ocean a stunning blue infinity.

It's gotten to a point where it's hard for me to see beauty without thinking of the alternative.

My guess was this case would be a tough one; the main hope for a solve was the bad guy screwing up and leaving behind some forensic tidbit: a unique tire tread, rare fiber, or biological remnant. A lot less likely than you'd think from watching TV. The most common print found at crime scenes is the palm, and police agencies have only started cataloging palm prints. DNA can work miracles but backlogs are ferocious and the data banks are less than comprehensive.

On top of that, criminals are wising up and using condoms, and this criminal sounded like a careful planner.

Cops watch the same shows everyone else does and sometimes they learn something. But Milo and other people in his position have a saying: *Forensics never solves crimes, detectives do.*

Milo would be happy this one wasn't his.

Then it was.

When the abduction became something else, the media started using names.

Michaela Brand, 23. Dylan Meserve, 24.

Mug shots do nothing for your looks but even with numbers around their necks and that trapped-animal brightness in their eyes, these two were soap-opera fodder.

They'd produced a reality show episode that backfired.

The scheme unraveled when a clerk at Krentz Hardware in West Hollywood read the abduction story in the *Times* and re-called a young couple paying cash for a coil of yellow nylon rope three days before the alleged carjacking.

A store video confirmed the I.D. and analysis of the rope revealed a perfect match to bindings found at the scene and to ligature marks around Michaela and Dylan's limbs and necks.

Sheriff's investigators followed the trail and located a Wilderness Outfitters in Santa

Monica where the couple had purchased a flashlight, bottled water, dehydrated food packets designed for hikers. A 7-Eleven near Century City verified that Michaela Brand's nearly depleted debit card had been used to buy a dozen Snickers bars, two packets of beef jerky, and a six-pack of Miller Lite less than an hour before the reported time of the abduction. Wrappers and empty cans found a half mile up the ridge from where the couple had staged their confinement filled in the picture.

The final blow was the report of an emergency room physician at Saint John's Hospital: Meserve and Brand claimed to have gone without food for two days but their electrolyte tests were normal. Furthermore, neither victim exhibited signs of serious injury other than rope burn and some "mild" bruising of Michaela's vagina that could've been consistent with "self-infliction."

Faced with the evidence, the couple broke down, admitted the hoax, and were charged with obstructing officers and filing a false police report. Both pleaded poverty, and public defenders were assigned.

Michaela's D.P.D. was a man named Lauritz Montez. He and I had met nearly a decade ago on a particularly repellent case: the murder of a two-year-old girl by two preadolescent boys, one of whom had been Montez's client. The ugliness had resurfaced last year when one of the killers, now a young man, had phoned me out within days of his release from prison and turned up dead hours later.

Lauritz Montez hadn't liked me to begin with and my digging up the past had made matters worse. So I was puzzled when he called and asked me to evaluate Michaela Brand.

"Why would I kid, Doctor?"

"We didn't exactly hit it off."

"I'm not inviting you to hang out," he said. "You're a smart shrink and I want her to have a solid report behind her."

"She's charged with misdemeanors," I said.

"Yeah, but the sheriff's pissed and is pushing the D.A. to go for jail time. We're talking a mixed-up kid who did something stupid. She feels bad enough."

"You want me to say she was mentally incapacitated."

Montez laughed. "Temporary raving-lunacy-insanity would be great but I know you're all pissy-anty about small details like facts. So just tell it like it was: She was addled, caught in a weak moment, swept along. I'm sure there's some technical term for it."

"The truth," I said.

He laughed again. "Will you do it?"

The plastic surgeons' little girl had started talking, but both parents' lawyers had phoned this morning and informed me the case had been resolved and my services were no longer necessary.

"Sure," I said.

"Seriously?" said Montez.

"Why not?"

"It didn't go that smoothly on Duchay."

"How could it?"

"True. Okay, I'll have her call and make an appointment. Do my best to get you some kind of reimbursement. Within reason."

"Reason's always good."

"And so rare."

CHAPTER
4

Michaela Brand came to see me four days later.

I work out of my house above Beverly Glen. In mid-November the whole city's pretty, nowhere more so than the Glen.

She smiled and said, "Hi, Dr. Delaware. Wow, what a great place, my name's pronounced Mick-*aah*-la."

The smile was heavy firepower in the battle to be noticed. I walked her through high, white, hollow space to my office at the back.

Tall and narrow-hipped and busty, she put a lot of roll-and-sway into her walk. If her breasts weren't real, their free move-ment was an ad for a great scalpel artist. Her face was oval and smooth, blessed by wide-set aquamarine eyes that could feign spontaneous fascination without much ef-fort, balanced perfectly on a long, smooth stalk of a neck.

Faint bruising along the sides of the neck were masked by body makeup. The rest of her skin was bronze velvet stretched across fine bones. Tanning bed or one of those spray jobs that last for a week. Tiny, mocha freckles sprinkled across her nose hinted at her natural complexion. Wide lips were en-larged by gloss. A mass of honey-colored hair trailed past her shoulder blades. Some stylist had taken a long time to texturize the 'do and make it look careless. Half a dozen shades of blond aped nature.

Her black, stovepipe jeans hung nearly low enough to require a pubic wax. Her hip bones were smooth little knobs calling out for a tango partner. A black jersey, cap-sleeved T-shirt rhinestoned *Porn Star* ended an inch above a wry smile of navel. The same flawless golden dermis sheathed a drum-tight abdomen. Her nails were long and French-tipped, her false lashes perfect.

Plucked brows added to the illusion of permanent surprise.

Lots of time and money spent to augment lucky chromosomes. She'd convinced the court system she was poor. Turned out she was, the debit card finished, two hundred bucks left in her checking account.

"I got my landlord to extend me a month," she said, "but unless I clear this up soon and get another job, I'm going to get evicted."

Tears welled in the blue-green eyes. Clouds of hair tossed and fluffed and resettled. Despite her long legs, she'd managed to curl up in the big leather patient's chair and look small.

"What does clearing it up mean to you?" I said.

"Pardon?"

"Clearing it up."

"You know," she said. "I need to get rid of . . . this, this mess."

I nodded and she cocked her head like a puppy. "Lauritz said you were the best."

First-name basis with her lawyer. I wondered if Montez had been motivated by more than professional responsibility.

Stop, suspicious fellow. Focus on the patient.

This patient was leaning forward and smiling shyly, loose breasts cupping black jersey. I said, "What did Mr. Montez tell you about this evaluation?"

"That I should open myself up emotionally." She poked at a corner of one eye. Dropped her hand and ran her finger along a black-denim knee.

"Open yourself up how?"

"You know, not hold back from you, just basically be myself. I'm . . ."

I waited.

She said, "I'm glad it's you. You seem kind." She curled one leg under the other.

I said, "Tell me how it happened, Michaela."

"How what happened?"

"The phony abduction."

She flinched. "You don't want to know about my childhood or anything?"

"We may get into that later, but it's best to start with the hoax itself. I'd like to hear what happened in your words."

"My words. Boy." Half smile. "No foreplay, huh?"

I smiled back. She unfolded her legs and

a pair of high-heeled black Skechers alit on the carpet. She flexed one foot. Looked around the office. "I know I did wrong but I'm a good girl, Doctor. I *really* am."

She crossed her arms over the *Porn Star* logo. "Where to start . . . I have to tell you, I feel so exposed."

I pictured her rushing onto the road, naked, nearly causing an old man to drive his truck off a cliff. "I know it's tough to think about what you did, Michaela, but it could be really helpful to get used to talking about it."

"So you can understand me?"

"That," I said, "but also at some point you might be required to allocate."

"What's that?"

"To tell the judge what you did."

"Confession," she said. "It's a fancy word for confession?"

"I guess it is."

"All these words they use." She laughed softly. "At least I'm learning stuff."

"Probably not the way you wanted to."

"That's for sure . . . lawyers, cops. I don't even remember who I told what."

"It's pretty confusing," I said.

"Totally, Doctor. I have a thing for that."

"For what?"

"Confusion. Back in Phoenix—in high school—some people used to think I was an airhead. The brainiacs, you know? Truth is, I got confused a lot. Still do. Maybe it's because I fell on my head when I was a little kid. Fell off a swing and passed out. After that I never really did too good in school."

"Sounds like a bad fall."

"I don't remember much about it, Doctor, but they told me I was unconscious for half a day."

"How old were you?"

"Maybe three. Four. I was swinging high, used to love to swing. Must've let go or something and went flying. I hit my head other times, too. I was always falling, tripping over myself. My legs grew so fast, when I was fifteen I went from five feet to five eight in six months."

"You're accident-prone."

"My mom used to say I was an accident waiting to happen. I'd get her to buy me good jeans, and then I'd rip the knees and she'd get upset and promise never to buy me anything anymore."

She touched her left temple. Caught

some hair between her fingers and twisted. Pouted. That reminded me of someone. I watched her fidget and it finally came to me: young Brigitte Bardot.

Would she know who that was?

She said, "My head's been spinning. Since the mess. It's like someone else's screenplay and I'm drifting through the scenes."

"The legal system can be overwhelming."

"I never thought I'd be *in* the system! I mean, I don't even watch crime stuff on TV. My mom reads mysteries but I hate them."

"What do you read?"

She'd turned aside, didn't answer. I repeated the question.

"Oh, sorry, I spaced out. What do I read . . . *Us* magazine. *People, Elle,* you know."

"How about we talk about what happened?"

"Sure, sure . . . it was just supposed to be . . . maybe Dylan and I took it too far but my acting teacher, her big thing is that the whole point of the training is to lose yourself and enter the scene, you really need to abandon the self, you know, the ego. Just give yourself up to the scene and flow."

"That's what you and Dylan were doing," I said.

"I guess I started out *thinking* we were doing that and I guess . . . I really don't know what happened. It's so crazy, how did I get into this *craziness*?"

She slammed a fist into an open hand, shuddered, threw up her arms. Began crying softly. A vein throbbed in her neck, pumping through cover-up, accentuating a bruise.

I handed her a tissue. Her fingers lingered on my knuckles. She sniffled. "Thanks."

I sat back down. "So you thought you were doing what Nora Dowd taught you."

"You know Nora?"

"I've read the court documents."

"Nora's in the documents?"

"She's mentioned. So you're saying the false abduction was related to your training."

"You keep calling it false," she said.

"What would you like me to call it?"

"I don't know . . . something else. The exercise. How about that? That's really what it started out as."

"An acting exercise."

"Uh-huh." She crossed her legs. "Nora

never came out and told us to do an exercise but we thought—she was always pushing us to get into the core of our feelings.
Dylan and I figured we'd . . ." She bit her lip.
"It was never supposed to go that far."

She touched her temple again. "I must've
been whack. Dylan and I were just trying to
be artistically authentic. Like when I tied him
up and wrapped the rope around myself, I
held it around my neck for a while to make
sure it would leave marks." She frowned,
touched a bruise.

"I see it."

"I knew it wouldn't take long. To make a
bruise. I bruise real easily. Maybe that's why
I don't do pain very well."

"What do you mean?"

"I'm a crybaby about pain so I stay away
from it." She touched a spot where the
scoop neck of the T-shirt met skin. "Dylan
feels nothing, I mean, he's like stone. When
I tied him up, he kept saying tighter, he
wanted to *feel* it."

"Pain?"

"Oh, yeah," she said. "Not his neck at
first, just his legs and arms. But even that
hurts when you go tight enough, right? But
he kept telling me tighter, tighter. Finally I

screamed at him, I'm doing it as tight as I can." She gazed up at the ceiling. "He just laid there. Then he smiled and said maybe you should do my neck the same way."

"Dylan has a death wish?"

"Dylan's a freak . . . it was freaky up there, dark, cold, this emptiness in the air. You could hear things crawling around." She hugged herself. "I said this is too weird, maybe it wasn't a good idea."

"What did Dylan say?"

"He just laid there with his head to the side." She closed her eyes and demonstrated. Let her mouth grow slack and showed a half inch of pointed, pink tongue. "Pretending to be dead, you know? I said, 'Cut it out, that's gross,' but he refused to talk or move and finally it got to me. I rolled over to him and touched his head and he just flopped, you know?"

"Method acting," I said.

Puzzled stare.

"It's when you live a role completely, Michaela."

Her eyes were somewhere else. "Whatever . . ."

"How soon into the exercise did you tie him up?"

"Second night, it was all the second night. He was okay before that, then he started punking me. I was letting him because I was scared. The whole thing . . . I was so, so stupid."

She folded wings of golden hair forward, masking her face. I thought of a show spaniel in the ring. Handlers manipulating the ears over the nose to offer the judge a choice view of the skull.

"Dylan scared you."

"He didn't move for a *long* time," she said.

"Were you worried you'd tied him too tight?"

She released the hair but kept her gaze low. "Honestly, I can't tell you, even now what his motivation was. Maybe he really *was* unconscious, maybe he was punking me a hundred percent. He's . . . it was really his idea, Doctor. I promise."

"Dylan thought the whole thing up?"

"Everything. Like getting rope and where to go."

"How'd he pick Latigo Canyon?"

"He said he hiked there, he likes to hike by himself, it helps him get in character."

The tongue tip glided across her lower lip, left behind a snail-trail of moisture.

"He also says one day he's going to have a place there."

"Latigo Canyon?"

"Malibu, but on the beach, like the Colony. He's crazy intense."

"About his career?"

"There are some people who put everything into a scene, you know? But later they know when to stop? Dylan can be cool when he's just being himself, but he's got these *ambitions.* Cover of *People,* take the place of Johnny Depp."

"What are your ambitions, Michaela?"

"Me? I just want to work. TV, big screen, episodic, commercials, whatever."

"Dylan wouldn't be happy with that."

"Dylan wants to be number one on the Sexiest Man List."

"Have you talked to him since the exercise?"

"No."

"Whose decision was that?"

"Lauritz told me to stay away."

"Were you and Dylan pretty close before?"

"I guess. Dylan said we had natural

chemistry. That's probably why I got . . . swept along. The whole thing was his idea but he freaked me out up there. I'm talking to him and shaking him and he looks really . . . you know."

"Dead."

"Not that I've ever seen anyone really dead but when I was young I liked to watch splatter flicks. Not now, though. I get grossed out easily."

"What'd you do when you thought Dylan looked dead?"

"I went crazy and started untying the neck rope, and he still wasn't moving and he held his mouth open and was looking really . . ." She shook her head. "The atmosphere up there, I was getting freaked *out*. I started slapping his face and yelling at him to stop it. His head just kept flopping back and forth. Like one of those loosening exercises Nora has us do before a big scene."

"Scary," I said.

"Scary-terrifying. I'm dyslexic, not intense dyslexic, like illiterate or illegible, I can read okay. But it takes me a long time to memorize words. I can't sound anything out. I mean, I can memorize my lines but I really work hard."

"Being dyslexic made it scarier to see Dylan like that?"

"Because my head felt all scrambled up and I couldn't think straight. And then being scared blurred it. Like my thoughts weren't making sense—like being in another language, you know?"

"Disoriented."

"I mean, look what I did," she said. "Untied myself and climbed up that hill and ran out to the road without even putting my clothes on. I had to be disoriented. If I was thinking normal, would I do that? Then, after that old guy, the one on the road who . . ." Her frown made it as far as the left side of her mouth before retracting.

"The old man who . . ."

"I was going to say the old guy saved me but I wasn't in real danger. Still, I *was* pretty terrified. Because I still didn't know if Dylan was okay. By the time the old guy called the rescue squad and they got there, Dylan was out of the ropes and standing there. When no one was looking, he gave a little smile. Like ha-ha, good joke."

"You feel Dylan manipulated you."

"That's the saddest thing. Losing trust. The whole thing was supposed to *be* about trust. Nora's always teaching us about the artist's life as constant danger. You're always working without a net. Dylan was my partner and I trusted him. That's why I went along with it in the first place."

"Did it take him a while to talk you into it?"

She frowned. "He made it like an adventure. Buying all that stuff. He made me feel like a kid having fun."

"Planning was fun," I said.

"Exactly."

"Buying the rope and the food."

"Uh-huh."

"Careful plan."

Her shoulders tightened. "What do you mean?"

"You guys paid cash and used several different stores in different neighborhoods."

"That was all Dylan," she said.

"Did he explain why he'd planned it that way?"

"We really didn't talk about it. It was like . . . we did so many exercises before, this was just another one. I felt I had to use my right side. Of my brain. Nora taught us to concentrate on using the right side of the brain, just kind of slip into right-brain stuff."

"The creative side," I said.

"Exactly. Don't think too much, just throw yourself in."

"Nora keeps coming up."

Silence.

"How do you think she feels about what happened, Michaela?"

"I know how she feels. She's pissed. After the police took me in, I called her. She said getting caught was amateurish and stupid, don't come back. Then she hung up."

"Getting caught," I said. "She wasn't angry at the scheme itself?"

"That's what she told me. It was stupid to get caught." Her eyes moistened.

"Hearing that from her must've been tough," I said.

"She's in a power role vis-à-vis me."

"You try talking to her again?"

"She won't return my calls. So now I can't go to the PlayHouse. Not that it matters. I guess."

"Time to move on?"

Tears ran down her face. "I can't afford to study, 'cause I'm broke. Gonna have to put my name in with one of those agencies. Be a personal assistant or a nanny. Or flip burgers or something."

"Those are your only choices?"

"Who's gonna hire me for a good job when I need to go out on auditions? And also until *this* is over."

I handed her another tissue.

"I sure wasn't out to hurt anyone, believe me, Doctor. I know I should've thought more and felt less, but Dylan . . ." She drew up her legs again. Negligible body fat allowed her to fold like paper. With that lack of insulation, two nights up in the hills must've chilled her. Even if she was lying about her fear, the experience hadn't been pleasant: The final police report had cited fresh human excrement under a nearby tree, leaves and candy wrappers used for toilet paper.

"Now," she said, "everyone will think I'm a dumb blonde."

"Some people say there's no such thing as bad publicity."

"They do?" she said. "You think so?"

"I think people can turn themselves around."

She fixed her eyes on mine. "I was stupid and I'm so, so sorry."

I said, "Whatever you guys intended, it ended up being a rough couple of nights."

"What do you mean?"

"Being out there in the cold. No bathroom."

"That was *gross,*" she said. "It was *freezing* and I felt like creepy-crawlies were all over me, just eating me up. Afterward my arms and legs and my neck *hurt.* Because I tied myself too tight." She grimaced. "I wanted to be authentic. To show Dylan."

"Show him what?"

"That I was a serious actor."

"Were you out to please anyone else, Michaela?"

"What do you mean?"

"You had to figure the story would get exposure. Did you consider how other people would react?"

"Like who?"

"Let's start with Nora."

"I honestly felt she'd respect us. For having integrity. Instead she's pissed."

"What about your mother?"

She waved that off.

"You didn't think about your mother?"

"I don't talk to her. She's not in my life."

"Does she know about what happened?"

"She doesn't read the papers but I guess if it's in the *Phoenix Sun* and somebody shows it to her."

"You haven't called her?"

"She can't do anything to help me." She mumbled.

"Why's that, Michaela?"

"She's sick. Lung disease. My whole childhood she was sick with something. Even when I fell on my head it was a neighbor took me to the doctor."

"Mom wasn't there for you."

She glanced to the side. "When she was stoned she'd hit me."

"Mom was into drugs."

"Mostly weed, sometimes she'd take pills for her moods. Mostly, she liked to smoke. Weed *and* tobacco *and* Courvoisier. Her lungs are seriously burned away. She breathes with a tank."

"Tough childhood."

She mumbled again.

I said, "I missed that."

"My childhood. I don't like talking about it but I'm being totally honest with you. No illusions, no emotional curtain, you know? It's like a mantra. I kept telling myself, 'honesty honesty honesty.' Lauritz told me to keep that here, right in front." A tapered finger touched a smooth, bronze brow.

"What *did* you figure would happen when the story got out?"

Silence.

"Michaela?"

"Maybe TV."

"Getting on TV?"

"Reality TV. Like a mixture of *Punk'd* and *Survivor* and *Fear Factor* but with no one knowing what's real and what isn't. It's not like we were trying to be mean. We were just trying to get a breakthrough."

"What kind of breakthrough?"

"Mentally."

"What about as a career move?"

"What do you mean?"

"Did you think it might get you a part on a reality show?"

"Dylan thought it might," she said.

"You didn't?"

"I didn't think, period . . . maybe down deep—unconsciously—I thought it might help get through the wall."

"What wall is that?"

"The success wall. You go on auditions and they look at you like you're not there, and even when they say they might call they don't. You're just as talented as the girl who gets called, there's no reason anything happens. So why not? Get yourself noticed, do something special or weird or terrific. *Make yourself special for being special.*"

She got up, circled the office. Kicked one shoe with the other and nearly lost balance. Maybe she'd been telling the truth about being clumsy.

"It's a suck life," she said.

"Being an actor."

"Being any kind of artist. Everyone loves artists but they also hate them!"

Grabbing her hair with both hands, she yanked, stretching her beautiful face into something reptilian.

"Do you have any idea how hard it is?" she said through elongated lips.

"What?"

She released the hair. Looked down on me as if I was thick.

"To. Get. Anyone. To. Pay. *Attention!*"

CHAPTER

5

I saw Michaela for three more sessions. She spent most of the time drifting back to a childhood tainted by neglect and loneliness. Her mother's promiscuity and various pathologies enlarged with each appointment. She recalled year after year of academic failure, adolescent slights, chronic isolation brought on by "looking like a giraffe with zits."

Psychometric testing revealed her to be of average intelligence with poor impulse control and a tendency to manipulate. No sign of learning disability or attention deficit, and her MMPI Lie Scale was elevated, meaning that she'd never stopped acting.

Despite that, she seemed a sad, scared, vulnerable young woman. That didn't stop me from asking what needed to be asked.

"Michaela, the doctor found some bruising around your vagina."

"If you say so."

"The doctor who examined you said so."

"Maybe *he* bruised me when he was checking me out."

"Was he rough?"

"He had rough fingers. This Asian guy. I could tell he didn't like me."

"Why wouldn't he like you?"

"You'd have to ask him." She glanced at her watch.

I said, "Is that the story you want to stick with?"

She stretched. Blue jeans, today, riding low on her hips, midriff-baring white lace V-top. Her nipples were faint gray dots.

"Do I need a story?"

"It could come up."

"It could if you mention it."

"It has nothing to do with me, Michaela. It's in the case file."

"Case file," she said. "Like I did some big crime."

I didn't answer.

She plucked at lace. "Who cares about any of that? Why do *you* care?"

"I'd like to understand what happened up in Latigo Canyon."

"What happened was Dylan getting crazy," she said.

"Crazy physically?"

"He got all passionate and bruised me."

"What happened?" I said.

"What usually happened."

"Meaning . . ."

"It's what we *did.*" She wiggled the fingers of one hand. "Touching each other. The few times."

"The few times you were intimate."

"We were never *intimate.* Once in a while we got horny and touched each other. Of *course* he wanted more, but I never let him." She stuck out her tongue. "A few times I let him go down on me but mostly it was finger time because I didn't want to get close to him."

"What happened in Latigo Canyon?"

"I don't see what that has to do with . . . what happened."

"Your relationship with Dylan is bound to—"

"Fine, fine," she said. "In the canyon it

was all fingers and he got too rough. When I complained he said he was doing it on purpose. For realism."

"For when you were discovered."

"I guess," she said.

She looked away.

I waited.

She said, "It was the first night. What else was there to do? It was so boring, just sitting up there, getting talked out."

"How soon did you get talked out?" I said.

"Real soon. 'Cause he was into this whole Zen *silence* thing. Preparing for the second night. He said we needed to cook images in our heads. Heat up our *emotions* by not crowding our heads with words."

Her laughter was harsh. "Big Zen silence thing. Until he got horny. Then he had no trouble telling me what he wanted. He thought being up there would make things different. Like I'd do him. As if."

Her eyes got hard. "I pretty much hate him now."

I took a day before writing an outline of my report.

Her story boiled down to diminished capacity combined with that time-honored tactic, the TODDI Defense: *The Other Dude Did It.*

Wondering if Lauritz Montez was her new acting coach, I phoned his office at the Beverly Hills court building. "I'm not going to make you happy."

"Actually, it doesn't matter," he said.

"The case settled?"

"Better. Sixty-day continuance, thanks to my colleague who's representing Meserve. Marjani Coolidge—know her?"

"Nope."

"She's scheduled on a roots trip to Africa, asked to put everything off. Once the sixty days are up, we'll get another continuance. And another. The media scrutiny's faded and the docket's jammed with serious felonies, no problem keeping trivial crap at bay. By the time we get to trial no one will give a shit. It's all pressure from the sheriffs, and those guys have the attention span of gnats on smack. I'm figuring the worst the two of them will get is teaching Shakespeare to inner-city kids."

"Shakespeare's not her thing."

"What is?"

"Improvisation."

"Yeah, well, I'm sure she'll figure it out. Thanks for your time."

"No report necessary?"

"You can send one but I can't tell you it'll ever get read. Which shouldn't bother you because turns out all I can get you paid for is straight session time at forty bucks per full hour, no portal-to-portal, no write-up fees."

I kept silent.

"Hey," he said, "budget cuts and all that. Sorry, man."

"Don't be."

"You're okay with it?"

"I'm not much for showbiz."

CHAPTER

6

Two weeks after Michaela's final session, I spotted a paragraph at the back of the Metro section.

Abduction Hoax Couple Sentenced

A pair of would-be actors accused of faking their own kidnapping in order to garner attention for their careers has been sentenced to community service as part of a plea-deal arranged between the Sheriff's Department, the District Attor-

*ney, and the Public Defender's
Office.*

*Dylan Roger Meserve, 24, and
Michaela Ally Brand, 23, had
been charged with a series of
misdemeanors that could have
led to jail time, stemming from
false claims of being carjacked in
West Los Angeles and driven to
Latigo Canyon in Malibu by a
masked gunman. Subsequent investigation revealed that the duo
had set up the incident, going so
far as to tie themselves up and
simulate two days of starvation.*

*"This was the best resolu-
tion," said Deputy D.A. Heather
Bally, in charge of prosecuting
the duo. She cited the couple's
youth and the absence of prior
criminal record, and emphasized
the benefits Meserve and Brand
could provide to the "theater
community," citing two summer
theater programs to which the
pair might be assigned: The-
aterKids in Baldwin Hills and The
Drama Posse in East Los Angeles.*

Calls to the sheriff's office were not returned.

One continuance had done the trick. I wondered if the two of them would bother to stay in town. Probably, if visions of stardom still stuffed their heads.

I'd sent my $160 invoice to Lauritz Montez's office, still hadn't gotten paid. I called him, left a polite message with a machine, and went about forgetting the case.

Lieutenant Detective Milo Sturgis had different ideas.

I'd spent New Year's alone and the ensuing weeks had been nothing to warble about.

The dog I shared with Robin Castagna turned ancient overnight.

Spike, a twenty-five-pound French bulldog with fire-log physique and the discerning eye of a practiced snob, had scoffed at the notion of joint custody and gone to live with Robin. During his last few months of life, his self-absorbed worldview had faded pathetically as he'd slipped into sleepy passivity. When he started to go downhill, Robin let me know. I began dropping by her house in Venice, sat on her saggy couch while she built and restored stringed instruments in her studio down the hall.

Spike actually allowed me to hold him, rested his cement-block head under my arm. Looking up from time to time with eyes turned filmy gray by cataracts.

Each time I left, Robin and I smiled at each other for the briefest of moments, never discussed what was imminent, or anything else.

The last time I saw Spike, neither the tap-tap of Robin's mallet nor the whine of her power tools roused him and his muscle tone was bad. Offers of food treats dangled near his crusted nose evoked no response. I watched the slow, labored heave of his rib cage, listened to the rasp of his breathing.

Congestive heart failure. The vet said he was tired but not in pain, there was no reason to put him down unless we couldn't tolerate watching him go this way.

He fell asleep in my lap and when I lifted his paw it felt cold. I rubbed it warmer, sat for a while, carried him to his bed, placed him down gently, and kissed his knobby forehead. He smelled surprisingly good, like a freshly showered athlete.

As I saw myself out, Robin kept working

on an old Gibson F5 mandolin. Six-figure instrument, heavy concentration required.

I stopped at the door and looked back. Spike's eyes were closed and his flat face was peaceful, almost childlike.

The next morning, he gasped three times and passed away in Robin's arms. She phoned me and cried out the details. I drove to Venice, wrapped the body, called the cremation service, stood by as a nice man carried the pathetically small bundle away. Robin was in her bedroom, still weeping. When the man left, I went in there. One thing led to another.

During the time Robin and I were apart, she hooked up with another man and I fell in and out of love with a smart, beautiful psychologist named Allison Gwynn.

I still saw Allison from time to time. Occasionally the physical pull we'd both felt asserted itself. As far as I knew, she wasn't seeing anyone else. I figured it was only a matter of time.

New Years she'd been in Connecticut with her grandmother and a host of cousins.

She'd sent me a necktie for Christmas. I'd reciprocated with a Victorian garnet brooch. I still wasn't sure what had gone wrong. From time to time it bothered me that I couldn't seem to hold on to a relationship. Sometimes I wondered what I'd say if I was sitting in The Other Chair.

I told myself introspection could rot your brain, better to concentrate on other people's problems.

It was Milo who ended up providing distraction, at nine a.m. on a cold, dry Monday morning, one week after the hoax settlement.

"That girl you evaluated—Mikki Brand, the one who faked her abduction? They found her body last night. Strangled and stabbed."

"Didn't know her nickname was Mikki." The things you say when you're caught off guard.

"That's what her mother calls her."

"She'd know," I said.

I met him at the scene forty minutes later. The murder had taken place sometime Sunday night. By now, the area had been cleaned and scraped and analyzed, yellow tape taken down.

The sole remnants of brutality were short

pieces of the white rope the coroner's drivers use to bind the body after they wrap it in heavy-duty translucent plastic. Filmy gray plastic. Same hue, I realized, as cataract-dimmed eyes.

Michaela Brand had been found in a grassy area fifty feet west of Bagley Avenue, north of National Boulevard, where the streets cut under the 10 freeway. A faint, oblong gloss caught sunlight where the body had compressed the weeds. The overpass provided cold shade and relentless noise. Graffiti boasted and raged on concrete walls. In some places the vegetation was waist high, crabgrass vying for nutrition with ragweed and dandelions and low, creeping things I couldn't identify.

This was city property, part of the freeway easement, sandwiched between the tailored, affluent streets of Beverlywood to the north and the working-class apartment buildings of Culver City to the south. A few years back, there'd been some gang problems, but I hadn't heard of anything lately. Still, it wouldn't be a place where I'd walk at night, and I wondered what had brought Michaela here.

Her apartment on Holt was a couple of

miles away. In L.A., that's a drive, not a walk. Her five-year-old Honda hadn't been located, and I wondered if she'd been jacked.

For real, this time.

Too ironic.

Milo said, "What're you thinking?"

I shrugged.

"You look contemplative. Let it out, man."

"Nothing to say."

He ran his hand over his big, lumpy face, squinted at me as if we'd just been intro-duced. He was dressed for messy work: rust-colored nylon windbreaker, wash-and-wear white shirt with a curling collar, skinny oxblood tie that resembled two lengths of beef jerky, baggy brown trousers, and tan desert boots with pink rubber soles.

His fresh haircut was the usual "style," meaning skinned at the sides, which em-phasized all the white, thick and black on top, a cockscomb of competing cowlicks. His sideburns now drooped a half inch be-low fleshy earlobes, suggesting the worst type of Elvis impersonator. His weight had stabilized; my guess was two sixty on his seventyfour-inch frame, a lot of it abdomen.

When he stepped away from the overpass, sunlight amplified his acne pits and gravity's cruel tendencies. We were months apart in age. He liked to tell me I was aging a lot more slowly than he was. I usually replied that circumstances had a way of changing fast.

He makes a big deal about not caring how he looks, but I've long suspected there's a self-image buried down deep in his psyche: *Gay But Not What You Expect.*

Rick Silverman's long given up on buying him clothes that never get worn. Rick gets his hair trimmed every two weeks at a high-priced West Hollywood salon. Milo drives, every two months, to La Brea and Washington where he hands his seven bucks plus tip to an eighty-nine-year-old barber who claims to have cut Eisenhower's hair during World War II.

I visited the shop once, with its gray linoleum floors, creaky chairs, yellowed Brylcreem posters featuring smiling, toothy white guys, and similarly antique pitches for Murray's straightening pomade aimed at the majority black clientele.

Milo liked to brag about the Ike connection.

"Probably a one-shot deal," I said.

"Why's that?"

"So Maurice could avoid a court-martial."

That conversation, we'd been in an Irish bar on Fairfax near Olympic, drinking Chivas and convincing ourselves we were lofty thinkers. A man and a woman he'd been pretending to look for had been nabbed at a traffic stop in Montana and were fighting extradition. They'd slain a vicious murderer, a predator who'd sorely needed killing. The law had no use for moral subtlety and news of the capture led Milo to deliver a cranky, philosophical sermon. Downing a double, he apologized for the lapse and changed the subject to barbering.

"Maurice isn't *courant* enough for you?"

"Wait long enough, and everything becomes *courant.*"

"Maurice is an artist."

"I'm sure George Washington thought so."

"Don't be an ageist. He can still handle those scissors."

"Such dexterity," I said. "He should've gone to med school."

His green eyes grew bright with amusement and grain alcohol. "Couple of weeks ago, I was giving a talk to a Neighborhood

Watch group in West Hollywood Park. Crime prevention, basic stuff. I got the feeling some of the young guys weren't paying attention. Later, one of them came up to me. Skinny, tan, Oriental tats on the arm, all that cut muscle. Said he dug the message but I was the stodgiest gay man he'd ever met."

"Sounds like a come-on."

"Oh, sure." He tugged at a saggy jowl, released skin, took a swallow. "I told him I appreciated the compliment but he should be paying more attention to watching his back when he cruised. He thought that was a double entendre and left cracking up."

"West Hollywood's the sheriff," I said. "Why you?"

"You know how it is. Sometimes I'm the unofficial spokesman for law enforcement when the audience is alternative."

"Captain pressured you."

"That, too," he said.

I walked over to where Michaela had been found. Milo remained several feet back, reading the notes he'd taken last night.

A flash of white stood out among the weeds. Another nub of coroner's rope. The drivers had trimmed the bindings because Michaela had been a slim girl.

I knew what had happened at the scene: her pockets emptied, her nails cleaned of detritus, hair combed out, any "product" collected. Finally, attendants had packaged her and lifted her onto a gurney and wheeled her up into a white coroner's van. By now she'd be waiting, along with dozens of other plastic bundles, stacked neatly on a shelf in one of the large, cool rooms that line the gray hallways of the basement crypt on Mission Road.

They treat the dead with respect at Mission Road, but the backlog—the sheer volume of bodies—can't help but leach out the dignity.

I picked up the rope. Smooth, substantial. As it had to be. How did it compare to the yellow binding Michaela and Dylan had purchased for their "exercise"?

Where was Dylan now?

I asked Milo if he had any idea.

He said, "First thing I did was call the number on his arrest form. Disconnected. Haven't located his landlord. Michaela's, either."

"She told me she was running out of

money, had a month's grace before eviction."

"If she did get evicted, be good to know where she's been crashing. Think they could've moved in together?"

"Not if she was leveling with me," I said. "She blamed the whole thing on him."

I scanned the dump site. "Not much blood. Killed somewhere else?"

"Looks that way."

"Who found the body?"

"Woman walking her poodle. Dog sniffed it out, pronto."

"Strangled and stabbed."

"Manual strangulation, hard enough to crush the larynx. The follow-up was five stab wounds to the chest and one to the neck."

"Nothing around the genitalia?"

"She was fully clothed, nothing overtly sexual about the pose."

Strangulation itself can be a sexual thing. Some lust killers describe it as the ultimate dominance. It takes a long time to stare into the face of a struggling, gasping human being and watch the life force seep out. One monster I interviewed laughed about it.

"Time goes quickly when you're having fun, Doc."

I said, "Anything under her nails?"

"Nothing overly interesting, let's see what the lab comes up with. No hair fibers, either. Not even from the dog. Apparently, poodles don't shed much."

"Any of the wounds defensive?"

"No, she was dead before the cutting started. The neck wound was a little stick to the side, but it got the jugular."

"Five's too many for impulse cuts but less than you'd expect from an overkill frenzy. Any pattern?"

"With her clothes on, it was hard to see much of anything except wrinkles and blood. I'll be at the autopsy, let you know."

I stared at the glossy spot.

Milo said, "So she blamed Meserve for the hoax. Lots of love lost?"

"She said she'd come to hate him."

"Hatred's a fine motive. Let's try to locate this movie star."

CHAPTER

7

Dylan Meserve had cleared out of his Culver City apartment six weeks ago, failing to give notice to the company that owned the place. The firm, represented by a pinch-featured man named Ralph Jabber, had been more lax than Michaela's landlord: Dylan owed three months back rent.

We encountered Jabber walking through the empty flat and jotting notes on a clipboard. The unit was one of fifty-eight in a three-story complex the color of ripe cantaloupe. The Seville's tripometer put it three miles from where Michaela's body had been found. That placed the murder scene roughly equidistant from the couple's respective apartments and I said so to Milo.

"What, the two of them reaching some kind of common ground?"

"I'm pointing out, not interpreting."

He grunted and we walked through un-guarded double glass doors into a musty-smelling lobby done up in copper foil wall-paper, pumpkin-colored industrial carpet, and U-build Scandinavian furniture made of something yellow that yearned to be wood.

Dylan Meserve's unit was on the far end of a dark, narrow hallway. From ten yards away I could see the open door, hear the supercharged whine of an industrial vac-uum cleaner.

Milo said, "So much for trace evidence," and walked faster.

Ralph Jabber motioned to the dark little woman pushing the vacuum. She flipped a switch that quieted but didn't silence the machine.

"What can I do for you?"

Milo flashed the badge and Jabber low-ered his clipboard. I caught a glimpse of the checklist. *1. FLOORS: A. Normal Wear B. Tenant Liability 2. WALLS . . .*

Jabber was sallow, short, and sunken-chested, in a shiny black four-button suit over a white silk T-shirt, brown mesh loafers without socks. He had nothing to offer about his former tenant, other than the outstanding rent.

Milo asked the woman what she knew and got an uncomprehending smile. She was less than five feet tall, sturdily built, with a carved-teak face.

Ralph Jabber said, "She doesn't know the tenants."

The vacuum idled like a hot rod. The woman pointed to the carpet. Jabber shook his head, glanced at a Rolex too huge and diamond-encrusted to be genuine. *"El otro apartmente."*

The woman wheeled the machine out of the apartment.

Dylan Meserve had lived in a rectangular white room, maybe three hundred square feet. A single aluminum window set high on one of the long walls granted a view of gray stucco. The carpeting was coarse and oat-colored. The vest-pocket kitchenette sported orange Formica counters chipped white along various corners, prefab white cabinets smudged gray near the handles, a brown space-saver refrigerator left open.

Empty fridge. Bottles of Windex and Easy-Off and a generic brand of disinfectant sat on the counter. Scuff marks bottomed some of the walls. Little square indentations compressed the carpet where furniture had sat. From the number of dents, not much furniture.

Ralph Jabber's clipboard lay flat against his thigh now. I wondered how he'd scored the scene.

"Three months back rent," said Milo. "You guys are pretty flexible."

"It's business," said Jabber, without enthusiasm.

"What is?"

"We don't like evictions. Prefer to keep the vacancy rate low."

"So you let him ride."

"Yeah."

"Anyone talk to Mr. Meserve about it?"

"I wouldn't know."

"How long would Mr. Meserve have had to go before you threw him out?"

Jabber frowned. "Every situation is different."

"Mr. Meserve asked for an extension?"

"It's possible. Like I said, I don't know."

"How come?"

"I don't handle the rents. I'm the termination-transition manager," said Jabber.

That sounded like a euphemism for mortician.

Milo said, "Meaning . . ."

"I fix the place up when it's vacant, get it ready for the new tenant."

"Got a new tenant for this one?"

Jabber shrugged. "It won't take long. The place is high-demand."

Milo looked around the small dismal room. "Location, location, location."

"You got it. Close to everything, Lieutenant. The studios, the freeways, the beach, Beverly Hills."

"I know it's not your area of expertise, sir, but I'm trying to trace Mr. Meserve's activities. If he hadn't asked for an extension, would there be some reason you'd simply let him go for three months?"

Jabber's eyelids half closed.

Milo moved closer, used his height and bulk to advantage. Jabber stepped back. "Off the record?"

"Is it a sensitive topic, Mr. Jabber?"

"No, no, not that . . . to be honest, this is

a big building and we've got others even bigger. Sometimes things get . . . over-looked."

"So maybe Meserve got lucky and just sneaked by."

Jabber shrugged.

"But eventually," said Milo, "his failure to pay rent would've caught up with him."

"Of course, yeah. Anyway, we got at least his first month and damage deposit. He's not getting nothing back 'cause he didn't give notice."

"How'd you find out he was gone?"

"Phone and electricity got shut off for nonpayment. We pay the gas but the utilities notify us when the other stuff goes."

"Kind of an early warning system."

Jabber smiled uneasily. "Not early enough."

"When did the phone and electricity get shut off?"

"You'd have to call the main office."

"Or you could."

Jabber frowned, pulled out a cell phone, punched an auto-dial three-digit code. "Samir, there? Hey, Sammy, Ralph. I am, yeah, the usual . . . tell me, when did the juice get squeezed off at Overland D 14?

Why? 'Cause the cops wanna know. Yeah . . . who knows, Sammy, they're here now, want to talk to them yourself . . . okay, then, just tell me so I can get them outta— so they can find out what they wanna know. Listen, I got six more to deal with, Sammy, including two in the Valley and it's already eleven . . . yeah, yeah . . ."

Ninety seconds passed. Phone tucked between his ear and his shoulder, Jabber walked into the kitchenette, opened cabinets, ran his finger inside drawers. "Fine. Yeah. Okay. Yeah, I will, yeah."

He clicked off. "Utilities went four weeks ago. One of our inspectors said there'd been no mail for six weeks."

"Four weeks ago and you just came by today."

Jabber colored. "Like I said, it's a big company."

"You the owner?"

"I wish. My father-in-law."

"That him you were talking to?"

Jabber shook his head. "Brother-in-law."

"Family affair," said Milo.

"By marriage," said Jabber. His lips twisted into a tight, pale blossom. "Okay? I gotta lock up."

"Who's the inspector?"

"My sister-in-law. Samir's wife. Samir has her come around, check things out. She's not too bright, never told anyone about the no-mail."

"You have any idea where Mr. Meserve went?"

"I wouldn't know him if he walked in right now. Why all the questions? What'd he do?"

Milo said, "Would anyone at the company have information about him?"

"No way," said Jabber.

"Who rented to him?"

"He probably used one of the services. Rent-Search, or one of them. It's on-line or you can call, mostly people do it on-line."

"How's it work?"

"Applicant submits an application to the service, service passes it along to us. Applicant qualifies, he puts down the deposit and the first month and moves in. Once we get occupancy, we pay a commission to the service."

"Meserve have a lease?"

"Month to month, we don't do leases."

"Leases don't keep the vacancy rate down?"

"You get a bum," said Jabber, "doesn't matter what's on paper."

"What does it take to qualify as a tenant?"

"Hey," said Jabber. "Lots of homeless would kill for a place like this."

"You ask for references?"

"Sure."

"Who did Meserve give?"

"Like I said, I'm just the—"

"Call your brother-in-law. Please."

Three references: a previous landlord in Brooklyn, the manager of the Foot Locker where Dylan Meserve had worked before getting arrested, and Nora Dowd, Artistic Director of the PlayHouse, in West L.A., where the young man had been listed as a "creative consultant."

Jabber examined what he'd written down before passing it along to Milo.

"Guy's an actor?" He laughed.

"You rent to a lot of actors?"

"Actor means bum. Samir's stupid."

I followed Milo to the West L.A. station, where he parked his unmarked in the staff lot and got into the Seville.

"Meserve stopped his mail soon after he got busted," he said. "Probably planning to rabbit if things didn't work out in court." He searched his notepad for the acting school's address. "What do you think of that 'creative consultant' business?"

"Maybe he apprenticed to earn extra money. Michaela blamed Dylan for the hoax but obviously Nora Dowd didn't."

"How'd Michaela feel about that?"

"She didn't talk about Nora's reaction to Dylan. She was surprised at Nora's angry reaction to her."

"Dowd boots her but keeps him on as consultant?"

"If it's true."

"Meserve faked the reference?"

"Meserve's been known to embellish."

Milo phoned Brooklyn, located the landlord Dylan had cited as a reference. "Guy said he knew Dylan's father because he's a part-time musician himself and they used to gig. He has a vague memory of Dylan as a kid but never rented him an apartment."

"Creative consultant," I said.

"Let's talk to the consultee."

CHAPTER

8

The PlayHouse was an old one-story Craftsman house on an oversized lot, just north of Venice Boulevard, in West L.A. Plank siding painted deep green with cream trim, low-set bulk topped by sweeping eaves that created a small, dim porch. The garage to the left had old-fashioned barn doors but looked freshly painted. The landscaping was from another age: a couple of four-story cocoa palms, indifferently pruned bird of paradise grown ragged, agapanthus, and calla lilies surrounding a flat, brown lawn.

The neighborhood was working-class rental residential, mostly boxy multi-units and boxy houses awaiting demolition. Nothing denoted the acting school's function. The windows were dark.

Milo said, "Guess she doesn't need to advertise. Or keep daytime hours."

I said, "If most of the aspirants have day jobs, it's an evening business."

"Let's check it out, anyway."

We walked up to the porch. Floored with green board, thickly varnished. The window in the paneled oak door was blocked with opaque lace. A hand-hammered copper mailbox perched to the right. Milo flipped the lid and peered inside. Empty.

He pushed a button and chimes sounded. No answer.

Two doors down an old Dodge Dart backed out toward the street. Hispanic man around thirty at the wheel, leaving a pale blue bungalow. Milo walked over, rolled his arm.

No badge, but people tend to obey him. The man lowered his window.

"Morning, sir. Know anything about your neighbor?"

Big shrug. Nervous smile. *"No hablo Ingles."*

Milo pointed. "The school. *La Escuela.*"

Another shrug. *"No se."*

Milo looked into his eyes, waved him away. As the Dart sped off, we returned to the porch, where Milo jabbed the button several more times. A chime sonata went unanswered.

"Okay, I'll try again tonight."

As we turned, footsteps sounded from inside the PlayHouse. Lace wiggled in the window but didn't part.

Then nothing.

Milo swiveled and rapped the door hard. Scratches, as a bolt turned. The door swung open and a heavy man holding a broom and looking distracted said, "Yeah?" Before the word was out of his mouth, his eyes tightened and distraction gave way to calculation.

This time Milo had the badge out. The heavy man barely glanced at it. His second "Yeah?" was softer, wary.

He had a splotchy, pie-tin face, a meaty, off-kilter nose, brambles of curly graying hair that flew from his temples, muttonchops that petered to a colorless grizzle. The mustache atop parched lips was the sole bit of disciplined hair: clipped, precise, a gray-brown hyphen. Tight eyes the color of strong tea managed to be active without moving.

Wrinkled gray work shirt and matching pants, open sandals, thick white socks. Dust and sweepings flecked white cotton toes. The tattoos that embroidered his fleshy hands promised to snake up under his sleeves. Blue-black skin art, crude and square-edged. Hard to decipher, but I made out a tiny little grinning demon's head, more impish than satanic, leering at a puckered knuckle.

Milo said, "Is Nora Dowd here?"

"Nope."

"What about Dylan Meserve?"

"Nope."

"You know Mr. Meserve?"

"I know who he is." Low, slurred voice, slight delay before forming syllables. His right hand gripped the broom handle. The left had gathered shirt fabric and stretched it over his substantial belly.

"What do you know about Mr. Meserve?" said Milo.

The same hesitation. "One of the students."

"He doesn't work here?"

"Never saw that."

"We were told he's a creative consultant."

No answer.

"When's the last time you saw him?"

Small yellow teeth made a play at a cracked upper lip. "A while."

"Days?"

"Yeah."

"Weeks?"

"Could be."

"Where's Ms. Dowd?"

"Dunno."

"No idea?"

"Nossir."

"She's your boss."

"Yessir."

"Want to guess where she might be?"

Shrug.

"When did you see her last?"

"I work days, she's here at night."

Out came Milo's pad. "Your name, please."

No answer.

Milo edged closer. The man stepped back, just as Ralph Jabber had.

"Sir?"

"Reynold."

"First name, please."

"Reynold. Last name's Peaty."

"Reynold Peaty."

"Yessir."

"Is that Peaty with two e's or e-a?"

"P-E-A-T-Y."

"You work here full-time, Mr. Peaty?"

"I do the clean up and the lawn mowing."

"Full-time?"

"Part-time."

"Got another job?"

"I clean buildings."

"Where do you live, Mr. Peaty?"

Peaty's left hand flexed. Gray shirt fabric shimmied. "Guthrie."

"Guthrie Avenue in L.A.?"

"Yessir."

Milo asked for the address. Reynold Peaty thought for a moment before giving it up. Just east of Robertson. A short walk from Michaela Brand's apartment on Holt. Close to the death scene, too.

"Know why we're here, Mr. Peaty?"

"Nossir."

"How long have you been working here?"

"Five years."

"So you know Michaela Brand."

"One of the girls," said Peaty. His bushy eyebrows twitched. The fabric over his gut vibrated harder.

"Seen her around?"

"Coupla times."

"While you were working days?"

"Sometimes it stretches," said Peaty. "If I get here late."

"You know her by name."

"She was the one did that thing with him."

"That thing."

"With him," Peaty repeated. "Pretending to be kidnapped."

"She's dead," said Milo. "Murdered."

Reynold Peaty's lower jaw jutted like a bulldog's, rotated as if chewing gristle.

"Any reaction to that, sir?" said Milo.

"Terrible."

"Any idea who'd want to do something like that?"

Peaty shook his head and ran his hand up and down the broom shaft.

"Yeah, it is terrible," said Milo. "Such a pretty girl."

Peaty's small eyes narrowed to pupil-glint. "You think he did it?"

"Who?"

"Meserve."

"Any reason we should think that?"

"You asked about him."

Milo waited.

Peaty rolled the broom. "They did that thing together."

"That thing."

"It was on TV."

"You think that might be connected to Michaela's murder, Mr. Peaty?"

"Maybe."

"Why would it be?"

Peaty licked his lips. "They didn't come here together no more."

"For acting lessons."

"Yessir."

"Did they come separately?"

"Just him."

"Meserve kept coming but not Michaela."

"Yessir."

"Sounds like a lot of your days stretch into nights."

"Sometimes he's here in the day."

"Mr. Meserve?"

"Yessir."

"By himself?"

Head shake.

"Who's he with?"

Peaty shifted the broom from hand to hand. "I don' wanna get in trouble."

"Why would you?"

"You know."

"I don't, Mr. Peaty."

"Her. Ms. Dowd."

"Nora Dowd comes here during the day with Dylan Meserve."

"Sometimes," said Peaty.

"Anyone else here?"

"Nossir."

"Except you."

"I leave when she tells me I done enough."

"What do she and Meserve do when they're here?"

Peaty shook his head. "I work."

"What else can you tell me?" said Milo.

"About what?"

"Michaela, Dylan Meserve, anything else that comes to mind."

"Nothing," said Peaty.

"The hoax Michaela and Dylan tried to pull off," said Milo. "What'd you think about that?"

"It was on TV."

"What do *you* think of it?"

Peaty tried to chew on his mustache but the clipped hair was too short for a tooth hold. He tugged at his right muttonchop. I tried to think of the last time I'd seen a set that overgrown. College days? Portrait of Martin Van Buren?

Peaty said, "It ain't good to lie."

"I agree with you there. My job, people

are always lying to me and it really gets on my nerves."

Peaty's eyes dropped to the porch planks.

"Where were you last night, Mr. Peaty, say between eight p.m. and two a.m.?"

"Home."

"Your place on Guthrie."

"Yessir."

"Doing what?"

"Eating," said Peaty. "Chicken fingers."

"Takeout?"

"Frozen. I heat 'em up. I had a beer."

"What brand?"

"Old Milwaukee. I had three. Then I watched TV, then I went to sleep."

"What'd you watch?"

Family Feud.

"What time did you pop off?"

"Dunno. The TV was goin' when I woke up."

"What time was that?"

Peaty curled a muttonchop. "Maybe three."

One hour past the bracket Milo had given him.

"How do you know it was three?"

"You asked so I said something."

"Anything special about three?"

"Sometimes when I get up I look at the clock and it's three, or three thirty. Even if I don't drink a lot, I gotta get up." Peaty looked at the floor again. "To piss. Sometimes twice or three times."

"Let's hear it for middle age," said Milo.

Peaty didn't answer.

"How old are you, Mr. Peaty?"

"Thirty-eight."

Milo smiled. "You're a young guy."

No answer.

"How well did you know Michaela Brand?"

"I didn't do it," said Peaty.

"I didn't ask you that, sir."

"This other stuff you're asking. Where was I." Peaty shook his head. "I don't wanna talk no more."

"Just routine," said Milo, "no reason to get—"

Shaking his head, Peaty backed away, toward the door.

Milo said, "Here we were having a nice conversation, then I ask you how well you knew Michaela Brand and all of a sudden you don't want to talk. That's only gonna make me wonder."

"It ain't," said Peaty, groping for the door

handle. He'd left the oak panel slightly ajar and the handle was inches out of reach.

"Ain't what?" said Milo.

"Right. Talking like I did something." Peaty edged back, found the handle, and shoved, revealing oak floors and walls, a glimmer of stained glass. "I had a beer and went to sleep."

"Three beers."

No answer.

"Listen," said Milo. "No offense intended, but it's my job to ask questions."

Peaty shook his head. "I eat and watch TV. That don't mean nothing."

He stepped into the house, started to close the door. Milo checked it with his shoe. Peaty tensed but let go. His grip on the broom handle swelled his knuckles. He shook his head and stray hairs floated free, landing on thick, rounded shoulders.

"Mr. Peaty—"

"Leave me alone." More whimper than demand.

"All we're trying to do is get some basic facts. So how about we come in and—"

Peaty's hand grabbed the door's edge. "Not allowed!"

"We can't come in?"

"No! The rules!"

"Whose rules?"

"Ms. Dowd's."

"How about I call her? What's her number?"

"Dunno."

"You work for her but don't—"

"Dunno!"

Peaty danced backward and shoved the door hard. Milo let it slam.

We stood on the porch for a few moments. Cars drove up and down the street.

Milo said, "For all I know he's got rope and a bloody knife in there. But no damn way to find out."

I said nothing.

He said, "You could argue with me."

"There is the fact that he's weird," I said.

"Yeah, yeah," he said. "Guy lives on Guthrie off Robertson. You visualizing the same map I am?"

"Blocks from Michaela. Not much farther to the crime scene."

"*And* he's weird." He glanced back at the door. Rang the bell several times.

No response.

"Wonder what time he got to work this morning." Another bell-push. We waited. He put his pad away. "I'd love to check this place out but I'm not even gonna think about heading round back and giving some lawyer an illegal entry angle."

He grinned. "One day in and I've got trial fantasies. Okay, let's see what we can do within the boundaries of The Law."

We descended the porch and headed for the car.

"It's probably no big deal," he said. "Not getting inside. Even if Peaty is the bad guy, why would he bring evidence to work? What do you think of him probability-wise?"

"A definite maybe," I said. "Talking about Michaela clearly made him nervous."

"Like he had a crush on her?"

"She was a beautiful girl."

"And way out of his league," he said. "Working around all those starlet wannabes could be frustrating for a guy like that."

We got into the Seville.

I said, "When Peaty shook his head, stray hairs fell out. Fellow that hirsute and unruly, you'd think he'd have left some trace on the body, or at least at the scene."

"Maybe he had time to clean up."

"Guess so."

"There was some wind last night," he

said. "The body coulda been there a while before the poodle came by. For all we know, the damned *dog* licked up trace evidence."

"The owner let it nose the body?"

Milo rubbed his face. "The owner claims she yanked it away the minute she saw what it was. Still . . ."

I started up the car.

He said, "I need to be careful not to tunnel in on anyone too quickly."

"Makes sense."

"Sometimes I do that."

CHAPTER

9

A DMV check revealed no vehicles currently registered to Reynold Peaty. No California driver's license. Ever.

"Hard to transport a body without wheels," I said.

Milo said, "Wonder how he gets to work."

"The bus. Or a stretch limo."

"Your attempt at humor is refreshing. If he bears further watching, I'll check out the bus routes, see if he's a regular." He laughed.

I said, "What?"

"He comes across dumb and weird but

think about it: He sweeps up at an *acting* school."

"He was playing us?"

"The world's a stage," he said. "Sure be nice to have the script."

"If he was performing, why would he put on a weird act?" I said.

"True . . . let's head back."

I drove toward the West L.A. station as he phoned the MTA and learned which buses Peaty would've taken from Pico-Robertson to the PlayHouse. Transfers and the need to cover several blocks on foot stretched a half-hour car trip to at least a ninety-minute journey.

I said, "Michaela's Honda show up yet?"

"Nope . . . you're thinking Peaty coulda jacked her?"

"The hoax might've given him ideas."

"Life imitating art." He punched numbers on his cell, talked briefly, hung up. "No sign of it yet. But we're not talking conspicuous. A Civic, black no less. If the plates are off or replaced, it could take a long time to spot it."

"If Peaty is the bad guy," I said, "maybe he decided to drive to work this morning and ditched it within walking distance of the PlayHouse."

"That would be pretty damned stupid."

"Yes, it would."

He chewed his cheek. "Mind turning around?"

We cruised the half-mile radius surrounding the acting school, peering up and down streets and alleys, driveways and parking lots. Taking more than an hour, then expanding to another half mile and spending another hundred minutes. Spotting lots of Civics, three of them black, all with plates that checked out.

On the way back to the station, Milo tried the coroner's office and learned that Michaela's autopsy was scheduled in four days, maybe longer if the body count stayed high. "Any way to prioritize? Yeah, yeah, I know . . . but if there's anything you can do. Appreciate it, this one could get complicated."

I sat in the spare chair of Milo's tiny, windowless office as he tried to plug Reynold Peaty into the data banks. His computer took a long time to sputter to life, even longer for icons to fill the screen. Then they disappeared and the screen went black and he started all over again.

Fourth PC in eight months, yet another hand-me-down, this one from a prep school in Pacific Palisades. The last few donated machines had enjoyed the shelf life of raw milk. In between Clunkers Two and Three, Milo had paid for a high-priced laptop with his own money, only to see some glitch in the station's electrical system fry his hard drive.

As the disk drives ground on, he sprang up, muttering about "advanced middle age" and "plumbing," and left for a few minutes. Returning with two cups of coffee, he handed one to me, drank his, snatched a cheap cigarillo from his desk drawer, unwrapped it, and jammed the unlit cylinder between his incisors. Tapping his fingers as he stared at the screen, he bit down too hard, splintered the cigar, wiped tobacco shreds from his lips. Tossing the Nicaraguan pacifier, he got himself another.

Smoking's prohibited anywhere in the building. Sometimes he lights up, anyway. Today he was too antsy to enjoy the fruits of misdemeanor. As the computer struggled to resuscitate, he sorted through his messages and I reviewed the prelim on Michaela Brand, studied the crime scene photos.

Beautiful golden face turned a familiar green-gray.

Milo grimaced as the screen flashed and dimmed and flashed. "If you want to translate *War and Peace,* feel free to do so."

I tasted the coffee, put it aside, closed my eyes, and tried to think of nothing. Sound came through the walls, too murky to classify.

Milo's space is at the end of a hall on the second floor, set well apart from the detectives' room. Not an overcrowding issue; *he's* set apart. Listed on the books as a lieutenant, but he's got no administrative duties and continues to work cases.

It's part of a deal he made with the former police chief, a cozy bit of politics that allowed the chief to retire rich and unbothered by criminal charges and Milo to remain in the department.

As long as his clearance rate stays high, and he doesn't flaunt his sexual preferences, no one bothers him. But the new chief's big on drastic change and Milo keeps waiting for the memo that will disrupt his life.

Meanwhile, he works.

Whir-whir, burp, click-click. He sat up. "Okay, here we go . . ." He typed. "No state record, too bad . . . let's try NCIC. C'mon baby, give it to Uncle Milo . . . yes!"

He pushed a button and the old dot-matrix printer near his feet began scrolling paper. Yanking out the sheets, he tore on the perforated line, read, handed them to me.

Reynold Peaty had accumulated four felony convictions in Nevada. Burglary thirteen years ago in Reno, a Peeping Tom three years later in that same city pled down to public intoxication/disturbing the peace, two drunk driving violations in Laughlin, seven and eight years ago.

"He's still drinking," I said. "Three beers he admits to. A long-standing alcohol problem would account for no driver's license."

"Booze-hound peeper. You see those tattoos?"

"Jailbird. But no felonies on record since he crossed the border five years ago."

"That impress you mightily?"

"Nope."

"What impresses *me*," he said, "is the combination of burglary and voyeurism."

"Breaking in for the sexual thrill," I said. "All those DNA matches that end up turning burglars into rapists."

"Booze to lower inhibitions, young sexy girls parading in and out. It's a lovely combination."

We drove to Reynold Peaty's place on Guthrie Avenue, clocking the route from the dump site along the way. In moderate traffic, only a seven-minute traverse of Beverlywood's impeccable, tree-lined streets. After dark, even shorter.

On the first block east of Roberston the neighborhood was apartments and the maintenance was sketchier. Peaty's second-floor unit was one of ten in an ash-colored two-story box. The live-in manager was a woman in her seventies named Ertha Stadlbraun. Tall, thin, angular, with skin the color of bittersweet chocolate and marcelled gray hair, she said, "The crazy white fellow."

She invited us into her ground-floor flat for tea and sat us on a lemon-colored, pressed-velvet, camelback couch. The living room was compulsively ordered, with olive carpeting, ceramic lamps, bric-a-brac on open shelves. A suite of what used to be called Mediterranean furniture crowded the space. An airbrushed portrait of Martin Luther King dominated the wall over the couch, flanked by school photos of a dozen or so smiling children.

Ertha Stadlbraun had come to the door wearing a housecoat. Excusing herself, she disappeared into a bedroom and came back wearing a blue shift patterned with clocks, matching pumps with chunky heels. Her cologne evoked the cosmetics counter at some midsized department store from my Midwest childhood. What my mother used to call "toilet water."

"Thanks for the tea, ma'am," said Milo.

"Hot enough, gentlemen?"

"Perfect," said Milo, sipping orange pekoe to demonstrate. He eyed the school pictures. "Grandchildren?"

"Grandchildren and godchildren," said Ertha Stadlbraun. "And two neighbor children I raised after their mother died young. Sure you don't want sugar? Or fruit or cookies?"

"No, thanks, Mrs. Stadlbraun. Nice of you."

"What is?"

"Taking in a neighbor's kids."

Ertha Stadlbraun waved away the praise and reached for the sugar bowl. "My glucose level, I shouldn't do this, but I'm going to, anyway." Two heaping teaspoons of white powder snowed into her cup. "So what is it you want to know about the crazy fellow?"

"How crazy is he, ma'am?"

Stadlbraun sat back, smoothed the shift over her knees. "Let me explain why I pointed out he was white. It's not because I resent him for that. It's because he's the only white person here."

"Is that unusual?" said Milo.

"Are you familiar with this neighborhood?"

Milo nodded.

Ertha Stadlbraun said, "Then you know. Some of the single houses are going white again but the rentals are Mexican. Once in a while you get a hippie type with no credit rating wanting to rent. Mostly we've got the Mexicans coming in. Waves of them. Our building is me and Mrs. Lowery and Mr. and

Mrs. Johnson, who're really old, on the black side. The rest are Mexican. Except for him."

"Does that pose problems?"

"People think he's strange. Not because he raves and rants, because he's too quiet. You can't *communicate* with the man."

"Never talks at all?"

"Person won't look another person in the eye," said Ertha Stadlbraun, "makes everyone nervous."

"Antisocial," I said.

"Someone walks your way, you say hello because when you were a child, you learned proper manners from your mama. But this person didn't learn and doesn't have the courtesy to reply. He lurks around—that's the word for it. Lurk. Like that butler on that old TV show. He reminds me of that fellow."

"The Addams Family," said Milo. "Lurch."

"Lurch, lurk, same difference. The point is, he's always got his head down, staring at the ground, like he's looking for some treasure." She pushed her head forward, turtle-like, bent her neck sharply and gawked at her carpet. "Just like this. How he sees where he's going is a mystery to me."

"He do anything else that makes you nervous, ma'am?"

"These questions of yours are making me nervous."

"Routine, ma'am. Does he do—"

"It's not what he does. He's just an odd one."

"Why'd you rent to him, ma'am?"

"I didn't. He was already here before I moved in."

"How long is that?"

"I arrived shortly after my husband died, which was four years ago. I used to have my own house in Crenshaw, nice neighborhood, then it got bad, now it's getting nice again. After Walter passed on, I said who needs all this space, a big yard to take care of. A fast-talking real estate agent offered me what I thought was a good price so I sold. Big mistake. At least I've got the money invested, been thinking about getting another house. Maybe out in Riverside, where my daughter lives, you get more for your money there."

She patted her hair. "Meanwhile, I'm here, and what they pay me to manage covers my expenses and then some."

"Who's they?"

"The owners. Couple of brothers, rich kids, inherited the building from their parents along with a whole lot of other buildings."

"Does Mr. Peaty pay his rent on time?"

"That's one thing he does do," said Stadlbraun. "First day of the month, postal money order."

"He go to work every day?"

Stadlbraun nodded.

"Where?"

"I have no idea."

"Does he ever entertain visitors?"

"Him?" She laughed. "Where would he entertain? If I could show you his place, you'd see what I mean, teeny-weeny. Used to be a laundry room until the owners converted it to a single. There's barely room for his bed and all he's got besides the bed is a hot plate and a little TV and a dresser."

"When were you inside last?"

"Must've been a couple of years ago. His toilet backed up and I called a rooter service to snake it. I was ready to blame it on him— you know, overstuffing the commode like some fools do?" Regret made her eyes droop. "Turns out it was lint. When they converted it, no one had the sense to clean the traps and somehow the lint got wadded up and moved round and caused a godawful mess. I remember thinking what a *teeny* little place, how can anyone live like this."

Milo said, "Sounds like a cell."

"That's exactly what it is." Stadlbraun squinted. Sat back. Folded her arms across her chest. "You should've told me from the beginning, young man."

"Told you what, ma'am?"

"Like a cell? He's an ex-*con,* right? What'd he do that sent him to prison? More important, what'd he do to bring you around now?"

"Nothing, ma'am. We just need to ask a few questions."

"Come on, now," said Ertha Stadlbraun. "No shilly-shallying."

"At this point—"

"Young man, you are *not* asking me questions because that one's thinking of running for *president.* What'd he *do*?"

"Nothing that we know of. That's the truth, Mrs. Stadlbraun."

"You don't *know* anything for certain, but you sure *suspect* something."

"I really can't say more, Mrs. Stadlbraun."

"This is not right, sir. Your job is to protect

citizens so you *should* say. He's a crazy person and an ex-con living in the same building with normal folks."

"Ma'am, he's done nothing. This is part of a preliminary investigation and he's one of several people we're talking to."

She folded her arms across her dress. "Is he dangerous? Tell me yes or no."

"There's no reason to think that—"

"That's a lawyer answer. What if he's one of those ticking time bombs you hear about on the news, real quiet until he explodes? Some of the Mexicans have kids. What if he's one of those perverts and you didn't tell me?"

"Why would you think that, ma'am?"

"He *is*?" said Stadlbraun. "A *pervert*? *That's* what this is about?"

"No, ma'am, and it would be a real bad idea—"

"It's in the news every day, all these perverts. It wasn't like that in my day. Where did they all *come* from?"

Milo didn't answer.

Ertha Stadlbraun shook her head. "He gives me the willies. And now you're telling me he's an ex-con child molester."

Milo leaned in closer. "I am definitely *not*

telling you that, ma'am. It would be a *terrible* idea to spread those kinds of rumors."

"You're saying he could sue me?"

"I'm saying that Mr. Peaty is not suspected of anything. He may be a material witness and we're not even sure of that. This is what we call a background check. We do it all the time to be thorough. Mostly it ends up going nowhere."

Ertha Stadlbraun considered that. "Some job you've got."

Milo suppressed a smile. "If you were in danger, I'd tell you. I promise, ma'am."

Another hair pat. "Well, I've got nothing more to tell you. Wouldn't want to be careless and spread *rumors.*"

She stood.

Milo said, "May I ask a few more questions?"

"Such as?"

"When he comes home from work, does he ever leave again?"

Her chest heaved. "He's an innocent lamb but you want to know about his schedule . . . oh, never mind, you're clearly not going to tell me the truth."

She turned her back on us.

"Does he ever leave once he's home?" said Milo.

"Not that I've seen but I don't keep tabs."

"What about last night?"

She faced us again, shot a disgusted look. "Last night I was busy cooking. Three whole chickens, green beans with onions, yams, coleslaw with bacon shreds, four pies. I freeze early in the week so I can relax on Sunday when the kids come to visit. That way I can defrost Sunday morning before church, get back and heat up and we have a real dinner, not that greasy fast food."

"So you didn't notice what time Mr. Peaty came in."

"I *never* notice," she said.

"Never?"

"I might see him come in occasionally."

"What time does he usually get here from work?"

"Six, seven."

"And weekends?"

"Far as I can tell, weekends he stays inside all day. But I'm not going to promise you he never leaves. It's not like he'd stop by to say hello, him with those eyes aiming down like he's counting ants on a hill. I *certainly* can't tell you about last night. While I cooked, I had music on, then I watched the news, then I watched the Essence Awards, then I did a crossword and went to sleep. So if you're looking for me to alibi that nut, forget it."

CHAPTER
10

Much has been made of geographical profiling—criminals remaining within a comfort zone. Like any theory, sometimes it pans out, sometimes it doesn't and you get killers prowling the interstate or venturing far from home so they can establish a comfort zone *far* from prying eyes.

With any alleged rules about human behavior, you're lucky if you do better than chance. But the four-minute drive from Peaty's apartment to Michaela Brand's place on Holt was hard to ignore.

Her building was a mint-green fifties dingbat. The front was an open carport set behind

oil-specked concrete. Six parking slots, unoc-
cupied but for a dusty brown Dodge minivan.
The facade was spanned by two olive-green
diamonds. Speckles in the stucco caught afternoon light. Way too giddy.

A bank of key-lock mailboxes set into the
wall just south of the parking area bore no
names, only unit numbers. No manager designation. Michaela's compartment was shut
tight. Milo squinted through the slot. "Lots of
stuff inside."

Her apartment was at the back. Louvre
windows as old as the building were a burglar's dream. The glass slats were folded
shut but green curtains had been left slightly
parted. Dark inside, but the outlines of furniture were clear.

Milo began knocking on doors.

The only tenant at home was a woman in her
twenties wearing a stiff, brandy-colored wig
and a calf-length denim jumper over a white,
long-sleeved sweater. The wig made me
wonder about chemotherapy, but she was
buxom and her gray eyes were clear. The
same kind of lightly freckled complexion
Michaela Brand had been blessed with.
Open face tightened by surprise.

I saw the side curls and yarmulke on the squirming blond boy she was holding and got it: Some Orthodox Jewish women covered their natural hair out of modesty.

The badge made her press her son to her chest. "Yes?"

The boy's arms and feet shot out simultaneously and she nearly lost her grip. He looked to be three or so. Stocky and sturdy, twisting and turning, emitting little growly noises.

"Calm down, Gershie Yoel!"

The boy waved a fist. "Hero hero *Yehudah*! Fall the elephant!"

He squirmed some more and she gave up and set him down. He rocked on his feet and growled some more. Eyed us and said, "Fall!"

"Gershie Yoel, go in the kitchen and take a cookie—but only one. And don't wake up the babies!"

"Hero-hero! *Yehudah HaMa*kawbee gonna spear you bad Greek!"

"Go *now,* good boy, or no cookie!"

"Grr!" Gershie Yoel ran off, past walls covered with bookshelves. Books on every table and the couch. Any remaining space

was filled with playpens and toys and packages of disposable diapers.

The boy's shouts diminished.

"He's still celebrating the holidays," said
the young woman.

"Hanukkah?" said Milo.

She smiled. "Yes. He thinks he's Yehudah—Judah Maccabee. That's a big hero in
the Hannukah story. The elephant is from
a story about one of his brothers—" She
stopped, blushed. "What can I do for you?"

"We're here about one of your neighbors,
Mrs. . . ."

"Winograd. Shayndie Winograd."

Milo had her spell it and wrote it down.

She said, "You need my name?"

"Just for the record, ma'am."

"Which neighbors, the punk rockers?"

"Which punk rockers are those?"

She pointed to an upstairs unit two doors
down. "Over there, Unit Four. Three of them,
they think they're musicians. My husband
tells me they're punk rockers, I don't know
from such things." She held her ears.

"Noise problem?" said Milo.

"There was before," said Shayndie Winograd. "Everyone complained to the owner
and it's been okay . . . excuse me a second,

I need to check on the babies, please come in."

We cleared books from a brown corduroy couch. Leatherette-bound volumes gold-embossed with Hebrew titles.

Shayndie Winograd returned. "Still sleeping, *boruch*—thank God."

"How many babies?" said Milo.

"Twins," she said. "Seven months ago."

"Mazel tov," said Milo. "Three's a lot to handle."

Shayndie Winograd smiled. "Three would be easy. I've got six, five are school-age. Gershie Yoel should be in school but he was coughing this morning and I thought maybe he had a cold. Then, wouldn't you know, he got miraculously better."

Milo said, "The Lord works in mysterious ways."

Her smile widened. "Maybe I should have you talk to him about honesty . . . so is the problem the punk rockers?"

"This is about Ms. Brand, the tenant in Unit Three."

"The model?" said Shayndie Winograd.

"She modeled?"

"I call her that because she looks like a

model. Pretty, very skinny? What's the problem?"

"Unfortunately, ma'am, she was murdered last night."

Shayndie Winograd's hand flew to her
mouth. "Oh, my God—oh, no." She reached
back for an armchair, removed a toy truck,
and sat down. "Who did it?"

"That's what we're trying to find out, Mrs.
Winograd."

"Maybe her boyfriend?"

"Who's that?"

"Another skinny one."

Out of Milo's attaché came Dylan
Meserve's book shot from the hoax.

Winograd glanced at the photo. "That's
him. He was arrested? He's a criminal?"

"He and Ms. Brand were involved in a situation. It was in the papers."

"We don't read the papers. What kind of
situation?"

Milo gave her a summary of the phony
abduction.

She said, "Why would they do such a
thing?"

"It seems to have been a publicity stunt."

Shayndie Winograd's stare was blank.

"To help their acting careers," said Milo.

"I don't understand."

"It's hard to understand, ma'am. They thought the attention might help them get noticed in Hollywood. So why would you think Mr. Meserve would hurt Ms. Brand?"

"Sometimes they screamed at each other."

"You heard it up here on the second floor?"

"It was loud."

"What did they scream about?"

Shayndie Winograd shook her head. "I didn't hear the words, just the noise."

"Were these fights frequent?"

"Is he a bad person? Dangerous?"

"You're not in any danger, ma'am. How often did he and Ms. Brand scream at each other?"

"I don't know—he didn't live here, he just came over."

"How often?"

"Once in a while."

"When's the last time you saw him?"

She thought. "Weeks."

"When's the last time they had an argument?"

"Even longer . . . I'd say a month, maybe

more?" She shrugged. "I'm sorry. I try not to notice things."

"Not wanting to pry," said Milo.

"I don't want *nahrish*—foolish things in my life."

"So Mr. Meserve hasn't been here for a few weeks."

"At least," said Shayndie Winograd.

"And when did you last see Ms. Brand?"

"Her . . . let me think . . . not recently. But she used to come in late. The only time I ever noticed her was when I was out late with my husband and that's not often."

"The children."

"The children get up early, everyone's always needing something."

"Don't know how you do it, ma'am."

"You concentrate on what's important."

Milo nodded. "So you haven't seen Ms. Brand recently. Could you think back, maybe come up with something more specific?"

The young woman pushed back a lock of tight-sprayed, supplementary hair. "Maybe two weeks, three. I really can't say more than that. Don't want to give you false testimony."

Milo suppressed a smile. The young

woman shook her head. "I go out. To work. I just don't look at things that aren't important."

"With six kids you have time to work?"

"At the preschool, I stay half a day. What happened to her, it's terrible. Was it the way she lived?"

"What do you mean, ma'am?"

"I'm not insulting her, but we live one way, they live another way."

"They?"

"The outside world." Shayndie Winograd reddened. "I shouldn't be talking like this. My husband says each person should pay attention to their own actions, not what other people do."

"Your husband's a rabbi?"

"He has *smicha*—he's a rabbi but he doesn't work as a rabbi. Half a day he does bookkeeping, the rest of the time he learns."

"Learns what?"

Shayndie Winograd smiled again. "Torah, Judaism. He goes to a *kollel*—it's like a graduate school."

"Working on an advanced degree," said Milo.

"He learns for the sake of learning."

"Ah . . . anyway, sounds like you guys

have your hands full . . . so, tell me about Michaela Brand's way of life."

"She was the normal way. What's the American way now."

"Meaning?"

"Tight clothes, short skirts, going out all the time."

"Going out with who?"

"The only one I saw was the one in the picture. Sometimes she went out alone." Shayndie Winograd blinked. "A few times we said hello. She said my children were cute. Once she offered Chaim Sholom—my six-year-old—a candy bar. I took it because I didn't want to insult her but it wasn't kosher so I gave it to a Mexican lady who works at the day care . . . she always smiled at the children. Seemed like a nice girl." Deep sigh. "So terrible for her family."

"She ever talk about family?"

"No, sir. We never really had a conversation, just to say hello and smile."

Milo put his pad away. He hadn't written anything down. "Anything else you can tell me, ma'am?"

"Like what?"

"Whatever comes to mind."

"No, that's it," said Shayndie Winograd.

Another deep blush. "She was beautiful but I felt sorry for her. Showing a lot of . . . herself. But she was nice, smiled at the babies, one time I let her hold one because I was getting into the car and had lots of packages."

"So you had no problems with her."

"No, no, not at all. She was nice. I felt sorry for her, that's all."

"Why?"

"Living by herself. All the going out. People think they can go out and do anything they want but the world is dangerous. This proves it, no?"

Squalls sounded from a bedroom. "Uh-oh." We followed her into a ten-by-ten room taken up by two cribs. The occupants were a pair of infants, purple with indignation and, from the aroma, freshly soiled. Gershie Yoel bounced like a Slinky toy and tried to butt his mother as she changed diapers.

"Stop it! These men are policemen and if you don't behave they can take you to the *Beis Hasohar* like *Yosef Aveenu.*"

The little boy growled.

"*Beis Hasohar,* I mean it, you good boy." To us: "That's jail. Yosef—Joseph, from the

Bible, he ended up there, seven years until Pharaoh took him out."

"What'd he do?" said Milo.

"Nothing," she said. "But he was accused. By a woman." She rolled up a filthy diaper, wiped her hands. "Bad things. Even then there were bad things."

Milo left his card at the other apartments. When we got to the ground floor the mail carrier was distributing envelopes.

"Afternoon," said Milo.

The postman was a gray-haired Filipino, short and slight. His U.S. Postal Service van was parked at the curb. His right hand grasped one of several keys on a chain attached to his belt as the left pressed bound stacks of mail against his torso.

"H'lo," he said.

Milo identified himself. "What's the situation in Box Three?"

"What do you mean?"

"When's the last time she emptied it?"

The carrier opened Michaela's compartment. "Looks like not for a while." He let the keychain drop and used both hands to separate the stacks. "Two for her today. It's not my regular route . . . lucky this is all she got, not much room left."

Milo pointed to the two envelopes. "Can I take a look at those?"

The mailman said, "You know I cannot do that."

"I don't wanna open them," said Milo. "She got murdered last night. I just wanna see who's writing to her."

"Murdered?"

"That's right."

"It's not my regular route."

"You already said that."

The carrier hesitated, handed over the envelopes.

Bulk solicitation to apply for a low-interest home loan and a "Last Chance!" pitch to resubscribe to *InStyle* magazine.

Milo handed them back.

"How about the stuff inside?"

"That's private property," said the mailman.

"What happens when you come back in a few days and there's no more room?"

"We leave a notice."

"Where does the mail go?"

"Stays in the station."

"I can get a warrant and come by and open it all up."

"If you say."

"I say I just wanna look at the envelopes that are in there. Seeing as the box is already open."

"Privacy—"

"When she got killed she lost her privacy."

The carrier made a show of ignoring us as he went about delivering mail to the other tenants. Milo reached into Box Three, removed a thick stack wedged so tightly he had to ease it out, and thumbed through.

"Mostly junk . . . a few bills . . . urgent one from the gas company meaning she was overdue . . . same deal with the phone company."

He inspected the postmarks. "Ten days' worth. Looks like she was gone well before she died."

"A vacation's not likely," I said. "She was broke."

He looked at me. Both of us thinking the same thing.

Maybe someone had kept her for a while.

CHAPTER

11

We sat in the car, in front of Michaela's building.

I said, "Dylan Meserve cleared out of his place weeks ago. The neighbor heard him and Michaela arguing and Michaela told me she hated him."

"Maybe he came and got her," said Milo. "Took her on another adventure."

"What about Mr. Sex Criminal Peaty? Maybe he snatched both of them."

"If Peaty did abduct anyone, he didn't take them to his place," I said. "No way to keep that from Mrs. Stadlbraun and the other tenants."

"Too small to entertain."

"Still, he's the one with the record."

"And he's weird. So now I've got two high-priority bins."

As we drove away, he said, "Coffee would prop my eyelids."

I stopped at a place on Santa Monica near Bundy. Scrawled the possibilities as I saw them on a napkin and slid it across the table as Milo returned from making some calls.

1. *Dylan Meserve abducts and murders Michaela, then flees.*
2. *Reynold Peaty abducts and murders Michaela and Dylan.*
3. *Reynold Peaty abducts and murders Michaela and Dylan's disappearance is a coincidence.*
4. *None of the above.*

"It's that last one I love." Milo waved for the waitress, ordered pecan pie à la mode. Finishing most of the wedge in three gulps, he nibbled the rest with excruciating care, as if that proved self-restraint.

"I called Michaela's mother again, it was

all about her, big time woe-is-me. Too sick to come out to claim the body. The way she was gasping I figure it's probably true."

I summarized Michaela's account of her childhood.

"Ugly duckling?" he said. "Every gorgeous girl says that . . . what that Jewish lady said, the lifestyle issue, maybe she had a point."

"Michaela got caught up in the Hollywood thing."

"You know what that does to the ninety-nine-point-nine percent who fall on their asses. The question is, did it snag her or was it just one of those bad-luck deals."

"Like running into Peaty."

He ate the last bit of pie, wiped his mouth, put way too much money on the table, and extricated himself from the booth. "Back to the salt mine. Lots of boring stuff to do."

Boring was his code word for *I need to be alone.* I drove him to the station and went home.

That evening Michaela's murder was the lead story on every local broadcast, blow-dried news readers half smiling as they intoned about the "shocking crime" and exhumed mock-solemn memories of Michaela and Dylan's "publicity stunt."

Dylan was cited as "a person of interest, not a suspect." The implication was clear, as it always is when the police phrase it that way. I knew Milo hadn't given them the quote. Probably some public relations officer, issuing yet another boilerplate release.

Next morning's paper ran a page-three story with five times the ink space the hoax had merited, graced by two pictures of Michaela: a sultry, airbrushed head-shot taken by a photographer who churned them out for Hollywood hopefuls, and her LAPD booking photo. I wondered if either or both would resurface in the tabloids or on the Internet.

One way to get famous is to die the wrong way.

I didn't hear from Milo that day, figured the tips would be pouring in and he'd either learn a lot or nothing. I filled my time polishing up reports, thought about getting a dog, took a new referral from an attorney named Erica Weiss.

Weiss had filed suit against a Santa Monica psychologist named Patrick Hauser for molesting three female patients who'd attended his encounter groups. Chances were it would settle and there'd be no court appearance. I negotiated a high hourly fee and felt pretty good about the deal.

I looked up Hauser's office address. Santa Monica and Seventh. Allison also practiced in Santa Monica, a few miles away on Montana. I wondered if she knew Hauser, thought about calling her. Figured she might see it as an excuse to get in touch and decided against it.

At a quarter to six, when she was likely to be between patients, I changed my mind. Her private line was still on speed dial.

"Hi, it's me."

"Hi," she said. "How've you been?"

"Fine. You?"

"Fine . . . I was about to say, 'How've you been, handsome.' Got to watch those little slips."

"All compliments will be received with gratitude, oh Gorgeous One."

"Listen to this smarmy mutual admiration society."

"If I'm lyin', I'm flyin'."

Silence.

I said, "I'm actually calling on a professional matter, Ali. Do you know an esteemed colleague named Patrick Hauser?"

"I've seen him at a few meetings. Why?" I told her.

She said, "I guess I'm not surprised. Rumor has it he drinks. An encounter group, huh? That does surprise me."

"Why?"

"He seems more the corporate consultant type. How many patients are we talking about?"

"Three."

"That's pretty damning."

"Hauser claims it's a group delusion. There's no physical evidence, so it boils down to a he said/they said. The State Board's been sitting on it for months, still hasn't handed down a disposition. The women got impatient and contacted a lawyer."

"All three have one lawyer?"

"They're framing it as a mini–class action, hoping others will hear about it and come forward."

"How'd they find out they'd had similar experiences with Hauser?"

"They hung around after session, went for drinks, it came out."

"Not too smart of Hauser to put them in the same room."

"Fondling patients is no act of genius."

"So you think he did it."

"I'm open-minded but all three were seeing Hauser for mild depression, nothing delusional."

"Like I said, he's known to imbibe. That's all I can tell you."

"Thanks . . . so how's it been?"

"Life in general?" she said. "It's been okay."

"Want to join me for dinner?"

Where had *that* come from?

She didn't answer.

I said, "Sorry. Rewind the tape."

"No," she said. "I'm thinking about the offer. When did you mean?"

"I'm open. Including tonight."

"Hmm . . . I'll be free in an hour, have to eat anyway. Where?"

"You name it."

"How about that steak place?" she said. "The one where we met the first time."

I asked for a booth away from the mahogany bar with its low-pitched alkie chatter and sports on TV. By the time Allison showed up ten minutes later, I'd finished my Chivas, was working on my second glass of water.

The restaurant was dim and she stood there for a few seconds letting her eyes adjust. Her long, black hair swung free and her ivory face was serious. I thought I saw tension around the shoulders.

She stepped forward, revealed color. An orange pantsuit hugged her trim little body. Tangerine-orange. With that hair of hers, Halloween Costume could've been a problem but she made it work.

She spotted me, strode forward on high heels. The usual adornments sparkled at earlobes, wrists, and neck. Gold and sapphire; the stones brought out the deep blue of her eyes and played off the orange. Her makeup was perfect and her nails were French-tipped. The smile that parted her lips was hard to read.

A substantive woman but she takes a long time getting herself together.

The kiss on my cheek was quick and cool. She slid into the booth, just close enough to make conversation feasible but too distant for easy touching. Before we could talk the waiter had planted himself in front of us. Eduardo, the feisty one. Eighty-year-old Argentinian immigrant who claimed he could cook seafood better than the chef.

He bowed before Allison. "Evening, Dr. Gwynn. The usual?"

"No, thanks," she said. "It's a little chilly outside, so I think I'll have an Irish coffee. Make it decaf, Eduardo, or I'll be calling you up at three a.m. to play cards."

His smile said that wasn't a dreaded outcome. "Very good, Doctor. Another Chivas, sir?"

"Please."

He marched off. I said, "Been coming here a lot?"

"No. Why?"

"He used your name."

"I guess I'm here every three weeks or so."

Alone or with another guy?

She said, "The T-bone made a lasting impression on me."

Eduardo returned with drinks and menus. Extra whipped cream for Allison's Irish coffee. Bowing again, he left.

We touched glasses and drank. Allison licked foam from her up-per lip. Her face was smooth and white as fresh cream. She's thirty-nine but when she eases up on the jewelry, she can pass for ten years younger.

She pushed her drink away. "How's Robin?"

I worked at a casual shrug. "I guess she's okay."

"Haven't seen her much?"

"Not much."

"Sleeping with her?"

I put my scotch down.

She said, "That means yes."

When in doubt, revert to shrink tactics. I kept quiet.

"Sorry, that was totally inappropriate." She smoothed hair away from her face. "I knew it and felt like asking, anyway."

Bending over her coffee, she inhaled steam. "You're entitled to sleep with anyone you want, I just yearned to be bitchy. Sometimes I wouldn't mind sleeping with you myself."

"Sometimes is better than never."

"On the face of it, why shouldn't we?" she said. "Two healthy, libidinous people. We were great together." Faint smile. "Except when we weren't . . . not very profound, is it?"

We drank in silence. The second Chivas

brought on a nice warm buzz. Maybe that's why I said, "So what the hell happened?"

"You tell me."

"I'm asking you."

"And I'm asking you back."

I shook my head.

She drank, laughed. "Not that anything's funny."

Eduardo came over to take the food order, saw the looks on our faces, and turned heel.

Allison said, "Maybe nothing went wrong, it was just evolution."

"Devolution."

"Alex, when we started out, there was this rush of feeling every time I saw you. All I had to do was hear your voice and this sympathetic nervous system thing kicked in—this incredible *flood* of emotion. Sometimes when the doorbell rang and I knew it was you there'd be this heat—like a hot flash. I started to worry I was going through early menopause." She looked into her Irish coffee. "Sometimes I'd get sopping wet. *That* was something."

I touched her hand. Cool.

She said, "Maybe we just had some kind of hormonal thing going on and it faded.

Maybe every damn thing boils down to hormones and we're in the wrong damn field."

She turned away. Grabbed for her purse, fumbled for a tissue, and poked at her eyes. "One drink and my filter goes bye-bye."

Her mouth set in a way that thinned her lips. "I'll probably regret saying this but what really bothered me when I felt things diminishing was that it wasn't that way with Grant."

Her dead husband. Wharton grad, rich kid, successful financial type. He'd succumbed young to a freakishly rare cancer. Even when Allison loved me she'd talked about him adoringly.

"You had something great with him," I said.

"You weren't a replacement, Alex. I swear."

"Worse things to be."

"Don't be noble," she said. "It makes me feel worse."

I said nothing.

She said, "I just lied big time. It *did* fade with Grant. After I buried him he stopped being physical to me and turned into a . . . a . . . wraith. I felt—still feel guilty about that."

I groped for a reply. Every option sounded like shrinky cant. Coming here had been a mistake.

Suddenly, Allison's hip was touching mine and she was taking my face in her hands, kissing me hard. She retreated, ended up even farther down the booth.

We sat there.

"Alex, what I felt about you in the beginning was every bit as intense as with Grant. More intense on the physical level. Which also made me feel guilty. I started to think about us in a long-term sense. Wondering what it would be like. Then we had that problem on the Malley case and things just started to change. I know that alone couldn't have done it, there must've been . . . oh, listen to me, I sound like every other talky broad . . . it's confusing. The work stuff was part of what turned me on, and then all of a sudden it repulsed me."

The Malley case was the eight-year-old child murder. One of Allison's patients—a fragile young woman—had been drawn in. I'd deceived her. All in the name of truth, justice . . .

Robin had never liked hearing about *the*

work stuff. Allison had chased gory details with a vengeance.

I said, "Things change."

"They do. Dammit." She looked away. "If I said your place or mine, would you feel manipulated?"

"Maybe for a nanosecond."

"I'm not going to say it. Not tonight. I'm feeling really unattractive."

"There's a delusion for you."

"*Inside* I'm unattractive," she said. "I wouldn't be good, believe me."

I raised my glass. "To brutal honesty."

"Sorry. Want to forget about dinner?"

"Dinner wasn't a ploy to get you in the sack."

"What was it?"

"I don't know . . . maybe a ploy to get you in the sack."

She smiled. I smiled.

Eduardo had positioned himself across the room, spying on us while pretending to be above it all.

I said, "I could eat."

"I could, too." She waved him over. "Dinner with a former lover. How civilized in that French-movie kind of way."

Shifting closer, she lifted my left hand,

traced the outline of my thumbnail. "Still here."

"What is?"

"That split in the crescent—the little Pac-Man growing out of your nail. I always thought it was cute."

My body part, I'd never noticed it.

She said, "It's the same you."

CHAPTER

12

I spent the next day interviewing the three women who'd filed suit against Dr. Patrick Hauser. Individually, they came across vulnerable. As a group they were calmly credible.

Time for Hauser's insurance company to settle and cut its losses.

The following morning, I got to work on my report, was still in the thinking phase when Milo called.

"How's it going, big guy?"

"It's going nowhere at warp speed. Still haven't gotten into Michaela's place, landlord doesn't like leaving La Jolla. If he doesn't get here soon, I'm popping the lock. I talked to the Reno detective who nabbed Reynold Peaty for peeping. The story was Peaty was in an alley behind an apartment building, drunk as a skunk, looking through the drapes of a rear unit bedroom. The objects of his affliction were three college girls. Some guy walking his dog saw Peaty wagging his weenie and yelled. Peaty ran, the guy gave chase, knocked Peaty to the ground, called the cops."

"Brave citizen."

"Defensive tackle on the U. Nevada football team," he said, "Student neighborhood."

"Ground-floor rear unit?" I said.

"Just like Michaela's. The girls were a little younger than Michaela but you could make a case for victim similarity. What got Peaty off light was that these three had a history of being less than careful about the drapes. Also, the prosecutors never got word of Peaty's burglary conviction years before. That was a daylight break-in, cash and ladies' undies."

"Voyeur meets up with exhibitionists and everyone goes home happy?"

"Because the exhibitionists didn't want to

testify. The girls' exuberance extended to getting creative with videotape. Their main concern was their parents finding out. Peaty's a definite creep and I've promoted him to the penthouse of the high-priority bin."

"Time for a second interview."

"I tried. No sign of him or anyone else at the PlayHouse this morning, ditto for his apartment. Mrs. Stadlbraun wanted to have tea again. I drank enough to constipate a rhino and she talked about her grandkids and her godkids and the lamentable state of modern morality. She said she'd started watching Peaty more closely but he's gone most of the day. I'm gonna have Binchy tail him."

"Any decent phone tips?"

"Mostly the usual Martians and maniacs and morons, but there was one I'm following up on. That's why I called. Wire service picked up the *Times* story and some guy in New York phoned me yesterday. Couple of years ago his daughter went missing out here. What got me interested was she was going to acting school, too."

"The PlayHouse?"

"Father has no idea. There seems to be

lots he doesn't know. An MP report was filed on this girl—Tori Giacomo—but it doesn't look like anyone pursued it. No surprise, given her age and no sign of foul play. The guy insisted on flying out so I figure I can spare him some time. We're scheduled at three p.m., hope he likes Indian food. If you've got time, I could use some supplementary intuition."

"About what?"

"Ruling his daughter out. Listen to him but don't tell me what I want to hear."

"Do I ever?"

"No," he said. "That's why you're my pal."

Pink madras curtains separate Café Moghul's interior from the traffic and light of Santa Monica Boulevard. The shadowy storefront is walking distance from the station and when Milo needs to bolt the confines of his office, he uses it as an alternative work site.

The owners are convinced the presence of a large, menacing-looking detective serves the same purpose as a well-trained rottweiler. Once in a while Milo obliges them by handling homeless schizophrenics who wander in and try to sample the all-you-can-eat lunch buffet.

The buffet's a recent introduction. I'm not convinced it wasn't put in place for Milo.

When I got there at three p.m., he was seated behind three plates heaped with vegetables, rice, curried lobster, and some kind of tandoori meat. A basket of onion naan was half full. A pitcher of clove-flavored tea sat at his right elbow. Napkin tied around his neck. Only a few sauce specks.

Off-hour for lunch and he was the only diner. The smiling, bespectacled woman who runs the place said, "He's here, sir," and led me to his usual table at the rear.

He chewed and swallowed. "Try the lamb."

"A little early for me."

"Chai tea?" said the bespectacled woman.

I pointed to the pitcher. "Just a glass."

"Very good."

Last time I'd seen her, she'd been trying out contact lenses.

She said, "I had allergies to the cleaning solution. My nephew's an ophthalmologist, he says LASIK's safe."

Milo tried to hide his wince but I caught it.

He lives with a surgeon but blanches at the thought of doctor visits.

"Good luck," I said.

The woman said, "I'm still not sure," and left to get my glass.

Milo wiped his mouth and pulled a blue folder from his attaché. "Copy of Tori Giacomo's missing person file. Feel free to read but I can summarize in a minute."

"Go ahead."

"She was living in North Hollywood, alone in a single, working as a waitress at a seafood place in Burbank. She told her parents she was coming out to be a star but no one's aware of any parts she got and she had no agent. When she disappeared, the landlord stored her junk for thirty days then dumped it. By the time MP got around to checking, there was nothing left."

"The parents weren't notified when she skipped?"

"She was twenty-seven, didn't leave their number on her rental application."

"Who did she give as a reference?"

"File doesn't say. We're talking two years ago." He consulted his Timex. "Her father phoned from the airport an hour ago. Un-

less there was some disaster on the freeway, he shoulda been here already."

He squinted at numbers he'd scrawled on
the cover of the folder, punched his cell
phone. "Mr. Giacomo? Lieutenant Sturgis.
I'm ready for you . . . where? What's the cross
street? No, sir, that's *Little* Santa Monica, it's
a short street that starts in Beverly Hills,
which is where you are . . . three miles east of
here . . . yes, there are two of them. Little and
Big . . . I agree, it doesn't make . . . yeah, L.A.
can be a little strange . . . just turn around and
go north to Big Santa Monica . . . there's some
construction but you can get through . . . see
you, sir."

He hung up. "Poor guy thinks he's confused now."

Twenty minutes later a compact, dark-
haired man in his fifties pushed the restaurant door open, sniffed the air, and walked
straight toward us as if he had a score to
settle.

Short legs but big strides. Racewalking
to what?

He wore a brown tweed sportcoat that fit
around the shoulders but was too roomy
everywhere else, a faded blue plaid shirt,

navy chinos, bubble-toed work shoes. The dark hair was flat-black with reddish tints that betrayed the use of dye. Dense at the sides but sparse on top—just a few strands over a shiny dome. His chin was oversized and cleft, his nose fleshy and flattened. Brooding eyes looked us over as he approached. No taller than five nine but his hands were huge, sausage-fingered, furred at the knuckles with more black hair.

In one hand was a cheap red suitcase. The other shot out. "Lou Giacomo."

Choosing me first. I introduced myself, minus the doctorate, and he shifted quickly to Milo.

"Lieutenant." Going for rank. Military experience or plain old logic.

"Good to meet you, Mr. Giacomo. Hungry?"

Giacomo's nose wrinkled. "They got beer?"

"All kinds." Milo summoned the bespectacled woman.

Lou Giacomo told her, "Bud. Regular, not Light." Removing his jacket, he draped it over the back of his seat, tweaked the arms and the shoulders and the lapel until it hung straight. The plaid shirt was short-sleeved.

His forearms were muscled, hirsute cud-gels. Producing a billfold, he withdrew a pale blue business card and handed it to Milo.

Milo passed it over.

LOUIS A. GIACOMO, JR.
Appliance and Small Engine Repair
You Smash 'Em, We Patch 'Em

Red wrench logo in the center. Address and phone number in Bayside, Queens.

Giacomo's beer arrived in a tall, chilled glass. He looked at it but didn't drink. When the bespectacled woman left, he wiped the rim of the glass with his napkin, squinted, swabbed some more.

"Appreciate you meeting with me, Lieu-tenant. Learn anything about Tori?"

"Not yet, sir. Why don't you fill me in?"

Giacomo's hands clenched. He bared teeth too even and white to be anything but porcelain. "First thing you gotta know: No one looked for Tori. I called your department a bunch of times, talked to all these differ-ent people, finally I reached some detec-tive—some guy named Mortensen. He told me nothing but I kept calling. He got sick of hearing from me, made it real clear Tori wasn't high-priority, it was missing kids he was into. Then he stopped answering my calls, so I flew out but by that time he'd retired and moved to Oregon or somewhere. I lost my patience, said something to the detective they transferred me to, to the effect of what's wrong with you, you care more about traffic tickets than people? He had nothing to say."

Giacomo frowned into his beer. "Sometimes I lose my patience. Not that it woulda made a difference. I coulda been the nicest guy in the world, no one was gonna do anything to find Tori. So I have to go back and tell my wife I got nothing and she goes and has a nervous breakdown on me."

He pinged a thumbnail on the side of his glass.

Milo said, "Sorry."

"She got over it," said Giacomo. "Doctors gave her antidepressants, counseling, whatever. Plus, she had five other kids to deal with—the baby's thirteen, still in the house. Keeping busy, that's the best thing. Helps her not think about Tori."

Milo nodded and drank tea. Giacomo finally lifted his glass and drank.

"Tastes like Bud," he said. "What is this place, Pakistani?"

"Indian."

"We got those where I come from."

"Indians?"

"Them and their restaurants. I never been."

"Bayside," said Milo.

"Grew up there, stayed there. Hasn't changed that bad except now on top of your Italians and your Jews you get Chinese and other Orientals and Indians. I fixed a coupla their washing machines. Ever been to Bayside?"

Milo shook his head.

Giacomo looked at me.

I said, "Been to Manhattan, that's it."

"That's the city. The city's for the filthy rich people and homeless poor people, you got no room for the normal people in between." He took a generous swallow of beer. "Definitely Bud." Rolling a fist on the table, he flexed his forearms. Tendons jumped. The big, white teeth again. Eager to bite something.

"Tori wanted to be noticed. Since she was a little girl, my wife told her she was special. Taking her to these baby beauty contests, sometime she won a ribbon, it made the wife happy. Dancing and singing lessons, all these school plays. Problem was, Tori's grades weren't so great, one semester they threatened her she'd have to drop out of theater arts unless she passed math. She passed with a D, but that's what it took, threats."

I said, "Acting was her main thing."

"Her mother was always telling her she could be this big movie star. Encouraging her, for the whatchmacallit, the self-esteem. Sounds good but it also put ideas in Tori's head."

"Ambitions," I said.

Giacomo pushed his glass away. "Tori shoulda never come out here, what did she know about being on her own? It was the first time she was ever on a plane. This is a crazy place, right? You guys tell me if I'm wrong."

Milo said, "It can be rough."

"Crazy," Giacomo repeated. "Tori never worked a day in her life before she came out here. Until the baby came along she was the only girl, it's not like she's gonna work with *me*. Right?"

"Did she live at home before she came out here?"

"Always, with her mother doing everything for her. She never made her own bed. That's why it was crazy, picking up out of the blue."

"Was it a sudden decision?" I said.

Giacomo frowned. "Her mother was putting it in her head for years, but, yeah, when she announced it, it was sudden. Tori was nine years outta high school but she done nothing except for getting married and that didn't last."

"When'd she get married?" said Milo.

"When she was nineteen. A kid she dated in high school, not a bad guy but not too bright." Giacomo tapped his head. "At first, Mikey worked for me, I was trying to help out. Kid couldn't figure out how to use a frickin' Allen wrench. So he went to work with his uncle instead."

"Doing what?"

"Sanitation Department, like the rest of his family. Good pay and benefits, you get in the union, it's all about who you know. Used to do it myself but you come home stinkin' and I got tired of that. Tori said Mikey stunk when he came home, it wouldn't wash off.

Maybe that's why she got it annulled, I dunno."

"How long did the marriage last?" said Milo.

"Three years. Then she's back at home sitting around, doing nothing for five years except going out on auditions for commercials, modeling, whatever."

"She ever get anything?"

Giacomo shook his head. Bending, he unzipped a compartment of the red suitcase and drew out two head-shots.

Tori Giacomo's face was millimeters longer than the perfect oval. Huge dark eyes were topped by feathery, fake lashes. Too-dark eye shadow from another era. Same cleft chin as her father. Pretty, maybe borderline beautiful. It had taken me a few seconds to come to that conclusion, and in a world of flash impressions that wouldn't be enough.

In one photo, her hair was long, dark, and wavy. In the other, she'd switched to a shoulder-length, feathery platinum cut.

"She's always been a gorgeous kid," said Lou Giacomo. "But that ain't enough, right? You gotta *do* immoral stuff to get ahead. Tori's a good girl, never missed mass on

Sunday and that's not 'cause we forced her. My oldest sister became a nun and Tori was always close to Mary Agnes. Mary Agnes pulled strings with the monsignor to get the annulment through."

"Tori had a spiritual side," I said.

"Very, very spiritual. When I was out here I found out where the churches were near her apartment and went to all of them." Giacomo's eyes narrowed. "No one knew her, not the priests, the secretaries, no one. So right away I knew something was wrong."

His expression said he meant that on more than one level.

I said, "Tori'd stopped going to church."

Giacomo sat up straighter. "Some of those churches, they weren't much to look at, not like St. Robert Bellarmine, where my wife goes, that's a *church*. So maybe Tori wanted a nice church, like she was used to, I dunno. I went to the biggest one you guys got, downtown. Talked to an assistant to the assistant to the cardinal or whatever. Thinking maybe they had some records. No one knew a damn thing there, either."

He sat back. "That's it. Ask me whatever you want."

Milo began with the usual questions,

starting with Tori's ex-husband, the not-too-bright, odiferous Mikey.

Lou Giacomo said, "Mortensen wanted to know the same thing. So I'll tell you what I told him: No way. First off, I know the family and they're good people. Second, Mikey's a good kid, the soft type, you know? Third, he and Tori stayed friendly, there was no problem, they were just too young. Fourth, he never been out of New York."

He huffed, glanced over his shoulder. "Not much business in this place. The food got a problem?"

"How often did Tori call home?"

"Coupla times a week she talked to her mother. She knew I wasn't real happy about her picking up and leaving. She thought I didn't understand nothing."

"What'd she tell her mother?"

"That she was making a living on tips and learning how to act."

"Learning where?"

Giacomo frowned. "She never said. I double-checked with the wife after I talked to you. You can call her and ask any questions you like, but all she's gonna do is cry, believe me."

"Give me Mikey's last name," said Milo. "For the record."

"Michael Caravanza. Works at the Forest Hills branch. He and Tori looked happier split up than at the wedding. Like both of them were free, or something." He snorted. "Like you can ever be free. Go ahead, ask me more."

Ten more minutes of questioning revealed a sad truth: Louis Giacomo Junior knew precious little about his daughter's life since she'd come out to L.A.

Milo said, "The article on Michaela Brand caught your attention."

"The acting thing, you know." Giacomo's shoulders dropped. "I read it, got sick in the stomach. I don't wanna think the worst but it's been two years. No matter what her mother says, Tori woulda called."

"What does her mother say?"

"Arlene gets crazy theories in her head. Tori met some billionaire and she's off on some yacht. Stupid stuff like that." The whites of Giacomo's eyes had pinkened around the edges. He choked back a surge of emotion with a furious growl.

"So what do you think?" he demanded of

Milo. "This dead girl have something to do with Tori?"

"I don't know enough to think anything yet, sir."

"But you figure Tori's dead, right?"

"I couldn't say that either, Mr. Giacomo."

"You couldn't say but *you* know it and *I* know it. Two years. No way she wouldn't call her mother."

Milo didn't answer.

"The other girl," said Giacomo. "Who killed her?"

"The investigation just opened."

"You get a lot of those? Girls wanna be movie stars getting into big trouble?"

"It happens—"

"Bet it happens plenty. What's the name of the acting school the other girl went to?"

Milo rubbed his face. "Sir, it really wouldn't be a good idea for you to go over there—"

"Why not?"

"Like I said, it's a new investigation—"

"All I wanna do is ask if they knew Tori."

"I'll ask for you, sir. If I learn something, I'll call you. That's a promise."

"Promises, promises," said Giacomo. "It's

a free country. Nothing illegal about going over there."

"Interfering with an investigation's illegal, sir. Please don't complicate your life."

"That a kinda threat?"

"It's a request not to interfere. If I learn anything about Tori, I'll tell you." Milo put money on the table and stood.

Lou Giacomo got up, too. Picked up his red suitcase and fished in a rear pants pocket. "I'll pay for my own beer."

"Don't worry about it."

"I don't worry, worrying's a waste of time. I'll pay for my own *beer*." Giacomo pulled out a wallet stuffed so thick it was nearly round. Taking out a five, he tossed it near Milo's cash.

"If I call your medical examiners, ask about unclaimed bodies, what're they gonna tell me?"

"What makes you think that happened to Tori, Mr. Giacomo?"

"I was watching this show on cable. Forensics detectives, something like that. They said bodies don't get claimed, sometimes you do a DNA, solve an old case. So what would they tell me if I asked?"

"If a decedent is identified and someone

offers proof of family relationship, they're given forms to fill out and the body can be released."

"Is it one of those long pain-in-the-ass red-tape things?"

"It can usually be done in two, three days."

"How long do they keep 'em around?" said Giacomo. "Unclaimed bodies."

Milo didn't answer.

"How long, Lieutenant?"

"Legally, the maximum's a year but it's usually sooner."

"How much sooner?"

"It can be thirty to ninety days."

"Whoa. In and out, huh?" said Giacomo. "What, you got a dead body traffic jam?"

Milo was impassive.

"Even if it's a murder?" pressed Giacomo. "For a murder they got to keep it around, right?"

"No, sir."

"Don't they need to hold on to it for all that forensic stuff?"

"Evidence is collected and stored. What's not . . . necessary isn't kept."

"What, some union flunky's getting paid off to ditch bodies?" said Giacomo.

"There's a space issue."

"Same deal even with murder?"

"Same deal," said Milo.

"Okay, then what? Where does the body go if nobody claims it?"

"Sir—"

"Just tell me." Giacomo buttoned his jacket. "I'm one of those people, meets crap face-to-face, don't do no running away. I never fought in no wars but the marines trained me to deal. What's the next step?"

"The county crematorium."

"They burn it . . . okay, what happens to the ashes?"

"They're placed in an urn and kept for two years. If a verified relative steps forward and pays $541 to cover transportation costs, they get the urn. If no one claims the urn, the ashes are scattered in a mass grave at the Evergreen Memorial Cemetery in Boyle Heights—that's East L.A., near the coroner's office. The graves are marked with numbers. It's a group scattering, no individual identification is possible. Not all the unclaimed bodies are kept at the main crypt. Some are out in Sylmar, which is a suburb north of L.A., and others are even farther out in Lancaster, which is a city in the Antelope Valley—the high desert, maybe seventy miles east."

Rattling off the facts in the low, emotionless voice of a reluctant penitent.

Giacomo took it without flinching. Seemed almost to revel in the details. I thought about the cheap plastic urns the county used. Bundles stacked in room after room of the cold-storage basement on Mission Road, bound by sturdy white rope. The inevitable rot that sets in because refrigeration slows decomposition but doesn't stop it.

During my first visit to the crypt, I hadn't thought that through and expressed surprise to Milo at the greenish patches mottling a corpse lying on a gurney in the basement hallway.

Middle-aged man with a John Doe designation, awaiting transfer to the crematorium. Paperwork laid across his decaying torso, listing the meager details known.

Milo's answer had been painfully glib: "What happens to steak when you leave it in the fridge too long, Alex?"

Now he told Lou Giacomo: "I'm really sorry for your situation, sir. If there's anything else you want to tell us about Tori, I'd like to hear it."

"Like what?"

"Anything that would help find her."

"The restaurant she worked, her mother thinks it had something with 'Lobster' in it."

"The Lobster Pot," said Milo. "Riverside Drive, in Burbank. It went out of business eighteen months ago."

"You checked it out," said Giacomo, surprised. "You're looking for Tori because you *do* think it had something to do with the other girl."

"I'm exploring all the possibilities, sir."

Giacomo stared at him. "You got something you're not telling me?"

"No, sir. When are you going back home?"

"Who knows?"

"Where are you staying?"

"Same answer," said Giacomo. "I'll find something."

"There's a Holiday Inn on Pico past Sepulveda," said Milo. "Not far from here."

"Why would I wanna be close to here?" said Giacomo.

"No reason."

"What, you wanna keep tabs on me?"

"No, sir. Got plenty to do." Milo motioned to me. The two of us headed for the door.

The bespectacled woman said, "Was everything tasty, Lieutenant?"

Milo said, "Great."

Lou Giacomo said, "Yeah, everything's fantastic."

CHAPTER

13

Giacomo's rental Escort was parked in a loading zone ten yards from Café Moghul, the predictable ticket secured by a wiper blade. Milo and I watched him snatch the citation and rip it into confetti. Paper snow floated to the curb.

He shot Milo a defiant look. Milo pretended not to notice.

Giacomo stooped, picked up the shreds, put them in his pocket. Rolling his shoulders, he got in the Escort and drove off.

Milo said, "Every time I start off in one of those situations I tell myself to be sensitive. Somehow, it gets messed up."

"You did fine."

He laughed.

I said, "With all his frustration and grief it couldn't have gone any differently."

"That's exactly what you were supposed to say."

"At least something in life's predictable."

We walked east on Santa Monica, passed an Asian import shop where Milo stopped and pretended to be fascinated by bamboo.

When we resumed walking, I said, "Think Giacomo's right about Tori being dead?"

"It's a distinct possibility, but maybe her mother's right and she's off partying in Capri or Dubai. What do you think of the acting-school angle?"

"Lots of those in L.A.," I said.

"Lots of young waitpersons aiming for bigger and better. Be interesting if Tori took classes at the PlayHouse but short of that you see any stunning parallels?"

"A few similarities but more differences. Michaela's body was left out in the open. If Tori was murdered, the killer sure didn't want her discovered."

We turned right and walked south on Butler.

"What if we're looking at an escalation thing, Alex? Our bad boy started off hiding his handiwork but acquired confidence and decided to advertise?"

"Someone like Peaty moving from peeping to assault," I said. "Getting progressively more violent and brazen."

"That does come to mind."

"A sexual aspect to Michaela's killing would support it. There was no positioning and she was left fully clothed. But maybe she was played with at the kill-spot, tidied up before being transported. Autopsy's due soon, right?"

"It just got kicked up another day or two. Or four."

"Busy time at the crypt."

"Always."

"Are they really moving the bodies out that fast?"

"If only the freeways worked as well."

"Wonder how many Jane Does are in storage?" I said.

"If Tori ever was there, she's long gone. As her daddy will learn soon enough. What are the odds he's calling them right now?"

"If she was my daughter, that's what I'd be doing."

He sniffed, cleared his throat, scratched the side of his nose. Raised a pink, wormy welt that faded as quickly as it had materialized.

"Got a cold?" I said.

"Nah, air's been itching me, probably some crap blown in by the Santa Susannas . . . yeah, I'd be hounding them, too."

Back at his office, he tried the coroner's office again and asked for a rundown on young Caucasian Jane Does in the crypt. The attendant said the computer was down, they were short-staffed, a hand search of the records would take a long time.

"Any calls from a guy named Louis Giacomo? Father of a missing girl . . . well, he probably will. He's having a hard time, go easy . . . yeah, thanks, Turo. Let me ask you something else: What's the average transfer time to cremation nowadays? Just an estimate, I'm not gonna use it in court. That's what I thought . . . when you do check the inventory, go back a couple of years, okay? Twenties, Caucasian, five five, a hundred twenty. Giacomo, first name Tori." He spelled it. "She could be a blonde or brunette or anything in between. Thanks, man."

He hung up, swiveled in his chair. "Sixty, seventy days and it's off to the furnace." Spinning back to his phone, he called the PlayHouse again, listened for a few seconds, slammed the receiver down. "Last time, it just rang. This time I got sultry female voice on tape. The next class—something called 'Spontaneous Ingathering'—is tomorrow night at nine."

"Nocturnal schedule, like we guessed," I said. "Sultry, huh?"

"Think Lauren Bacall getting over the flu. Maybe it's Ms. Dowd. If she's an actor herself, velvety pipes wouldn't hurt."

"Voice-overs are a mainstay for unemployed actors," I said. "So are coaching gigs, for that matter."

"Those who can't do, teach?"

"Entire universities operate on that premise."

He laughed. "Okay, let's see what DMV has to say about the golden-throated Ms. Dowd."

Nora Dowd's DOB made her thirty-six, five two, a hundred and ten pounds, brown and brown. One registered vehicle, a six-month-old, silver Range Rover MK III. Home address on McCadden Place in Hancock Park.

"Nice neighborhood," he said.

"Bit of a drive to the school. Hollywood's just across Melrose from Hancock Park, you'd think a Hollywood address would attract screen-hopefuls."

"Maybe Dowd got a break on the rent. Or she owns the place. McCadden and her wheels says she's got bucks."

"A wealthy dilettante who does it for fun," I said.

"Hardly a rare bird," he said. "Let's see if this one sings."

Wilshire Boulevard near Museum Mile was disrupted by filming and we sat with the engine idling, an audience for nothing. Half a dozen triple-sized trailers filled an entire block. A fleet of carelessly parked smaller vehicles choked an eastbound lane. A squadron of cameramen, sound techs, gaffers, gofers, retired cops, and unionized hangers-on laughed and loafed and stalked the catered buffet. Two large men walked past, each carrying a lightweight, folding director's chair. Stenciled names on the canvas backs that I didn't recognize.

Public space commandeered with the usual insouciance. The motoring public on Wilshire wasn't happy and tempers flared in the single open lane. I managed to escape onto Detroit Street, hooked a right on Sixth Street, cruised across La Brea. A few blocks later: Highland, the western border of Hancock Park.

The next block was McCadden, wide and peaceful and sunny. A vintage Mercedes rolled out of a driveway. A nanny walked a baby in a navy blue, chrome-plated stroller. Birds swooped and settled and chirped gratitude. Cold winds had been whipping the city for a couple of days but the sun had broken through.

Nora Dowd's address put her half a block south of Beverly. Most of the neighboring residences were beautifully maintained Tudors and Spanish revivals set behind brilliant emerald lawns.

Dowd's was a two-story Craftsman, cream with dark green trim.

Inverse color scheme of her acting school and, like the PlayHouse, girded by a covered porch and shadowed by generous eaves. A low rock wall at the curb was centered by an open gate of weathered iron grillwork. Splitting the lawn was a wide flag-stone walkway. Similar old-school land-scaping: birds of paradise, camellias, azal-eas, fifteen-foot eugenia hedges on both sides of the property, a monumental deodor cedar fringing the double garage.

Barn doors on this garage, too. Nora Dowd's house was twice the size of her school but anyone scoring above nine on the Glasgow Coma Scale could see the par-allels.

"Consistent in her taste," I said. "An oa-sis of stability in this hazy, crazy town."

"Mr. Hollywood," he said. "You should write for *Variety*."

"If I wanted to lie for a living, I'd have gone into politics."

This porch was nicely lacquered, decorated with green wicker furniture and potted ferns. The pots were hand-painted Mexican ceramics and looked antique. The double doors were quartersawn oak stained dark brown.

Milky white leaded panes comprised the door window. Milo used his knuckles on the oak. The doors were hefty and his hard raps diminished to feeble clicks. He tried the bell. Dead.

He muttered, "So what else is new?" and stuck his business card in the split between the doors. As we returned to the Seville, he yanked his phone from his pocket as if it were a saddle burr. Nothing to report on Michaela's Honda, or Dylan Meserve's Toyota.

We returned to the car. As I opened the driver's door, a sound from the house turned our heads.

Female voice, low, affectionate, talking to something white and fluffy, cradled to her chest.

She stepped out to the porch, saw us, placed the object of her affection on the floor. Looked at us some more and walked toward the sidewalk.

The physical dimensions fit Nora Dowd's DMV stats but her hair was a blue-gray pageboy, the back cut high on the neck. She wore an oversized plum sweater over gray leggings and bright white running shoes.

Bouncy step but she faltered a couple of times.

She gave us a wide berth, started to walk south.

Milo said, "Ms. Dowd?"

She stopped. "Yes?" One single syllable didn't justify a diagnosis of sultry, but her voice was low and throaty.

Milo produced another card. Nora Dowd read it, handed it back. "This is about poor Michaela?"

"Yes, ma'am."

Under the shiny gray cap of hair, Nora Dowd's face was round and rosy. Her eyes were big and slightly unfocused. Bloodshot; not the pink of Lou Giacomo's orbs, these were almost scarlet at the rims. Elfin ears protruded past fine, gray strands. Her nose was a pert button.

Middle-aged woman trying to hold on to a bit of little girl. She seemed well past thirty-six. Turning her head, she caught some light and a corona of peach fuzz softened her chin. Lines tugged at her eyes, puckers cinched both lips. The ring around her neck was conclusive. The age on her driver's license was a fantasy. Standard Operating Procedure in a company town where the product was false promises.

The white thing sat still, too still for any

kind of dog I knew. Maybe a fur hat? Then
why had she talked to it?

Milo said, "Could we speak to you about
Michaela, ma'am?"

Nora Dowd blinked. "You sound a little
like Joe Friday. But he was a sergeant, you
outrank him." She cocked a firm hip. "I met
Jack Webb once. Even when he wasn't
working, he liked those skinny black ties."

"Jack was a prince, helped finance the
Police Academy. About Michae—"

"Let's walk. I need my exercise."

She surged ahead of us, swung her arms
exuberantly. "Michaela was all right if you
gave her enough structure. Her improv skills
left something to be desired. Frustrated, always frustrated."

"About what?"

"Not being a star."

"She have any talent?"

Nora Dowd's smile was hard to read.

Milo said, "The one big improv she tried
didn't work out so well."

"Pardon?"

"The hoax she and Meserve pulled."

"Yes, that." Flat expression.

"What'd you think of that, Ms. Dowd?"

Dowd walked faster. Exposure to sunlight

had irritated her bloodshot eyes and she blinked several times. Seemed to lose balance for a second, caught herself.

Milo said, "The hoax—"

"What do I think? I think it was shoddy."

"Shoddy how?"

"Poorly structured. In terms of theater."

"I'm still not—"

"Lack of imagination," she said. "The goal of any true performance is openness. Revealing the self. What Michaela did insulted all that."

"Michaela and Dylan."

Nora Dowd again surged forward. Several steps later, she nodded.

I said, "Michaela thought you'd appreciate the creativity."

"Who told you that?"

"A psychologist she talked to."

"Michaela was in therapy?"

"That surprises you?"

"I don't encourage therapy," said Dowd. "It closes as many channels as it opens."

"The psychologist evaluated her as part of her court case."

"How silly."

"What *about* Meserve?" said Milo. "He didn't fail you?"

"No one failed me. Michaela failed herself. Yes, Dylan should have known better but he got swept along. And he comes from a different place."

"How so?"

"The gifted are allowed more leeway."

"Was the hoax his idea or Michaela's?"

Five more steps. "No sense speaking ill of the dead." A beat. "Poor thing." Dowd's mouth turned down. If she was trying to project empathy, her chops were rusty.

Milo said, "How long did Michaela take classes with you?"

"I don't give classes."

"What are they?"

"They're performance experiences."

"How long was Michaela involved in the experiences?"

"I'm not sure—maybe a year, give or take."

"Any way to fix that more precisely?"

"Pree-cise-lee. Hmm . . . no, I don't think so."

"Could you check your records?"

"I don't do records."

"Not at all?"

"Nothing 'tall," Dowd sang. She rotated

her arms, breathed in deeply, said, "Ahh. I like the air today."

. "How do you run a business without records, ma'am?"

Nora Dowd smiled. "It's not a business. I don't take money."

"You teach—present experiences for free?"

"I *avail* myself, provide a time and place and a selectively judgmental atmosphere for those with courage."

"What kind of courage?"

"The kind that enables one to accept selective judgment. The *balls* to dig deep inside here." She cupped her left breast with her right hand. "It's all about self-revelation."

"Acting."

"*Performing.* Acting is an artificial word. As if life is here"—cocking her head to the left—"and performance is out here, on another galaxy. Everything's part of the same gestalt. That's a German word for the whole being bigger than the sum of the parts. I'm blessed."

Milo said, "With teaching—availing talent?"

"With an uncluttered consciousness and freedom from worry."

"Freedom from record-keeping's pretty good, too."

Dowd smiled. "That, as well."

"Does not charging mean freedom from financial worry?"

"Money's an attitude," said Nora Dowd brightly.

Milo pulled out the photo of Tori Giacomo and held it in front of her face. Her pace didn't falter and he had to speed up to keep it in her line of vision.

"Not bad looking in a *Saturday Night Fever* kind of way." Dowd fended off the photo and Milo dropped his arm.

"You don't know her?"

"I really can't say. Why?"

"Her name is Tori Giacomo. She came to L.A. to be an actress, took lessons, disappeared."

Nora Dowd said, "Disappeared? As in poof?"

"Did she ever avail herself at the Play-House?"

"Tori Giacomo . . . the name doesn't ring a bell but I can't give you a yes or no because we don't take attendance."

"You don't recognize her but you can't say no?"

"All sorts of people show up, especially on nights when we do group exercises. The room's dark and I certainly can't be expected to remember every face. There is a sameness, you know."

"Young and eager?"

"Young and oh-so hungry."

"Could you take another look, ma'am?"

Dowd sighed, grabbed the photo, stared for a second. "I simply can't say yes or no."

Milo said, "Big crowds show up but you did know Michaela."

"Michaela was a regular. Made sure to introduce herself to me."

"Ambitious?"

"High level of hunger, I'll give her that. Without serious *want* there's no chance of reaching the bottom of the funnel."

"What funnel is that?"

Dowd stopped, faltered again, regained her balance, and shaped a cone with her hands. "At the top are all the strivers. Most of them give up right away, which allows those who remain to sink down a little more." Her hands dropped. "But there are still far too many and they bump against each other, collide, everyone hungry for the spout. Some tumble out, others get crushed."

Milo said, "More room in the funnel for those with balls."

Dowd looked up at him. "You've got a Charles Laughton thing going on. Ever think of performing?"

He smiled. "So who gets to the bottom of the funnel?"

"Those who are karmically destined."

"For celebrity."

"That's not a disease, Lieutenant. Or should I call you Charles?"

"What's not?"

"Celebrity," said Dowd. "Anyone who makes it is a gifted winner. Even if it doesn't last long. The funnel's always shifting. Like a star on its axis."

Stars didn't have axes. I kept that nugget to myself.

Milo said, "Did Michaela have the potential to make it all the way to the spout?"

"As I said, I don't want to diss the dead."

"Did you get along with her, Ms. Dowd?"

Dowd squinted. Her eyes looked raw and inflamed. "That's a strange question."

"Maybe I'm missing something, ma'am,

but you don't seem too shaken up by her murder."

Dowd exhaled. "Of course I'm sad. I see no reason to reveal myself to you. Now if you'll let me complete my—"

"In a sec, ma'am. When's the last time you saw Dylan Meserve?"

"Saw him?"

"At the PlayHouse," said Milo. "Or anywhere else."

"Hmm," said Dowd. "Hmm, the last time . . . a week or so? Ten days? He helps out from time to time."

"Helps how?"

"Arranging chairs, that sort of thing. Now I need to get some cleansing exercise, Charles. All this talk has polluted the good air."

She jogged away from us, moving fast, but with a choppy, knock-kneed stride. The quicker she ran, the more pronounced was her clumsiness. When she was half a block away, she began shadowboxing. Swung her head from side to side.

Clumsy but loose. Oblivious to any notion of imperfection.

CHAPTER
14

Milo said, "Don't need you for a diagnosis. She's loony. Even without the dope."

"What dope?"

"You didn't smell it on her? She stinks of devil weed, dude. Those eyes?"

Red rims, lack of coordination, answers that seemed just a bit off-time. "I must be slipping."

"You didn't get close enough to smell it. When I handed her my business card, she reeked. Must've just finished toking."

"Probably why she didn't answer the door."

He gazed down the block. The speck that

was Nora Dowd had vanished. "Nuts and stoned and doesn't keep records. Wonder if she married money or inherited it. Or maybe she had her time at the bottom of the funnel and invested well."

"Never heard of her."

"Like she said, the axis shifts."

"Planets have axes, stars don't."

"Whatever. Not very sympathetic to Michaela, was she?"

"Not even faking it. When Dylan Meserve came up she bolted. Maybe because he avails himself in all sorts of ways."

"Creative consultant," he said. "Yeah, they're doing the nasty."

"Situation like that," I said, "a gorgeous young woman could be a threat to a woman of her age."

"Couple of good-looking kids, up in the hills, naked . . . Dowd's gotta be what, forty-five, fifty?"

"That would be my guess."

"Rich lady gets her strokes playing guru to the lean and hungry and pretty . . . she picks Dylan out of the fold, he goes and fools with Michaela. Yeah, it's a motive, ain't it? Maybe she told Dylan to clean things up. For all we know, he's right there, holed up in that big house of hers, got his wheels stashed in her garage."

I glanced back at the big, cream house. "It would also be a nice quiet place to keep Michaela while they figured out what to do with her."

"Load her in the Range Rover and dump her near her apartment to distance themselves." He crammed his hands in his pockets. "Wouldn't that be ugger-ly. Okay, let's see what the neighbors have to say about Ms. Stoner."

Three bell rings brought three cleaning ladies to the door, each one intoning, *"Senora no esta en la casa."*

At the well-kept brick Tudor three doors north of Nora Dowd's house, an elderly man wearing a bright green cardigan, a red wool shirt, gray plaid pants, and burgundy house slippers studied us over the rim of his old-fashioned. The toes of his slippers were embroidered with black wolves' heads. The dim marble entry behind him gave off a whiff of *eau de codger.*

He took a long time to examine Milo's business card. Reacted to Milo's inquiry about Nora Dowd with, "That one? Why?" A voice like gravel under heavy footsteps.

"Routine questions, sir."

"Don't give me that malarkey." Tall but bent, he had foxed-paper skin, coarse white hair, and clouded blue eyes. Stiff fingers bent the card in half and palmed it. A fleshy, open-pored nose dipped toward a lopsided twig of an upper lip. "Albert Beamish, formerly of Martin, Crutch, and Melvyn and ninety-three other partners until the mandatory out-to-pasture clause kicked in and they sentenced me to 'emeritus.' That was eighteen years ago so do the arithmetic and choose your words efficiently. I could drop dead right in front of you and you'd have to lie to someone else."

"Till a hundred and twenty, sir."

Albert Beamish said, "Get on with it, kiddo. What'd that one do?"

"One of her students was murdered and we're getting background information from people who knew the victim."

"And you spoke to her and you saw what a lunatic she is."

Milo chuckled.

Albert Beamish said, "Students? They let her teach? When did that start?"

"She runs her own acting school."

Beamish's laughter was jagged. It took a while for his cocktail to reach his lips. "Acting. That's just more of the same."

"The same what?"

"Being the indolent, spoiled brat she's always been."

Milo said, "You've known her for a while."

"She grew up in that overgrown log cabin. Her grandfather built it back in the twenties, a blight on the neighborhood then, just as it is now. Doesn't fit, should be in Pasadena or some place where they like that kind of thing." Beamish's filmy irises aimed across the street. "You see any others like it around here?"

"No, sir."

"There's a reason for that, kiddo. Doesn't *fit*. Try telling that to Bill Dowd Senior—the grandfather. No sophistication. Came from Oklahoma, made money in groceries, dry goods, something of that sort. His wife was low-class, uneducated, thought she could buy her way in spending money. Same with the daughter-in-law—that one's mother. Blond tramp, always throwing ostentatious parties."

Beamish drank some more. "Damned elephant."

Milo said, "Sir?"

"One time they brought in a damned elephant. For one of their birthdays, don't remember which one. Filthied up the street, the stench lasted for days." His nostrils quivered. "Bill Junior never worked a day in his life, fooled around on his daddy's money, married late. Woman just like his mother, no class. Now you're telling me *that* one teaches acting. Where does this travesty take place?"

"West L.A.," said Milo. "The PlayHouse."

"I never venture that far from civilization," said Beamish. "A play house? Sounds damned frivolous."

"It's a Craftsman building, same as the house," I said.

"Does it fit in over there?"

"The neighorhood's pretty hetero—"

"Piles of logs. All that gloomy wood and stained glass belongs in a church, where the intent is to simultaneously impress and depress. Bill Dowd Senior made his fortune with canned peas, whatever, nailed up that heap of timber. Probably got the idea when he was buying up properties in Pasadena,

South Pasadena, Altadena, Lord knows what other 'denas. That's what they've all been living off. She and her brothers. None of them worked a day in their lives."

"How many brothers?" I said.

"Two. Bill the Third and Bradley. One's a fool and the other's shifty. The shifty one sneaked into my yard and stole my persimmons." Pinpoints of anger livened the milky blue eyes. "Stripped the damn tree bare. He denied it but everyone knew."

Milo said, "How long ago was this, sir?"

"Thanksgiving of '72. Delinquent never owned up to it but my wife and I knew it was him."

"Why's that?" said Milo.

"Because he'd done it before."

"Stole from you?"

"From others. Don't ask me the who and what, never heard the details, just general woman's talk. They must have believed it, too. They boarded him out. Some sort of military academy."

"Because of the persimmons?"

"No," said Beamish, exasperated. "We never told them about the persimmons. No sense being obtrusive."

'What about Nora Dowd?" said Milo. "Any problems with her?"

"She's the youngest and the most spoiled. Always had those *ideas.*"

"What ideas, sir?"

"Being an *actress.*" Beamish's lips curled. "Running around trying to get parts in movies. I always thought her mother was the one behind all that."

"She ever get any parts?"

"Not that I heard. Do fools actually pay to hear what she has to say at her play house?"

"Seems to be that way," said Milo. "Did she ever marry?"

"Negative."

"Does she live with anyone?"

"She's got that heap of sticks all to herself."

Milo showed him the snap of Dylan Meserve.

Beamish said, "Who's that?"

"One of her students."

"Looks like a delinquent, himself. Are they fornicating?"

Milo said, "What about visitors?"

Beamish snatched the picture from between Milo's fingers. "Numbers around his neck. He's a damned felon?"

"Misdemeanor arrest."

Beamish said, "Nowadays, that could include homicide."

"You don't like Ms. Dowd."

"Don't have use for any of them," said Beamish. "Those persimmons. I'm talking the Japanese variety, tart, firm, nothing like those gelatinous abominations you get in the market. When my wife was alive she loved making compote for Thanksgiving. She was looking forward to Thanksgiving. That wastrel filched every one. Stripped the tree *naked*."

He returned the photo. "Never seen him but I'll keep an eye out."

"Thanks, sir."

"What'd you think of that pet of hers?"

"What pet, sir?"

Albert Beamish laughed so hard he began coughing.

Milo said, "You okay, sir?"

Beamish slammed the door.

15

The white fluffy thing Nora Dowd had left on her porch was a stuffed toy. Some sort of bichon or Maltese. Flat brown eyes.

Milo picked it up, had a close look. Said, "Oh, man," and handed it over.

Not a toy. A real dog, stuffed and preserved. The pink ribbon around its neck supported a heart-shaped, silver pendant.

Stan

Birth and death dates. Stan had lived thirteen years.

Blank look on the white fluffy face. Maybe

it was the glass eyes. Or the limits of taxidermy.

I said, "Could be Stan as in Stanislavsky. She probably talks to it and takes it with her on walks. Saw us and thought better of it."

"What does that mean?"

"Eccentric rather than psychotic."

"I'm so impressed." He took the dog and put it back on the floor. "Stanislavsky, eh? Let's method act the hell out of here."

As we drove past Albert Beamish's Tudor, the drapes across the living room window fluttered.

Milo said, "Neighborhood crank, love it. Too bad he didn't recognize Meserve. But with his vision, that means nothing. He sure hates the Dowds."

I said, "Nora has two brothers who own a lot of property. Ertha Stadlbraun said Peaty's landlords are a pair of brothers."

"So she did."

By the time we reached Sixth Street and La Cienega, he'd confirmed it. William Dowd III, Nora Dowd, and Bradley Dowd, doing business as BNB Properties, owned the apartment building on Guthrie. It took several other calls to get an idea of their holdings. At least forty-three properties registered in L.A. County. Multiple residences and office buildings and the converted house on the Westside where Nora availed herself to would-be stars.

"The school's probably a concession to Crazy Sister," he said. "Keeps her out of their hair."

"And far from their other properties," I said. "Something else: All those buildings mean lots of janitorial work."

"Reynold Peaty looking in all kinds of windows . . . if he's moved from peeping to violence, lots of potential victims. Yeah, let's check it out."

Corporate headquarters for BNB Properties was on Ocean Park Boulevard near the Santa Monica Airport. Not one of the Dowd sibs' properties, this one was owned by a national real estate syndicate that owned half of downtown.

"Wonder why?" said Milo.

"Maybe some sort of tax dodge," I said. "Or they held on to what their father left them, didn't add more."

"Lazy rich kids? Yeah, makes sense."

It was four forty-five and the drive at this

hour would be brutal. Milo called the listed number, hung up quickly.

" 'You've reached the office, blah blah blah. If it's a plumbing emergency, press 1. Electrical, press 2.' Lazy rich kids are probably drinking at the country club. You up for a try, anyway?"

"Sure," I said.

Olympic Boulevard seemed the optimal route. The lights are timed and parking restrictions keep all six lanes open during L.A.'s ever-expanding rush hour. The boulevard was designed back in the forties as a quick way to get from downtown to the beach. People old enough to remember when that promise was kept get teary-eyed.

This afternoon, traffic was moving at twenty miles per. When I stopped at Doheny, Milo said, "The love-triangle angle fits, given Nora's narcissism and nuttiness. This woman thinks her dog's precious enough to be turned into a damned mummy."

"Michaela insisted she and Dylan weren't lovers."

"She'd want to keep that from Nora. Maybe from you, too."

"If so, the hoax was really stupid."

"Two naked kids," he said. "The publicity wouldn't have thrilled Dowd."

"Especially," I said, "if she really doesn't feel that blessed."

"Never made it to the bottom of the funnel."

"Never made it, lives alone in a big house, no stable relationships. Needs to smoke up before greeting the world. Maybe clinging to a stuffed dog is just massive insecurity."

"Playing a role," he said. "Availing herself. Okay, let's see if we can tête-à-tête with the rest of this glorious family."

The site was a two-story strip mall on the northeast corner of Ocean Park and Twenty-eighth, directly opposite the lush, industrial park that fronted Santa Monica's private airport. BNB Properties was a door and window on the second floor.

Cheaply built mall, lemon-yellow sprayed-stucco walls stained by rust around the gutters, brown iron railings rimming an open balcony, plastic tile roof pretending to evoke colonial Spain.

The ground floor was a take-out pizza joint, a Thai café and its Mexican counterpart,

and a coin-op laundry. BNB's upstairs neighbors were a chiropractor touting treatment for
"workplace injuries," Zip Technical Assis-
tance, and Sunny Sky Travel, windows fes-
tooned by posters in bright, come-on colors.

As we climbed pebble-grained steps, a
sleek, white corporate jet shot into the sky.

"Aspen or Vail or Telluride," said Milo.
"Someone's having fun."

"Maybe it's a business trip and they're
going to Podunk."

"That tax bracket, *everything's* fun. Wonder if the Dowd brothers are in that league.
If they are, they're skimping on ambience."

He pointed at BNB's plain brown door.
Chipped and gouged and cracking toward
the bottom. The corporate signage consisted of six U-stick, silver foil parallelo-
grams aligned carelessly.

BNBinc

A single, aluminum-framed window was
blocked by cheap, white mini-blinds. The
slats tilted to the left, left a triangle of peep-
space. Milo took advantage, shading his
eyes with his hands and peering in.

"Looks like one room . . . and a bathroom

with the light on." He straightened. "Some guy's in there peeing, let's give him time to zip up."

Another plane took off.

"That one's Aspen for sure," he said.

"How can you tell?"

"Happy sound from the engines." He knocked and opened the door.

A man stood by a cheap, wooden desk staring at us. He'd forgotten to zip the fly of his khaki Dockers and a corner of blue shirt peeked out. The shirt was silk, oversized and baggy, a stone-washed texture that had been fashionable a decade ago. The khakis sagged on his skinny frame. No belt. Scuffed brown penny loafers, white socks.

He was short—five five or six—looked to be around fifty, with down-slanted medium brown eyes and curly gray hair cut in a tight Caesar cap. White fuzz on the back of his neck said it was time for a trim. Same for a two-day growth of salt-and-pepper beard. Hollow cheeks, angular features, except for his nose.

Shiny little button that gave his face an elfin cast. Either he'd used the same surgeon as his sister or stingy nasal endowment was a dominant Dowd trait.

Milo said, "Mr. Dowd?"

Shy smile. "I'm Billy." The badge made him blink. His hand brushed the corner of shirttail and he stiffened. Zipped his fly. "Oops."

Billy Dowd breathed into his hand. "Need my Altoids . . . where did I *put* them?"

Turning four pockets inside out, he produced nothing but lint that landed on thin, gray carpet. A check of his shirt pocket finally located the mints. Popping one in his mouth and chewing, he held out the tin. "Want some?"

"No, thanks, sir."

Billy Dowd perched on the edge of his desk. Across the room was a larger, more substantial work station: carved oak replica of a rolltop, flat-screen computer monitor, the rest of the components tucked out of view.

Brown walls. The only thing hanging a Humane Society calendar. Trio of tabby kittens staking a claim on ultimate cute.

Billy Dowd chewed another mint. "So . . . what's happening?"

"You don't seem surprised we're here, Mr. Dowd."

Billy blinked some more. "It's not the only time."

"That you've spoken to police?"

"Yup."

"When were the others?"

Billy's brow creased. "The second I'd have to say was last year? One of the tenants—we've got a lot of tenants, my brother and sister and me, and last year one of them was stealing computer stuff. A policeman from Pasadena came over and talked to us. We said okay, arrest him, he pays late anyway."

"Did they?"

"Uh-uh. He ran away and escaped. Took the lightbulbs, messed the place up, Brad was *not* happy. But then we got another tenant pretty soon and he got happy. Real nice people. Insurance agents, Mr. and Mrs. Rose, they pay on time."

"What was the name of the dishonest tenant?"

"I'd have to say . . ." Slowly spreading smile. "I'd have to say I don't know. You can ask my brother, he'll be here soon."

"What was the other time the police visited?" said Milo.

"Pardon me?"

"You said the second was last year. When was the first?"

"Oh. Right. The first was *long* ago, I'd have to say five years, could be even six?"

He waited for confirmation.

I said, "What happened a long time ago?"

"That was different," he said. "Someone hit someone else in the hallway, so they called the police. Not tenants, two visitors, they got into a fight or something. So what happened this time?"

"A student of your sister's was murdered and we're looking into people who knew her."

The word "murdered" drew Billy Dowd's hand to his mouth. He held it there and his fingers muffled his voice. "That's *awful*!" The hand dropped to his chin, clawed the stubbly surface. Nails gnawed short. "My sister, she's okay?"

"She's fine," said Milo.

"You're *sure*?"

"Absolutely, sir. The murder didn't take place at the PlayHouse."

"Phew." Billy drew a hand across his brow. "You scared me, I nearly pissed my pants." He laughed nervously. Looked down at his crotch, verifying continence.

A voice from the doorway said, "What's going on?"

Billy Dowd said, "Hey, Brad, it's the police again."

The man who walked in was half a foot taller than Billy and solidly built. He wore a well-cut navy suit and a yellow shirt with a stiff spread collar, soft brown calfskin loafers.

Mid forties but his hair was snow-white. Dense and straight and clipped short.

Crinkly dark eyes, full lips, square chin, beak nose. Nora and Billy Dowd had been modeled from soft clay. Their brother was hewn from stone.

Bradley Dowd stood next to his brother and buttoned his jacket. "Again?"

"You remember," said Billy. "That guy, the one who stole computers and took all the lights—what was his name, Brad? Was he Italian?"

"Polish," said Brad Dowd. He looked at us. "Edgar Grabowski's back in town?"

"It's not *about* him, Brad," said Billy. "I was just explaining why I was surprised but not totally surprised when they came in here, because it wasn't the first—"

"Got it," said Brad, patting his brother's shoulder. "What's up, gentlemen?"

Milo said, "There's been a murder . . . one of your sister's students—"

"My God, that's *horrible*—Nora's okay?"

Same protective reflex as Billy.

"I already asked him that, Brad. Nora's good."

Brad must've put some weight on Billy's shoulder because the smaller man sagged.

"Where did this happen and who exactly did it happen to?"

"West L.A. The victim's a young woman named Michaela Brand."

"The one who faked being kidnapped?" said Brad.

His brother stared up at him. "You never told me about that, Bra—"

"It was in the news, Bill." To us: "Did her murder have something to do with that?"

"Any reason it would?" said Milo.

"I'm not saying it did," said Brad Dowd. "I'm just asking—it's a natural question, don't you think? Someone garners publicity, it has the potential to bring out the weirdos."

"Did Nora talk about the hoax?"

Brad shook his head. "Murdered . . . terrible." He frowned. "It must've hit Nora hard, I'd better call her."

"She's okay," said Milo. "We just talked to her."

"You're sure?"

"Your sister's fine. We're here, sir, because we need to talk to anyone who might've had contact with Ms. Brand."

"Of course," said Brad Dowd. He smiled at his brother. "Billy, would you do me a favor and go down and get a sandwich from DiGiorgio's—you know how I like it."

Billy Dowd got off the desk and looked up at his brother. "Peppers, egg, eggplant, and tomato. A lot of pesto or just a medium amount?"

"A lot, bro."

"You got it, bro. Nice to meet you guys." Billy hurried off.

When the door closed, Brad Dowd said, "He doesn't need to hear about this kind of thing. What else can I help you with?"

"Your janitor, Reynold Peaty. Anything to say about him?"

"You're asking because of his arrests?"

Milo nodded.

"Well," said Brad, "he was up-front about them when he applied for a job. I gave him points for honesty and he's been a good worker. Why?"

"Just routine, sir. How'd you find him?"

"Agency. *They* weren't up-front about his past, so we dropped them."

"How long's he been working for you?"

"Five years."

"Not that long after his last arrest in Nevada."

"He said he'd had a drinking problem and had gotten clean and sober. He doesn't drive, so any DUI problems aren't going to happen."

Milo said, "Are you aware of his arrest for peeping through a window?"

"He told me about everything," said Brad. "Claimed that was also the drinking. And the only time he'd done something like that." He flexed his shoulders. "Many of our tenants are women and families with children, I'm not naive, keep my eyes out on all the employees. Now that the Megan's Law database is up and operating, I check it regularly. I assume you do, too, so you know Reynold isn't on there. Is there some reason you're asking about him, other than routine?"

"No, sir."

Brad Dowd inspected his fingertips. Unlike his brother's, beautifully manicured. "Please be up-front, Detective. Do you have the slightest bit of evidence implicating

Reynold? Because he circulates among lots of our buildings and as much as I'd like to trust him, I'd hate to incur any liability. Not to mention the human cost."

"No evidence," said Milo.

"You're sure."

"That's the way it looks, so far."

"So far," said Brad Dowd. "Not exactly encouraging."

"There's no reason to suspect him, sir. If I hear otherwise, I'll let you know."

Dowd fiddled with a hand-stitched lapel. "There's no subtext here, is there, Detective? You're not suggesting I fire him?"

"I'd prefer that you don't."

"Why's that?"

"No sense stirring things up, Mr. Dowd. If Peaty's turned his life around, more power to him."

"That's how I feel . . . that poor girl. How was she killed?"

"Strangled and stabbed."

Dowd winced. "Any idea by who?"

"No, sir. Here's another routine question: Do you know Dylan Meserve?"

"I'm aware of who he is. Is there any sense asking why he's part of your routine?"

"He hasn't been seen for a while and

when we tried to talk to your sister about him, she ended the conversation."

"Nora," said Brad wearily. His eyes shot to the doorway. "Hey, bro. Smells good, thanks."

Billy Dowd toted an open cardboard carton, using both hands, as if his cargo was precious. Inside was a hero-sized sandwich wrapped in orange paper. Aromas of tomato paste, oregano, and basil filled the office.

Brad turned so his brother couldn't see and slipped Milo a yellow business card. Perfect match to his shirt. "Anything I can do to help, Detective. Feel free to call me if you have any further questions—that smells fantastic, Billy. You're the man."

"*You're* the man," said Billy gravely.

"You, too, Bill."

Billy Dowd's mouth screwed up.

Brad said, "Hey, we can both be the man." He took the sandwich and cuffed his brother's shoulder lightly. "Right?"

Billy considered that. "Okay."

16

By the time we made it to the door, Brad Dowd had his dinner unwrapped and was saying, "This hits the spot, Bill."

As we climbed down to the strip mall's first level, Milo said, "That sandwich smelled good."

We parked near the far west end of the airport. The coffee from Café DiGiorgio was dark and strong. Milo pushed the seat back as far as it would go and got to work on his meatball and pepper sandwich.

After four ferocious bites, he stopped to

breathe. "Looks like ol' Bradley watches out for his sibs."

"Looks like they both bear watching."

"What's your diagnosis on Billy?"

"The best word's probably 'simple.' "

"And Nora's a spacey doper."

"You're ready to take the state boards," I said.

He scanned blue sky. No sleek white jets to feed his fantasies. He fished out Brad Dowd's yellow business card and handed it over.

Crisp, substantial paper. Bradley Dowd's name embossed in chocolate italics, above a phone number with an 825 prefix.

"Gentleman's calling card," I said. "You don't see that too often."

"Once a rich kid, always a rich kid. I'll call him tonight, find out what he didn't want to talk about in front of his brother."

I got home at six, cleared a tapeful of junk messages, listened to one from Robin that had come in ten minutes ago.

"I could tell you this is about shared grief for our late pooch but it's really . . . a booty call. I guess. Hopefully, you're the only one listening to this. Please erase it. Bye."

I called her back. "I erased it."

"I'm lonely," she said.

"Me, too."

"Should we do something about it?"

"I think so."

"That's not exactly rabid desire, but I'll take what I can get."

I was at her house in Venice by seven. We spent the next hour in bed, the rest of the evening reading the paper and watching the last third of *Humoresque* on The Movie Channel.

When the film was over, she got up without a word and left for her studio.

I tried to sleep, didn't have much success until she returned to bed. I was up just after seven when western light streaming through her curtains couldn't be denied.

She stood naked, by the window, holding a cup of tea. She'd always been a coffee drinker.

I croaked something that approximated "Morning."

"You dreamed a lot."

"I was noisy?"

"Active. I'll get you some coffee."

"Come back to bed, I'll get it."

"No, relax." She padded out and returned with a mug, stood by the bed.

I drank and cleared my throat. "Thanks. You're into tea, now?"

"Sometimes."

"How long have you been awake?"

"Couple of hours."

"My activity?"

"No, I've turned into an early riser."

"Cows to milk, eggs to collect."

She smiled, put on a robe, sat on the bed.

I said, "Come back in."

"No, once I'm up, I'm up." She forced a smile. I could smell the effort.

"Want me to leave?"

"Of course not," she said too quickly. "Stay as long as you like. I don't have much for breakfast."

"Not hungry," I said. "You've got work to do."

"Eventually."

She kissed my forehead, got up, and moved to her closet and began getting dressed. I went to shower. By the time I was out and dried and dressed, her band saw was humming.

◆

I had breakfast at John O'Groats on Pico, going out of my way because I was in the mood for Irish oatmeal, and the company of strangers seemed like a good idea. I sat at the counter and read the paper. Nothing on Michaela. No reason for there to be.

Back home, I did some paperwork and thought about Nora Dowd's flat responses to Milo's questions.

Not bothering to fake sympathy or interest in Michaela's murder. The same for Tori Giacomo's disappearance.

But Dylan Meserve's name had pulled out some emotion and Brother Brad didn't want to talk about Dylan in front of the most vulnerable Dowd sib.

I got on the computer. Nora's name pulled up a single citation: inclusion in a list of acting workshops listed by city that appeared on a site called StarHopefuls.com.

I printed the list, called all the West Coast programs, fabricated a casting-director cover story and asked if Tori Giacomo had ever been a student. Mostly, I got confusion. A few times, I got hang-ups, meaning I could use some acting lessons myself.

By noon, I had nothing. Better to stick with what I was getting paid to do.

I finished the report on Dr. Patrick Hauser and took a run down to the nearest mailbox. I was back at my desk, clearing paper, when Milo rang the doorbell.

"I called first," he said.

"Out jogging."

"I envy your knees."

"Believe me, don't. What's up?"

"Michaela's landlord promises to be there tomorrow morning, I got subpoenas for her phone records but my contact at the phone company says I'm wasting my time. Account was shut off for nonpayment weeks before she died. If she had a cell account, I can't find it. On the positive side, God bless the angels at the coroner's." He stomped in. "Your knees really hurt?"

"Sometimes."

"If you weren't my buddy, I'd gloat."

I followed him into the kitchen. Instead of raiding the fridge he sat down and loosened his tie.

"Michaela's autopsy was prioritized?" I said.

"Nope, more interesting. My buddies at the crypt looked through the Doe files, found some possibles and traced one of 'em to a bone analyst doing research on identification. Forensic anthropologist on a grant, what she does is collect samples from various cases and try to classify them ethnically. In her trove was an intact skull with most of the teeth still embedded. Young, Caucasian female homicide victim found nineteen months ago, the rest of the body was incinerated six months after discovery. Their forensic odontologist said the dentition was distinctive. Lots of cosmetic bridgework, unusual for someone that young."

"Someone trying to look their best. Like an aspiring actress."

"I got the name of Tori Giacomo's dentist in Bayside and thanks to the magic of digital photography and e-mail, we had a positive I.D. within the hour."

"How's her dad taking it?"

"Don't know," he said. "I had no way to reach him here in L.A., so I called his wife. Contrary to what Giacomo told us, she comes across like a sensible, stable lady. Has been expecting the worst for a while." He slumped. "Prince that I am, I didn't disappoint her."

He got up, filled a glass with water from the tap. "Got any lemon?"

I sliced one, dropped a wedge into his glass.

"Rick says I should keep my kidneys hydrated but plain water tastes like plain water . . . anyway, Tori is no longer Jane Doe 342-003. Wish I had the rest of the body but she was listed as an unsolved Hollywood homicide and the D's report spelled things out pretty clearly."

He drank some more, put the glass in the sink.

"She was found four months after she disappeared, dumped in some brush on the L.A. side of Griffith Park. All that was left were scattered bones. Coroner thought he spotted damage to some of the cervical vertebrae and there are definitely some relatively superficial knife cuts in her sternum and a couple in the thoracic ribs. Tentative cause of death is strangulation/stabbing."

I said, "Two young, female acting students, similar wounds and Nora Dowd didn't rule out Tori attending her classes."

"No answer at Nora's home or the school. I'll be at the PlayHouse tonight, mingling with the beautiful people. After I meet with Brad Dowd. He called, apologized for cutting off the conversation, invited me to his house."

"Eager to talk about Dylan," I said. "Where does he live?"

"Santa Monica Canyon. Care to join me? I'll drive."

Bradley Dowd lived on Gumtree Lane, a mile north of Channel Road, just east of where Channel descends steeply to Pacific Coast Highway.

A darkening sky and a tree canopy brought early night. The air was still and unseasonably warm and no ocean aroma brined the canyon.

Usually it's ten degrees cooler near the coast. Maybe it's me, but patterns seem to be shaking up more often.

The house was a one-story redwood and glass box set in a low spot along the leafy road, well back from the street. The wealth of vegetation made it hard to make out where the property began and ended.

High-end box, with polished-copper trim and a porch supported by carved beams. Carefully placed spots illuminated flower beds and luxuriant ferns. The wooden address plate imbedded in the fieldstone gatepost was hand-painted. A gray or beige Porsche sat in the front of the gravel driveway. Hanging succulents graced the porch, which was set up with Adirondack chairs.

Brad Dowd stood near one of the chairs, one leg bent so that his shoulders sloped to the right. He wore a T-shirt and cutoffs, held a long-necked bottle in one hand.

"Park right behind me, Detective."

When we got to the porch, he hoisted the bottle. Corona. The T-shirt said *Hobie-Cat.* His feet were bare. Muscular legs, knobby, misshapen knees. "Join me?"

"No, thanks."

Dowd sat, gave another wave. We repositioned two chairs and faced him.

"Any problem finding me?"

"None," said Milo. "Thanks for calling."

Dowd nodded and drank. Crickets chirped. A hint of gardenia blew by and dissipated.

"Pretty out here, sir."

"Love it," said Brad. "Nothing like peace and quiet after a day dealing with leaks, short circuits, and various other minor disasters."

"Trials and tribulations of being a landlord."

"Are you one, too, Detective?"

"God forbid."

Brad laughed. "It beats honest labor. The key is to keep things organized."

He'd left the front door cracked six inches. Serape throws on chairs, a kilim ottoman, lots of leather. Propped in a corner was a white surfboard. Longboard, the type you don't see much anymore.

The knobs on Dowd's knees made sense. Surfer's knots.

Milo said, "There was something about Dylan Meserve you wanted to tell us."

"Thanks for waiting. I didn't want Billy to hear."

"Protecting Billy," I said.

Dowd turned to me. "Billy needs protection. Sometimes it's hard for him to put things in perspective."

"Something about Meserve bother him?" said Milo.

Brad Dowd's brow creased. "No, I just like to keep him away from what he doesn't need to know . . . sure I can't get you guys one of these?"

"We're fine," said Milo. "You take care of Billy."

"He doesn't need special care—he's not

retarded or anything like that. When he was born, there was an oxygen problem. We used to live together, then a couple of years ago I realized he needed his independence, so I got him his own place. A nice lady lives upstairs. Billy thinks they're just neighbors, but she gets paid to be there for him. Anyway, about Meserve, it's no big deal. My sister had a thing for him and I consider him a first-class sleazeball."

"A mutual thing?"

Dowd stretched his legs, pointed his toes, massaged a knot. Maybe calcium explained the wince. "In some ways, Nora can be a bit of an adolescent. All the time she spends with young people doesn't help."

I said, "Dylan wasn't her first thing?"

"I didn't say that."

I smiled.

Brad Dowd drank beer. "No sense bullshitting. You know how it is, a woman gets to a certain age, the whole youth culture thing. Nora's entitled to her fun. But with Meserve it was getting a little out of hand, so I talked to her and she realized I was right."

"You didn't want Billy to hear this because . . ."

Brad Dowd's mouth got tight. "It was a bit of a hassle. Convincing Nora. She'd have been a lot more upset if Billy got involved. If he tried to comfort her or something like that."

"Why's that?" said Milo.

"Nora and Billy aren't close . . . the truth is, when we were kids, Billy was a source of embarrassment to Nora. But Billy *thinks* they're close—" He stopped. "This is family stuff you don't need to know."

Milo said, "So Nora broke up with Meserve?"

"It didn't require a formal declaration because the two of them were never officially . . ." He smiled. "I almost said 'going steady.' "

"How'd Nora end it with Meserve?"

"By keeping her distance. Ignoring him. Eventually, he got the point."

"How was their relationship getting out of hand?" I said.

Brad frowned. "Is this really relevant to that poor girl's murder?"

"Probably not, sir. We ask all sorts of questions and hope for the best."

"Is Meserve a suspect?"

"No, but close friends of the victim are

considered individuals of interest, and we haven't been able to locate Meserve to talk to him."

"I understand, Detective. But I still don't see why my sister's private life needs to be aired."

I said, "Was there something about Meserve that bothered you more than her other 'things'?"

Dowd sighed. "In the past, Nora's relationships were short-lived. Mostly because the men who interest Nora aren't the type with long-term plans. Meserve seemed different to me. Manipulative, as if he was planning something. That hoax he pulled proves it, right?"

Milo said, "Planning what?"

"Isn't it obvious?"

"You suspected he was out for Nora's money."

"I started to get concerned when Nora gave him a paid job at the PlayHouse. Creative consultant." Dowd snorted. "You need to understand: Nora doesn't charge a penny for her classes. That's a crucial point, tax-wise, because the PlayHouse—the building, the upkeep, any supplies—is funded by a foundation we set up."

"You and your sibs."

"Basically, I did it for Nora, because acting's her passion. We're not talking some huge financial undertaking, there's just enough endowment to keep the classes going. The building's one of many we inherited from our parents and the rent we forego is a nice deduction against the profit from some other rentals in our portfolio. I'm the nominal head of the foundation so I approve expenditures. Which is why when Nora came to me wanting salary for Meserve, I knew it was time to talk. There was simply nothing in the budget to accommodate that. And it confirmed my suspicions that Meserve was out for something."

"How much did she want to pay him?"

"Eight hundred a week."

"Very creative consultant," said Milo.

"No kidding," said Dowd. "That's my point. Nora has no concept of finances. Like a lot of artistic folk."

"How long ago did she ask for the money?"

"After she offered him the job. A week or so before Meserve and the girl pulled that stunt. Maybe that's why he did it."

"What do you mean?"

"Trying to win Nora's affections with a creative performance. If that was the idea, it backfired."

"Nora wasn't pleased."

"I'd say not."

"Was she upset at the hoax or something else?"

"Such as?"

"Meserve being with another woman."

"Jealous? I seriously doubt it. By that time Nora was finished with him."

"She gets over 'things' quickly."

"Nothing to get over," said Brad Dowd. "She saw my point, stopped paying attention to him, and he stopped hanging around."

"What bothered Nora about the hoax?"

"The exposure."

"Most actresses like publicity."

Brad placed his beer on the porch deck. "Detective, the extent of Nora's acting career was a single walk-on part on a sitcom thirty-five years ago when she was ten. She got the part because a friend of our mother's was connected. After that, Nora went on audition after audition. When she decided to channel her efforts into teaching, it was a healthy move."

"Adapting," said Milo.

"That's what it's all about, Detective. My sister has talent but so do a hundred thousand other people."

I said, "So she prefers to stay out of the public eye."

"We're a private bunch." Dowd took a long swallow and finished his beer. "Is there anything else, guys?"

"Did Nora ever talk about Michaela Brand?"

"Not to me. No way she was jealous. Gorgeous young people stream in and out of Nora's world. Now, I really think I should stop talking about her personal life."

"Fair enough," said Milo. "Let's concentrate on Meserve."

"Like I said, a gold digger," said Dowd. "I meddled but sometimes meddling is called for. In the end my sister was grateful not to get involved with someone like that. Maybe you should be looking at him for the girl's murder."

"Why's that, sir?"

"His view of women, he had a relationship with the victim, and you just said he's missing. Doesn't running away imply guilt?"

"What view of women are we talking about?" said Milo.

"You know the type. Easy smile, cruising on looks. He flirted with my sister shamelessly. I'll be blunt: He kissed up and Nora bought it because Nora's . . ."

"Impressionable."

"Unfortunately. Any time I'd drop by the PlayHouse, he'd be there alone with Nora. Following her around, flattering her, sitting at her feet, shooting her adoring glances. Then he began giving her cheap little gifts— doodads, tacky tourist junk. A snow globe, do you believe that? Hollywood and *Vine*, for God's sake, when's the last time there was snow in Hollywood?" Dowd laughed. "I'd love to think it was Nora's soul and inner beauty that attracted him, but let's get real. She's naive, menopausal, and financially independent."

I said, "How'd you convince her Meserve's intentions weren't pure?"

"I was calm and persistent." He stood. "I hope you catch whoever killed that girl, but please don't involve my brother and sister in it. You couldn't find two more harmless people on the face of the earth. In terms of Reynold Peaty, I've been asking tenants and the only complaints I've received are along the lines of not emptying garbage in a timely manner. He shows up diligently, minds his own business, has been a first-class worker. I'll keep my eyes open, though."

He cocked his head toward the open door. "Coffee or a soft drink for the road?"

"We're good," said Milo, getting up.

"Then I'm hitting the sack. *Buenas noches.*"

"Early to bed?"

"Busy day ahead."

"Beats honest labor," Milo said.

Brad Dowd laughed.

CHAPTER
17

Milo took Channel Road down toward the coastline. "There's time till the class at the PlayHouse. How about we grab a couple of beers at a place I know."

"Coronas?"

"Good brand."

"As long as Brad Dowd's not offering."

"Never fraternize with the citizenry. What'd you think of our grown-up surfer dude?"

"You saw the knots, too."

"And the board."

"He's the family guardian, takes well to the job."

He reached PCH, stopped at the long red

light that can keep you there for what seems to be hours. The ocean's always changing. Tonight the water was flat and gray and infinite. Slow, easy tide, steady and metallic as a drum machine.

"Maybe I'm making too big a deal out of this, Alex, but Brad's parting words seemed off: asking me to keep both Nora and Billy out of the investigation. We'd been focused on Nora, why bring in Billy?"

"Could be force of habit," I said. "He lumps the two of them together because they both need protection."

"Maybe that's it."

"Billy interests you?"

"Adult male with immature social skills who needs to be supervised covertly?" As we waited, he ran a DMV check on William Dowd III, hung up before the light changed. "Wanna guess how many vehicles are registered to Billy?"

"None."

"And just like Peaty, never had a license."

"Tagging along with Brother Brad," I said. "When Brad drops in at the PlayHouse, Billy's right there with him. All those good-looking starlets-in-training."

"Getting an eyeful of girls like Michaela

and Tori Giacomo, could be overstimulat-
ing."

"Billy seemed gentle," I said. "But crank
up the id and who knows?"

"What if the real reason Brad didn't want
to talk to us in front of Billy was because
he was afraid Billy would give something
away? And here's something else: Billy lives
in an apartment in Beverly Hills. Reeves
Drive, just off Olympic."

"Couple of miles from Michaela's place."

"A guy with no wheels could walk it."

"Same problem as Peaty," I said. "How to
transport a body. And I don't see Billy getting away with an unregistered ride. Not
with Brad that protective."

That turned him silent until we reached
Santa Monica's gold coast. Beachside mansions, once private enclaves, were now exposed to the clamor and the reality of the
public sand that fronted them. The clap-
board monster William Hearst had built for
Marion Davies was ready to crumble after
years of Santa Monica city council dithering.
A moment later, the exoskeleton of the pier
came into view, lit up like Christmas. The
Ferris wheel rotated, slow as bureaucracy.

Milo drove the ramp up to Ocean Front,

continued onto Pacific Avenue, crossed into Venice. "So now I've got two strange guys with access to the PlayHouse."

I thought about that. "Billy stopped living with Brad two years ago, right before Tori's disappearance."

"Why would Brad get Billy out of his house at this point in their lives? These guys are middle-aged, all of a sudden it's time for a change?"

"Brad wanted to keep his distance from Billy? But if he suspected something, he'd tighten the leash."

"So what's the answer?"

"Don't know."

"For all we know," he said, "Brad *did* try to clamp down and Billy's a lot more difficult than he seems. Hell, maybe *Billy* insisted on breaking away. Brad pays some nice lady to 'look after him,' because he knows Billy bears watching. Meanwhile, if something does happen, he's across town in Santa Monica Canyon."

"Less liability," I said.

"He thinks in those terms—foundations, tax breaks, keeping things organized. That rung of the social ladder, it's a whole different world."

He looked at his watch. "Let's see how Nora reacts when I push her a bit. How long it takes for her to cry to Brother Brad."

Over the years I've accompanied Milo to lots of taverns and beer joints and cocktail lounges. A couple of gay bars as well. It's an illuminating experience watching him function in that sphere.

This was a new dive, a narrow, dark tunnel of a place called Jody Z's, at the southern edge of Pacific, just above the Marina. Arena rock on the jukebox, silent football rerun on TV, tired men at the urethane bar, rough paneling and fishnets and glass globes.

Plastic sawdust on the floor. What was the point of that?

A short drive to Robin's house on Rennie. In another time and place, Milo might have mentioned that. The set of his jaw said the only things on his mind were the murders of two young women.

Once we'd finished a couple of beers and rehashed what we knew, there was little to talk about and he started to blend in with the dispirited clientele.

Phoning Michaela's landlord in La Jolla, he confirmed the appointment tomorrow morning. Ground his teeth. "Bastard's doing me a big, freaking favor."

He looked over at the blackboard. Three specials, including the promise of fresh clam chowder. He chanced it.

"Not too bad," he said, spooning.

" 'Not too bad' and 'seafood' shouldn't be uttered in the same sentence," I said.

"If I die, you get the first eulogy. I wonder if Nora really gave in when Brad asked her to cool it with Meserve. Brad did raise one good point: Meserve's nowhere to be found."

"He seemed eager to steer you to Meserve as a suspect," I said. "That's in his best interest if he's covering for Billy, but it doesn't mean he's wrong. Michaela told me she hated Meserve and Mrs. Winograd heard them fighting more than once."

"Any theory about Dylan's motive? For Michaela *and* Tori."

"Maybe he's just a bad guy who picks off girls at acting class. He played death games with Michaela up in Latigo and if Michaela was being at all truthful, he planned a calculated hoax. Toss in Brad's suspicions about gold digging and it doesn't add up to a character reference."

"Michaela tell you why she went from being naked in the hills with him to seeing him as the enemy?"

"At the time, I assumed she was dumping the blame on him as trial strategy."

"Lawyer games."

"Guess who her lawyer was. Lauritz Montez."

"That guy from the Malley case? Thought you two had friction."

"We did but I'm the biggest, baddest, smartest shrink in the whole wild world. Gee willikers."

"He schmeared you and you bought it?"

"The case interested me."

"That's a good reason."

"As good as any."

"Mind talking to Montez again, see if Michaela had more to say about her partner in crime?"

"Don't mind at all," I said. I'd been thinking of doing it, anyway.

He pushed aside a half bowl of chowder. Waved for another beer, then altered it to a Coke.

The sixty-five-year-old barmaid laughed. "When did you ever have self-control?"

Milo said, "Don't be cruel," and she laughed some more and left.

I realized all the patrons were men. Wondered about that as Milo ticked an index finger. "Meserve, Peaty, Brother Billy. Investigation 101 teaches you to narrow the suspect pool. I seem to be doing just the opposite."

"The search for truth," I said.

"Ah, the agony."

CHAPTER
18

By eight fifty-three p.m., we were parked four blocks west of the PlayHouse. As we headed to the school on foot, Milo's bulk slanted forward, as if marching into a blizzard.

Scoping out streets and driveways and alleys for Michaela Brand's little black Honda.

The alert for the car had been expanded statewide. Milo and I had cruised these same streets just a few days ago, no reason to look now.

The ability to put logic aside sometimes makes for a great detective.

◆

We got to the building at five after nine, found people milling.

Dim porch light allowed me to count as we neared the front steps. Eight females, five males. Each one slim, young, gorgeous.

Milo muttered, "Mutants," as he bounded up the stairs. Thirteen pairs of eyes turned to watch. A few of the women shrank back.

The men occupied a narrow height range: six to six two. Broad, square shoulders, narrow hips, angular faces that seemed curiously static. The women varied more in stature but their body shape was uniform: long legs, flat bellies, wasp waists, high-tucked butts, high puffy bosoms.

Manicured hands gripped plastic bottles of water and cell phones. Wide hungry eyes questioned our presence. Milo stepped into the middle of the porch and the acting students cleared space. The light played up every crease, pit and pucker and pore. He looked heavier and older than ever.

"Evening, folks."

Dubious stares, general confusion, smirks and side glances of the kind you see in middle-school cafeterias.

One of the young men said, "What's up," with practiced slur.

Brando in *On the Waterfront*? Or was that ancient history?

"Crime's up, friend." Milo moved the badge so that it caught light.

Someone said, "Whoa." Snickers petered to silence.

Milo checked his Timex. "Wasn't class supposed to start ten minutes ago?"

"Coach not here," said another Adonis. He jiggled the front door handle.

"Waiting for Nora," said Milo.

"Better than Godot."

"Hopefully, unlike him, she'll show up." Milo's wolf-grin caused a reflexive tooth-bare from the young man. The guy threw back his head and a sheet of dark hair billowed, then flapped back in place.

"Nora late a lot?"

Shrug.

"Sometimes," said a young woman with curly yellow hair and lips so bulbous they resembled tiny buttocks. That and blue saucer eyes gave her a stunned mien. Inflatable doll barely come to life.

"Well," said Milo, "this gives us time to chat."

Swigs from water bottles. Flips of cell

phone covers nursed forth a series of electronic mouse-squeaks.

Milo said, "I assume you guys heard about Michaela Brand."

Silence. A nod, then two. Then ten.

"Anybody has something to say, it would be much appreciated."

A car drove west. Several of the acting students followed its diminishing taillights, grateful for distraction.

"Anything, people?"

Slow head shakes.

"Nothing at all?"

"Everyone's freaked out," said a dark, pointy-chinned girl with coyote eyes. Deep sigh. Her breasts rose and fell as a unit.

"I saw her a couple of times but didn't know her," said a man with a shaved head and bone structure so pronounced he seemed carved out of ivory.

"That's 'cause you just started, Juaquin," said the pillowly-lipped, curly-haired girl.

"That's what I'm saying, Brandy."

"Briana."

"Whatever."

"You knew her, Briana?" said Milo.

"Just from here. We didn't hang out."

"Any of you know Michaela outside of here?" said Milo.

Head shakes.

"She was, like, quiet," said a redheaded woman.

"What about Dylan Meserve?"

Silence. Notable edginess.

"None of you knew Dylan?"

"They were friends," said the redhead. "Her and him."

"Any of you see Dylan recently?"

The red-haired girl pulled a watch out of her purse and squinted at it.

"Nine sixteen," said Milo. "Nora generally this late?"

"Sometimes," said Curly Blonde.

Someone else said, "Nora's Nora."

Silence.

Milo said, "What's on the agenda tonight?"

"There is no agenda," said the hair-flipper. He wore a plaid flannel shirt tailored tight to his V-frame, faded jeans, clean, crisp hiking boots that had never encountered mud.

"Nothing's planned?" said Milo.

"It's free-form."

"Improv?"

Impish smile from Plaid. "Something like that, Officer."

"How often you guys come here?"

No answer.

"Once a week for me," said Briana Pillowlips. "For other people it's more."

"Same here," said Plaid.

"Once a week."

"More when I have time. Like I said, it's free form."

And free.

I said, "No rules."

"No constrictions."

Milo said, "There are no constrictions helping the police, either."

An olive-skinned guy with a face that managed to be reptilian and handsome said, "No one knows anything."

Milo handed out business cards. A few of the beautiful people bothered to read them.

We left them waiting on the porch, walked halfway down the block until darkness concealed us, and watched the building.

Milo said, "It's like they're extruded from machines."

We waited in silence. By nine twenty-three Nora Dowd still hadn't showed and her students began to drift away. When the young woman named Briana headed toward us, Milo said, "Karma."

We stepped out of the shadows well in time for her to see us.

Despite that, she jumped. Gripped her purse, held on to her balance. "You scared me!"

"Sorry. Have a minute?"

Inflated lips parted. How much collagen had it taken for them to get that way? She hadn't reached thirty, but tuck lines around her ears said she wasn't relying on youth. "I have nothing to say and you really *scared* me." She walked past us to a battered white Nissan, headed for the driver's door, groped for her keys.

Milo followed her. "We really are sorry, it's just that we haven't learned much about Michaela's murder and you seemed to know her best."

"All I said was I knew who she was."

"Your fellow students didn't know her at all."

"That's because they're new."

"Freshmen?"

Curls shook. "It's not like college—"

"I know, free-form," said Milo. "What's the problem helping us, Briana?"

"There's no problem, I just don't know anything." She unlocked the driver's door.

"Is there some reason you *don't* want to help?"

She looked at him. "Like what?"

"Someone told you not to help?"

"Of course not. Who would do that?"

Milo shrugged.

"No way," she said. "I just don't know anything and I don't want any hassle."

"No hassle involved. I'm just trying to solve a murder. Pretty nasty one, at that."

Big lips trembled. "I'm really sorry. But we weren't tight. Like I said before, she kept to herself."

"She and Dylan."

"Right."

"And now she's dead and he's gone. Any idea where he might be?"

"Definitely not."

"*Definitely* not?"

"I definitely don't know. He could be any-where."

Milo edged closer, pressed his hip against the hinges of the driver's door. "What sur-prises me is the lack of curiosity. All you guys. Someone you know gets killed, you'd think there'd be some interest." He sliced air horizontally. "Zippo, no one cares. Is it something about actors?"

She frowned. "Just the opposite. You need to *be* curious."

"To act."

"To learn about our feelings."

"Nora tells you that."

"Anyone who knows anything tells you that."

"Let me get this," said Milo. "You're curious about playing parts, but not about real life?"

"Look," said the girl, "sure, I'd like to know. It scares me. The whole murder thing. Just talking about it. I mean, come on."

"Come on?"

"If it happened to Michaela, it could happen to anyone."

I said, "You see it as a random crime?"

She turned to me. "What do you mean?"

"As opposed to something that had to do with Michaela."

"I—she was—I don't know, maybe."

Milo said, "Was there something about Michaela that made her a likely victim?"

"That thing she—they did. Her and Dylan. Lying."

"Why would that put her in danger?"

"Maybe they ticked someone off."

"Are you aware of someone that angry?"

"Nope." Too quickly.

"No one, Briana?"

"No one. I got to go."

"In a sec," said Milo. "What's your last name?"

She looked ready to cry. "Do I have to say?"

Milo tried for a soft smile. "It's routine, Briana. Address and phone number, too."

"Briana Szemencic." She spelled it. "Can this be off the record?"

"Don't worry about that. Live around here, Briana?"

"Reseda."

"Bit of a drive."

"I work in Santa Monica. With the traffic it's easier to stay in the city and go back later."

"What kind of work do you do, Briana?"

"Shitty work." Rueful smile. "I'm an assistant at an insurance agency. I file, I get coffee, I gofer. Beaucoup excitement."

"Hey," said Milo, "pays the bills."

"Barely." She touched her lips.

"So who was pissed off about the hoax, Briana?"

Long pause. "No one that much."

"But . . ."

"Nora was a little frosted."

"How could you tell?"

"When someone asked her about it she got this real tight look and changed the subject. Can you blame her? It sucked, using the PlayHouse like that. Nora's a private person. When Michaela never came back, I figured Nora gave her the boot."

"Dylan came back."

"Yeah," she said. "That was the funny thing. She wasn't mad at Dylan, kept treating him nice."

Milo said, "Even though the hoax was mostly his idea."

"That's not what he said."

"Dylan blamed it on Michaela?"

"Totally, he said she really worked on him. Nora must've believed him because she . . . like you said, he came back."

"Does Nora like Dylan more than the other guys?"

Fragile shoulders rose and fell. Briana

Szemencic gazed up the block. "I don't think I should go there."

"Touchy business?"

"Not *my* business," said Briana. "Anyway, Nora would never hurt anyone. If you're thinking that, you're totally wrong."

"Why would we be thinking that?"

"You're asking was she mad. She was but not that type of mad."

"Not the jealous type of mad?"

Briana didn't answer.

Milo said, "Nora and Dylan, Dylan and Michaela. But no jealousy."

"Nora had the hots for Dylan, okay? It's no crime, she's a *woman.*"

"Had or has?"

"I don't know."

"Same question, Briana."

"Has. Okay?"

"How'd Nora feel about Dylan and Michaela hanging out?"

Briana shook her head. "She never said anything. It's not like we were tight. Can I go now? *Please?*"

"Nora didn't like Dylan and Michaela hanging but she wasn't really pissed off about it."

"She'd never hurt Michaela. Never, ever.

You need to understand Nora, she's . . . she's kind of, really, like, she's not, you know . . . she's *here.*" Tapping her pretty forehead.

"Intellectual?"

Tush lips struggled to form words. Finally, she said, "That's not what I mean, I'm talking more, like, you know, she's intensely *right brain.* Intuitionalistic. That's the point of the workshops, she shows us how to tap into ourselves, free the inner . . ." Pillow lips wriggled as she struggled for vocabulary. "Nora's all about *scenes,* she's always telling us to break everything into scenes, that way it's not so huge, you can deal with it until you get the whole gestalt—that means the big picture. I think she kind of lives that way herself."

"Scene by scene," said Milo.

"She's not paying attention to down here." Pointing to the asphalt.

"Reality."

The word seemed to bother Briana Szemencic. "All the crap below the right brain, whatever you want to call it. Nora would never hurt anyone."

"You like her."

"She's helped me. A lot."

"As an actor."

"As a person." Sharp little lower teeth got hold of gluteal lip and held on.

I said, "Nora's supportive."

"Not—it's not that. I was real shy, okay? She helped me step out of myself. Sometimes it wasn't fun. But it helped—can I go now?"

Milo nodded. "Reseda, huh? Valley girl?"

"Nebraska."

"Flatlands," said Milo.

"You know Nebraska?"

"Been to Omaha."

"I'm from Lincoln but same difference," said Briana Szemencic. "You stare at forever and there's nothing at the end. Can I *go* now? I'm *really* tired."

Milo stepped back. "Thanks for stepping out of that silent thing your friends were into."

"They're not my friends."

"No?"

"No one's anyone's friend over there." She glanced back at the PlayHouse. The empty porch looked gloomy. Staged for gloomy, like a movie set.

"Not a friendly atmosphere?" said Milo.

"We're supposed to concentrate on the work."

"So when Dylan and Michaela started hanging out they broke a rule."

"There are no rules. Michaela was being stupid."

"How so?"

"Hooking up with Dylan."

"Because Nora liked him?"

"Because he's totally shallow."

"You don't share Nora's enthusiasm."

A beat. "Not really."

"How come?"

"He's hanging with Michaela but he's also been getting into Nora? Gimme a break."

"But no jealousy on Nora's part."

Yellow curls shook violently. She reached for the Nissan's door handle. Milo said, "What about Reynold Peaty?"

"Who?"

"The janitor."

"The fat guy?" Her arm dropped. "What about him?"

"He ever bother you?"

"Like perve-bother? No. But he stares, it's creepy. He's sweeping, mopping, whatever, and out of the corner of your eye you can see him staring. If you look at him, he turns away fast, like he knows he shouldn't be doing it." She shuddered. "Is he, like, serious-creepy? Like *America's Most Wanted* creepy?"

"I couldn't say that."

Briana Szemencic's slender frame stiffened. "But you couldn't say no?"

"I have no evidence he's ever done something violent, Briana."

"If he's not a perve, how come you *asked* about him?"

"My job is asking questions, Briana. Most of them turn out to be useless but I can't take chances. Guess it's kinda like acting."

"What do you mean?"

"A little improv, a lot of hard work. Does Peaty hang out at the PlayHouse a lot?"

"When he's cleaning."

"Days as well as nights?"

"I'm only there nights."

"Anyone else drop by?"

"Just people applying for workshops. Mostly Nora turns them away but there can still be crowds."

"No talent."

Another lip bite. "Yeah."

"Any other reason she turns them away?"

"You'd have to ask her."

Milo said, "Well, thanks again—it's a cool thing, Nora giving away her skills for free."

"Very cool."

"Guess she can do that because her brothers fund the PlayHouse."

"Her brothers *and* her," said Briana Szemencic. "It's like a whole family thing. They're filthy rich but they're artistic and generous."

"The brothers ever drop by to see how it's spent?"

"I've seen them a few times."

"Sitting in?"

"More like walking around. Dropping by to visit Nora." She gripped her purse with both hands. "Tell me the truth about that fat guy."

"I already have, Briana."

"He's not a perve? You can guarantee me that?"

"He really scares you."

"Like I said, he's *staring* all the time."

"I told you the truth, Briana."

"But you were punking me about the other stuff."

"What other stuff?"

"What you said about cop stuff being like acting. That was b.s., right?"

"You know a girl named Tori Giacomo?" said Milo.

"Who's that?"

"Maybe a student here once."

"I've only been here a year. You didn't answer my question. That was total bullshit, right?"

"Nope, I meant it," said Milo. "There are all kinds of similarities between cop work and acting. Like frustration. It's a big part of my job just like it is for you."

Big blue eyes filmed with confusion.

"I start off with a new case, Briana, all I can do is ask my questions, see if something takes shape. It's just like reading a brand-new script."

"Whatever." She opened her car door.

"We both know one thing, Briana. It's all about the work. You do your best, try to make it to the bottom of the funnel, but no guarantees."

"I guess."

Milo smiled. "Thanks for talking to us. Drive safely."

As we began to walk away a high, tight voice from the Nissan said, "What's the funnel?"

"A kitchen implement."

◆

She drove away. He pulled out his pad and jotted.

I said, "Off the record, huh?"

"She must've confused me for a reporter . . . guess Nora didn't share the funnel analogy with her flock."

I said, "Too anxiety-provoking. One thing Nora *didn't* keep to herself was her attraction to Meserve. Past and present. Looks like Brad overestimated his control. Nora and Dylan still being together means when Dylan blamed the hoax on Michaela, Nora would've believed it. The question is, does that have anything to do with Michaela ending up in a pile of weeds."

"No matter what that little genius just said, I think the jealousy thing's worth looking into."

"It does, but other scenarios come to mind. If Nora resented Michaela, Dylan might have taken it upon himself to keep Nora happy. Or Michaela became a threat to Dylan by threatening to go to Brad and telling him bad stuff about Dylan. Or to Nora herself—spinning some erotic details of her nights up in Latigo with Dylan."

"Spin? The two of them were naked up there for two nights."

"Michaela told me they never had intercourse."

"You're a trusting soul. Either way, why would Michaela threaten Dylan like that?"

"Maybe more trial strategy," I said. "Pressuring him to shoulder all the blame for the hoax. In the end, the case settled. But if he stayed angry, he might've acted out."

"And the motive for doing Tori is his just being a nasty guy?"

"That or he and Tori also had something going and it went bad."

"He does her, finds it easier the second time around . . . he *is* gone as hell. And Nora knows where—or she's hiding him. That would explain her getting squirrely when we brought him up. Okay, enough theory for one night."

We walked to the car.

He said, "There's still Peaty."

"Stare at the girls and make them cry."

"Got him in trouble before. Let's see if Sean's surveillance pulled up anything."

He drove with one hand, phoned Binchy with the other. The young detective was still parked a few feet up from Reynold Peaty's apartment. The janitor had come home at seven and had stayed inside.

"Three hours watching a building," said Milo, hanging up. "I'd be out of my mind. Sean's as happy as if he's playing his bass."

Sean Binchy was a former ska punk who'd embraced religion and law enforcement simultaneously.

"How is he at working his own cases?" I said.

"He's great at the routine but it's hard to get him to think independently."

"Send him to Nora. Get him to open up his right side."

"Yeah," he said. "Meanwhile, *my* brain hurts. Gonna check for messages and call it a night."

Two messages, no respite.

The expected call from Lou Giacomo and a request to phone *Mister* Albert Beamish.

"Maybe he wants compensation for his persimmons." He punched the number, waited, clicked off. "No answer." He sighed. "Okay, now for the fun."

◆

Lou Giacomo was staying at the Holiday Inn Milo had suggested. Milo was hoping for a brief condolence chat but Giacomo wanted to meet and Milo lacked the will to refuse him.

Giacomo was standing outside the hotel wearing the same clothes he'd had on yesterday. When we pulled up, he said, "Can we go somewhere, maybe get a drink? This place is driving me up the wall."

"The hotel?" said Milo.

"Your frickin' city."

19

Our second drinking hole tonight, this one a dank, would-be Irish tavern on Pico.

Lou Giacomo took in the décor. "This could be Queens."

The three of us settled in a stiff-backed booth with Naugahyde cushions. Milo asked for a Diet Coke and I had coffee.

Giacomo said, "Bud, not Light, regular."

This barmaid was young, with a lip-pierce. "I'd never take you for a Light guy."

Giacomo ignored her. She shot him a sharp look and left.

He said, "You guys reformed drunks or something?"

Milo spread his shoulders and took up more space in the booth.

Giacomo massaged a thick wrist. "No offense intended, I'm not at my best, okay?"

"Sorry about Tori," said Milo. "I mean that."

"Like I told you the first time, I already knew. Now the wife claims she knew, too."

"How's she doing?"

"She wants me home a-sap. Probably gonna greet me with another nervous breakdown. I ain't going back until I'm sure Tori gets a proper burial."

His eyes watered. "What a stupid thing to say, it's a fuckin' *skull,* how the fuck can it get a proper *burial*? I went over there, to your coroner. They didn't wanna show it to me, gave me all this bullshit, it ain't like TV, you don't have to see it. I *made* 'em show it to me."

Spade-shaped hands shaped a shaky oval in the air. "Fuckin' *thing.* Only reason they even had it was some lady was working with it, some fuckin' science project, she's putting *holes* in it, digging out the . . ."

His loss of composure was sudden as a stroke. Pale and sweating, he pressed himself against the seat, gasping as if he'd been sucker punched.

Milo said, "Mr. Giacomo?"

Giacomo clenched his eyes shut and waved him off.

When the young barmaid brought the drinks, he was still sobbing and she was mature enough to look the other way.

"Sorry about that faggy shit."

"Don't be," said Milo.

"Well I fuckin' *am.*" Giacomo rubbed his eyes, ran his jacket sleeve over the lids. The tweed left red trails across his cheeks. "What they told me is I gotta fill out forms so I can take it with me. After that, I'm outta here."

He gazed at his beer as if it were a urine sample. Drank anyway.

"I got this to tell you: The few times Tori called, her mother bugged her—getting any parts, sleeping enough, dating anyone. I try to tell Arlene. Don't bug her. She says 'I do it 'cause I *care.*' Meaning I *don't.*"

Giacomo swallowed more beer. "Now all of a sudden, she's telling me Tori was maybe dating someone. How does she know? Tori didn't say so but she didn't deny it."

"Any details?"

Giacomo's lip curled. "Mother's intuition." He rotated his mug. "That place stinks. Your coroner's. Smells like garbage left out for a month. Any way you can use what I just told you?"

"Not without some kind of evidence."

"Figures—I'm not trying to bust your balls, but what I got to look forward to when I get home ain't no picnic. Dealing with the church, who knows what the pope's position is on burying—my sister's gonna talk to the monsignor, we'll see."

Milo sipped his Diet Coke.

Lou Giacomo said, "I keep telling myself Tori's in a better place. If I can't convince myself of that, I might as well . . ."

Milo said, "If I call your wife, is it possible she can tell me more?"

Giacomo shook his head. "But suit yourself. She was always bugging Tori—are you eating, are you exercising, how're your teeth. What she never *got* was Tori finally wanted to grow up. So what do you think, is Tori connected to that other girl?"

Milo's lie was smooth. "I can't say that, Mr. Giacomo."

"But you're not *not* saying it."

"Everything's an open issue at this point."

"Meaning you don't know shit."

"That's a pretty accurate appraisal."

Giacomo's smile was queasy. "You're probably gonna get pissed but I did something."

"What's that?"

"I went over there. To Tori's apartment. Knocked on all the doors and asked if they remembered Tori, or seen any guy hanging around. What a dump. Mostly you got Mexicans living there, I'm gettin' all these confused looks, no speaky English. You could get hold of the landlords and ask 'em to pull their rental records."

"Seeing as you already tried and they said no?"

"Hey—"

Milo said, "Don't worry about it, just tell me what they said."

"They said diddly." Giacomo handed over a scrap of paper. Holiday Inn stationery. A name and a 323 number.

Milo said, "Home-Rite Management."

Giacomo said, "Bunch of Chinese, I

talked to some woman with an accent. She claimed they didn't own the building two years ago. I try to explain to her this is important but I got nowhere." He ran his hands along the sides of his head. "Stupid bitch— it's like my brain's gonna explode. I'm bringing Tori back home in a fuckin' *carry-on.*"

We drove him back to the Holiday Inn, let the engine idle, and walked him to the hotel's glass doors.

"I'm sorry about that alkie crack, okay? That other time, that Indian place, you guys had tea, I was just . . ." He shrugged. "Out of line, none of my business."

Milo placed a hand on his shoulder. "No apologies necessary. What you've gone through, I couldn't hope to understand."

Giacomo didn't repel the contact. "Be straight with me: Would you consider this a bad one? Compared to most of them that you get?"

"They're all bad."

"Yeah, of course, sure. Like someone else's kid ain't as important as mine. But my kid's what *I'm* thinking about—think I'll ever be able to not think about it?"

Milo said, "People tell me it gets easier."

"Hope so. You find anything, you'll let me know?"

"Of course."

Giacomo nodded and shook Milo's hand. "You guys are all right."

We watched him enter the hotel lobby, pass the desk without word, and stand fidgeting in front of the elevator without touching the button. Thirty seconds later, he slapped his temple and pushed. Turned around, saw us, and mouthed the word "stooopid."

Milo smiled. We got back in the car and drove off.

" 'People tell me it gets easier'," said Milo. "Pretty therapeutic, huh? Speaking of lies, I need to get to the office, chart all that stuff Little Brie thought was off the record. Don't wanna bore you."

"Want me to meet you at Michaela's apartment tomorrow morning?"

"Nah, that could be boring, too. But how about you phone Tori's mom, see if a Ph.D. helps. The ex-husband, too. Here's the numbers."

I made the calls the following morning. Arlene Giacomo was a thoughtful, sane woman.

She said, "Lou drive you nuts?"

"Not yet."

"He needs me," she said. "I want him home."

I let her talk for a while. Eulogizing Tori but providing nothing new. When I brought up the dating issue, she said, "A mother can tell, believe me. But I've got no details, Tori was really into being free, no more girl talk with Mama. That was something her father couldn't grasp, he always bugged her."

I thanked her and punched in Michael Caravanza's number. A woman answered.

"Hold on—*Mii*-keee!"

Moments later a slurred, "Yeah?"

I explained why I was calling. He said, "Hold on—one second, babe. This is about Tori? You found her?"

"Her remains were identified yesterday."

"Remains—oh, shit, I don't wanna tell Sandy, she knew Tori."

"Did she know her well?"

"Nah," said Caravanza, "just from church. What happened?"

"That's what we're trying to figure out. Did you have contact with her after she moved to L.A.?"

"We were divorced, but we were getting along, you know? Like they say, amicable.

She called me a coupla times, maybe the first month. Then it stopped."

"No more loneliness."

"I figured she hooked up with someone."

"She say that?"

"Nah, but I know—knew Tori. When she had that voice it meant she was excited about something. And it sure wasn't her acting career, she wasn't getting shit. That she told me."

"No idea who she was seeing?"

"You think he did it to her?"

"Any lead would be helpful."

"Well," said Michael Caravanza, "if she did what she said she was gonna do, she hooked up with some movie star. That was the plan. Go to Hollywood, the right clubs, whatever, meet some movie star and show him she could be a star, too."

"Ambitious."

"Ambitious is what split us up. I'm a working guy, Tori thought her shit was—she thought she was gonna be Angelina Jolie or something—what's that—hold on, babe, just a sec—sorry, Sandy's my fiancée."

"Congratulations," I said.

"Yeah, I'm gonna try the marriage thing again. Sandy's nice and she wants kids. No big church deal, this time, we're just gonna do it with some judge then go off to Aruba or something."

"Sounds nice."

"Hope so. Don't get me wrong, Tori was a nice girl. She just thought she could be someone else."

"The few times she did call," I said, "did she say anything that could help us?"

"Let me think," said Caravanza. "It was only three times, four, whatever . . . what did she say . . . mostly she said she was lonely. That was basically it, lonely. In some shitty little apartment. She didn't miss me or want to get back together, nothing like that. She just wanted to tell me she was feeling shitty."

"What did you say?"

"Nothing, I listened. Mostly that's what I did when I was married. She talked, I listened."

I reached Milo's cell and reported both conversations.

"Hooking up with a movie star, huh?"

"Maybe she settled for someone who looked like one."

"Meserve or another PlayHouse Adonis."

"With her level of naiveté, someone who'd been around just a bit longer could've seemed impressive."

"Wonder how long Meserve's been getting insight from Nora Dowd."

"Longer than two years," I said. "He was there before Michaela arrived."

"And when Tori showed up. So where the hell is he . . . okay, thanks, let me toss this around while I wait for Michaela's landlord."

The day floated by with all the importance of a cork in the ocean. I considered calling Allison, then Robin, then Allison again. Settled for neither and filled Saturday by running and sleeping, doing scutwork around the house.

Sunday's balm and glorious blue skies made matters worse; this was a day to be with someone.

I drove to the beach. The sun had brought people and cars to the coastline. Golden-haired girls promenaded in bikini tops and sarongs, surfer dudes peeled in and out of wetsuits, tourists gawked at natural wonders of all types.

On PCH, a conspicuously crawling highway patrol car lowered the pace to racewalk from Carbon Beach to Malibu Road. The southern entry to Latigo Canyon was closer but that meant more miles of winding road. I kept going to Kanan Dume and turned off.

Alone.

I tooled up the canyon, both hands on the wheel as the twists tested the Seville's mushy suspension. Despite being up here years ago, the sharpness of the curves and the dead drops if you steered wrong surprised me.

Not a spot for a leisurely cruise and after dark the route would be treacherous unless you knew it well. Dylan Meserve had hiked up here and returned to play out a fraudulent kidnapping.

Maybe because of the isolation. I had yet to encounter another vehicle challenging the mountains.

I drove another few miles, managed to turn around on a skinny ribbon of asphalt, hooked right on Kanan, and drove into the Valley.

Tori Giacomo's last known address was a dingy white multiplex. Old cars and trucks filled the street. True to her father's description, the people I saw were mostly brown-skinned. Some were dressed for church. Others looked as if faith was the last thing on their minds.

Laurel Canyon south led me back into the city and Beverly Boulevard east took me to Hancock Park. No Range Rover in Nora Dowd's driveway and when I walked up to the door and knocked, no response.

Go west, aimless man.

The weeds where Michaela had been dumped had fluffed, obscuring any history of violence. I stared at plants and dirt, got back in the car.

On Holt Avenue, I spotted Shayndie Winograd and a young, sparsely bearded man in a black suit and a broad-brimmed hat walking four small children and steering a double stroller north toward Pico. The allegedly ailing Gershie Yoel was the picture of health as he tried to shinny up his father's trousers. Rabbi Winograd fended him off, finally lifted the boy and slung him over his shoulder like a sack of flour. The kid loved it.

A short drive away, on Reynold Peaty's block of Guthrie, I looked for Sean Binchy but couldn't find him. Was the guy that good? Or had born-again obligations prevailed on Sunday?

As I coasted past Peaty's building, a young Hispanic family came down the stairs and headed for a dented blue van. Definite church garb, including three chubby kids under five. These parents looked even younger than the Winograds—barely out of their teens. The father's shaved head and stone-faced swagger were at odds with his stiff gray suit. He and his wife were heavy. She had tired eyes and blond-streaked hair.

Back in my intern days, the psych staff had favored a smug, knowing line: *Kids having kids.* The unspoken tsk-tsk.

Here I was, driving around by myself.

Who was to say?

I'd stopped without meaning to in front of Peaty's building. One of the little kids waved at me and I waved back and both parents turned. Shaved-head Dad glared. I sped off.

No action at the PlayHouse, same for the big cantaloupe-painted complex on Overland that Dylan Meserve had left without notice.

Shabby place. Rust streaks beneath the gutters I hadn't noticed the first time. Front grid of stingy little windows, no hint anyone lived behind them.

That exhumed memories of my student days living on Overland, alone and faceless and so full of self-doubt that entire weeks could slog by in a narcotic haze.

I pictured Tori Giacomo mustering the courage for a cross-country move and ending up in a small, sad room on a street full of strangers. Fueled by ambition—or delusions. Was there a difference?

Lonely, everyone lonely.

I recalled a line I'd used on girls back then.

No, I don't do drugs, more into the natural low.

Mr. Sardonic. Every so often, it had worked.

Monday morning at eleven, Milo phoned from his car. "Damn landlord stood me up Saturday, too much traffic from La Jolla. Finally, he tells me I can get a key from his sister who lives in Westwood. Asshole. I waited for the techies, just finished doing my own toss."

"Learn anything?"

"She wasn't living large. No food in the

fridge, granola bars and canned diet shakes in the pantry. Mydol, Advil, Motrin, Pepto-Bismol, Tums, a little marijuana in her night-stand. No birth control. Not much of a reader, the extent of her library was back issues of *Us* and *People* and *Glamour.* TV but no cable hookup and the phone was dead. My subpoena for her calls is paying off in a few days but like I said her land line was disconnected for nonpayment and I can't find any cell account. One thing she did have was nice clothes. Not a lot, but nice, she probably spent all her dough on duds. Manager of the restaurant she worked at said she was fine, no problems, didn't make much of an impression. No guys he remembers seeing her with. Meserve's shoe-store boss said Meserve was unreliable and could be snotty to customers. Anyway, we'll see if any interesting prints come up. No signs of violence or struggle, doesn't look as if she was killed there. How was your weekend?"

"Quiet."

"Sounds nice."

I told him about driving up to Latigo, left out the rest of my motor tour and the memories it had evoked.

He said, "No kidding. I was up there my-self, early in the morning. Pretty, no?"

"And out of the way."

"I talked to a few neighbors, including the old guy Michaela scared when she jumped out naked. No one had ever seen her or Meserve there before. Also, I got Mr. Albert Beamish on the phone this morning. Satur-day and Sunday he spends at his place in Palm Desert. Sunshine did nothing for his disposition. What he was itching to tell me was he spotted Nora's Range Rover leaving her house Friday around nine."

"Right after our meeting at Brad's house."

"Maybe Brad advised her to take a vaca-tion. Or she just felt like some down time and didn't bother to tell her students be-cause she's an indolent rich girl. I asked Beamish to keep an eye out, thanked him for being observant. He barks back at me, 'Show your gratitude by doing your job with minimal competence.' "

I laughed. "Did his powers of observation lead to checking the Rover's occupants?"

"If only. Meserve's car still hasn't shown up but if he's with Nora, the two of them could be using hers and stashing his. As in

Nora's garage, or the one at the PlayHouse. Maybe I can pry a door and take a peek. On a whole other tack, Reynold Peaty is being true to his loser-loner self. Stayed in his apartment all weekend. I gave Sean Sunday off because he's religious, so it's possible we missed something. But I did watch the place in the afternoon around four."

Missing me by a couple of hours. Again.

"Last and possibly least," he said, "Tori Giacomo's building has changed ownership twice since she lived there. The original owners were a couple of nonagenarian sisters who passed on naturally. The property went to probate, a speculator from Vegas picked it up cheap then resold to a consortium of businessmen from Koreatown. No records of any old tenants, the aroma of futility fills the air."

"When are you heading over to Nora's?"

"Pulling up as we speak . . ." A car door slammed. "I am now heading for her door. Knock knock—" He raised his voice to an androgynous alto: "Who's there? Lieutenant Sturgis. Lieutenant Sturgis who? . . . Hear that, Alex?"

"Hear what?"

"Exactly. Okay, now I'm at the garage . . .

no give, locked . . . where's a battering ram when you need it? Tha-tha-that's all, folks, this has been a presentation of the Useless Travel Channel."

CHAPTER

20

Tuesday morning, I called Robin, got her machine, hung up.

In my office, a dusty stack of psych journals beckoned. A twenty-page treatise on the eye-blink reflex in schizophrenic Hooded rats lowered *my* eyelids.

I went down to the pond and fed the koi. For fish, they're smart, have learned to swarm the moment I come down the stairs. It's nice to be wanted.

Warm air and sloshing water put me under again. The next thing I saw was Milo's big face crowding my visual field.

Smile as wide as a continent. Scariest

clown in the known world. I mumbled some kind of greeting.

"What's with you?" he said. "Snoozing midday like a codger?"

"What time is it?"

He told me. An hour had vanished. "What's next, white shoes and dinner at four?"

"Robin naps."

"Robin has a real job."

I got to my feet and yawned. The fish sped toward me. Milo hummed the theme from *Jaws.* In his hand was a folder. Unmistakable shade of blue.

"A new one?" I said.

Instead of answering, he climbed back up to the house. I cleared my head and followed.

He sat himself at the kitchen table, napkin tucked into his collar, dishes and utensils set for one. Half a dozen slices of toast, runny Vesuvius of scrambled eggs, sixteen-ounce glass of orange juice, half emptied.

He wiped pulp from his lips. "Love this place. Breakfast served any time."

"How long have you been here?"

"Long enough to rob you blind if such

were my intention. Why can't I convince you to lock your door?"

"No one drops in but you."

"This isn't a visit, it's business." He stabbed the egg mound, slid the blue folder across the table. A second file separated from the first. "Read 'em and wake."

A pair of missing persons cases. *Gaidelas, A. Gaidelas, C.*

Consecutive case numbers.

"Two more girls?" I said. "Sisters?"

"Read."

Andrew and Catherine Gaidelas, forty-eight and forty-five, respectively, had disappeared two months after Tori Giacomo.

The couple, married twenty years with no children, were owners of a beauty parlor in Toledo, Ohio, called Locks of Luck. In L.A. for a spring vacation, they'd been staying in Sherman Oaks with Cathy's sister and brother-in-law, Dr. and Mrs. Barry Palmer. On a clear, crisp Tuesday in April the Palmers went to work and the Gaidelases left to go hiking in the Malibu mountains. They hadn't been seen since.

Identical report in both files. I read Catherine's. "Doesn't say where in Malibu."

"Doesn't say a lot of things. Keep going."

The facts were sketchy, with no apparent links to Michaela or Tori. Was I missing something? Then I came to the final paragraph.

Subject C. Gaidelas's sister, Susan Palmer, reports Cathy and Andy said they were coming out to Calif for vacation but after they got there talked about staying for a while so they could "break into acting." S. Palmer reports her sister did some "modeling and theater" after high school and used to talk about becoming an actress. A. Gaidelas didn't have acting experience but everyone back home thought he was a handsome guy who "looked like Dennis Quaid." S. Palmer reports Andy and Cathy were tired of running a beauty parlor and didn't like the cold weather in Ohio. Cathy said she thought they could get some commercials because they looked "all-American." She also talked about "getting serious and taking acting lessons" and S. Palmer thinks Cathy contacted some acting schools but doesn't know which ones.

At the rear were two color head-shots. Cathy and Andy Gaidelas were both fair-haired and blue-eyed with disarming smiles. Cathy had posed in a sleeveless black dress trimmed with rhinestones and matching pendant earrings. Full-faced, with plump shoulders, she had teased platinum hair, a strong chin, a thin, straight nose.

Her husband was a tousled gray-blond, long-faced and craggy in a white button-down shirt that exposed curls of pale chest hair. I supposed his off-kilter grin had a Dennis Quaid charm. Any other similarities to the actor eluded me.

All-American couple well into middle age. They might qualify for Mom and Dad parts on commercials. Pitches for dog food, TV dinners, garbage bags . . .

I shut the file.

Milo said, "Wannabe stars and now they're gone. Am I reaching?"

"How'd you come across it?"

"Checking out other MP cases with either an acting connection or a Malibu link. As usual, the computer flagged nothing, but a sheriff's detective remembered the Gaidelases as would-be thespians. In his mind, no homicide, two adults rabbiting. I reached the brother-in-law, plastic surgeon. The Gaidelases are still missing, family got fed up with the sheriffs, tried the P.I. route, went through three investigators. The first two gave them zilch, the third turned up the fact that the Gaidelases' rental car had showed up five weeks after the disappearance, sent them a big bill and said that's all she could do."

"The sheriffs never thought to tell the family about the car?"

"Ventura police auto-recovery case, sheriffs weren't even aware of it."

"Where was it found?"

"Camarillo. One of the parking lots at that big discount shopping outlet they've got there."

"Huge place," I said.

"You shop there?"

Twice. With Allison. Waiting as she tried on outfits at Ralph Lauren and Versace. "Five weeks and no one noticed the car?"

He said, "For all we know, it was stashed somewhere and moved. The Gaidelases' rental contract was for two weeks and when they didn't return it, the company started phoning the number on the form, got no answer. When the company tried to bill for late charges, they found out the Gaidelases' credit card and cell phone had been canceled the day after they disappeared. Company kept tacking on fees at a usurious rate of interest. The bill compounded seriously and after thirty days, the debt got assigned to a collection agency. The agency found out the Gaidelases' number in Ohio, got another disconnect. What's it sound like to you?"

"A skip."

"Ten points. Anyway, a lien got put on the Gaidelases' assets, screwed up their credit rating. Private Sleuth Number Three pulled a credit check and back traced. The Palmers say no way the Gaidelases skipped, the two of them were hyped up about making it as actors, loved California."

"Did the car get checked for evidence?"

He shook his head. "No reason to check a recovered rental. By now, no one knows where it is. Probably put up for auction and shipped to Mexico."

"The Camarillo outlet's miles up the coast from Malibu," I said. "The Gaidelases could've gone hiking and followed up with a shopping trip—duds for auditions. Or they never got out of the hills."

"Shopping's unlikely, Alex. The last credit card purchase they made before the account was canceled was lunch at an Italian place in Pacific Palisades the day before. My vote's for a nature walk turned nasty. Couple of tourists digging the view, never figuring on a predator."

He pushed eggs around his plate. "Never liked nature. Think it's worth pursuing?"

"Malibu and a possible acting school link say it needs to be."

"Dr. Palmer said he'd ask his wife if she was willing to talk. Two minutes later, Dr. *Susan* Palmer's secretary phones, says the sooner the better. Susan's got a dental practice in Brentwood. I'm meeting her for coffee in forty minutes. Let me finish my breakfast. Am I expected to wash my own dishes?"

Dr. Susan Palmer was a thinner, plainer version of her sister. More subdued shade of blond in her short, layered hair, true-blue eyes, a frame that looked too meager for her wide face. She wore a ribbed white silk turtleneck, navy slacks, blue suede loafers with golden buckles. Worry lines framed the eyes and tugged at her mouth.

We were in a Mocha Merchant on San Vicente, in the heart of Brentwood. Sleek people ordered complex six-dollar lattes and pastries the size of an infant's head. Reproductions of antique coffee grinders hung from cedar-paneled walls. Smooth jazz alternated with Peruvian flute on tape-loop. The scorched smell of overdone beans bittered the air.

Susan Palmer had ordered a "half-caf iced Sumatran Vanilla Blendinesse, part soy, part whole milk, make sure it's whole, not low-fat."

My request for a "medium coffee" had confused the kid behind the counter.

I scanned the menu board. "Brew of the day, extra-hot, Medio."

Milo said, "The same."

The kid looked as if he'd been cheated out of something.

We brought our drinks to the pine table Susan Palmer had selected at the front of the coffeehouse.

Milo said, "Thanks for meeting with us, Doctor."

Palmer looked down at her iced drink and stirred. "I should thank you—finally someone's interested."

Her smile was abrupt and obligatory. Her hands looked strong. Scrubbed pink, the nails trimmed close and smooth. Dentist's hands.

"Happy to listen, ma'am."

"Lieutenant, I've come to accept that Cathy and Andy are dead. Maybe that sounds terrible, but after all this time, there's no other logical explanation. I know about the credit card cancellation and the utilities back in Toledo, but you have to believe me: Cathy and Andy did *not* run away to start a new life. No way would they do that, it's not in either of their characters." She sighed. "Cathy would have no *idea* where to run."

"Why's that, Doctor?"

"My sister was the *sweetest* person. But unsophisticated."

"Escape isn't always sophisticated, Dr. Palmer."

"Escape would be beyond Cathy. *And* Andy." More stirring. The beige concoction foamed unpleasantly. "Let me give you some family background. Our parents are retired professors. Dad taught anatomy at the Medical College of Ohio and Mom taught English at the University of Toledo. My brother, Eric, is an M.D.-Ph.D. doing bioengineering research at Rockefeller U., and I'm a cosmetic orthodontist."

Another sigh. "Cathy barely made it out of high school."

"Not a student," I said.

"Cathy had what I now realize were learning disabilities and with that came all the self-esteem issues you'd expect. Back then we just thought she was . . . not as sharp as the rest of us. We didn't mistreat her, just the opposite, we *coddled* her. She and I had a great relationship, we never fought. She's two years older but I always felt like the big sister. Everyone in the family was loving and kind but there was this . . . Cathy *had* to feel it. Way too much sympathy. When she announced her plans to learn to be a cosmetologist, our parents made such a big deal you'd think she'd gotten into Harvard."

She tasted her drink, nudged the cup a few inches away. "Mom and Dad are not ebullient people. When my brother *did* get into Harvard, their reaction was low-key. Cathy had to know she was being patronized."

Milo said, "She and her husband ran a business. In terms of her ability to plan—"

Susan Palmer moved her head rapidly,

more quiver than shake. "In any other family, Cathy would've been able to think of herself as successful. But in ours . . . the business came about after a long . . . how can I say this . . . Cathy got into difficulties. When she was younger."

"Teenage difficulties?" said Milo.

"Cathy had an extended adolescence. Drugs, drinking, hanging with the wrong crowd. Eight years after high school she still lived at home and did nothing but sleep late and party. A couple of times, she ended up in the E.R. That's why my parents were *thrilled* when she went to beauty school. That's where she met Andy. Perfect match."

"Andy wasn't a student, either?" said Milo.

"Andy also struggled through high school," said Susan Palmer. "He's nice enough—nice to Cathy, that's what's important. They both got jobs as stylists at local salons. But their incomes never progressed much and after ten years, they were still living in a cruddy little apartment. So we set them up. Barry and I, my brother and his wife, Mom and Dad. We found an old commercial building, renovated it, bought beauty equipment. Officially it was a loan but no one's ever discussed repayment."

"Locks of Luck," I said.

"Corny, no? That was Andy's inspiration."

"They make money?" said Milo.

"The last few years they were turning a small profit. Mom and Dad still helping out."

"Mom and Dad are in Toledo?"

"Geographically in Toledo. Psychologically in Denial."

"They think Cathy and Andy are alive."

"I'm sure sometimes they even *believe* it," said Susan Palmer. "Other times . . . let's just say it's been tough. Mom's health has deteriorated and Dad's aged terribly. If you could learn *anything,* you'd be helping some really nice people."

Milo said, "Do you have any theories about what happened?"

"The only one that makes sense is that Cathy and Andy went hiking and met some psycho." Susan Palmer shut and opened her eyes. "I can only imagine. I don't *want* to imagine."

"The morning they went hiking, did anything unusual occur?"

"No, it was just a regular morning. Barry and I both had a full day of patients, we were really rushed. Cathy and Andy were just waking up when we were about to leave. All excited about exploring nature. Barry and I were so hurried, we didn't pay much attention." Her eyes misted. "How could I know it would be the last time I'd see my sister?"

She tasted her drink. "I *specifically* said *whole* milk, this is *low*-fat. *Idiots.*"

Milo said, "I'll get you another."

"Forget it," she snapped. On the brink of tears. Her face softened. "No, thanks, Lieutenant. What else can I tell you?"

"Did Cathy and Andy mention where in Malibu they were headed?"

"Barry and I thought they'd enjoy the ocean, but they had a Triple-A book and wanted to hike somewhere at the top of Kanan Dume Road."

"Where atop Kanan Dume?"

"I couldn't tell you," said Susan Palmer. "I just remember them showing us a map in the book. It looked pretty curvy but that's what they wanted. We told the sheriffs all this and they said they drove up and checked the area. Frankly, I don't trust them, they never took us seriously. Barry and I have spent hours driving all over land-side Malibu." She exhaled. "So much space."

I said, "Their car was found around twenty-five miles north of Kanan Dume."

"Which is why I've come to believe what-ever happened was up in the hills. It had to be that way, right? Why else would some-one cancel Cathy and Andy's credit card if they weren't trying to cover up something terrible? Same for ditching the car. It was to throw us off the trail."

"Were Cathy and Andy aware of the dis-count outlets?"

"We never told them about it, but maybe from the Triple-A book." She placed both el-bows on the table. "My sister and brother-in-law were simple, direct people. If they said they were going hiking up in Malibu, they went hiking up in Malibu. No *way* would they just disappear and go off on some crazy adventure."

"They did have one fantasy," I said.

"What do you mean?"

"Acting."

"That," she said. "During those eight years after high school Cathy managed to convince herself she was going to be an ac-tress. Or a model, depending on what day it was. Not that she ever did anything to pur-sue those goals beyond reading fan maga-

zines. My mother knew the owner of Dillman's department store and they gave
Cathy a runway job modeling spring fash-
ions. Cathy's pretty, when she was young
she was gorgeous. But by that time a few
years older and not exactly anorexic."

She sniffed and held her breath for several seconds. "I flew out to attend the show.
Mom and I sat in the front row and we both
bought clothing we didn't need. The following spring, Dillman's didn't ask Cathy back."

"How'd she react?" I said.

"She didn't. Which was Cathy's way,
she'd just take every bit of indignity as if she
deserved to be disappointed. We all *hated*
when Cathy got disappointed. That's why
Mom encouraged her to take some acting
lessons. Adult Ed at the community center,
musical revivals, that kind of thing. Mom
wanted Cathy *engaged* in something and
Cathy finally agreed. She seemed to be
having a good time. Then she stopped and
announced she was going to become a
cosmetologist. That's why Barry and I were
shocked when she and Andy got here and
announced they'd come to pursue acting."

"Was it Andy's dream, as well?"

"It was Cathy's dream but Andy got with the program, like he always did."

Milo said, "That can make for a good marriage."

"Andy and Cathy were best friends. It was almost . . . I don't want to say platonic, but the truth is, I've always wondered, and so did my husband and my brother and anyone who's met Andy."

"Wondered about what?"

"His being gay."

"Because he's a hairdresser," said Milo.

"It's more than that. Andy has a definite feminine side to him. He's really good at clothes and decorating and cooking and that sounds prejudiced but if you met him, you'd understand." She blinked. "Maybe he was one of those effeminate straight men. It doesn't matter, does it? He *loved* my sister. They adored each other."

Milo said, "The missing persons file mentioned something about acting schools."

"It did?"

"You're surprised, Doctor?"

"I told the sheriff that but I had no idea he actually wrote it down. Is it important?"

"Anything that fills in Cathy and Andy's

activities during their trip to L.A. could be important. They mention specific schools?"

"No, the only thing they talked about was tourist stuff. Disneyland, Universal City Walk, Hollywood and Vine—they went to the Hollywood museum on Vine, the old Max Factor building. That they loved, because of the emphasis on hair and makeup. Andy kept talking about the Blonde Room, the Brunette Room—" She brightened. "Maybe they found an acting school in Hollywood. There's bound to be some there, right?"

"More than a few."

"I'd be willing to check, Lieutenant. I'll call every single one."

"I'll do it, Dr. Palmer."

She eyed him warily.

"Cross my heart."

"Sorry, it's just . . . I need to relax and trust someone. I get a good feeling about you, Lieutenant."

Milo's turn to blush.

"I hope I'm right," said Susan Palmer.

CHAPTER

21

Milo talked to Susan Palmer for another ten minutes, easing into open-ended questions, putting pauses and silences to work.

Good technique but it didn't produce. She talked about how much she missed her sister, lapsed into exclusive past tense. When she shot to her feet, her eyes looked bruised. "Got an office full of malocclusions. Please stay in touch."

We watched her cross the parking lot and get into a silver BMW 740. The license plate read: I STR8 10.

Milo said, "Her office is two blocks away but she drove."

"California girl," I said. "Something her sister wanted to be."

"Acting lessons and a hike above Kanan Dume. Can't be coincidence. The question is how do the Gaidelases figure in with a couple of pretty-face female victims?"

"That girl we spoke to—Briana—said Nora rejected applicants for reasons other than talent."

"Wanting 'em young and pretty," he said. "Cathy and Andy were both too old and Cathy was too fat. So what, they got turned away from the PlayHouse *and* killed? Talk about flunking an audition."

"Maybe their obvious vulnerability got a predator sniffing."

"Someone at the school spots 'em and stalks 'em?" He gazed out the window and back at me.

I said, "Could be the same way Tori Giacomo was spotted. If her ex is right about her dating someone, you'd think that person would've surfaced when she went missing. Unless he had something to do with her death."

"A good-looking predator. As in Meserve. What, he proposed a three-way to the Gaidelases and the party went bad?"

"Or he just offered to help them with their careers."

"Yeah," he said, "that would work."

"On the other hand," I said, "Reynold Peaty had plenty of opportunity to check out the flock at the PlayHouse."

"Him . . . let's see if Sean's seen anything." He tried Binchy's number, scowled, clicked off. "No connection. Maybe the cell waves are upset by environmentally conscious mochalicious fumes."

I said, "Nora's attachment to youth is interesting."

"Why? That just makes her like everyone else in showbiz."

"But she has no profit motive. The school's a make-work project, so why get picky? Unless what she really wanted was a personal dating pool."

"Sample the studs," he said.

"And when they get too close, Brother Brad chases them off. Or thinks he does."

"Okay, she's a middle-aged horn-dog. How do the Gaidelases figure in with that?"

"I don't know, but when Susan Palmer was describing her family situation, I was struck by parallels between Cathy and Nora. Both floundered well into adulthood.

Family connections got Cathy a runway gig that she couldn't hold on to. Nora's got her a single sit-com walk-on that went nowhere. Cathy had long-standing drug problems. Nora smokes dope to get her day going. Eventually, both women were set up in business. Cathy's salon had been making a profit recently. Meaning it lost money for years. The Dowd family fortune has relieved Nora from any financial pressure, but bottom line, we've got a couple of prodigal daughters. Maybe Cathy showing up at the PlayHouse evoked something in Nora that Nora didn't want to see."

"Cathy's too much like her, so she kills her? That's a little abstract, Alex. Why would Nora even know about Cathy's history if she turned her away?"

"What if Cathy did have a chance to audition?" I said. "Nora's a big one for opening the soul."

"Cathy emoted and it made Nora squirm? Fine, but I don't see flashpoint epiphany as a motive for murder. All Nora has to do is send her and Andy away and move on to the next stud. And if uncomfortable memories are the issue, how does Michaela fit in? Or Tori Giacomo who disappeared *before* the Gaidelases? This feels more like a sexual thing, Alex. Just what you said: Some psychopath scopes out the herd and picks off the weak ones. Cathy may have been over the hill for a starlet, but she wasn't a bad-looking woman. To a guy like Peaty she coulda looked downright sexy, no?"

"Peaty was caught peeping at college girls. Michaela and Tori would fit, but—"

"Cathy wouldn't. So maybe he's not as limited as that oafish demeanor suggests. Or Cathy set something off—fond memories of a barroom floozy who rejected him back in Reno. Hell, maybe Cathy reminded him of his *mother* and he snapped. You guys still believe in the Oedipal thing?"

"It has its place."

"No telling what goes on in the old cranio, right?" He got up and paced. "If it's a sexual thing, there could be more victims out there. But let's concentrate on the victims we know about. What they have in common is acting school and/or the Malibu hills."

"One person with links to both is Meserve," I said. "He picked Latigo for his hoax allegedly because he'd hiked up there. Nora was angry at the hoax, but instead of kicking him out, she promoted him. Maybe she wasn't clueless after all."

"Dylan and Nora planned the hoax together? Why?"

"The real performance game. Two failed actors writing a script. Discarding the bit players—*that* sounds like Hollywood."

"Nora choreographs, Meserve acts it out."

"Nora *directs.* It's what everyone in the industry aims for."

The coffeehouse got warmer and noisier as every table filled. Sleek people began milling at the entrance. Lots of peeved glances aimed our way.

Milo hooked his finger and we left. A woman muttered, "Finally."

We drove to the station and ran into Sean Binchy exiting Milo's office. Binchy's Doc Martens gleamed as shiny as his rusty, gelled hair.

"Hey, Loot. I just took a call for you."

"I tried to call *you,*" said Milo. "Anything new on Peaty?"

Binchy beamed. "We can arrest him if you want. Driving without a license."

"He has a car?"

"Red Datsun minivan, old and messed-up looking. He parks it on the street, three blocks from his apartment. Which shows intent to conceal, right? The plates are inactive, originally came from a Chrysler sedan that was supposed to be junked ten years ago. Your basic little old lady from Pasadena. Literally, Loot. And guess what, that's exactly where Peaty drove this morning. Ten East to the 110 North, off at Arroyo Parkway, and then he took surface streets."

"Where?"

"Apartment building on the east side of town. He pulled mops and cleaning stuff out of the van and went in there to work. I tried to call you but your cell wasn't receiving."

"Designer coffee messed up the air," said Milo.

"Pardon?"

"Go back to Peaty's tonight, Sean. See if you can get a VIN number from the van and trace it."

"Sure," said Binchy. "Did I do wrong by terminating the surveillance, Loot? There were a few things I needed to do back here."

"Like what?" said Milo.

Sean shifted his weight. "Captain called

me in yesterday, I've been wanting to tell you. He wants me to work a new case with Hal Prinski, liquor store robbery and pistol-whipping on Sepulveda. Robberies aren't my thing but Captain says I need breadth of experience. I'm not sure what Detective Prinski will want from me. All I can say is I'll do my best to get back to Peaty."

"Appreciate it, Sean."

"I'm really sorry, Loot, if it was up to me, I'd be doing nothing but your stuff. Your stuff's interesting." He shrugged. "That illegal car buttresses Peaty being lowlife."

"Buttresses," said Milo.

Binchy's freckles receded as the skin behind them deepened. "New word a day. Tasha's idea. She read somewhere the brain starts deteriorating after puberty—like we're all rotting, you know? She's into crosswords, word games, to stay mentally challenged. To me, reading the Bible's plenty challenging."

Milo said, "The van buttresses, Sean. If you can't spend any more time on Peaty, don't sweat it but let me know right away."

"For sure. About that call, the one that just came in? It's related to Peaty, too. Indi-

vidual named Bradley Dowd. Name's in the
Michaela Brand file. He's Peaty's boss."

"What'd he want?"

"Wouldn't say, just that it might be important. He sounded real rushed, wouldn't talk
to me, only you. The number he left's a cell,
not in the file."

"Where is it?"

"Next to your computer. Which I noticed
was turned off."

"So?"

"Well," said Binchy, "I don't want to tell
you how to operate, but sometimes it's better to just leave it on all the time, especially
with an outmoded machine. 'Cause booting
up by itself can cause power surges and—"

Milo edged past him. Slammed his door.

"—drain energy." Binchy smiled at me.

I said, "He's had a busy day."

"He usually does, Dr. Delaware." Shooting a French cuff, Binchy examined a bright
orange Swatch watch. "Whoa, noon already. All of a sudden, I got a burrito Jones.
Hello, vending machine. Have a nice day,
Doc."

I opened Milo's door, nearly collided with
him as he stormed out. He kept walking and
I hurried to keep pace.

"Where to?"

"The PlayHouse. Just got a call from Brad Dowd. He's got something to show us. Talking fast but he didn't sound rushed to me. More like scared."

"He say why?"

"Something about Nora. I asked if she was hurt and he said no, then he hung up. I figured I'd wait till we were face-to-face before applying my powers of detection."

CHAPTER
22

The gate to the PlayHouse property was open. A sky heavy with marine fog browned the grass and deepened the house's green siding to mustard.

Bradley Dowd stood in front of the garage. One of the barn doors was ajar. Dowd wore a black cashmere crewneck over fawn slacks and black sandals. The fog turned his white hair sooty.

No sign of his Porsche on the street. A red, split-windowed, sixties Corvette was parked up a bit. All the other vehicles in sight were as glamorous as oatmeal.

Dowd waved as we pulled to the curb.

Something metallic glinted in his hand. When we reached the garage, he flung the door open. The structure's aged exterior was deceiving. Inside were black cement floors polished to a gloss and cedar-plank walls adorned with racing posters. Halogen lights glinted from the ceiling rafters.

Triple garage, all three spaces occupied.

To the left was an impeccably restored green Austin Healy, low-slung, waspishly aggressive. Next to that, another Vette, white, happily chromed. Softer body style than the one on the street. Nipple taillights. One of my grad school profs had tooled around in a car like that. He'd bragged about it being a '53.

A dust filter hummed between the two sports cars. It hadn't done much for the dented brown Toyota Corolla in the right-hand slot.

Brad Dowd said, "I got here an hour ago, bringing my '63 Sting Ray back from valve work." The shiny thing in his grip was a combination padlock. "This piece of crap was sitting where the Stinger's supposed to go. The doors were unlocked so I checked the reg. It's Meserve's. There's something on the front seat that spooks me a little."

Milo walked past him, circled the Corolla, squinted inside the car, returned.

"See it?" said Brad Dowd.

"Snow globe."

"It's the one I told you about. When Nora broke off with him she must've given it back. Don't you think it's a little weird that he kept it in his damned heap? And parked the heap in my space?" Dowd's jaw trembled. "I called Nora yesterday, no answer. Same thing today. She doesn't have to inform me of her comings and goings, but usually she returns calls. I'm going over to her house but first I wanted you to see this."

Albert Beamish had spied Nora driving away four days ago. Milo said nothing about that. "Meserve ever leave his car here before, Mr. Dowd?"

"Hell, no. Nora uses the main building for the school but the garage is mine. I'm always in a space crunch."

"Lots of cars?"

"A few. Sometimes I set aside slots in my buildings, but it's not always enough. I used to keep a hangar at the airport, which was perfect because it's right near the office. Then all the demand from the jet owners drove the rentals up."

He jiggled the padlock. "What bothers me is that only Nora and I know the combination. I wanted her to have it in case of fire or some other disaster. She wouldn't give it out to *him.*"

"You're sure of that," said Milo.

"What do you mean?"

"Nora's an adult, sir. Maybe she chose to disregard your advice."

"About Meserve? No way, Nora agreed with me about that lowlife." Brad lowered his hand and swung the padlock. "What if he forced her to open up?"

"Why would he do that, sir?"

"To hide that *thing,*" said Dowd. He eyed the Toyota. "Leaving that stupid globe, there . . . there's something off about it. What are you going to do about it?"

"Any idea how long the car's been here?"

"No more than two weeks because that's when I took the Stinger in for valve work."

Milo circled the car again. "Doesn't seem to be much in here other than the globe."

"There isn't," said Dowd, wringing his hands. The padlock clicked. He hung it on the door hasp and returned, shaking his head. "I *warned* her about him."

Milo said, "All we've got is his car."

"I know, I know—think I'm overreacting?"

"It's normal to worry about your sister but let's not jump to conclusions."

"What do I do with the heap?"

"We'll have the heap towed to the police impound lot."

"When?"

"I'll phone right now."

"Thanks." Brad Dowd tapped his foot as Milo made the call.

"Within half an hour, Mr. Dowd."

"Fine, fine—you know what else is bothering me? That girl—the Brand girl. She got mixed up with Meserve and look what happened to *her.* Nora's too damned trusting, Lieutenant. What if he showed up and she let him in and he got violent?"

"We'll check the car for signs of violence. Are you sure your sister and yourself are the only ones with the combination?"

"Damned sure."

"No way Nora could've given it to Meserve? Back when she was still interested in him?"

"She was never *interested* in him—we're talking a brief flirtation." Dowd chewed his lip. "She'd never give him the combination. I explicitly forbade her to give it out. It's not logical, anyway. If she wanted to open the garage, she could do it herself. Which she wouldn't, because she knew the Stinger would be coming back."

"Did she know when?"

"That's what I was calling her about yesterday. To tell her I'd be driving it back. She didn't answer."

"So she didn't know," said Milo.

"Let me try her house again." He produced a shiny black cell phone, punched a two-digit speed-dial code. "Still no answer."

"Could Reynold Peaty have learned the combination, sir? From working here?"

Dowd's eyes widened. "Reynold? Why would he want it? Is there something you haven't told me about him?"

"Turns out he does drive. Has an unregistered vehicle."

"What? Why the hell would he do that? I pay for a van pool to pick him up and take him to work."

"He drove himself to a job in Pasadena today." Milo read off the address from his pad.

"Yeah, that's one of mine. Oh, Jesus— you're sure—of course you are, you've obviously been watching him." Dowd ran a thumb through his white hair. His other hand clenched. "I asked you the first time if I should worry about him. Now you're telling me I should." Brad shaded his eyes with a shaky hand. "He's been alone with my sister. This is a nightmare—I can't tell Billy."

"Where is Billy?"

"Waiting for me at the office—the key is to find *Nora.* What the hell are you going to do about that, Lieutenant?"

Milo eyed the PlayHouse. "Have you checked in there?"

"There? No—oh, man!" Brad Dowd bolted toward the building, running around the porch rails with long, smooth strides, fumbling in his pockets as he vaulted steps two at a time. Milo went after him and when Dowd turned the key, Milo stilled his hand.

"Me first, sir."

Dowd stiffened, then backed away. "Fine. Go. Hurry."

He positioned himself on the east end of the porch where he leaned on the rail and stared at the garage. Sun peeked out from under the marine layer. Foliage was green again. Dowd's red Corvette took on an orange sheen.

Six silent minutes passed before the door opened. Milo said, "Doesn't appear to be any crime scene, but I'll call the techs and have them take a look if you'd like."

"What would that entail? Would they tear the place up?"

"There'd be fingerprint dust but no structural damage unless something came up."

"Like what?"

"Signs of violence."

"But you don't see any?"

"No, sir."

"You need my permission to bring in your people?"

"With no probable cause I do."

"Then I don't see the point. Let me go in, I'll tell you right away if anything's off."

Polished oak, everywhere.

Paneled walls, broad-plank flooring, beamed ceilings, window casements. Vigorously grained, quarter-sawn wood milled a century ago, mellowed the color of old bourbon and held together by mortise and tenon joints. Darker wood—black walnut—had been used for the pegs. Fringed brown velvet drapes covered some of the windows.

Others had been left clear, revealing stained glass insets. Flowers and fruit and greenery, high-quality work, maybe Tiffany.

Not much natural light flowed in. The house was dim, silent, smaller than it appeared from the street with a modest entry hall centering two front rooms. What had once been the dining room was set up with old overstuffed thrift-shop chairs, vinyl beanbags, rolled up futons, rubber exercise pads. An open doorway offered a glimpse of a white kitchen.

A stage had been constructed at the rear of the former parlor. Ragged plywood affair on raw fir joists made even cruder by its contrast to the precision joinery and gleaming surfaces everywhere else. Three rows of folding chairs for the audience. Photos taped to the outer wall, many of them black-and-white. What looked to be stills from old movies.

Brad Dowd said, "Everything looks normal." His eyes shifted to an open door, stage right. "Did you check in back?"

Milo nodded. "Yup, but feel free."

Dowd went in there and I followed. A short, dark hallway led to two small rooms with an old lav between them. Once-upon-a-time bedrooms paneled with bead board below the chair rail, painted pea green above. One chamber was vacant, the other stored additional folding chairs and was decorated with more movie stills. Both closets were empty.

Brad Dowd moved in and out quickly. The aging-surfer insouciance I'd seen at his house had given way to gamecock jumpiness.

Nothing like family to shake you up.

He left. I lingered and glanced at the photos. Mae West, Harold Lloyd, John Barrymore. Doris Day and James Cagney in *Love Me or Leave Me*. Veronica Lake and Alan Ladd in *The Blue Dahlia*. Voight and Hoffman in *Midnight Cowboy*. Black-and-white faces I didn't recognize. A section devoted to youth acts. The Lennon Sisters. The Brady Bunch. The Partridge Family. The Cowsills. A quartet of grinning kids in bell-bottoms called the Kolor Krew.

I returned to the front room. Milo and Brad Dowd sat at the edge of the stage. Dowd's head was down. Milo was saying, "You can help by trying to remember where your sister goes when she travels."

"She wouldn't let that thing in the garage and just go off somewhere."

"Covering bases, Mr. Dowd."

"Traveling . . . okay, she flies to Paris every year. Later in the year, mid-April. She stays at the Crillon, costs a fortune. Sometimes she goes on to the south, rents a little chateau. The longest she's been away is a month."

"Anywhere else?"

"She used to go everywhere—England, Italy, Germany—but France is the only place she really likes. She speaks high school French, never had any of those problems you hear about."

"What about here in the States?"

"She's been to a health spa in Mexico a few times," said Dowd. "Down in Tecate. I think she also goes to a place in Ojai. Or Santa Barbara, somewhere in that vicinity. She likes the whole spa thing—you think that could be it? She just wanted to be pampered and I'm worrying about nothing? Hell, maybe Meserve did learn the combination and stashed that piece of shit and Nora knows nothing about it and is getting a mud pack or whatever."

His fingers drummed his knees. "I'll get

on the horn, call every damn spa in the state."

"We'll do that, sir."

"I want to do *something.*"

"Help me by thinking back," said Milo. "Did Nora mention *anything* about traveling recently?"

"Definitely not." Brad bounded up. "I'm going to check on Billy, then it's over to Nora's house, Lieutenant. She doesn't like me using my key but what if she fell and needs help?"

Milo said, "When's the last time you remember seeing her with Meserve?"

"After Meserve pulled that stunt and she assured me it was over."

Milo said nothing.

Dowd's laugh was bitter. "So what's his damn car doing here, right? You think I'm clueless."

"Your sister's an adult."

"So to speak," said Brad Dowd softly.

"It's tough being in charge," I said.

"Yeah, it's a day at the beach."

Milo said, "So you have a key to Nora's house."

"In my safe at the office but I've never used it. She gave it to me years ago—same reason I gave her the combination to the garage. If she's not home, maybe I'll look around just a little. See if I can find her passport. I'm not sure where she keeps it but I can try. Though I guess you could find out faster—just call the airlines."

"After Nine-Eleven, it's a little complicated," said Milo.

"Bureaucratic bullshit?"

"Yes, sir. I can't even go into your sister's house with you, unless she explicitly gave you permission to bring in guests."

"Guests," said Brad Dowd. "Like we're having a goddamn party—no, she never did that. Truth is, I've never gone in there myself without Nora. Never thought I'd *need* to."

He brushed invisible dust from his sweater. "I'm firing Reynold."

"Please don't," said Milo.

"But—"

"There's no evidence against him, Mr. Dowd, and I don't want to alert him."

"He's a goddamn *pervert,*" said Brad Dowd. "What if he does something on the job? Who gets sued for liability? What else haven't you told me?"

"Nothing, sir."

Dowd stared at Milo. "Lieutenant, I'm

sorry if it messes up your case, but I *am* going to fire him. Once I've talked to my lawyer
and my accountant, make sure everything's
by the book. It's my prerogative to handle
my business any—"

"We're watching Peaty," said Milo, "so
the likelihood of his stepping out of line is
next to nil. I'd strongly prefer you to hold
off."

"You'd *prefer,*" said Dowd. "*I'd* prefer not
having to deal with everyone else's shit."

He left us, passed the rows of folding
chairs. Kicked a metal leg. Cursed under his
breath.

Milo remained on the stage, chin in hand.

One-man show. The Sad Detective.

Brad Dowd made it to the entry hall and
looked back. "You planning on sleeping
here? C'mon, I need to lock up."

Milo toed the curb and watched as the Corvette sped off.

I said, "You wanted Brad to take Peaty more seriously."

He reached behind and slapped his rear. "C.Y.A. time. If it turns out something bad happened to Nora, he'll be looking for someone to blame."

"You didn't tell him Nora left Friday night."

"There are limits to my honesty. First of all, Beamish never saw who was in the car. Second, there's no law keeping her inside her house. She coulda been going out for drinks. Or she did have travel plans. Or she got abducted by aliens."

"If Meserve snatched her, why would he leave his wheels at her school and broadcast the fact? And if the snow globe's some kind of trophy, he'd take it with him."

"If?" he said. "What else could it be?"

"Maybe a defiant message to Brad from Dylan *and* Nora: 'We're still together.' That also fits with planting the Toyota in one of Brother's Treasured Spaces. Is there some reason you don't trust Brad?"

"Because I didn't tell him everything? No, I just don't know enough to be sharing. Why, does he bug you?"

"No, but I think his value as a source of data is limited. He clearly overestimates his authority with Nora."

"Not so take-charge sib."

"He assumed the caretaker role because Billy and Nora aren't competent. That allowed them to remain adult children. Nora's more of a perpetual adolescent—self-centered, casually sexual, smokes up. And what do rebellious teens do when they're cornered? They resist passively or fight back. When Brad insisted she break off with Meserve, Nora chose passive."

"Tooling off in her Range Rover and leaving lover boy's heap behind so they can travel in style? Yeah, could be. So what do we have, just a road trip? Bonnie and Clyde in fancy wheels cutting town because they've been doing bad things."

"Don't know," I said. "People who attend Nora's school keep disappearing, but now that we know Peaty's got wheels he's got to remain center focus."

"A van. Your basic psycho meat wagon. And soon he's gonna be unemployed. If Sean's yanked off surveillance and that bastard sneaks away, I'm further back than when I started."

He folded his arms across his chest. "I screwed up by telling Brad about Peaty's van."

"Peaty cleans lots of buildings," I said. "It was the right thing to do, morally."

"Weren't you listening? I was covering my own ass."

"Sorry, can't hear you."

While we waited for the LAPD tow truck to arrive, Milo tried phoning Binchy. Again no connection. He said something about the "high-tech big lie" and paced up and down the block.

The truck appeared, moving slowly as the driver searched for the address. Milo's wave went unheeded. Finally, the rig pulled up and a sleepy-looking driver around nineteen got out.

"In there, the Toyota," Milo told him. "Consider it a crime scene and take it directly to the forensics garage."

The driver rubbed his eyes and shuffled paper. "Them wasn't my orders."

"Them is now." Milo handed him gloves. The driver slipped them on and slouched toward the little car's driver's door.

Milo said, "There's a snow globe on the seat. It's evidence."

"A wha?"

"One of those doohickeys that snows when you turn it upside down."

The driver looked baffled. Opened the door and drew out the globe. Upending the toy, he watched plastic flakes flutter. Peered at the writing at the base and wrinkled his brow.

Milo gloved up, snatched it away, and dropped it in an evidence bag. His face was flushed.

The driver said, "I'm supposed to take that in?"

"No, Professor, I keep it."

"Snow," said the driver. "Hollywood and Vine? Never seen no snow there."

As I drove back to the station, Milo said, "Do me a favor and contact that lawyer— Montez—soon as you can. Find out if Michaela told him anything about Meserve and Nora that she didn't tell you. Any idea who Meserve's P.D. was?"

"Marjani Coolidge."

"Don't know her."

"Me neither, but I can try."

"Try is great."

The second call to Binchy connected. Milo told him, "Check out your phone, Sean. You still on him? Nah, don't worry about it, he's probably working. I'll figure something out for nights. What you *can* do for me is start calling health spas from Santa Barbara County down to mid-Baja and see if Nora Dowd or Dylan Meserve have checked in . . . spas—like in massages and health food. What? . . . no, it's *fine,* Sean."

He jammed the phone in his pocket.

"Stuck on robbery detail?" I said.

"Seems to be." He beat a fast cha-cha rhythm on the dashboard. I could feel the vibrations through the steering wheel.

"Better get over to Peaty's place myself tonight. The unregistered van's grounds to arrest him. Maybe we can chat in his apartment so I get a look at the dump. Meanwhile, I make those spa calls myself—hello, ear cancer."

"I can do that. Leave the big-strong-guy detective work to you."

"Such as?"

"Finding out if Nora used her passport. Is it really tougher post Nine-Eleven? I'd think there'd be more interagency communication."

"What a sage," he said. "Yeah, I fibbed to Bradley, figuring he'd be motivated to get into Nora's house, let me know if anything's off. Technically, nothing's changed, you still need a search warrant to access passenger lists. And the airlines, being busy figuring out ways to torment their passengers, still take their sweet time complying. But there is more buddy-buddy stuff. Remember that granny shooting I closed last year?"

"Sweet old lady subbing for her son at the liquor store."

"Alma Napier. Eighty-two years old, perfect health, some meth-addled dungball unloads a shotgun on her. The search of said dungball's dump turns up a carton of video cameras from Indonesia hollowed out inside with pistol-shaped compartments. I thought the Federal Air Marshals might want to hear about that, got to know one of the supervisors there."

He retrieved the phone, asked for Commander Budowski.

"Bud? Milo Sturgis . . . fine. You? Terrific. Listen, I need a favor."

Fifteen minutes after we got to his office, a civilian clerk brought in the fax. We'd split the task of locating and phoning spas, were coming up empty.

Milo read Budowski's report, handed it to me, got back on the phone.

Nora Dowd hadn't used her passport for foreign travel since the previous April. Three-week trip to France, just as Brad had said.

Dylan Meserve had never applied for a passport.

Neither Nora nor Dylan's name appeared on any domestic flights out of LAX, Long Beach, Burbank, John Wayne, Lindbergh, or Santa Barbara.

Budowski had left a handwritten note at the bottom. If Nora had sprung for a private jet, that fact might never emerge. Some air-charter companies were less than meticulous checking I.D.s.

Milo said, "There's everyone. Then there's the rich."

He made a few more calls to resorts, broke for coffee at two p.m. Instead of continuing, he leafed through his notepad, found a number, and phoned.

"Mrs. Stadlbraun? Detective Sturgis, I was by last week to talk about . . . he is? How so? I see. No, that's not very politet . . . yes, it is. Has there been anything beyond thatt . . . no, there's nothing new but I was figuring to stop by and talk to him. If you could call me when he gets in, I'd appreciate it. Still have my card? I'll holdt . . . yes, that's perfect, ma'am, either of those numbers. Thankst . . . no, ma'am, there's nothing to worry about, just routine follow-up."

He clicked off, rotated the phone receiver, twisting the cord and letting it recoil.

"Ol' Ertha says Peaty's been acting 'even weirder.' He used to just keep his head down, pretended not to hear. Now he looks her in the eye with what she claims is 'nastiness.' What do you make of that?"

"Maybe he spotted Sean watching him and is getting nervous," I said.

"I suppose, but one thing Sean's an ace at is not getting made." He wheeled his chair the few inches the cramped space permitted. "Would 'nervous' make Peaty more dangerous?"

"It could."

"Think I should caution Stadlbraun?"

"I don't know what you could say that wouldn't cause panic. No doubt Brad will evict Peaty in addition to firing him."

"So we've got ourselves a homeless, jobless, angry guy with illegal wheels. Time to grovel and ask the captain for help with surveillance."

He disappeared, came back, shaking his head. "At a meeting downtown."

I was on the line with the Wellness Inn of Big Sur, enduring a voice mail message about seaweed wrap and Ayurvedic massage and waiting for a human voice.

By three thirty, we were both finished.

Nora Dowd hadn't checked into any posh retreat we could find under her name or Dylan Meserve's.

I tried Lauritz Montez at the Beverly Hills Public Defender's office.

In court, expected back in half an hour.

Too much sitting around. I got up and told Milo where I was go-ing. His reply was a finger wave. I didn't bother to reciprocate.

I reached the Beverly Hills court building by five to four. Closing time for most sessions. The hallways were filled with attorneys, cops, defendants, and witnesses.

Montez was in the middle of it, pushing a black leather case on wheels. Thin and sallow as ever, gray hair drawn back in a ponytail. Giant drooping mustache and wispy chin-beard whitening around the edges. The lenses of his glasses were hexagonal and cobalt blue.

Walking alongside him was a pallid young woman in a filmy pink granny dress. Long black hair, beautiful face, old woman's stoop. She kept talking to Montez. If he cared about what she had to say, he wasn't showing it.

I blended with the crowd, managed to get behind the two of them.

Every time I'd seen Montez he'd gone for foppery. Today's costume was a fitted, black velvet suit with an Edwardian cut, wide, peaked lapels trimmed with satin. The pink of his shirt brought painful memories of childhood sunburns. His peacock-blue bowtie was glossy silk.

The pallid girl said something that made him stop. The two of them veered to the right and stepped behind an open court-room door. I edged closer to the other side and pretended to study a wall directory. The crowd had thinned, and I could make out their conversation through the jamb.

"What the continuance means, Jessica, is I bought some time for you to get clean and stay clean. You can also find yourself a job and try to con the judge into thinking you want to be a solid citizen."

"What kinda job?"

"Anything, Jessica. Flip burgers at Mc-Donalds."

"What about Johnny Rockets? It's, like, close by."

"If you can get a job at Johnny Rockets, that would be great."

"I never flipped burgers."

"What have you done?"

"I danced."

"Ballet?"

"Topless."

"I'm sure you were great on the pole, Jessica, but that's not going to help you."

He walked away. The girl didn't.

I moved from behind the door and said, "Afternoon."

Montez turned. The girl had her back to the wall, as if pressed there by an unseen hand. "Go look for a job, Jessica."

She flinched and left.

I said, "Did Michaela say anything about Dylan and Nora Dowd having a relationship?"

"You stalking me, Doc? Or is this happy coincidence?"

"We need to talk—"

"I need to go home and forget about work. That includes you." He took hold of his luggage rack.

"Meserve's missing," I said. "Given the fact that your client was murdered last week, you might reconsider being a glib wiseass."

His jaw tightened. "It sucks, okay? Now leave me alone."

"Meserve could be in danger or he could be a bad guy. Did Michaela tell you anything that would clarify the situation?"

"She blamed him for the hoax."

I waited.

"Yeah, he was fucking Dowd. Okay?"

"How'd Michaela feel about that?"

"She thought Meserve had lost it," said Montez. "Going for a senior citizen. I believe her precise phrase was 'tired meat.' "

"Jealous?"

"No, she had no feelings for Meserve, just thought it was gross."

"Was there any indication Nora was in on the hoax?"

"Michaela never said so but I wondered. Because she *was* fucking Meserve and he didn't get kicked out of her school. You think he killed Michaela?"

"I don't know," I said.

"Would you look at that," he said. "Finally I get a shrink to be direct."

"Is Marjani Coolidge back from her trip to Africa?"

"She's right there." Pointing down the hall to a short, thin black woman in a powder-

blue suit. Two tall, gray-haired men were listening to what she had to say.

"Thanks." I turned to leave.

Montez said, "Just to show you I'm not
the asshole you think I am, here's another
tidbit: Dowd called me right after I got the
case. Offered to pay any bills the county
wasn't covering. I told her the county could
handle it, asked her why the generosity. She
said Meserve was a gifted artist, she
wanted to help him and if that meant clearing Michaela, she'd do it. I could smell the
hormones through the phone. She good-
looking?"

"Not bad."

"For her age?"

"Something like that," I said.

He laughed and wheeled his cart away
and I walked toward Marjani Coolidge. The
two men had left and she was examining
the contents of her own lawyer-luggage.
Double-case, scuffed brown leather, stuffed
so tight the stitching was unraveling.

I introduced myself, told her about
Michaela's murder.

She said, "I heard about that, the poor
kid," then interrogated me about my associ-
ation with LAPD. Appraising my words and

my body language with huge brown eyes. Her hair was elaborately braided, her skin smooth and taut.

I said, "Did Meserve tell you anything that could shed light on the murder?"

"You're serious."

"Something nonincriminating," I said. "Anything that could help locate him."

"Is he a suspect?"

"He could turn out to be a victim."

"Of the same person who killed Brand?"

"Maybe."

She smoothed her skirt. "Nonincriminating. Last I heard that animal was extinct."

"How about this," I said. "Without divulging content, can you tell me if Meserve's someone to be scared of?"

"Was I scared of him? Not in the least. Not the brightest star in the constellation but he did what he was told. That girlfriend of his, on the other hand . . ."

"Which girlfriend is that?"

"The acting teacher—Dowd."

"She caused problems?"

"Battleax," said Coolidge. "Phoned me right at the outset, said she'd hire a private attorney if I didn't give Pretty Boy high priority. I felt like saying, 'Is that a threat or a promise?' "

"What did you tell her?"

" 'Do what you want, ma-*dame*,' then I hung up. Never heard from her again. I represented Meserve the way I do any other client. Turned out just fine, wouldn't you say?"

"Meserve's codefendant's dead and he's missing."

"Irrelevant," she said. "We settled, my obligations are over."

"Just like that," I said.

"You better believe it. My job, you learn to stay in your own orbit."

"Orbit, constellation. You have an interest in astronomy?"

"Majored in it at Cornell. Then I moved here for law school and found out you can't see anything because of all the light pollution." She smiled. "Civilization, I think you call it."

CHAPTER
24

I exited the courthouse parking lot and took Rexford Drive through the Beverly Hills municipal complex. The light at Santa Monica was long enough for me to leave a message on Milo's cell.

Driving home, I wondered about the affair between Meserve and Nora. Partners in the worst kind of crime or just another May-December romance?

Wouldn't it be nice if Reynold Peaty got caught doing something nasty, confessed to multiple murder, and we could all move on.

I realized I was driving too fast and

slowed down. Switching on a CD, I listened to Mindy Smith's clear, sweet soprano. Waiting for her man to arrive on the next train.

The only thing waiting for me was mail and an unread newspaper. Maybe it was time to get another dog.

As I turned off Sunset, a brown Audi Quattro parked on the east side of Beverly Glen pulled behind me and stayed close. I sped up and so did the Audi, as it rode my tail close enough for a rear-view of bird dirt on the four-ring grille. A tinted windshield prevented further clarity. I swung to the right. Instead of passing, the Audi downshifted, drove alongside to my left for a second, then sped off in nasal acceleration. I made out a driver, no passengers. A rear bumper sticker sported red letters on a white background. Too brief for me to read the whole message but I thought I'd seen the word "therapy."

When I reached the bridle path that leads to my street, I looked for the car. Nowhere.

Just another friendly day on the roads of L.A. I'd been an obstruction and he'd felt compelled to tell me.

◆

The phone was ringing as I walked into the house.

Robin said, "Sorry I missed your call."

That threw me for a second. Then I remembered I'd called her this morning, hadn't left a message.

She understood the pause, said, "Caller I.D. What's up?"

"I was just saying hi."

"Want to get together? Just to talk?"

"Sure."

"How about talk *and* eat?" she said. "Nothing too intense, name the place."

Long time since she'd been in the house that she'd designed. I said, "I could make something here."

"If you don't mind, I'd rather go out."

"When should I pick you up?"

"How about seven—seven thirty? I'll wait outside."

Meaning don't come in? Or did she crave fresh air after hours of sawdust and varnish?

Did it matter?

Rose Avenue sported a few more boutiques and cute cafés tucked among the laundromats and fast food stands. The ocean air that blew through windows was sour but not unpleasant for that. The night sky was a swirl of gray and indigo, textured like pigments mixed haphazardly on a palette. Soon the the cute cafés would be overflowing, pretty people fortified by margaritas and possibilities spilling out to the curb.

Robin lived minutes from that scene. Did she ever participate?

Did *that* matter?

Her block on Rennie was quiet and inconsistently lit, lined with neatly tended little houses and side-by-side duplexes. I spotted the flower beds she'd planted out front before I saw her step out of the shadows.

Her hair bounced as she beelined to the car. Nighttime turned auburn rosy. Her curls reminded me, as they always did, of grapes on the vine.

She wore a second-skin top in some dark shade, form-fitted light jeans, boots with nasty looking heels that clump-clumped. As she opened the door the dome light told all: chocolate brown tank top, textured silk, one shade lighter than her almond eyes. The jeans were cream, the boots mocha. Silvery pink gloss ripened her lips. Blush on her cheekbones created something feline.

Those curves.

She flashed a wide, ambiguous smile and put on her seat belt. The strap cut diagonally between her breasts.

"Where to?" she said.

I'd taken her at her word about "nothing intense." Haute cuisine meant ritual and high expectations and we could do with neither.

Allison liked haute. Loved rolling the stem of a wineglass between manicured fingers as she engaged in earnest discussion of an elegant menu with snooty waiters, her toes trailing up my trousers . . .

I mentioned a seafood joint in the Marina that Robin and I had patronized back before the Ice Age. Spacious, dockside, no-sweat parking, nice view of a harbor full of big white boats, most of which seemed never to go anywhere.

She said, "That place. Sure."

We got a table outdoors, near the glass wall that keeps the wind out. The night had turned cool and butane heaters were switched on. The sports bar up front was packed but it was still early for the Marina dinner crowd and more than half the tables were empty. A chirpy waitress who looked around twelve took our drink order and brought Robin's wine and my Chivas before we had a chance to get awkward.

Drinking and gazing at the yachts postponed that a while longer.

Robin put her glass down. "You look fit."

"You look gorgeous."

She studied the water. Black and sleek and still, under a sky streaked with amethyst. "Must've been a great sunset."

"We had a few of those," I said. "That summer we lived at the beach."

The year we'd rebuilt the house. Robin had served as the contractor. Did she miss the place?

She said, "We had some spectacular ones at Big Sur. That crazy Zen place that was supposed to be luxurious, then they stuck us with chemical toilets and that terrible smell?"

"Rustic living." I wondered if the place had been on the resort list Milo and I had just run down. "What was it called?"

"The Great Mandala Lodge. Closed down last year." She looked away and I knew why. She'd gone back. With *him.*

She drank wine and said, "Even with the smell and the mosquitoes and that splinter in my toe from that stupid pinecone, it was fun. Who knew a *pinecone* could be lethal."

"You're forgetting *my* splinters," I said.

Oversized incisors flashed. "I didn't forget, I chose not to remind you." Her hand made circular motions in the air. "Rubbing that ointment into your cute butt. How could we know that other couple would be watching? All that other stuff they could see from their cabin."

"Should've charged them tuition," I said. "Crash course in Sex Ed for the honeymooners."

"They did seem pretty inept. All that tension at breakfast. Think the marriage lasted?"

I shrugged.

Robin's eyes turned down a bit. "The place deserved to tank. Charge that kind of money and smell like a cesspool."

More alcohol for both of us.

I said, "Nice to be with you."

"Just before you called this morning, I was thinking." Brief smile. "Always a risky thing, no?"

"Thinking about what?"

"The challenge of relationships. Not you and me. Me and him."

My gut twinged. I drained my scotch. Looked around for the baby-faced waitress.

Robin said, "Me and him as in What Was I Thinking."

"That's rarely useful."

"You don't engage in self-doubt?"

"Sure I do."

"I find it good for the soul," she said. "That old Catholic girl resurfacing. All I could come up with was he convinced himself that he loved me and his intensity half convinced *me.* I was the one who broke it off, you know. He took it really hard—but that's not your problem. Sorry for bringing it up."

"He's not a bad guy."

"You never liked him."

"Couldn't stand him. Where is he?"

"You care?"

"I'd like him to be far."

"Then you got your wish. London, teaching voice at the Royal Academy of Drama. His daughter's living with him—she's twelve, wanted the switch." She tugged at her curls. "It was rude, bringing him up."

"He's a twit," I said. "But the problem wasn't you and him, it was you and not *me*."

"I don't know what it was," she said. "All this time and I still can't figure it out. Just like the first time."

Breakup number one, years ago. Neither of us had wasted time finding new bed partners.

I said, "Maybe that's the way it has to be with us."

"What do you mean?"

"Eons together, centuries apart."

Somewhere out in the open water a ship's horn sounded.

She said, "It was mutual but for some reason I feel I should ask your forgiveness."

"You shouldn't."

"How's Allison?"

"Doing her thing."

Soft voice: "You two are really kaput?"

"That would be my bet."

"You're making it sound like you have no control," she said.

"In my limited experience," I said, "it's rarely been necessary to make a formal announcement."

"Sorry," she said.

I drank.

"You really see it as mutual, Alex, and not my fault?"

"I do. And I don't understand it any more than you do." Ditto for the break with Allison. Maybe with any other woman I'd find . . .

"You know I was never untrue to you. Didn't touch him until you and I were living apart."

"You don't owe me any explanation."

"Everything we've been through," she said, "I can't figure out what I owe you."

Footsteps approaching the table rescued me from having to answer. I looked up, expecting Ms. Chirpy. More than ready for another drink.

A man loomed over us.

Big-bellied, ruddy, balding, fifty or so. Black-framed eyeglasses slightly askew, sweaty forehead. He wore a maroon V-neck over a white polo shirt, gray slacks, brown loafers. Florid jowls settled over the shirt's soft collar.

Swaying, he placed broad, hairless hands on our table. Sausage digits, some kind of class ring on his left index ring finger.

He leaned down and his weight made the

table rock. Bleary eyes behind the specs stared down at us. He gave off a beery odor.

Some joker who'd wandered over from the sports bar.

Keep it friendly. My smile was wary.

He tried to straighten up, lost balance, and slapped a hand back on the table, hard enough to slosh water out of our glasses. Robin's arm shot out before her wine toppled.

The drunk looked at her and sneered.

I said, "Hey, friend—"

"I. Am. Not. Your. Friend."

Hoarse voice. I looked around for Ms. Perky. Anyone. Spotted a busboy up a ways, wiping tables. I arched my eyebrows. He continued wiping. The nearest couple, two tables down, was engaged in an eye-tango.

I told the drunk, "The bar's back in there."

He leaned in closer. "You. Don't. Know. Who. I. Am?"

I shook my head.

Robin had room to back away. I motioned her to leave. When she started to get up, the drunk roared, "Sit. Slut!"

My brain fired.

Conflicting messages from the prefrontal

cortex: rowdy young guys shouting: *"We're pumped, dude! Pound him to shit!"* A reedy old man's voice whispering: *"Careful. The consequences."*

Robin sank back.

I wondered how much karate I remembered.

The drunk demanded, "Who. Am. I?"

"I don't know." My tone said the old man was losing out to the prefrontal bad boys. Robin gave me a tiny head shake.

The drunk said, "What. Did. You. Say?"

"I don't know who you are and I'd appreciate—"

"I. Am. Doctor. Hauser. *Doctor.* Hauser. And. You. Are. A. Fucking. *Liar.*"

The old man whispered: *"Self-control. It's all about control."*

Hauser drew back his fist.

The old man whispered, *"Scratch all that."*

I caught him by the wrist, twisted hard and followed up with a heel-jab under his nose. Hard enough to stun him, well short of driving bone into his brain.

As he tumbled back I sprang up and took

hold of his shirt, breaking his fall to give him a soft landing.

My reward was a face full of beery spittle. I let go just before his ass hit the deck. Tomorrow, his tailbone would hurt like hell.

He sat up for a moment, frothing at the mouth and rubbing his nose. The spot where I'd hit him was pink and just a little bit swollen. He worked his mouth to gather more spit, closed his eyes and flopped down and rolled over and started to snore.

A perky voice said, "Wow. What happened?"

A nasal voice said, "That dude tried to hit the other dude and the other dude protected his lady."

The busboy, standing next to the waitress. I caught his eye and he smiled uneasily. He'd been watching all along.

"You were righteous, man. I gonna tell the cops."

The cops showed up eleven long minutes later.

CHAPTER

25

Patrol Officer *J. Hendricks,* stocky, clean-cut, black as polished ebony.

Patrol Officer *M. Minette,* curvy, clean-cut, beige hair ponytailed.

Hendricks eyed the spot where Patrick Hauser had fallen. "So both of you are doctors?" He stood just out of arm's reach, notepad in hand. My back was to the glass wall. The diners who'd remained in the restaurant pretended not to stare.

An ambulance had come for Hauser. He'd greeted the EMTs by cursing and spitting and they'd restrained him on the gurney. Change had fallen out of his pocket. Two quarters and a penny remained on the deck.

"We're both psychologists," I said, "but as I said, I've never seen him before."

"A total stranger assaulted you."

"He was drunk. A brown Audi Quattro followed me home this afternoon. If you find one in the parking lot, he stalked me, too."

"All 'cause of this . . ." Hendricks consulted his notes, "this report you wrote him up on."

I retold the story, kept my sentences short and clear. Dropped Milo's name. Again.

Hendricks said, "So you're saying you hit him once under the nose with your bare fist."

"Heel of my hand."

"That's kind of a martial arts move."

"It seemed the best way to handle it without inflicting serious damage."

"That kind of blow could've inflicted *real* serious damage."

"I was careful."

"You a martial arts guy?"

"Not hardly."

"A martial arts guy's hands are like deadly weapons, Doctor."

"I'm a psychologist."

"Sounds like you moved pretty good."

"It happened fast," I said.

Scribble scribble.

I looked over at Officer Minette, listening to the busboy and writing as well. She'd interviewed Robin, first, then the waitress. I was Hendricks's assignment.

No handcuffs, that was a good sign.

Minette let the busboy go and came over. "Everyone seems to be telling the same story." The narrative she recited matched what I'd told Hendricks. He relaxed.

"Okay, Doctor. I'm going to make a call and verify your address with DMV. That checks out, you're free to go."

"You might check if Hauser's got a Quattro."

Hendricks looked at me. "I might do that, sir."

I searched for Robin.

Minette said, "Your lady friend went to the little girls' room. She said the victim called her a slut."

"He did."

"That must've been irritating."

"He was drunk," I said. "I didn't take him seriously."

"Still," she said. "That's pretty annoying."

"It wasn't until he tried to hit me that I was forced to act."

"Loser insults your date like that, some guys would have reacted stronger."

"I'm a man of discretion."

She smiled. Her partner didn't join in.

She said, "I think we're finished here, John."

As Robin and I walked through the restaurant, someone whispered, "That's the guy."

Once we got outside, I exhaled. My ribs hurt. Hauser hadn't touched me; I'd been holding in air for a long time. "What a disaster."

Robin slipped her arm around my waist.

"You need to know," I said, "that this was a civil case, nothing to do with police work." I told her about the harassment charges against Hauser, my interview of his victims, the report I'd written.

"Why do I need to know?" she said.

"The way you feel about the ugly stuff. This was out of the blue, Robin."

We headed for the Seville and I scanned the lot for the brown Audi.

There it was, parked six slots south. The red letters on the bumper sticker said, *Get Therapy.*

I wanted to laugh but couldn't. Wasn't surprised when we reached the Seville and both of my rear tires were flat. No slash marks; the valves had been opened.

Robin said, "That's pathetic."

"I've got a pump in the trunk."

Part of the emergency kit Milo and Rick had gotten me last Christmas. Tire changing kit, flares, orange Day-Glo road markers, blankets, bottled water.

Rick taking me aside and confiding, "I'd have picked a nice sweater, but an *ahem* cooler head prevailed."

Milo's voice bellowing from the corner of their living room: "Haberdashery don't cut it when you're stranded out on some isolated road with no lights and wolves and God knows what other toothy carnivores are aiming their beady little predator eyes at your anatomy, just waiting to—"

"Then why didn't we get him a gun, Milo?"

"Next year. Some day you'll thank me, Alex. You're welcome in advance."

I hooked up the pump and got to work.

When I was finished, Robin said, "The way you handled it—just enough to defuse the situation and no one got hurt. Classy."

She took my face in her hands and kissed me hard.

We found a deli on Washington Boulevard, bought more takeout than we needed, drove back to Beverly Glen.

Robin walked into the house as if she lived there, entered the kitchen and set the table. We made it halfway through the food.

When she got out of bed, the movement woke me. Sweaty nap but my eyes were dry.

Through half-closed lids, I watched her slip on my ratty yellow robe and pad around the bedroom. Touching the tops of chairs and tables. Pausing by the dresser. Righting a framed print.

At the window, she drew back one side of the silk curtains she'd designed. She put her face against the glass, peered out at the foothills.

I said, "Pretty night."

"The view," she said without turning. "Still unobstructed."

"Looks like it's going to stay that way. Bob had his lower acre surveyed and it's definitely unfit for construction."

"Bob the Neighbor," she said. "How's he doing?"

"When he's in town, he seems well."

"Second home in Tahiti," she said.

"Main home in Tahiti. Nothing like inherited wealth."

"That's good news—about the view. I was hoping for that when I oriented the room that way." She let the curtain drop. Smoothed the pleats. "I did a decent job with this place. Like living here?"

"Not as much as I used to."

She cinched the robe tighter, half faced me. Her hair was wild, her lips slightly swollen. Faraway eyes.

"I thought it might be strange," she said. "Coming back. It's less strange than I would've predicted."

"It's your place, too," I said.

She didn't answer.

"I mean it."

She baby-stepped over to the far end of

the bed, played with the edges of the comforter. "You haven't thought that through."

I hadn't. "Sure I have. Many a long night."

She shrugged.

"The place echoes, Robin."

"It always did. We were aiming for great
acoustics."

"It can be musical," I said. "Or not."

She pulled at the comforter, squared the
seam with the edge of the mattress. "You
do all right by yourself."

"Says who?"

"You've always been self-contained."

"Like hell." My voice was harsh.

She looked up at me.

I said, "Come back. Keep the studio if
you need privacy, but live here."

She tugged at the comforter some more.
Her mouth twisted into a shape I couldn't
read. Loosening the robe, she let it fall to
the floor, reconsidered, picked it up, folded
it neatly over a chair. The organized mind of
someone who works with power tools.

Fluffing her hair, she got back in bed.

"No pressure, just think about it," I said.

"It's a lot to digest."

"You're a tough kid."

"Like hell." Pressing her flank to mine,

she laced her fingers and placed them over her belly.

I drew the covers over us.

"That's better, thanks," she said.

Neither of us moved.

CHAPTER

26

Once I'm roused, I'm restless for hours.

As Robin slept, I prowled the house. Ended up in my office and composed a mental list. Switched to a written list.

First thing tomorrow I'd contact Erica Weiss and tell her about Hauser. More ammunition for her civil suit. If Hauser's control was that loose, mounting legal problems might not stop him from harassing me. Or getting litigious himself.

This whole mess could cost me. I tried to convince myself it was the price of doing business.

Must be nice to be that serene.

Replaying the scene at the restaurant, I wondered how Hauser had lasted this long as a therapist. Maybe the smart thing would be filing a preemptive suit against him. Officers Hendricks and Minette had appeared to see things my way, so a police report would help. But you never knew.

Milo would know what to do but he had other things on his mind.

So did I.

My offer to Robin spilling out like Pentothal chatter. If she said yes, would that constitute a happy ending?

So many what-ifs.

Milo said, "I was just about to call you."

"Kismet."

"You don't want this type of kismet." He told me why.

I said, "I'll be right over."

The note I left on the nightstand read:

Dear R, Had to go out, a bit of the ugly stuff. Stay as long as you'd like. If you have to go, let's talk tomorrow.

I dressed quietly, tiptoed to the bed, and kissed her cheek. She stirred, reached up with one arm, let it drop as she rolled over.

Girl fragrance mixed with the smell of sex. I took one last look at her and left.

Reynold Peaty's corpse had been wrapped in translucent plastic, tied with stout twine, and loaded onto the right-hand stretcher in the white coroner's van. The vehicle remained parked in front of Peaty's apartment building, rear doors open. Bolted metal racks secured the body and the empty stretcher to its left.

Busy nights in L.A., double occupancy transport was a good idea.

Flanking the coroner's van were four black-and-whites, roof lights pulsing. Terse recitations from dispatch operators sparked the night but no one was listening.

Lots of uniforms standing around trying to look official. Milo and Sean Binchy conferred near the farthest cop car. Milo talked and Binchy listened. For the first time since I'd known the young detective, he looked upset.

Over the phone, Milo told me the shooting had taken place an hour ago. But the suspect was just being taken down the stairs of Peaty's building.

Young Hispanic guy, heavily built, broad skull helmeted by dark stubble. Escorted by two huge, gym-rat patrolmen who diminished him.

I'd seen him before, when I'd driven past the building last Sunday.

Father of the young family heading for church. Wife and three chubby little kids. Stiff gray suit that looked out of place.

Kids having kids.

He'd aimed hard eyes my way as I stopped in front of the building. No view of his eyes now. His arms were cuffed behind him and his head hung low.

Barefoot, wearing a black XXXXL T-shirt that nearly reached his knees, saggy gray sweatpants that threatened to slip off his hips, and a big gold fist on a chain that swung over the shirt's snarling pit bull *BaaadBoyz* logo.

Someone had forgotten to remove the bling. Milo went over and rectified the situation and the iron-pumper cops seemed abashed. The suspect looked up as Milo fiddled, heavy lids tenting. When Milo got the chain off, the kid smiled and said something. Milo smiled back. He checked behind the kid's ears. Waved the cops on and handed the necklace to an evidence tech who bagged it.

As the uniforms got the shooter into one of the idling cruisers and drove away, Mrs. Ertha Stadlbraun stepped out of her ground-floor flat and walked to the sidewalk. Standing just right of the taped perimeter, she shivered and hugged herself. Her dressing gown was custard-yellow and quilted. Fuzzy white mules encased her feet and yellow rollers turned her hair into white tortellini. Shiny bright skin; some kind of night cream.

She shivered again and tightened her arms. Tenants stared out of windows. So did a few residents of the dingbat next door.

Milo beckoned me over. His face was sweaty. Sean Binchy stayed behind, not doing much of anything. When I got there, he said, "Doctor," and chewed his lip.

Milo said, "Hot town, summer in the city."

"In February."

"That's why we live here."

I told him about seeing the suspect before. Described the kid's demeanor.

He said, "That fits."

A coroner's attendant slammed the van's doors shut, got in, drove away.

I said, "How close is his apartment to Peaty's?"

"Two doors down. His name's Armando Vasquez, he's got a sealed juvenile gang history, claims to be a steadily working, church-going married man for the past four years. Has a landscaping gig with a company that maintains some of the big B.H. properties north of Sunset. He used to just mow grass but this year he learned to trim trees. He's pretty proud of that."

"How old is he?"

"Twenty-one. Wife's nineteen, three kids under five. For the most part they stayed asleep while I tried to chat with their daddy. One time the oldest toddled in. I let Vasquez kiss the kid. Kid smiled at me." He sighed. "Vasquez has no adult sheet, so maybe he's telling the truth about finding God. The neighbors I've spoken to so far say the kids can be noisy but the family doesn't cause problems. No one liked Peaty. Apparently, everyone in the building's been jabbering about him, since we met with Stadlbraun."

He glanced at the old woman. Still hugging herself, staring out at the darkened street. She seemed to be fighting for composure.

I said, "She spread the word Peaty was dangerous."

Milo nodded. "The ol' gossip mill was chugging along. Before Vasquez dummied up, he told me Peaty always rubbed him the wrong way."

"Prior conflict?"

"No fights, just lots of tension. Vasquez didn't like Peaty living so close. The term he used was 'fuckin' crazy dude.' After he said that, he started moving his head back and forth and up and down. I said, 'What're you doing, Armando?' He says, 'Crossing myself. You got me cuffed so I'm doing it this way.' "

"Did Peaty ever bother his wife?"

"He stared at her, which is consistent with what everyone else says. 'Fuckin' crazy stare.' Unfortunately for Vasquez, it's not justification for blowing Peaty's brains out."

Sean Binchy came over, still looking uneasy. "Need me for anything more, Loot?"

"No, go home. Relax."

Binchy flinched. "Thanks. Hey, Doc. Bye."

Milo said, "You did fine, Sean."

"Whatever."

When he left, I said, "What's bothering him?"

"The lad has an overdeveloped sense of responsibility. He worked a robbery case all day, got off at eleven, and decided on his own to watch Peaty. He started here, didn't see Peaty's minivan, went out for a burger at a twenty-four-hour spot, got back just after midnight and spotted the van a block up that way."

He pointed east. "He was looking for a watch spot in the alley when he heard the three shots. Peaty caught all of 'em full-faced. You wouldn't figure that physiog could get any uglier but . . ."

"Sean's feeling guilty about not being here."

"About the burger. About nothing. No way he could've prevented it."

"Did he arrest Vasquez?"

"He called for backup then went up the stairs. Peaty's body was out on the walkway between the apartments. At that point, Sean waited for the blues and they went door to door. When they got to Vasquez's apartment, Vasquez was sitting on his couch watching TV, the gun's right next to him and so are the wife and the oldest kid. Vasquez puts up his hands and says, 'I killed his ass, do your thing.' The wife starts bawlin', the kid stays real quiet."

"How'd it happen?" I said.

"When I got to specifics, Vasquez got laryngitis. My sense is he's been stewing on Peaty for a while, started bubbling over when ol' Ertha told him about my visit. For some reason, tonight he got tired of doing nothing, saw Peaty come home, and went out to tell him to stay away from Mrs. Vasquez. As they say in the papers, a confrontation ensued. Vasquez claims Peaty made a move on him, he needed to defend himself, boom boom boom."

"Vasquez went out there armed."

"There is that minor detail," he said. "Maybe some lawyer will try to twist it as evidence Vasquez was scared of Peaty."

"Alcohol or dope involved?" I said.

"Vasquez admits to four beers and that fits with the empties in his trash basket. With his body weight that might or might not be relevant, depends what the blood-work turns up. Now let's see if the techies are through with Peaty's domicile."

◆

A room and a half bath, both tiny and putrid.

Fetid mélange of old cheese, charred tobacco, body gas, garlic, oregano.

An empty, grease-stained pizza box sat open on the metal-frame double bed. Crumbs dandruffed rumpled sheets the color of wet newsprint and green bedcovers printed with a repeating pattern of top hats and bowlers. Several, large, unpleasant stains on the sheets. Wads of dirty laundry filled most of the floor space. A waist-high stack of Old Milwaukee six-packs and the bed filled what was left. Fingerprint dust everywhere. That seemed unnecessary— the body had fallen outside—but you never knew about lawyers' creativity.

Milo kicked his way through the jumble and approached a wooden packing crate that served as a bed stand. Cluttering the top were oily takeout menus, balled-up tissues, crushed empty beer cans—I counted fourteen—a gallon bottle of Tyger fortified wine two-thirds empty, an economy-sized flask of Pepto-Bismol.

The only real furniture other than the bed was a ragged three-drawer dresser that supported a nineteen-inch TV and a VCR large enough to be quaint. Rabbit-ear antenna.

I said, "No cable box," and opened a dresser drawer. "His entertainment needs were simple."

Inside were boxed videotapes, stacked like books in a horizontal shelf. Loud colors. Lots of X's. *Not-So Legal Temptresses,* Volumes 1 through 11. *Shower Teen, Upskirt Adventures, X-Ray Journey, Voyeur's Village.*

The bottom two drawers held clothing that looked no fresher than the mess on the floor. Under a tangle of T-shirts, Milo found an envelope with $600 in cash and a small plastic box marked *Sewing Kit,* filled with five tightly round joints.

The half bath was a cubicle in the corner. My nose had accommodated to bedroom stench but this was a new challenge. The shower was fiberglass, barely big enough for a woman, let alone a man of Peaty's bulk. Originally beige, now brown, with a blackish-green crop of something flourishing at the drain. A streaked, spotted mirror was glued to the wall over the sink; no medicine cabinet. On the floor next to the cracked, grimy toilet was a small wicker box. Inside was an assortment of antacids and OTC analgesics, a toothbrush that looked as if it hadn't been used in a while, an amber pharmacy bottle containing two Vicodin pills. The original prescription had been for twenty-one tabs, prescribed by a doctor at a Las Vegas clinic seven years ago and filled at the clinic's pharmacy.

"Saving it for the bad times," I said. "Or the good."

"The occasional highball," said Milo. "Trailer-park style."

He returned to the bedroom, searched under the bed, came up dusty and empty-handed. Held his hands away from his slacks, glanced at the bathroom. "I'm not sure using that sink would make me cleaner . . . let's see if there's a hose outdoors."

Before we descended the stairs, he took me for a look at the kill-spot. Peaty had shed a lot of red. The spot where he'd fallen was demarcated by black tape.

A uniform stood outside the Vasquez apartment. Milo saluted her and we found a hose near Mrs. Stadlbraun's apartment. She was back inside, drapes drawn tight.

When he finished washing off, he said, "Any insights?"

"If Peaty's our bad guy, he didn't keep trophies or anything else of interest," I said.

But I was wrong.

In the rear of the rust-spotted red mini-van, Milo found boxes of cleaning supplies, tarps, brooms, mops, washcloths. Buried under the tarps was a brown, double-decker toolbox. A key-lock dangled from the hasp but it had been left unbolted.

Milo gloved up and opened the box. In the top foldaway rack were screwdrivers, hammers, wrenches, pliers, little plastic cylinders of screws and nails. In the compartments below were a set of burglar picks, two rolls of duct tape, a box cutter, a wire cutter, a push-button stiletto, a spool of thick, white nylon rope, four sets of women's panty hose, a blue steel automatic pistol wrapped in a grubby pink washcloth.

Loaded gun. Plenty of ammunition left in the box of .22-caliber bullets wedged into a corner of the toolbox.

Next to the bullets, something else wrapped in terry. Round, firm.

Milo unwrapped it. Souvenir snow globe.

The pink plastic base read *MALIBU, CALIF. SURF'S UP!*

He upended the sphere. White flakes fluttered over a cobalt ocean. He examined the underside of the base. "Made in U.S.A. New Hampshire. That explains it. Sons of bitches wanted to think of us frozen just like them."

He returned the globe to the box, walkie-talkied one of the techs at the murder scene. "Lucio? Drive up a ways. There's more."

While the crime scene crew did their thing with the van, Milo located the VIN number and did a search.

Stolen four years ago in Highland Park and never recovered, the registered owner Wendell A. Chong. Chong had a home address in South Pasadena that Milo copied down.

I said, "Peaty cleans lots of buildings on the east side, probably spotted an opportunity a year after he arrived in California and never bothered to tell the boss. Brad Dowd's paying for van-pool pickup. Peaty used the service most of the time. Meanwhile, he had an option."

"Equipped with a burglary/rape kit." He frowned. "Okay, let's boogie."

It was twelve thirty-four when I followed him to a Coco's at Pico and Wooster. He spent a long time in the men's room, came out with hands scrubbed pink and damp hair.

"Didn't know they provide showers," I said.

"I prayed to the sink." He ordered Boston cream pie and coffee for both of us.

I said, "Not hungry."

"Good. This way I get two without looking like a pig. So Peaty's an extremely bad guy. What does the globe mean?"

"The globe Dylan gave to Nora could've been part of a duo. Or a collection. One got left in Dylan's car because Peaty was bragging. The other he kept for masturbatory memories."

"Meaning, if you're Prudential, don't write a policy on Nora and Meserve. Any guesses where to start looking for their bodies?"

I shook my head. "The van and the kit say Peaty could've traveled anywhere. They also provide a scenario for Michaela. He targeted her at the PlayHouse, followed her home, found out she lived close to him. After that, it was easy for him to watch her from the van. When the time was right, he snagged her, drove her somewhere secluded, and strangled her. Maybe even in the van."

He frowned. "Abduction and seclusion sounds like bringing Dylan and Michaela's hoax to life. You think that's what stimulated Peaty?"

"He'd probably been watching Michaela for a while but the hoax clinched it. And Michaela getting kicked out of class meant she spent more evenings at home alone."

"Wherever he did her, Alex, he brought her back to the neighborhood. What's that, staying in his comfort zone?"

"Or just the opposite," I said. "Whoever killed Tori Giacomo dumped her in Griffith Park and concealed her body quite efficiently. The park's miles from Tori's apartment in the Valley and even farther from Peaty's. It's also a brief freeway detour from the Valley to Pasadena—get off the 101 and take the 5 for one exit, do your thing, get back on."

"Dropping her off on the way to work," he said. "Same way he stole the van."

"But getting away with Tori could've made him more daring with Michaela. With everyone thinking he had no wheels, he didn't worry about the body being traced back to him. So he left her right out in the open."

"The no-wheels lie wasn't hard to uncover."

"Wanting to brag overrode his caution," I said. "He was no criminal genius. Like most of them."

The pie arrived. He ate his, reached for mine. "Maybe with Michaela, he was just being lazy. Seeing as she lived so close to him, no reason to roam. Tori was in North Hollywood, no sense bringing her home. So what about the Gaidelases? Peaty's video collection is consistent with his Peeping Tom arrest. Good-looking young women."

I said, "It's hard to square the Gaidelases with that, but like I said before, he could've had other kinks. The car recovered in Camarillo's a tougher fit. If he left his van near the murder site and drove the Gaidelases' rental to the outlets, how'd he get back to Malibu?"

"To me that's no problem. He hitchhiked, stole another set of wheels, took a bus—or he never drove the rental in the first place. All he needed to do was leave it parked on

Kanan Dume, windows wide open, keys in the ignition. Open invitation for some joyriding kid."

"Joyride to the outlets?" I said. "Juvenile delinquents looking for bargains?"

"Why not? Shoplift some cool Nikes and hip-hop sweats. Any way you look at it, having Mr. Peaty swept off this mortal coil is no loss."

"True."

Several bites later: "What's on your mind?"

"The scenarios we've constructed depend on planning and patience. The way Peaty died—not backing off from an armed man—showed a lack of control."

"He was drunk. Or Vasquez didn't give him a chance to back off."

"Vasquez just went out there and shot him?"

"It happens."

"It does," I said. "But think about this: the Gaidelases' bodies have never been found and their credit cards were never used. Plus someone took the trouble to phone utilities in Ohio and have their power shut off. That's high-level calculation and discretion. Peaty was nabbed by a bystander watching college girls while beating off. He continued to stare openly at women and gave them the creeps. That sound discreet?"

"Even morons learn, Alex. But let's put the Gaidelases aside for a moment. Are you okay with Michaela and Tori as Peaty's handiwork?"

I nodded.

"Good, because stolen wheels, duct tape, rope, a knife, a loaded gun are the kind of evidence I can write up. Basic gear from your local Psycho Killer Emporium." He massaged a temple. Ate pie, drank coffee. Pushed the empty plate back in front of me and called for a refill.

The waitress said, "Boy, you guys were hungry."

Milo grinned. She thought it was sincere and smiled back.

When she was gone, his eyes clouded. "Almost two years passed between Tori and Michaela. The nasty old question resurfaces."

"How many others in between," I said.

"Peaty tags 'em at the PlayHouse. No curriculum, no attendance roster, people drop in and out. It's a predator's dream. I thought maybe Nora was being evasive

when she told me that. Now, with her looking more and more like a victim, I believe
her."

"We found no additional trophies in
Peaty's apartment or the van. So maybe
there are no other victims."

"Or he's got a storage bin somewhere."

"Could be. I'd start with the buildings
where Peaty did janitorial work."

"Grabbing freebie storage," he said.
"Maybe that explains stashing Meserve's
Toyota in Brad's garage. It also fits big-time
hostility toward authority. All those properties the Dowds own, Peaty doing the scut.
Be hard for Brad to monitor every bit of
space . . . so what were you calling me
about before I told you about Peaty?"

"Not important."

"It was important enough to call."

I recounted the scene with Hauser.

"You and Robin?"

"Yup."

He worked hard at stoicism. "Guy's a
shrink? Sounds like a nut."

"At the very least he's an ugly drunk."

"They arrest him?"

"Don't know," I said. "They took him
away in an ambulance."

"You clocked him good, huh?"

"I used discretion."

He squinted, turned his hands to blades, chopped the air, whispered, " 'Heeyah!' I thought you'd given up on all that black belt stuff."

"Never got past brown belt," I said. "It's like riding a bike."

"Hopefully the fool will wake up with a sore nose and realize the error of his ways. Want me to get the reports?"

"I was hoping."

"Any detectives show up?"

"Just uniforms. Hendricks and Minette. He-and-she team."

He phoned Pacific Division, asked to speak to the watch commander, explained the situation, listened, hung up smiling. "In the official police record, you are treated as a victim. Hauser was booked for creating a disturbance in a public place and released. What kind of car does he drive?"

"Don't waste time cruising by."

"A shrink, let's see . . . I'm guessing Volvo, maybe some kind of Volkswagen."

"Audi Quattro."

"Right continent," he said. "Yeah, I'll cruise by, you're welcome."

"It's unlikely he'll persist, Milo. When he sobers up he'll realize another disturbance will mess him up in civil court. If he doesn't, his lawyer will educate him."

"If he was that smart, Alex, he'd never have stalked you in the first place."

"Don't worry about it," I said. "I'm okay and you've got a full plate."

"Interesting," he said.

"What is?"

He loosened his belt and suppressed a belch. "Your choice of gastronomic imagery."

CHAPTER

27

No sign of Hauser's Audi when I got home at two a.m. The bed was made up and Robin was gone. I called her six hours later.

"I heard you leave," she said. "Went outside but you were driving away. What kind of ugly are we talking about?"

"You don't want to know."

"I do. The new me."

"The old you was fine."

"The ostrich's head has been lifted. What happened, Alex?"

"Someone got shot. An extremely bad guy. You could've stayed."

"I got antsy," she said. "It's a big house."

"Don't I know it."

"Last night was good, Alex."

"Except for the chop-socky interlude."

"Are you worried Hauser's going to cause more trouble?"

"Maybe he's smarter when he's sober. The police wrote it up in my favor. About what I asked you—"

"Have a change of heart?"

"Of course not."

"It wasn't just the moment, Alex?"

Maybe it had been. "No."

Couple of beats. "Would you be upset if I said I needed some time to think?"

"It's a big step," I said.

"It is. Which is kind of strange, given how much of our lives we've shared."

I didn't answer.

She said, "I won't take too long."

I left a message with Erica Weiss's secretary, saying I wanted to talk about Patrick Hauser. Just as I hung up, Milo clicked in.

He sounded exhausted. Probably up all night on Peaty. Maybe that's why he didn't bother with niceties.

"Wendell A. Chong, the guy whose van Peaty ripped off, is a software consultant who used to rent office space in a building owned by the Dowds. The van was boosted from his reserved tenant slot at night, while Chong was working late. Chong collected insurance, bought himself a new car, has no interest in reclaiming it."

"Peaty watched and seized the opportunity," I said. "Chong have any impressions of Peaty?"

"Never saw him. Who he does remember is Billy Dowd. He'd always wondered if Billy had something to do with the theft."

"Why?"

"Because Billy used to hang around aimlessly when Brad came by to collect rent. One time he drifted into Chong's office and just stood there, like he owned the place. Chong asked him what he wanted, Billy got a spaced-out look in his eyes and left without a word. Chong followed Billy out into the hall, saw him walking up and down, like he was patrolling. A couple of women stepped out of an office and Billy checked them out. Pretty intensely, according to Chong. Then Brad showed up, ushered Billy away. But he kept bringing Billy along, so Chong started locking his door. Interesting, huh?"

"Billy and Peaty?" I said.

"Weirdos finding common ground. It happens, right? Brad protects Billy but he can't be everywhere. And like you said, he overestimates his power. Maybe he takes Billy along with him when he checks out the garage at the PlayHouse. Or the PlayHouse itself. I don't see Billy getting laid on his own."

"Billy seemed gentle."

"Maybe he is," he said. "Except when he's not. In any event, I just got permission from Vasquez's D.P.D. to interview his client, on my way over to the jail. I'm betting on a quick plea, maybe involuntary manslaughter. Kinda nice to have one that closes easy."

"You could name Peaty as the bad guy on Michaela and close that," I said.

"Yet I wonder aloud about Billy," he said. "Why? Because I'm a self-destructive fool, no sleep in two days, I'm *vulnerable,* amigo. Tell me to forget about Billy and I will."

"Two bad guys could explain how the Gaidelases' car ended up twenty-five miles from Kanan Dume. Billy doesn't seem street-smart, but Peaty could've helped him there. Still, it's hard to imagine him getting away for any length of time. He and Brad seem to be together most of the day and at night there's a neighbor watching him."

"The 'nice lady.' Wonder how hard she looks. I was supposed to check that out but with all that's happened . . . do you think it's interesting that the bad stuff we know about started after Billy got his own place?"

"If the bad stuff was the product of a sick relationship," I said, "with Peaty gone, Billy might not act out again."

"There's comfort for you."

"I can drop by and talk to the neighbor."

"That would be great, I'm tied up with Vasquez all day." He read off Billy's address on Reeves Drive. "Any more problems from that asshole Hauser?"

"Not a one."

"Good."

"I'm still wondering about something," I said.

"Am I going to want to hear this?"

"Dylan Meserve picked Latigo for the hoax because he hiked up there. What led the Gaidelases to the same spot?"

"Aha," he said. "Already been there and back. Maybe Peaty overheard Dylan talking about hiking up there. While the Gaidelases were waiting for their audition, they mentioned wanting to hike and Peaty overheard again and gave them advice."

"That's a lot of overhearing."

"He's a watcher."

"Okay," I said.

"You're not buying it."

"What we know about Meserve suggests lack of conscience, or at the least a weak one. Michaela's description of his behavior those nights bothers me. Mind games, preoccupation with death, rough sex. I hate to add to your burden but—"

"It's not my burden. The Gaidelases were never my case."

A casual acquaintance might've bought that.

He said, "Peaty for the girls, Meserve for the Gaidelases? What, that damned school was a magnet for homicidal maniacs?"

"Something went on there."

He laughed. Not a pleasant sound.

CHAPTER
28

Erica Weiss phoned back while I was in the shower. I dried off and reached her at her office.

"What an experience, Doctor. You okay?" Like many referrals, she was just a phone voice to me. Fast-talking, high-energy, peppy as a cheerleader.

"I'm fine. Any word on Hauser?"

"Haven't checked yet. What exactly transpired?"

When I finished the re-tell, she was peppier. "His malpractice carrier will be thrilled to learn the ante just got upped. Idiot just cooked his goose well-*done.* When can I depose you?"

"Everything's in the police report," I said.

"Even so. When's convenient for you?"

Never. "How about tomorrow?"

"I was thinking more like today."

"It's short notice."

"Those poor women could use their settlements, Doctor."

"Try me late in the afternoon."

"You're a doll," she said. "I'll come to you with the court reporter. Just name the place."

"Let's talk later."

"Commitment-shy? Sure, whatever works, but please make it sooner rather than later."

Billy Dowd's address was on the south side of Beverly Hills, a short walk to Roxbury Park. Last year, I'd witnessed a shoot-out at the park that had never made the papers. This was Beverly Hills, with its aura of safety and ninety-second police response.

Lots of Spanish-style duplexes from the twenties on the block. Billy's was pink with leaded windows, a red-clay roof, and exuberant plaster moldings. An unfenced gateway led to a tile-inlaid stairway that climbed to the second floor. The overhang created a shaded entry nook for the ground-floor unit.

The wrought-iron mailbox inside the left-hand gatepost was unmarked. I climbed to the upstairs unit and knocked on a heavy carved door. The peep-window was blocked by a wooden slat but it stayed closed as the door opened.

A brunette in a white nylon uniform dress looked at me while combing her hair. Coarse hair chopped boyish meant short brisk strokes. She was fortyish with a dangerous tan, a beakish nose, and close-set black eyes. Santa Monica Hospital name tag above her left breast: *A. Holzer, R.N.*

A strange man showing up unannounced didn't perturb her.

"Can I help you?" Some kind of Teutonic accent.

"Billy Dowd lives downstairs?"

"Yes, but he's not here."

I showed her my police consultant I.D. Expired six months ago. Very few people are detail-oriented. A. Holzer barely glanced at it. "Police? About Billy?"

"One of Billy and his brother's employees was involved in some trouble."

"Oh—you wish to speak to Billy about that?"

"Actually, I'm here to see you."

"Me? Why?"

"You look after Billy?"

"Look after?" She laughed. "He's a grown man."

"Physically he is," I said.

The hand around the hairbrush turned glossy. "I don't understand why you are asking these questions. Billy is all right?"

"He's fine. These are routine questions. Sounds as if you like him."

"Of course I do, Billy is very nice," she said. "Listen, I am very tired, got off shift early this morning. I would like to sleep—"

"Eleven-to-seven shift your usual?"

"Yes. That's why I would like to sleep." New smile. Frosty.

"Sounds like you deserve it. What unit do you work on?"

"Cardiac Care—"

"Eight hours of CCU care, then all the time you spend with Billy."

"It's not—Billy doesn't require—why is this important?" She placed a hand on the door.

"It probably isn't," I said. "But when

something really bad happens, lots of questions need to be asked. About everyone who knew the victim."

"There was a victim. Someone was hurt?"

"Someone was murdered."

Her hand flew to her mouth. *"Gott en Himmel*—who?"

"A man named Reynold Peaty."

Head shake. "I don't know this person."

"He did janitorial work at some of Brad and Billy's buildings." I described Peaty.

When I got to the muttonchops, she said, "Oh, him."

"You've met him."

"Not a meeting, just seeing."

"He came here," I said.

She plucked at her badge. Gave her hair a few more whacks.

"Ms. Holzer—"

"Annalise Holzer." Lower voice, soft, guarded. I half expected a rank and serial number.

I said, "Reynold Peaty came to see Billy."

"No, no, not to see, to bring things back."

"Things?"

"Things Billy forgets. At the office. Some-

times Mr. Dowd brings them himself, sometimes I guess he sends this man."

"Reynold Peaty."

"Billy didn't kill him, that is for sure. Billy
opens the windows to let flies out so he
doesn't have to hit them."

"Gentle."

"Gentle," Annalise Holzer agreed. "Like a
nice little boy."

"But forgetful," I said.

"Everyone forgets."

"What does Billy forget?"

"The watch, the wallet. Lots of times the
wallet."

"Mr. Peaty came by and gave you the
wallet?"

"No," she said. "He tells me Billy lost the
wallet and he is returning the wallet."

"How many times did that happen?"

"A few," she said. "I do not count."

Lots of times the wallet. I raised an eye-
brow.

Annalise Holzer said, "A few times, that's
all."

"Those times, did Mr. Peaty go inside
Billy's apartment?"

"I don't know."

"You watch him."

"Nein," she said. "Not watching, not baby-sitting. Mr. Dowd asks me to help if Billy needs something."

"Sounds like a good job."

Shrug.

"Good salary?"

"No money, only less rent."

"Mr. Dowd's your landlord?"

"Very nice landlord, some of them are like . . . snakes."

Milo hadn't mentioned any Beverly Hills properties in the Dowds' holdings.

I said, "So you get a discount on the rent in return for looking in on Billy."

"Yes, exactly."

"What does that involve day to day?"

"Being here," said Annalise Holzer. "If he needs something."

"How does Billy get around?"

"Get around?"

"Go from place to place. He doesn't drive."

"He does not go out much," said Annalise Holzer. "Sometimes I take him to a movie on Sunday. Century City, I drop him off, pick him up. Mostly I rent him DVDs from the video store on Olympic near Almont Drive.

Billy has a big flat-screen TV, better than a movie theater, no?"

"Anyone else ever drive him?"

"Mr. Dowd picks him up in the morning and brings him home. Every day they work."

Wide circuit from Santa Monica Canyon to Beverly Hills and back to the beach city. Brad's unpaid job.

"Is there anyone else?"

"What do you mean?"

"Taxi, car service?"

"Never do I see that."

"So Billy doesn't go out much."

"Never by himself," said Annalise Holzer. "Never do I see him go out, even to walk. I like to walk, when I ask him does he want to walk with me, he tells me, 'Annalise, I did not like gym in school. I'm a big couch potato.' " She smiled. "I joke with him that he is lazy. He laughs."

"Does he have any friends?"

"No—but he is very friendly."

"A homebody," I said.

The word puzzled her.

"He comes home and stays here."

"Yes, yes, exactly. Watching the flat screen, DVDs, eating—I cook, sometimes. He likes some things . . . sauerbraten—

special veal meat. Spaetzle, it is a kind of noodle. I cook for two, bring it downstairs." She looked over her shoulder. The room behind her was tidy and bright. White porcelain figurines crowded the ledge of an arched, tiled mantel.

In the current market, the rent would be three, four thousand a month. Steep on a nurse's pay.

"You live alone, Ms. Holzer?"

"Yes."

"You're from Germany?"

"Lichtenstein." She pinched thumb to forefinger. "It is a teeny tiny little country between—"

"Austria and Switzerland," I said.

"You know Lichtenstein?"

"I've heard it's pretty. Banking, castles, Alps."

"It is pretty, yes," she agreed. "But I like it here better."

"L.A.'s more exciting."

"More to do, the music, the horses, the beach."

"You ride?"

"Anything with sunshine," she said.

"Working nights and sleeping days and doing things for Billy."

"Work is good. Sometimes I do a double shift."

"What are Billy's needs?" I said.

"Very easy. If he wants takeout and it is a long time for the restaurant to deliver, I get him his dinner. There is Domino Pizza on Doheny near Olympic. Billy likes Thai food, there's a nice place on La Cienega and Olympic. Sushi is also on Olympic. Nice place near Doheny. Very convenient, being near Olympic."

"Billy's a gourmet."

"Billy eats anything," said Annalise Holzer. "You must really think of him as a boy. A good boy."

When I was back on Olympic, I celled Milo, expecting voice mail because he was with Armando Vasquez.

"Canceled," he said. "Vasquez's D.P.D. had other plans but didn't bother to tell me. The prelim on Michaela's autopsy finally came in. I woulda been there but they did it earlier than scheduled. Bottom line is no sign of sexual assault, cause of death was strangulation, the stab wounds on her chest were relatively superficial. The neck wound was a puncture, pathologist can't say what caused it. Get to Billy's place yet?"

"Just finished with that and you're going to feel smart. The woman upstairs is a nurse on the night shift at Santa Monica Hospital, meaning she's gone by ten fifteen or so. Plus, she thinks L.A.'s an exciting city, likes art, the beach, riding horses. Her tan says she's out plenty during the day."

"Not much supervision."

"On top of that, Peaty came to Billy's apartment several times. Claimed he was sent by Brad to return things Billy left at the office. Brad told us he thought Peaty wasn't licensed to drive. Unless he lied about that, Peaty misrepresented his presence."

"How many times is several?"

"The woman couldn't quantify. Or wouldn't. She said Billy lost his wallet a lot. Then she backtracked to 'a few.' "

"What's her name?"

"Annalise Holzer. She's one of those people who gives you lots of details and ends up not telling you much. She considers Billy childlike, gracious, absolutely no problem. Some of that could be the rent-break Brad gives her. The building's another Dowd property."

"That so? Not on the BNB list."

"Maybe the Dowds have another corporation or a holding company that doesn't trace back to their names."

"All that real estate," he said. "These people have got to be hugely rich, and rich people get protected."

"Holzer was protective, all right. But I wouldn't trust her to know the details of Billy's life."

"Meaning Peaty coulda been a regular at Darling Billy's. I've *got* to take a serious look at the guy. After I speak to Vasquez's wife. That's the change in plans. All of a sudden, I can't have access to Armando until I talk to the missus."

"About what?"

"P.D.'s being cryptic. It'll probably turn out to be a stupid lawyer trick but the D.A. insists I check it out."

"D.A.'s office has their own investigators."

"Whom they pay. That's why I'm figuring it for scut palmed off on me."

"Where are you meeting the wife?"

"Right here in my office, half an hour."

"I'm twenty minutes away."

"Good."

CHAPTER

29

Jacalyn Vasquez, minus three kids and makeup and jewelry, looked even younger than when I'd seen her on Sunday. Streaked hair was tied back in a somber ponytail. She wore a loose white blouse, blue jeans, and sneakers. Florid acne played havoc with her forehead and cheeks. Her eyes had regressed into sooty sockets.

A tall honey-haired woman in her twenties held Vasquez's arm. The blonde's locks were long and silky. She wore a tight black suit that showcased a bikini figure. A ruby stud in her left nostril fought the suit's conservative cut. The pretty hair and tight body sparred with a monkeyish face the camera would savage.

She surveyed the tiny space and frowned. "How're we all going to fit in here?"

Milo smiled. "And you are?"

"Brittany Chamfer, Public Defender's Office."

"I thought Mr. Vasquez's attorney was Kevin Shuldiner."

"I'm a third-year law student," said Brittany Chamfer. "Working with the Exoneration Project." She amplified her frown. "This is like a closet."

"Well," said Milo, "one less body should help. Enjoy the fresh air, Ms. Chamfer. Come on in, Ms. Vasquez."

"My instruction was to stay with Jackie."

"My instruction is that you enjoy the fresh air." He stood and the chair squeaked. Silencing it with one hand, he offered the seat to Jacalyn Vasquez. "Right here, ma'am."

Brittany Chamfer said, "I'm *supposed* to stay."

"You're not an attorney and Ms. Vasquez hasn't been charged with anything."

"Still."

Milo took one big step that brought him

to the doorway. Brittany Chamfer had to step back to avoid collision, and the arm she'd used to support Jacalyn Vasquez pulled free.

Vasquez looked past me. The office could've been miles of glacier.

Brittany Chamfer said, "I'll have to call the office."

Milo ushered Vasquez in, closed the door.

By the time she sat down, Jacalyn Vasquez was crying.

Milo gave her a tissue. When her eyes dried, he said, "You have something to tell me, Ms. Vasquez?"

"Uh-huh."

"What is it, ma'am?"

"Armando was protecting us."

"Protecting the family?"

"Uh-huh."

"From . . ."

"Him."

"Mr. Peaty?"

"The pervert."

"You knew Mr. Peaty to be a pervert?"

Nod.

"How did you know that?"

"Everyone said."

"Everyone in the building."

"Yeah."

"Like Mrs. Stadlbraun."

"Yeah."

"Who else?"

"Everyone."

"Can you give me some names?"

Eyes down. "Everyone."

"Did Mr. Peaty ever do anything perverted that you know about personally?"

"He looked."

"At . . ."

Jacalyn Vasquez poked her left breast. Milo said, "He looked at you."

"A lot."

"He ever touch you?"

Head shake.

"His looks made you feel uncomfortable."

"Yeah."

"You tell Armando?"

"Uh-uh."

"Why not?"

"I didn't want to make him mad."

"Armando has a temper."

Silence.

"So Peaty looked at you," said Milo. "You figure that made it okay for Armando to shoot him?"

"Also the calls. That's what I'm here to tell you."

Milo's eyes narrowed. "What calls, ma'am?"

"The night. Calling, hanging up, calling, hanging up. I figured it was him."

"Peaty?"

"Yeah."

"Because . . ."

"He was a pervert." Her eyes dipped again.

"You figured it was Mr. Peaty harassing you," said Milo.

"Yeah."

"Had he done that before?"

Hesitation.

"Ms. Vasquez?"

"Uh-uh."

"He hadn't done it before but you suspected it was him. Did Mr. Shuldiner come up with that?"

"It coulda *been* him!"

Milo said, "Any other reason the calls bothered you?"

"They kept hanging up."

"They," said Milo. Stretching the word.

Vasquez looked up, confused.

Milo said, "Maybe you were worried about a 'they,' Jackie."

"Huh?"

"Armando's old homeboys."

"Armando don't have no homeboys."

"He used to, Jackie."

Silence.

"Everyone knows he used to run with the 88s, Jackie."

Vasquez sniffed.

"Everyone knows," Milo repeated.

"That was, like, a long time ago," said Vasquez. "Armando don't bang no more."

"Who's they?"

"The calls. There was a bunch."

"Any other calls last night?"

"My mother."

"What time?"

"Like six." Jacalyn Vasquez sat up straighter. "The other one wasn't no homeboys."

"What other one?"

"After the ones that hung up. Someone talked. Like a whisper, you know?"

"A whisper."

"Yeah."

"What'd they whisper about."

"*Him.* They said he was dangerous, liked to hurt women."

"Someone whispered that about Peaty?"

"Yeah."

"You heard this."

"They talked to Armando."

"What time did this whispering call come in, Jackie?"

"Like . . . we were in bed with the TV. Armando answered and he was pissed off 'cause a the other calls hanging up. He's, like, started yelling into the phone and then he's, like, stopped, listened. I said what, he waved his hand, like, you know? He listened and his face got all red. That was the last time."

"Armando got mad."

"Real mad."

" 'Cause of the whispering."

"Uh-huh."

"Did Armando tell you about the whispering after he hung up?"

Jacalyn Vasquez shook her head. "Later."

"When, later?"

"Last night."

"Calling from jail."

"Yeah."

"You never heard the whispering and Armando didn't tell you about it at the time. Then, after Armando shot Peaty, he decided to tell you."

"I ain't lyin'."

"I can understand your wanting to protect your husband—"

"I ain't lyin'."

"Let's say someone did whisper," said Milo. "You figure that made it okay to shoot Peaty?"

"Yeah."

"Why's that, Jackie?"

"He was dangerous."

"According to the whisperer."

"I ain't lyin'."

"Maybe Armando is."

"Armando ain't lyin'."

"Did Armando say if this whisperer was a man or a woman?"

"Armando said the whispering made so you couldn't tell."

"Pretty good whispering."

"I ain't lyin'." Jacalyn Vasquez folded her arms across her bosom and stared at Milo.

"You know, Jackie, that any calls to your apartment can be verified."

"Huh?"

"We can check your phone records."

"Fine," she said.

"The problem is," said Milo, "all we can know is that someone called you at a certain time. We can't verify what was said."

"It happened."

"According to Armando."

"Armando ain't lyin'."

"All those hang-ups," said Milo. "Then all of a sudden, someone's whispering about Peaty and Armando's listening."

Jacalyn Vasquez's hands, still crossed, climbed to her face and pushed against her cheeks. Her features turned rubbery. When she spoke through compressed lips, the words came out slurred, like a kid goofing.

"It happened. Armando told me. It happened."

Brittany Chamfer was waiting in the hall, playing with her nose stud. She whipped around, saw Jacalyn Vasquez dabbing her eyes. "You okay, Jackie?"

"He don' believe me."

Chamfer said, *"What?"*

Milo said, "Thanks for coming in."

Chamfer said, "We're looking for the truth."

"Common goal."

Chamfer considered her response. "What message should I give to Mr. Shuldiner?"

"Thank him for his civic duty."

"Pardon?"

"Thank him for creativity, too."

Brittany Chamfer said, "I'm not going to tell him *that*."

"Have a nice day."

"I will." Chamfer flipped her long hair. "Will *you*?"

Renewing her grip, she propelled Jacalyn Vasquez up the corridor.

Milo said, "That's why the D.A.'s office palmed it on me. What a crock."

"You're dismissing it out of hand?" I said.

"You're not?"

"If Vasquez's lying to exonerate himself, he could've picked something stronger. Like Peaty threatening him explicitly."

"So he's stupid."

"Maybe that's it," I said.

He leaned against the wall, scuffed the baseboard. "Even if someone did call Vasquez to prime the pump against Peaty, the right suspect's in jail. Let's say Ertha

Stadlbraun got things stoked up because Peaty had always creeped her out. My interview tipped her over and she stirred up the tenants. One of them was an incompletely reformed banger with a bad temper and boom boom boom."

"If you're comfortable not checking it out, so am I."

He turned his back on me, imbedded both hands in his hair and turned it into a fright wig. Smoothing it down was a partial success. He stomped back into his office.

When I entered, he had the phone receiver in hand but wasn't punching numbers. "Know what kept *me* up last night? Damned snow globe. Brad thought Meserve put it there but the one in the van says Peaty did. Would Peaty taunt Brad?"

"Maybe Peaty didn't leave it."

"What?"

"Meserve thinks he's an actor," I said. "Actors do voice-overs."

"The Infernal Whisperer? I can't get distracted by that kind of crap, Alex. Still have to check out all those buildings Peaty cleaned, stuff could be hidden anywhere. Can't ignore Billy either, because he hung with Peaty and I was masochistic enough to find out."

He passed the receiver from hand to hand. "What I'd love to do is get to Billy in his apartment, away from Brad, and gauge his reaction to Peaty's death." He huffed. "Let's take care of this whispering bullshit."

He called the phone company, talked to someone named Larry. "What I need is for you to tell me it's crap so I can avoid the whole subpoena thing. Thanks, yeah . . . you, too. I'll hold."

Moments later, his faced flushed and he was scribbling furiously in his pad. "Okay, Lorenzo, thanko mucho . . . no, I mean it . . . we'll forget this conversation took place and I'll get you the damned paper a-sap."

The receiver slammed down.

He ripped a page out of the pad and shoved it at me.

The first evening call to the Vasquez apartment had come in at five fifty-two p.m. and lasted thirty-two minutes. The caller's mid-city number was registered to Guadalupe Maldonado. The call from Jackie Vasquez's mom at "like six."

Milo closed his eyes and pretended to doze as I read on.

Five more calls between seven and ten p.m., all from a 310 area code that Milo had notated as *"stolen cell."* The first lasted eight seconds, the second, four. Then a trio of two-second entries that had to be hang-ups.

Armando Vasquez losing patience and slamming down the phone.

I said, "Stolen from who?"

"Don't know yet, but it happened the same day the call came in. Keep going."

Under the five calls was the doodle of an amoebic blob filled with crosses. Then something Milo had underlined so hard he'd torn paper.

Final call. 10:23 p.m. Forty-two seconds long.

Despite Vasquez's anger, something had managed to hold his interest.

Different caller, 805 area code.

Milo reached over and took the page, shredded it meticulously, and dropped it in his trash basket. "You have never seen that. You will see it once the goddamn subpoena that is now goddamn necessary produces legit evidence."

"Ventura County," I said. "Maybe Camarillo?"

"Not maybe, for sure. My man Lawrence says a pay phone in Camarillo."

"Near the outlets?"

"He wasn't able to be that precise, but we'll find out. Now I've got a possible link to the Gaidelases. Which should make you happy. All along, you never saw Peaty for them. So what're we talking about, an 805-based killer who prowls the coast and I've gotta start from scratch?"

"Only if the Gaidelases are victims," I said.

"As opposed to?"

"The sheriffs thought the facts pointed to a willful disappearance and maybe they were right. Armando told his wife the whispering made it impossible to identify the sex of the caller. If it's amateur theater we're talking about, Cathy Gaidelas could be a candidate."

His jaws bunched. He scooted forward on his chair, inches from my face. I thanked God we were friends.

"All of a sudden the Gaidelases have gone from victims to psycho *murderers*?"

"It solves several problems," I said. "No bodies recovered and the rental car was left in Camarillo because the Gaidelases ditched it, just as the company assumed. Who better to cancel credit cards than the legitimate owners? And to know which utilities to call back in Ohio?"

"Nice couple hiding out in Ventura County and venturing into L.A. to commit nasty? For starts, why would they home-base out there?"

"Proximity to the ocean and you don't have to be a millionaire. There are still places in Oxnard with low-rent housing."

He yanked his forelock up and stretched his brow tight. "Where the hell did all this *come* from, Alex?"

"My twisted mind," I said. "But think about it: The only reason we've considered the Gaidelases a nice couple is because Cathy's sister described them that way. But Susan Palmer also talked about an antisocial side—drug use, years of mooching off the family. Cathy married a man people suspect is gay. There's some complexity there."

"What I'm hearing is *minor* league complexity. What's their motive for turning *homicidal*?"

"How about extreme frustration coming to a head? We're talking two middle-aged people who've never achieved much on their own. They make the big move to L.A., delusional like thousands of other wannabes. Their age and looks make it even chancier but they take a methodical approach: acting lessons. Maybe they were rejected by other coaches and Nora was their last chance. What if she turned them away in less-than-diplomatic terms? Charlie Manson didn't take well to hearing he wasn't going to be a rock star."

"This is about revenge on Nora?" he said.

"Revenge on her and the symbols of youth and beauty she surrounded herself with."

"Tori Giacomo got killed *before* the Gaidelases disappeared."

"That wouldn't have stopped the Gaidelases from having contact with her. If not at the PlayHouse, at work. Maybe she served them a lobster dinner and that's how they *learned* about the PlayHouse."

"They do Tori, then wait nearly two years to do Michaela? That's a dish gone way cold, Alex."

"That's assuming no other students at the PlayHouse have gone missing."

He sighed.

I said, "The hoax could've served as

some kind of catalyst. Nora's name in the paper. Michaela's and Dylan's, too. Not to mention Latigo Canyon. I could be totally off base, but I don't think the 805 link can be overlooked. And neither can Armando Vasquez's story."

He stood, stretched, sat back down, buried his face in his hands for a while and looked up, bleary-eyed. "Creative, Alex. Fanciful, inventive, impressively outside the goddamn box. The problem it *doesn't* solve is Peaty. A definite bad guy with access to all of the victims and a rape kit in his van. If the Gaidelases were chasing stardom, why would they have anything to do with a loser like him, let alone set him up to be shot? And how the hell would they know to prime the pump by phoning Vasquez?"

I thought about that. "It's possible the Gaidelases met Peaty at the PlayHouse and some bonding took place—outsiders commiserating."

"That's a helluva lot going on during a failed audition. Assuming the Gaidelases were ever *at* the PlayHouse."

"Maybe Nora kept them waiting for a long time then dismissed them unceremoniously. If they did bond with Peaty, they could've had opportunity to visit his apartment and pick up on tension in the building. Or Peaty talked about his dislike for Vasquez."

"Ertha Stadlbraun said Peaty never had visitors."

"Ertha Stadlbraun goes to sleep by eleven," I said. "Be interesting to know if anyone at the apartment recognizes the Gaidelases' photos."

He stared at me.

"Peaty, Andy, and Cathy. And let's toss in Billy Dowd, because we're feeling generous. What, some kind of misfit club?"

"Look at all those schoolyard shootings committed by outsiders."

"Oh, Lord," he said. "Before I get sucked into this vortex of fantasy, I need to do some boring old police work. As in pinpointing the phone booth and trying to pull some prints. As in keep searching for any troves Peaty might've stashed God knows where. As in . . . let's not shmooze any more, okay? My head's splitting like a luau coconut."

Yanking his tie loose, he hauled himself up, crossed the tiny office, and threw back the door. It hit the wall, chunked out a disk of plaster, bounced a couple of times.

My ears were still ringing when he stuck

his head in, seconds later. "Where can I find one of those amino-acid concoctions that makes you smarter?"

"They don't work," I said.

"Thanks for your input."

CHAPTER
30

The Brazilian rosewood door of Erica Weiss's law firm should've been used for guitar backs. Twenty-six partners were listed in efficient pewter. Weiss's was near the top.

She kept me waiting for twenty minutes but came out to greet me personally. Late thirties, silver-haired, blue-eyed, statuesque in charcoal Armani and coral jewelry.

"Sorry for the delay, Doctor. I was willing to come to you."

"No problem."

"Coffee?"

"Black would be fine."

"Cookies? One of our paras whipped up some chocolate chips this morning. Cliff's a great baker."

"No, thanks."

"Coming up with black coffee." She crossed a field of soft, navy carpet to an entry square of hardwood. Her exit was a castanet solo of stiletto heels.

Her lair was a bright, cool, corner space on the eighth floor of a high-rise on Wilshire, just east of Rossmore in Hancock Park. Gray felt walls, Macassar ebony deco revival furniture, chrome and black leather chair that matched the finish of her computer monitor. Stanford law degree tucked in a corner where it was sure to be noticed.

A coffin-shaped rosewood conference table had been set up with four black club chairs on wheels. I took the head seat. Maybe it was meant for Erica Weiss; she could always tell me that.

An eastern wall of glass showcased a view of Koreatown and the distant gloss of downtown. To the west, out of sight, was Nora Dowd's house on McCadden.

Weiss returned with a blue mug bearing the law firm's name and logo in gold leaf. The icon was a helmet over a wreath filled with Latin script. Something to do with honor and loyalty. The coffee was strong and bitter.

She looked at the head chair for a second, settled to my right with no comment. A Filipina carrying a court-reporter's stenotype machine entered, followed by a young spike-haired man in a loose-fitting green suit who Weiss introduced as Cliff. "He'll be witnessing your oath. Ready, Doctor?"

"Sure."

She put on reading glasses and read a file while I sipped coffee. Then off came the specs, her face got tight, and the blue in her eyes turned to steel.

"First of all," she said and the change in her voice made me put my cup down. She concentrated on the top of my head, as if something odd had sprouted there. Pointing a finger, she turned *"Doctor"* into something unsavory.

For the next half hour, I fielded questions, all delivered in a strident rhythm dripping with insinuation. Scores of questions, many taking Patrick Hauser's point of view. No letup; Erica Weiss seemed to be able to speak without breathing.

Just as suddenly, she said, "Finished."

Big smile. "Sorry if I was a little curt, Doctor, but I consider depositions rehearsals and I like my witnesses prepared for court."

"You think it'll come to that?"

"I'd bet against it, but I don't bet anymore." She peeled back a cuff and studied a sapphire-ringed Lady Rolex. "In either event, you'll be ready. Now, if you'll excuse me, I've got an appointment."

Ten-minute ride to McCadden Place.

Still no Range Rover but the driveway wasn't empty.

A yacht-sized, baby-blue '59 Cadillac convertible hogged the space. Gleaming wire wheels, white top folded down, tailfins that should've been registered as lethal weapons. Old black-and-yellow plates bore a classic car designation.

Brad and Billy Dowd stood next to the car, their backs to me. Brad wore a light brown linen suit and gestured with his right hand. His left arm rested on Billy's shoulder. Billy wore the same blue shirt and baggy Dockers. Half a foot shorter than his brother. But for his gray hair, the two of them could've passed for father and son.

Dad talking, son listening.

The sound of my engine cutting made Brad look over his shoulder. A second later, Billy aped him.

By the time I got out, both brothers were facing me. The polo shirt under Brad's jacket was aquamarine pique. On his feet were perforated, peanut-butter-colored Italian sandals. Cloudy day but he'd dressed for a beachside power lunch. His white hair was ragged and he looked tense. Billy's face was blank. A grease stain rorschached the front of his pants.

He greeted me first. "Hi, Detective."

"How's it going, Billy?"

"Bad. Nora's nowhere and we're scared."

Brad said, "More worried than scared, Bill."

"You said—"

"Remember the brochures, Bill? What did I tell you?"

"Be positive," said Billy.

"Exactly."

I said, "Brochures?"

Billy pointed at the house. "Brad went in there again."

Brad said, "First time was superficial. This time I opened some drawers, found travel brochures in my sister's nightstand.

Nothing seems out of place except maybe some extra space in her clothes closet."

"Packed to go," I said.

"I hope that's it."

"What kind of brochures?" I said.

"Places in Latin America. Want to see them?"

"Please."

He jogged to the Caddy and brought back a stack of glossies.

Pelican's Pouch, Southwater Caye, Belize; Turneffe Island, Belize; Posada La Mandragora, Buzios, Brazil; Hotel Monasterio, Cusco, Peru; Tapir Lodge, Ecuador.

"Looks like vacation plans," I said.

"Still, you'd think she'd tell us," said Brad. "I was going to call you to see if you found any flights she took."

Nora's passport hadn't been used.

I said, "Nothing so far but still checking. Does Nora ever fly privately?"

"No. Why?"

"Covering all bases."

"We've talked about doing that," said Brad. "Mostly, I've talked about it. Being so close to Santa Monica Airport, you see those beauties take off and it looks real inviting."

Same thing Milo had said. For the Dowds it could be more than fantasy.

I said, "What did Nora think?"

"She was ready to do a time share. But once I found out the cost, I said forget it. The cool thing would be owning my own plane but that was never an option."

"How come?"

"We're not close to that financial league, Detective."

"Did Nora agree with that assessment?"

Brad smiled. "Nora isn't much for budgeting. Would she charter something on her own? I suppose it's possible. But she'd have to get the money from me."

"She doesn't have her own funds?"

"She has a checking account for day to day, but for serious money she comes to me. It works out better for all of us."

Billy's eyes rose to the sky. "I never get to go anywhere."

"Come on, Bill," said Brad. "We flew to San Francisco."

"That was a long time ago."

"It was two years ago."

"That's a long time." Billy's eyes got dreamy. One hand dropped toward his crotch. Brad cleared his throat and Billy jammed the hand in his pocket.

I turned back to Brad. "It's not in character for Nora to take off without telling you?"

"Nora does her own thing on a limited level, but she's never traveled for any length of time without letting me know."

"Those trips to Paris."

"Exactly." Brad glanced at the brochures. "I was going to contact those resorts, but if you want to do it, you can keep the information."

"Will do."

He rubbed the corner of one eye. "Maybe Nora will waltz in tomorrow with a—I was going to say with a terrific tan, but Nora doesn't like the sun."

I waved the brochures. "These are all sunny spots."

Brad glanced at Billy. Billy's eyes were still aimed at the sky. "I'm sure there's a logical explanation, Detective. Just wish I . . . anyway, thanks for stopping by. If you learn anything, please let me know."

"There's something you should know," I said. "Reynold Peaty was murdered last night."

Brad gasped. "What! That's crazy!"

Billy froze. Stayed that way but his eyes locked into mine. Nothing absent about his gaze now.

Brad said, "Billy?"

Bill continued to stare at me. Pointed a finger. "You just said something terrible."

"I'm sorry—"

"Reyn got murdered?" Billy's hands balled. "No *way!*"

Brad touched his arm but Billy shook him off and ran to the center of Nora's lawn, where he began punching his thighs.

Brad hurried over, talked in his brother's ear. Billy shook his head violently and walked several feet away. Brad followed, talking nonstop. Billy stepped away again. Brad persisted through a series of Billy's head shakes and grimaces. Finally, Billy allowed himself to be ushered back. Flared nostrils doubled the width of his pug nose. Thick white spittle flecked his lips.

"Who killed Reyn?" he demanded.

"A neighbor," I said. "They had an argument and—"

"A neighbor?" said Brad. "One of our *tenants? Who?*"

"A man named Armando Vasquez."

"*That* one. *Shit,* right from the get-go I

had a bad feeling about him, but his application was in order and nowadays you can't turn down a tenant based on intuition." He tugged at a lapel. "Jesus. What *happened*?"

"What worried you about Vasquez?"

"He seemed like . . . you know, the cholo thing."

"Where is he, Brad?" said Billy. "I wanna kill him back."

"Shh! An argument? How'd it get from talking to murdering?"

"Hard to say."

"Christ," said Brad. "Talking about what?"

Billy's eyes were slits. "Where's the *lowlife*?"

"In jail," said Brad. To me: "Right?"

"He's in custody."

"For how long?" said Billy.

"A long time," I said.

"Tell me when he gets out so I can shoot his ass."

Brad said, "Billy, *stop!*"

Billy glared. Breathed heavily.

Brad tried to touch him. Again, Billy shook him off. "I'll stop now, fine, okay. But when he gets out I'll shoot a bullet *up* his ass." He punched air.

"Billy, that's—"

"Reyn was my *friend*."

"Bill, he wasn't a real—okay, okay, whatever, Bill, I'm sorry. He was your friend, you have every right to be upset."

"I'm not upset. I'm *pissed*."

"Fine, be pissed." Back to me: "An *argument*? Jesus, I was going to go by that building today or tomorrow."

"Why?"

Brad cocked a head toward his brother. Billy was studying the grass. "Making the circuit."

About to fire and evict Peaty.

Billy punched his palm. "Reyn was my *friend. Now he's *dead. That's fucked *up.*"

I said, "What did you and Reyn do together, Billy?"

Brad tried to step between Billy and me but Billy twisted around him. "Reyn was polite to me."

Brad said, "Billy, Reyn had some problems. Remember I told you about them—"

"Driving too fast. So what, *you* do that, Brad."

"Billy . . ." Brad smiled and shrugged.

Billy cocked his head at the Cadillac. "Not in the '59, the '59's too fucking slow— that's what you always say, too fucking slow to move its big old fucking ass. You drive fast in the Sting Ray and the Porsche and the Austin—"

"Fine," Brad snapped. He smiled again. "The detective gets it, Bill."

"You say the Ray's as fast as that girl in your class . . . what was her name—er, er, er, Jocelyn . . . the Sting Ray's as fast as Jocelyn . . . Jocelyn . . . Olderson . . . Oldenson . . . and just as expensive. You always say that, the Sting—"

"That's a joke, Bill."

"*I'm* not laughing," said Billy. To me: "Reyn drove too fast a long time ago and got in trouble. Does that mean he has to get his *ass* killed?"

Brad said, "No one's saying that, Billy."

"I'm asking *him,* Brad."

"It doesn't mean that," I said.

"It fucking pisses me *off.*" Billy broke free again, headed for the driveway. Climbing over the Caddy's passenger door with some effort, he sank down, arms folded, and stared straight ahead.

Brad said, "Climbing in like that, he knows that's against the—he must really be upset, though for the life of me I can't tell you why."

"He considers Peaty his friend."

He lowered his voice. "Wishful thinking."

"What do you mean?"

"My brother has no peer group. When I first hired Peaty I noticed him staring at Billy like Billy was some kind of freak. I told him to stop doing that and he did and after that he was friendly to Billy. I figured he was kissing up to me. Anyway, that's probably what Billy's responding to. Anyone who treats him like half a man is his buddy. After you guys dropped in at the office, he told me *you* were his buddies."

Over in the Cadillac, Billy started rocking.

I said, "He's pretty upset for having no relationship at all with Peaty."

"My brother has trouble with change."

"Learning someone you know has been murdered is serious change."

"Yes, of course, I'm not minimizing it. All I'm saying is it's harder for Billy to process that kind of thing." He shook his head. "Shot to death over a stupid argument? Now that Billy's not listening, can you tell me what really happened?"

"Same answer," I said. "I wasn't protecting Billy."

"Oh. Okay, sorry. Look, I'd better go calm him down, so if—"

"You're sure Billy and Peaty didn't associate."

"I'm positive. Peaty was a *janitor,* for God's sake."

I said, "He's been to Billy's apartment."

Brad's lower lip dropped. "What are you talking about?"

I repeated what Annalise Holzer had told me.

"Lost articles?" he said. "That makes no sense at all."

"Is Billy absentminded?"

"Yes, but—"

"We were wondering if Peaty stopped by at your instruction."

"My instruction? Ridiculous. As far as I knew, he didn't drive, remember?" Brad wiped his brow. "Annalise said that?"

"Is she reliable?"

"God, I sure hope so." He scratched his head. "If she said Peaty dropped by, I guess he did. But I've got to tell you, I'm astonished."

"That Peaty and Billy would associate?"

"We don't know they *associated,* just that Peaty dropped things off. Yes, Billy's absentminded but usually he tells me when he's left something and I tell him don't worry, we'll get it tomorrow. If Peaty did drop something off I'm sure that's where it ended."

He looked over at Billy. Rocking harder. "First Nora taking off and now this . . ."

I said, "They're adults."

"Chronologically."

"Must be hard, being the protector."

"Mostly it's no big deal. Sometimes it's a challenge."

"This is one of those sometimes."

"This is a real *big* sometime."

"At some point," I said, "we'd like to talk to Billy about Peaty."

"Why? Peaty's dead and you know who shot him."

"Just to be thorough."

"What does it have to do with Billy?"

"Probably nothing."

"Is Peaty still a suspect for that girl's murder?"

"Still?"

"All those questions you asked about him when you came to my house. It was pretty obvious what you were getting at. Do you really think Peaty could've done something like that?"

"It's an open investigation," I said.

"Meaning you won't say. Look, I appreciate what you guys do but I can't just let you browbeat Billy."

"Browbeating's not on the agenda, Mr. Dowd. Just a few questions."

"Believe me, Detective, he has nothing to tell you."

"You're sure about that."

"Of course I am. I can't allow my brother to be drawn into anything sordid."

"Because he's chronologically an adult but . . ."

"Exactly."

"He doesn't seem retarded," I said.

"I told you, he isn't," said Brad. "What he *is* no one's ever been sure. Nowadays he'd probably be called some kind of autistic. Back when we were kids he was just 'different.' "

"Must've been tough."

"Whatever." His eyes shifted sideways toward the Cadillac. Billy rested his head down on the dashboard. "There isn't a mean bone in his body, Detective, but that didn't stop other kids from tormenting him.

I'm younger but I always felt like the older brother. That's the way it's remained and I'm going to have to ask you to respect our privacy."

"Maybe it would be good for Billy to talk," I said.

"Why?"

"He seemed pretty traumatized by the news. Sometimes getting it out helps."

"Now you sound like a shrink," said Brad. New edge in his voice.

"You've got experience with shrinks?"

"Back when we were kids Billy got taken to all kinds of quacks. Vitamin quacks, hypnosis quacks, exercise quacks, psychiatric quacks. No one did a damn thing for him. So let's all just stick to what we know best. You chase bad guys and I'll take care of my brother."

I walked over to the Caddy, Brad's protests at my back. Billy sat up, rigid. His eyes were shut and his hands clawed the placket of his shirt.

"Nice seeing you again, Billy."

"It wasn't nice. This is a bad news day."

Brad got in the driver's seat, started up the engine.

"Real bad news," I said.

Billy nodded. "Real real real bad."

Brad turned the ignition key. "I'm backing out, Detective."

I waited until they'd been gone for five minutes, then walked up to Nora Dowd's door and knocked. Got the silence I'd expected.

Empty mailbox. Brother Brad had collected Nora's correspondence. Cleaning up everyone's mess, as usual. He claimed Billy was harmless but his opinion was worthless.

I got back in the Seville and drove away, passing Albert Beamish's house. The old man's curtains were drawn but he opened his door.

Red shirt, green pants, drink in hand.

I stopped and lowered the car window. "How's it going?"

Beamish started to say something, shook his head in disgust, went back inside.

CHAPTER

31

Billy had been attached to Peaty. And Billy had a temper.

Was he too dull to realize the implication of a relationship with Reynold Peaty? Or *was* there no implication?

One thing was likely: The janitor's visits had been more than dropping off lost articles.

As I drove Sixth Street toward its terminus at San Vicente, I considered Billy's reaction. Shock, anger, desire for vengeance.

Another sib defying Brad.

A child's impulsiveness together with a grown man's hormones could be a danger-

424   JONATHAN KELLERMAN

ous combination. As Milo had pointed out, Billy had begun living on his own right around the time of Tori Giacomo's murder and the Gaidelases' disappearance.

Perfect opportunity for Billy and Peaty to take their friendship to a new level? If the two of them had become a murder team, Peaty was certain to have been the dominant one.

Some leadership. An outwardly creepy alcoholic voyeur and a dullard man-boy didn't add up to the kind of planning and care that had stripped Michaela's dumpsite of forensic detail, concealed Tori Giacomo's body long enough to reduce it to scattered bones.

Then there was the matter of the whispering phone call from Ventura County. No way Billy could've pulled that off.

Iago-prompt, courtesy of the phone lines. It had worked.

I'd hypothesized about a cruel side to the Gaidelases but there was another pair of performance buffs worth considering.

Nora Dowd was an eccentric dilettante and a failure as an actress, but she'd been skillful enough to fool her brother about breaking off with Dylan Meserve. Toss in a young lover with a penchant for rough sex and mind games and it cooked up interesting.

Maybe Brad had found no sign of struggle in Nora's house because there'd been none. Travel brochures in a nightstand drawer and missing clothes plus Dylan Meserve's skip on his rent weeks ago said a long-planned trip. Albert Beamish hadn't seen anyone living with Nora but someone entering and exiting the house after dark would have escaped his notice.

A woman who thought private flying was a nifty idea.

Her passport hadn't been used recently and Meserve had never applied for one. But he'd grown up on the streets of New York, could've known how to obtain fake paper. Getting through passport control at LAX might be a challenge. But jetting from Santa Monica to a landing strip in some south-of-the-border village with payoff cash would be another story.

Brochures in a drawer, no real attempt to conceal. Because Nora was confident no one would broach her privacy?

When I stopped for a red light at Melrose,

I took a closer look at the resorts she'd researched.

Pretty places in South America. Maybe for more than the climate.

I drove home as fast as Sunset would allow, barely took the time to look for Hauser's brown Audi. Moments after logging on to the Internet I learned that Belize, Brazil, and Ecuador all had extradition treaties with the U.S. and that nearly all the countries without treaties were in Africa and Asia.

Hiding out in Rwanda, Burkina Faso, or Uganda wouldn't be much fun, and I couldn't see Nora taking well to the feminine couture of Saudi Arabia.

I studied the brochures again. Each resort was in a remote jungle area.

To be extradited you had to be found.

I pictured the scene: May-December couple checks into a luxury suite, enjoys the beach, the bar, the pool. Nighttime's the right time for al fresco candlelight dinners, maybe a couple's massage. Long, hot, incandescent days allow plenty of time to search for a leafy suburb hospitable to affluent foreigners.

Nazi war criminals had hidden for decades

in Latin America, living like nobility. Why not a couple of low-profile thrill killers?

Still, if Nora and Dylan had escaped for the long run, why leave brochures anywhere to be discovered?

Unless the packets were a misdirect.

I looked up jet leasing, air charter, and time-share companies in Southern California, compiled a surprisingly long list, spent the next two hours claiming to be Bradley Dowd experiencing a "family emergency" and in dire need of finding his sister and his nephew, Dylan. Lots of turndowns and the few outfits who checked their passenger logs had no listing of Nora or Meserve. Which proved nothing if the couple had assumed new identities.

For Milo to get subpoenas of the records, he'd need evidence of criminal behavior and all Dowd and Meserve had done was disappear.

Unless Dylan's misdemeanor conviction could be used against him.

Milo would be tied up right now with "boring police stuff." I called him anyway and described Billy Dowd's behavior.

He said, "Interesting. Just got Michaela's full autopsy results. Also interesting."

◆

We met at nine p.m., at a pizza joint on Colorado Boulevard in the heart of Pasadena's Old Town. Hipsters and young business types feasted on thin crust and pitchers of beer.

Milo had been scoping out BNB buildings in the eastern suburbs for evidence of Peaty's unofficial storage, asked if I could meet him. When I left the house at eight fifteen, the phone rang but I ignored it.

When I arrived, he was at a front booth, apart from the action, working on an eighteen-inch disk crusted with unidentifiable foodstuffs, his own pitcher half full and frosted. He'd doodled a happy face on the glass. The features had melted to something morose and psychiatrically promising.

Before I could sit, he hoisted his battered attaché case, took out a coroner's file, and placed it across his lap. "When you're ready. Don't ruin your dinner." Munch munch.

"I ate already."

"Not very social of you." He massaged the pitcher, erased the face. "Wanna glass?"

I said, "No, thanks," but he went and got one anyway, left the file on his chair.

At the front were routine forms signed by

Deputy Coroner A.C. Yee, M.D. In the photos what had once been Michaela Brand
was a department-store manikin taken apart
in stages. See enough autopsy shots and
you learn to reduce the human body to its
components, try to forget it's ever been di-
vine. Think too much and you never sleep.

Milo returned and poured me a beer.
"She died of strangulation and all the cuts
were postmortem. What's interesting are
Numbers Six and Twelve."

Six was a close-up of the right side of the
neck. The wound was an inch or so long,
slightly puffed at the center, as if something
had been inserted in the slot and left there
long enough to create a small pouch. The
coroner had circled the lesion and written a
reference number above the ruler segment
used for scale. I paged to the summary,
found the notation.

Postmortem incision, superior border of
the sternoclavicular notch, evidence of tis-
sue-spreading and surface exploration of
the right jugular vein.

Twelve was a front view of a smooth, full-
breasted female chest. Michaela's implants
spread as if deflated.

Dr. Yee had pointed to the spots where

they'd been stitched up and noted, "Good healing." In the smooth plain between the mounds were five small wounds. No pouching. Yee's measurements made them shallow, a couple were barely beneath the skin.

I returned to the description of the neck lesion. " 'Surface exploration.' Playing around with the vein?"

"Maybe a special type of play," said Milo. "Yee wouldn't put it in writing but he said the cut reminded him of what an embalmer might do at the start of a body prep. The location was exactly what you'd choose if you wanted to expose the jugular and the carotid artery for drainage. After that, you spread the wound to expose the vessels and insert cannulas in both of 'em. Blood drains out of the vein while preservative's pumped into the artery."

"But that didn't happen here," I said.

"No, only a scratch on the vein."

"A would-be embalmer who lost his nerve?"

"Or changed his mind. Or lacked the equipment and knowledge to follow through. Yee said there was an 'immature' quality to the murder. The neck stuff and the chest lacerations he called dinky and ambivalent. He wouldn't put that in writing, either. Said it was for a shrink to decide."

He extended a palm.

I said, "Better find yourself a decisive shrink."

"Fear of commitment?"

"So I've been told."

He laughed and drank and ate. "Anyway, that's the extent of the weird stuff. There was no sexual penetration or fooling with the genitalia or overt sadism. Not much blood loss either, most of it settled, and the lividity showed the body was on its back for a while."

"Manual strangulation," I said. "Look in her eyes and choke the life out of her. It takes time. Maybe it's enough to get you off."

"Watching," he said. "Peaty's thing. With him and Billy being a couple of arrested-development losers—immature—I can see them fooling with a body but being afraid to dig too deep. Now you're telling me ol' Billy's got a temper."

"He does."

"But?"

"But what?"

"You're not convinced."

"I don't see Billy and Peaty being clever enough. More important, I don't see Billy setting up Peaty with that call."

"Maybe he's not as stupid as he comes across. The real actor in the family."

"Brad can obviously be fooled," I said, "but he and Billy lived together so I doubt to that extent. Learn anything new about the stolen cell phone?"

He flipped the attaché case open, got his notepad. "Motorola V551, Cingular wireless account, registered to Ms. Angeline Wasserman, Bundy Drive, Brentwood. Interior designer, married to an investment banker. The phone was in her purse when it got stolen the day of the call—nine hours before. Ms. Wasserman was shopping, got distracted, turned her head, and poof. Her big concern was the whole identity theft thing. The purse, too—four-figure Badgley-something number."

"Badgley Mischka."

"Your brand?"

"I've known a few women."

"Ha! Wanna guess where she was shopping?"

"Camarillo outlets," I said.

"The Barneys outlet, specifically. Tomorrow, when it opens at ten, I'll be there showing around pictures of Peaty and Billy, the Gaidelases, Nora and Meserve, Judge Crater, Amelia Earhart, anyone else you wanna suggest."

"Nora and Meserve may be cavorting as we speak." I told him about the travel brochures, my calls to the private jet outfits.

"Another subpoena called for, if I had grounds," he said. "The paper for Ms. Wasserman's cell came in fast because it'd been reported stolen but I'm still waiting on the phone booth trace. Hopefully I'll have it in hand tonight."

"Night owl judge?"

His smile was weary. "I've known a few jurists."

I said, "Meserve's hoax conviction won't help with the passenger logs?"

"Misdemeanor offense pled down to community service? Not hardly. You're liking him and Nora better now? Nor more Andy and Cathy as psychos?"

"Their leaving town puts them in my radar."

"Nora and Mr. Snow Globe. He hid his own car in Brad's treasured space, just like

Brad assumed, left the globe there for a screw-you."

"If he and Nora targeted Peaty, they could've learned about Peaty's unregistered van. Left the second globe as a misdirection."

"Rape kit too?"

"Why not?" I said. "Or it *was* Peaty's. Everyone at the PlayHouse seems to have known about Peaty's staring and Brad knew about Peaty's arrest record, so it's not a big stretch to assume Nora could've found out. If Nora and Dylan wanted a scapegoat, they had a perfect candidate."

"Years of picking off the weak ones and then they just decide to leave for the tropics?"

"Been there, done it. Time to explore new vistas," I suggested.

"Brad told you that Nora would have to come to him for serious dough."

"Brad's been wrong about lots of things."

He took the coroner's file back, leafed through it absently.

I said, "Dylan had Michaela bind him tight around the neck. He pretended to be dead so effectively it scared the hell out of her.

She also said pain didn't seem to be an issue for him."

"The old psychopath numbness," he said.

A young, black, cornrowed waitress came over and asked if we were okay.

Milo said, "Please wrap this to go, and I'll try that brownie sundae."

Closing the file. The waitress caught the *Coroner* label.

"You guys in TV?" she said. "*C.S.I.* or something like that?"

"Something like that," said Milo.

Deft fingering of cornrows. Eyelid flutter. "I'm an actor." Big smile. "Shock of shocks."

"Really?" said Milo.

"*Extremely* really. I've done a ton of regional theater in Santa Cruz and San Diego—including the Old Globe, where I was a main fairy in *Midsummer.* I've also done improv at the Groundlings and a nonunion commercial in San Francisco, but you'll never see that. It was for Amtrak and they never ran it."

She pouted.

I said, "It happens."

"It sure does. But, hey, it's all good. I've only been in L.A. for a few months and an agent at Starlight is just about ready to sign me."

"Good for you."

"D'Mitra," she said, extending her hand.

"Alex. This is Milo. He's the boss."

Milo glared at me, smiled at her. She sidled closer to him. "That's a great name, Milo. Pleased to meet you. Can I leave you my name and number?"

Milo said, "Sure."

"Cool. Thanks." Leaning in, she rested a breast on his shoulder and scrawled on her order book. "I'll bring your brownie sundae right now. Totally on the house."

CHAPTER

32

We set out for the outlets at nine a.m.

Taking the Seville because "you've got leather seats."

Beautiful day, sixty-five, sunny—if you had nothing on your mind you could pretend California was Eden.

Milo said, "Let's do the scenic route."

That meant Sunset to the coast highway and north through Malibu. When I approached Kanan Dume Road, I lifted my foot from the gas pedal.

"Keep going." Slouching, but his eyes had fixed on the odometer. Imagining the trip from a killer's perspective.

At Mulholland Highway we crossed over the Ventura County line. Sped past the beach house I'd rented with Robin years ago. The 8:15 call I'd walked out on last night had been from her. No message other than to phone. I'd tried. Not home.

The road compressed to two lanes and continued through miles of cliff-bordered state parkland and oceanfront campgrounds. At Sycamore Creek, the hills were pillowed by wet-year vegetation. Lupine and poppies and cactus played on the land-side. To the west was crashing Pacific and milkshake breakers. I spotted dolphins leaping twenty yards offshore.

"Glorious."

Milo said, "All that green stuff, when the fires take hold it's a barbecue. Remember a few years ago when this was charcoal?"

"Good morning to you, too."

An eastward turn on Las Posas Road took us through miles of vegetable fields. Green leafy rows in some of the acreage, the rest was brown and flat and dormant. U-pick sheds and produce stands were shuttered for the off season. Combines and other metal monsters perched out past the furrows, awaiting the signal to chew and churn and inseminate. At Camarillo's western edge, a southerly cruise on Factory Stores Drive led us to a peach-pink village of commerce.

A hundred twenty stores divided into north and south sections. Barneys New York occupied the western tip of the southern wing, a compact, well-lit space, attractively laid out, staffed well, nearly empty.

We'd walked three steps when a spike-haired young man in all black came up to us. "Can I help you?" He had sunken cheeks and mascaraed eyes, wore a cologne full of citrus. The platinum soul patch under his lip right-angled with each syllable, like a tiny diving board.

Milo said, "You carry Stefano Ricci ties? The five-hundred-buck deals with the real gold thread?"

"No, sir, I'm afraid we—"

"Just kidding, friend." Fingering the skinny, wrinkled polyester thing that hung down his paunch.

The young man was still working on a smile when Milo flashed the badge. Off to one side a pair of Persian saleswomen looked us over and spoke in low tones.

"Police?"

"We're here about a theft that occurred four days ago. A customer got her purse stolen."

"Sure. Ms. Wasserman."

"She's a regular?"

"Every month like clockwork. I find her purse for her all the time. This time I guess it really did get stolen."

"Absentminded lady?"

"I'll say," said the young man. "They're beautiful pieces, you'd think she'd . . . I don't want to gossip, she's a nice lady. This time it was a snakeskin Badge-Mish. She's got Missoni and Cavallo, vintage Judith Leiber day bags, Hermès, Chanel."

"You'd think," said Milo.

"I'm not putting her down, she's a really nice person. Perfect size zero and she tries to tip the staff even though it's not allowed. Did you find it?"

"Not yet. Those other times, where did she leave them, Mr. . . . ."

"Topher Lembell. I'm a designer so I'm always noticing details. The Badge was sweet. Anaconda, this you-better-notice-me pattern, the dye job was so good you could almost think a snake could really be mauve—"

"Where's Ms. Wasserman tend to leave her purses?"

"The dressing room. That's where I always find them. You know, under a pile of clothes? This time she claimed she last saw it over there." Pointing to a display counter in the middle of the store. Shiny things arrayed neatly under glass. Nearby was a display of last season's men's linen suits in earth tones, canvas shoes, straw hats, fifty-dollar T-shirts.

Milo said, "You doubt that."

"I guess she'd know," said Topher Lembell. "Though if she left it out in the open, you'd think someone would've noticed, what with it being so gorgeous. And everyone knowing about Ms. Wasserman's forgetfulness."

"Maybe someone did," said Milo.

"I meant *us,* Officer. We had a full staff that day because it was real busy, lots of stock came in, including stuff that didn't move at the warehouse sale and was deep-deep-discounted. The company advertised, plus preferred customers get e-mails."

"Like Ms. Wasserman."

"She's definitely preferred."

"A busy day could make it harder to notice things," said Milo.

"You'd think so but on super-heavy days we're super-*careful.* So, actually, theft rates go down. It's the medium days that are worse, enough people so we're outnumbered, you turn your back and someone's boosted something."

"Still, Ms. Wasserman's purse did get stolen."

Topher Lembell pouted. "No one's perfect. My bet's still on the dressing room. She was in and out all morning, trying on stuff, tossing it on the floor. When she's in that mode she can create a real mess— don't tell her I said that, okay? I'm one of her favorites. It's like she uses me for a personal shopper."

"Sealed lips," said Milo. "Now would you do me a favor and look at these photos and tell me if any of these people were in the store that day?"

"Suspects?" said Topher Lembell. "This is cool. Can I tell my friends about being part of an investigation or is it a big top-secret deal?"

"Tell anyone you want. Is everyone here who was working that day?"

"We had five more people, including one of *their* friends from the Valley." Eyeing the Persian women. "The others were Larissa, Christy, Andy, and Mo. They all go to college, come in weekends and on heavy days. Larissa and Christy are due in to pick up their check, I could call and see if they can come earlier. And maybe I can get Mo and Andy on the phone, they're roomies."

"Thanks for the help," said Milo.

"Sure, let's see those suspects. Like I said, I've got a great eye for detail."

As Milo produced the photos, Topher Lembell studied the wrinkled necktie and the wash-and-wear shirt beneath it. "By the way, we've still got some good deals on last season's goods. Lots of loose, comfy stuff."

Milo smiled and showed him DMV headshots of Nora Dowd and Dylan Meserve.

"He's younger and cuter than her."

The snaps of Cathy and Andy Gaidelas evoked, "Sorry, no. These two look kind of Wisconsin—I grew up in Kenosha. Are they really criminals?"

"How about this one?"

Lembell studied Reynold Peaty's arrest shot and stuck out his tongue. "Ugh. The moment *he* stepped inside, we'd be on the lookout. Uh-uh."

Milo said, "On a busy day, despite the extra staff, couldn't someone blend in with the crowd?"

"If it was me in charge, never. My eyes are like lasers. On the other hand, *some* people . . ." Another glance at the saleswomen, now idling silently near a rack of designer dresses.

One of them caught Milo's eye and waved tentatively.

He said, "Let's see what your colleagues have to say. And if you could make those calls to the temps right now, I'd appreciate it."

"I'm on it," said Topher Lembell, following along as we crossed the room. "By the way, I do custom couture. Men's suits, jackets, pants, made to precise measure, all I charge is five percent over the cost of fabric, and I've got surplus rolls from Dormeuil and Holland & Sherry, some really cool Super 100's. If you're a wee bit hard to fit—"

"I'm harder after a big meal," said Milo.

"No prob, I can create an expandable waistband with tons of stretch."

"Hmm," said Milo. "Let me think about it . . . hello, ladies."

Forty minutes later, we were parked near the food court at the northern edge of the complex drinking iced tea from twenty-ounce cups.

Milo removed his straw, bent it into segments, created a plastic tapeworm, pulled it tight.

His mood was low. No I.D.s on any of the photos by the staff, including the histrionic Larissa and Christy who arrived giggling and continued to view the process as hilarious. Roommates Andy and Mo were interviewed by phone in Goleta. Same for Fahriza Nourmand of Westlake Village. No one recalled anyone lurking near Angeline Wasserman's person or purse.

No suspicious characters that day, though someone had boosted a package of men's briefs.

Topher Lembell gave up Angeline Wasserman's phone number, scrawling on the back of his own baby-blue business card.

"Call me any time for a fitting but don't tell anyone here about it. Technically, I'm not allowed to do my own thing on company time but I don't think God really cares, do you?"

Now, Milo copied Wasserman's number into his pad, crumpled the card, and tossed it in my ashtray.

I said, "No interest in custom couture?"

"For that I call Omar the Tentmaker."

"How about Stefano Ricci? Five hundred bucks for a tie's a bargain."

"Rick," he said. "His cravats cost more than my suits. When I'm feeling vindictive, I use it against him."

He played with the straw, tried to rip the plastic, failed, and jammed it back through the lid of his drink. "Just before I came to your place, I got an I.D. on the phone booth used for the whispering crap. Let's have a look, it ain't exactly a trek."

Gas station at Las Posas and Ventura, a five-minute drive.

Trucks and cars lined up at the pumps, hungry motorists streamed in and out of an adjacent Stop & Shop. The booth was off to the side, near the bathrooms. No police tape or indication anyone had dusted for prints.

I remarked on that and he said, "Ventura

PD came by at six a.m., lifted a whole bunch of latents. Even with AFIS it'll be a while before that's untangled."

We went into the food store where he showed the photos to the clerks. Head shakes, apathy. Back outside, he said, "Any ideas?"

"Whoever stole the purse was careful enough to use the cell for the hang-ups then switch to the pay phone for the whispering. Or, we're talking two people working as a team. Either way, the caller stuck around in Camarillo, so how about checking over there?" I pointed across Ventura to a mass of other eateries.

"Sure, why not."

We made it through six restaurants before he said, "Enough. Maybe the absent-minded Ms. Wasserman will recognize someone."

"You didn't show any shots of Billy Dowd."

"Couldn't come up with any," he said. "Didn't figure it mattered 'cause I don't see Billy making his way out here by himself."

"Even if he managed to, the Barneys staff would've noticed him."

"Not cool enough. Just like junior high."

"Why'd you bother showing Peaty's picture? He didn't call Vasquez and tag himself as dangerous."

"I wanted to see if he's ever been out here. Looks like none of our parties of interest have been."

"Not necessarily," I said. "Angeline Wasserman is here every month, 'like clockwork.' The staff knew her as absentminded so maybe someone else did. Someone stylish enough to blend in, like Dylan Meserve."

"No one recognized his picture, Alex."

"Maybe he knows something about special effects."

"He shops in disguise?"

"A performance," I said. "That could be the whole point."

I took the 101 back to the city, making good time as Milo called in for messages. He had to introduce himself three times to whoever answered at the West L.A. station, hung up cursing.

"New receptionist?"

"Idiot nephew of a city councilman, still doesn't know who I am. For the last three days I've gotten no messages, which is fine, except when I'm actually trying to solve a case. Turns out all my slips ended up in someone else's box—a D named Sterling who's out on vacation. Luckily it was all junk."

He punched Angeline Wasserman's number. Barely had time to recite his name before he was listening nonstop. Finally, he broke through and set up an appointment to meet in an hour.

"Design Center, she's at a rug place, doing a 'high-level multi-level Wilshire Corridor condo.' The day she got ripped off she thinks some guy was checking her out in the outlet parking lot."

"Who?"

"All I got was a guy in an SUV, she said she'd work on her recollection. Wanna hypnotize her?" He laughed. "She sounded excited."

"Just like Topher the designer. You didn't know you were in a glam profession."

He showed his teeth to the rearview mirror, scraped an incisor. "Ready for my close-up, Mr. DeMille. Time to scare small children and household pets."

Manoosian Oriental Carpets was a cavernous space on the ground floor of the Design Center's Blue Building, crammed with hundreds of hand-loomed treasures and smelling of dust and brown paper.

Angeline Wasserman stood in the center of the gallery's main room, red-haired, cheerfully anorexic, facially tucked so many times her eyes had migrated, fishlike, toward the sides of her head. Lime-green shantung pants fit her stick legs like Saran around chicken bones. Her orange cashmere jacket would've flared if she had hips. Bouncing like a Slinky toy among hemp-bound rolls of rugs, she smiled orders at two young Hispanic guys unfurling a waist-high stack of 20 x 20 Sarouks.

As we approached her, she sang out, "I'll do it!" and launched herself at the rugs. Tossing back dense flaps of woven wool, she passed instantaneous judgment on each. "No. No. *Definitely* no. Maybe. No. No. No on that one, too—we've got to do better, Darius."

The stocky, bearded fellow she addressed said, "How about some Kashans, Ms. W?"

"If they're better than these."

Darius waved to the young guys and they left.

Angeline Wasserman noticed us, inspected a few more piles, finished, and patted her hair and said, "Hello, police people."

Milo thanked her for cooperating, showed her the photos.

Her index finger tapped. "No. No. No. No. No. So, tell me, how come LAPD's involved when it happened in Ventura?"

"It might be related to an L.A. crime, ma'am."

Wasserman's piscine eyes glowed. "Some sort of big-time crime ring? Figures."

"Why's that?"

"Someone who recognizes a Badgley Mischka is clearly a pro." She waved away the photos. "Think you'll ever find my little beauty?"

"Hard to say."

"In other words, no. Okay, that's life, it was a year old, anyway. But should a miracle come down from above, the one thing I ask is that you only return it if it's in perfect shape. If it's not, just donate it to some police charity and let me know so I can write it off. Here today, gone tomorrow, right, Lieutenant?"

"Good attitude, ma'am."

"My husband thinks I'm pathologically insouciant, but guess who looks forward to getting up in the morning and who doesn't? Anyway, there wasn't much cash in there, maybe eight, nine hundred dollars and I put a stop on the magic plastic."

"Had anyone tried to use the cards?"

"Thank God, no. My AmEx Black's limitless. The phone's no big deal, either, it was time for an upgrade. Now, let me tell you about that guy who was checking me out. He was already there when I pulled into the lot, so he wasn't stalking me or anything like that. What probably happened is he was casing the lot for a pigeon—that's the right term, isn't it?—and he saw me as a perfect little dove."

"Because of the purse."

"The purse, my clothes, my demeanor." Bony hands traversed bony flanks. "I was dolled out, guys. Even when hunting *le grande bargainne,* I refuse to dress down."

"How was this person checking you out?" said Milo.

"Looking at me. Right through his car window."

"His window was rolled up?"

"All the way. And it was tinted, so I couldn't get a good look. But I'm sure he had his eye on me." Curled lashes danced. "I'm not flattering myself, Lieutenant. Believe me, he was looking."

"What do you remember about him?"

"Caucasian. I couldn't make out details but the way he was turned I had a full view of his face." A red-nailed finger touched a collagen lip. "By Caucasian, I mean light skinned. I suppose he could've been a pale Latino or some kind of Asian. Not black, that I can tell you for sure."

"He stayed in the car the whole time?"

"And continued to watch me. I just *know* he was following me with his eyes."

"Was the engine idling?"

"Hmm . . . no, I don't think so . . . no, definitely not."

"Everything you saw was through the glass."

"Yes, but it wasn't just what I saw, it was what I *felt.* You know, that itchy tingle you get on the back of your neck when someone's watching you?"

"Sure," said Milo.

"I'm glad *you* understand because my husband doesn't. He's convinced I'm flattering myself."

"Husbands," said Milo, grinning.

Wasserman's return smile tested the outer limits of her skeletal face.

"Could there have been more than one person in the car, Ms. Wasserman?"

"I suppose so, but the *feeling* I got was one person."

"The feeling."

"There was just a . . . solitary flavor to him." She touched a concave abdomen. "I trust *this.*"

"Is there anything else you can say about him?"

"At first, I just figured it for *guy* behavior— checking out the goods. After the Badge got stolen was when I started thinking he could've been up to no good. Was the phone used?"

"Yes, ma'am."

"Where'd they call? Outer Mongolia or some crazy place?"

"L.A."

"Well," said Angeline Wasserman, "that shows a lack of creativity. Maybe I was wrong."

"About what?"

"Him being some high-level crime guy and not just a crook."

"High level because he knew what a Badge was," said Milo.

"The whole image—being at Barneys, driving a Rover."

"A Range Rover?"

"A real pretty one, shiny and new-y."

"What color?"

"Silver, mine's anthracite. That's why it didn't bother me at first, his looking at me. Both of us with Rovers, parked near each other? Kind of a twinsie karma, you know?"

CHAPTER
33

A new stack of rugs arrived. Angeline Wasserman inspected a fringe. "These knots are tangled."

Milo muttered, "Story of my life."

If she heard him, she didn't indicate. "Darius, are these the *best* you've got?"

Driving to Butler Avenue, I said, "AmEx Black, never used."

"I know, same as with the Gaidelases. But do you see them tooling around in a Range Rover that just happens to match Nora Dowd's?"

No need to answer.

When we arrived at the station, Milo demanded his messages from the new receptionist, a terrified bald man in his forties named Tom, who said, "There's nothing new, Lieutenant, I promise."

I followed Milo's chuffy climb up the stairs. When we reached his office, he unpacked his attaché, placed the autopsy file next to his computer, and requested a BOLO on the Range Rover, all before sitting down.

"How about this, Alex: Nora and Meserve have an 805 love nest and those brochures were a diversion. I'm thinking something on the beach because what's a rich girl without a beach house? Could be right there in Camarillo, or farther north—Oxnard Harbor, Ventura, Carpinteria, Mussel Shoals, Santa Barbara, or points beyond."

I said, "Could be points south, too. Maybe Meserve didn't know Latigo because *he'd* hiked there."

"Nora's a Malibu gal," he said. "Has a rural hideaway tucked in the mountains."

"Something registered to her individually, not part of the BNB partnership."

"Easy enough to find out what she pays property tax on." He flipped the computer on. The screen flashed blue, then black, sparked a couple of times, and died. Several attempts to reboot were greeted by silence.

He said, "Expelling profanities is a waste of oxygen. Let me borrow someone else's terminal."

I used the time to leave another message for Robin. Read through Michaela's autopsy findings again.

Playing with veins and arteries.

The PlayHouse.

Nora tiring of theatrical abstractions. Meeting Dylan Meserve and discovering common interests.

Embalming. Nora's taste in pets.

Milo returned.

"Good news?" I said.

"If failure's your idea of success. The circuit that feeds all the computers is down, tech support was summoned hours ago. I'm going downtown to the assessor's office to do it the old-fashioned way. If tax leeches communicate with their buds in other counties maybe I can get hooked up with Ventura and Santa Barbara. If not, I'm on the road again."

Humming the Willie Nelson song.

"You're taking this well."

"All part of my audition," he said.

"For what?"

"Mentally stable individual." Grabbing his jacket, he opened the door and held it for me.

I said, "Taxidermy."

"What?"

"The coroner's guess about embalming. Think Nora's fluffy dog."

He sat back down. "Some horrific arts and *crafts* thing?"

"I was thinking stage prop."

"For what?"

"Grand Guignol."

He shut his eyes, knuckled a temple. "Your mind . . ." The eyes opened. "If Dowd and Meserve have an evil hobby, why wasn't Michaela actually messed with?"

"She was rejected," I said. "Same for Tori Giacomo. Or not. Scattered bones make it impossible to know."

"Why?"

I shook my head. "That level of pathology, the symbolism can be beyond anyone else's comprehension."

"Two pretty girls wrong for the part," he said. "The Gaidelases, on the other hand, have never been found. Meaning maybe their heads are hanging on a damn wall?"

Another temple massage. "Okay, now that the images are firmly planted in my brain and I'm sure to have a lovely day, let's get the hell out of here."

I followed him up the hall. When we reached the stairwell, he said, "Snuff and stuff. I can always count on you to cheer me up."

On our way out, Tom the receptionist sang out, "Have a nice day, Lieutenant."

Milo's reply was sotto voce and obscene. He left me standing on the sidewalk and continued to the staff parking lot.

Seeing his irritation at the lost messages brought to mind the disgusted look on Albert Beamish's face yesterday.

Constitutional crankiness? Or had the old man, ever eager to spread dirt on the Dowds, poked around and actually learned something useful? Tried to tattle and got no callback?

No sense overloading Milo's circuits. I drove to Hancock Park.

◆

Beamish's doorbell was answered by a tiny Indonesian maid in a black uniform clutching a dust-clogged feather duster.

"Mr. Beamish, please."

"No home."

"Any idea when he'll be back?"

"No home."

Walking over to Nora's house, I took a close look at the barn doors of her garage. Bolted. I nudged the panels, felt some give, but my bare hands were unable to spread the doors wide enough. Milo had left it at that. I wasn't bound by the rules of evidence.

Fetching a crowbar from the trunk of the Seville, I carried it parallel to my leg, went back, and managed to pry the doors an inch apart.

A stale gasoline smell blew out. No Range Rover or any other vehicle. At least Milo could be spared the bother of a warrant.

My cell phone beeped. "Dr. Delaware? It's Karen from your exchange. I've got a message from Dr. Gwynn that was marked priority. He asked if you can come by his office soon as you have a chance."

"Dr. Gwynn's a she," I said.

"Oh . . . sorry. Louise wrote this one down, I'm new. Do you usually specify gender?"

"Don't worry about it. When was the call?"

"Twenty minutes ago, just before I came on."

"Did Dr. Gwynn give a reason for wanting me over?"

"It just says asap, Doctor. Want the number?"

"I know it."

For Allison to reach out, it had to be something bad. Her grandmother. Another stroke? Worst-case scenario?

Even so, why call me?

Maybe because she had no one else.

Her message tape picked up. I drove to Santa Monica.

Empty waiting room. The red light next to her name was unlit, meaning no session in progress. I pushed open the door to the inner offices, proceeded through a short hall to Allison's corner suite. Knocked on her door and didn't wait for an answer.

She wasn't at her desk. Or in one of the soft white patient chairs.

When I said, "Allison?" no one answered.

This felt wrong.

Before I could process that thoroughly, the back of my head exploded in pain.

Hammer-on-melon pain.

Cartoonists are right; you really do see stars.

I reeled, got smashed again. Back of the neck this time.

I sank to my knees, wobbled on Allison's soft carpet, fought for consciousness.

A *new* pain burned my right flank. Sharp, electric. Was I being cut?

Heavy breathing behind me, someone straining with effort, blur of dark trouser leg.

The second kick to my ribs took all the fight out of me and I went down on my face.

Hard leather continued to have its way with bone. My brain rang like a gong. I tried to ward off further blows but my arms were numb.

For some reason, I counted.

Three kicks, four, five, six for good meas—

CHAPTER
34

Gray soupy world, viewed from the bottom of a stockpot.

I drowned in my chair, blinked, trying to clear eyes that wouldn't open. Someone played a trombone solo. My eyelids finally cooperated. The ceiling swooped down, changed its mind, soared miles above, a white plaster sky.

Blue sky. No, the blue was off to the left.

A smudge of black on top.

Pale blue, same exact color as the burned cork smell in my throat.

The black, Allison's hair.

The pale blue, one of her suits. Memories

flooded my head. Fitted jacket, skirt short enough to show a nice bit of knee. Braiding around the lapels, covered buttons.

Lots of buttons; it could take a long, sweet time to free them.

The pain in my skull took over. My back and my right side—

Someone moved. Above Allison. To the right.

"Can't you see he needs help—"

"Shut up!"

My eyelids sank. I blinked some more. Turned it into an aerobic activity and finally achieved some focus.

There she was. In one of the soft white chairs where she hadn't been before . . . how long ago?

I tried to look at my watch. The face was a silver disk.

My vision cleared a bit. I'd been right: She was wearing the exact suit I'd pictured, give the boy an A for . . .

Movement from the right.

Standing over her was Dr. Patrick Hauser. One of his hands had vanished in her hair. The other held a knife pressed to her smooth white throat.

Red handle. Swiss Army knife, one of the

larger versions. For some reason, I found that ludicrously amateurish.

Hauser's clothes clinched it. White golf shirt, baggy brown pants, brown wingtips.

Hard-toed wingtips, way too dressy for the outfit. White was the wrong color if you wanted to avoid those stubborn blood-stains.

Hauser's shirt was sweat-splotched but free of red. Beginner's luck. No sense rubbing it in. I smiled at him.

"Something funny?"

I had *so* many snappy comebacks. Forgot all of them. Gong. Gong.

Allison's eyes shifted to the right. Past Hauser, toward her desk?

Nothing else there but a wall and a closet.

Closet blocked by the door when you opened it.

Deep blue irises moved again. Definitely the desk. The far end, where her purse sat.

Hauser said, "Sit up and get that pen."

I was already sitting. Silly man.

I spread my arms to show him, hit an arm of the wooden desk chair.

Not sitting at all. Slumped, nearly prone, head tilted back, spine in an odd position.

Maybe that's why everything hurt so bad. I tried to straighten, nearly passed out.

"C'mon, up, up, up," barked Hauser.

Every inch of movement heated the toaster coils that had replaced my spinal nerves. It took years to reach a sitting position and the ordeal robbed me of breath. Inhaling was hellish, breathing out, worse.

A few more centuries and my eyes got clearer. I gained a sense of context: Allison and Hauser fifteen feet away. My chair pushed up to Allison's desk. The side where a new patient might sit, seeking consultation.

Therapy charts and Allison's desktop doodads on the pale oak surface. She'd been doing paperwork when he'd—

Hauser said, "Get the pen and start writing."

What pen? Ah, there it was, hiding among the noise and the color. Next to a clean, white sheet of paper.

Some comical guy's voice said, *"Wri-whuh?"*

I cleared my throat. Licked my lips. The rephrase came out: *"Writ . . . tuh whuh?"*

Hauser said, "Cut the theatrics, you're fine."

Allison moved her left shoe. Mouthed something that looked like "Sorry." She winced as the knife blade pressed into her skin. Hauser didn't seem to be aware of his own movement or her reaction.

"Write, you sonofabitch."

"Sure," I said. "Bun cun you crew—cue me in?"

"You're going to retract everything you told that bitch lawyer, label the other bitches for the malingering bitches they are, sign and date."

"Ah theh?"

"Then what?"

"Whah happahs aftah I chew thah?"

"Then we'll see, you unethical asshole."

"Alethical."

"Once you're exposed," said Hauser, "life will be cream and sugar."

"For who?"

His glasses slid down his nose and he flicked his head to right them. The movement distanced the blade from Allison's neck.

Then it was back.

A low sound fluttered his lips. "Shut up and write or I'll cut her and set it up like you did it."

"You're serious."

"Do I look as if I'm kidding?" His eyes watered. His lower lip vibrated. "I was doing just fine until everyone started lying. All my life I've done for others. Now it's time to take care of number one."

I managed to pick up the pen, nearly dropped it. Heavy little sucker—were they making them of lead nowadays? Wasn't lead bad for kids? No, that was pencils. No, that was graphite . . .

I flexed my right arm and its mate. No more numbness. The pain hadn't abated but I was starting to feel human.

I said, "For this to be cruda—credulab—cred-i-ble shouldn't it be notary publicked?"

Hauser licked his lips. His glasses had slid down again but he didn't try to adjust them. "Stop faking. I didn't hit you that hard."

"Thanks," I said. "But the question is still . . . revelant . . ."

"You write, I'll worry about what's relevant."

The pen had stopped trying to escape my hand, settled awkwardly between ring finger and pinky. I managed to roll it into writing position.

Allison watched me.

I was scaring her.

A pen made of lead; what would the EPA think of that?

I said, "So I write. Now. How?"

Hauser said, "What do you mean, how?"

"What words do I tell?"

"Start by acknowledging that you're a pathological liar unfit to practice."

"Should I use first person?"

"Isn't that what I just said?" Hauser's jowls shook with rage. His arm did, too, and once more the knife danced away from Allison's skin.

Not a good multitasker.

His right hand dug in and twisted Allison's hair. She gasped, closed her eyes, and bit her lip.

I said, "Please stop hurting her."

"I'm not hurting her—"

"You're pulling her hair," I said.

Hauser looked down at his hand. Stopped twisting. "This isn't about her."

"My point."

"You don't have a point," he said. "You owe me. If I wanted to hurt you, I could've used a club or something. All I did was sucker punch you with my bare hand. Same way you did me. I hurt my knuckles doing it. I'm not a violent person, all I want is justice."

"Kicked me in the ribs, " I said, sounding like a petulant child.

"When you punched me at that restaurant, you escalated the level of violence. All I wanted to do was talk rationally. Blame yourself."

"You scared me at the restaurant," I said.

That brought a smile to his lips. "Are you scared now?"

"Yeah."

"Then harness the fear—sublimate. Start writing and we can all go home."

I knew he was lying but I believed him. Tried another smile.

He stared past me.

Allison glanced at her purse. Blinked several times.

I said, "How 'bout I start like this: My name is Alex Demlaware, I'm a crinical psychologist licensed by the state of California, my license number is 45 . . ."

Droning on. Hauser followed with choppy movements of his head. Warming to the recitation because it was everything he wanted to hear.

"Fine. Write."

I leaned over the desk, shielding his view of my right hand with my left arm. Lowering the nib of the pen to just above the paper, I made writing motions.

"Oops," I said. "Out of ink."

"Bullshit, don't try—"

I held up the pen. "Tell me what you want me to do."

Hauser thought. The knife drifted. "Get another one out of the drawer. Don't agitate me."

I struggled to my feet, holding the chair for support. "Should I lean over the desk or go around?"

"Go around. That way." Pointing to the right.

Circling toward the front of the desk, I grazed Allison's purse with my sleeve. Opened the drawer, took out several pens, rested for breath. No act; my ribs felt like bonemeal.

On the return trip, I touched the purse again, hazarded a look.

Unzipped. Allison's bad habit. I'd given up lecturing to her about it.

I pretended to bang my knee against the

desk corner. Cried out in pain and dropped the pens.

"Idiot!"

"My balance is off. I think you knocked something loose."

"Bullshit, I didn't hit you that hard."

"I passed out. Maybe I've got a concussion."

"Your head was stationary and if you had a rudimentary knowledge of neuropsych you'd know that severe concussions result most often from two objects in motion colliding."

I looked at the carpet.

"Pick them up!"

I bent, collected the pens. Straightened and made my way back as Hauser watched.

The knife had shifted a few inches from Allison's throat but his right hand kept a firm hold on her hair.

I met her eyes. Edged to the right, farther from Hauser. That relaxed him.

Allison blinked.

I said, "One thing . . ."

Before Hauser could answer, Allison struck out at his knife arm, twisted away, and slid out of his grasp.

He shouted. She ran toward the door. He

went after her. I had the purse, groped with tingling fingers, found it.

Allison's shiny little automatic, perfect for her small hand, too small for mine. She'd oiled it recently and maybe some of the lubricant had made its way to the grip. Or my motor skills were shot and that's why my shaking arms bobbled the weapon.

I caught it, used both hands to steady my aim.

Hauser was a foot behind Allison, flushed and huffing, knife held high. He made a grab for her, caught another handful of hair, yanked her head back, chopped down.

I shot him in the back of the knee.

He didn't fall immediately so I blew out the other knee.

For good measure.

CHAPTER
35

I'd spent ten years working in a hospital. Some smells never change.

Robin and Allison sat across from my bed.

Next to each other. Like friends.

Robin in black, Allison still in the baby-blue suit.

I remembered pokes and probes and other indignities but not being transported here.

The CAT scan and X-rays had been boring, the MRI a bit of claustrophobic fun. The spinal tap was no kind of fun at all.

No more pain, though. What a tough guy I was.

Robin and Allison—or maybe it was Allison and Robin—smiled.

I said, "What is this, some kind of beauty contest?"

Milo stepped into view.

I said, "I redact and retract and refract any former statement vis-à-vis aesthetic compete-tition."

Smiles all around. I was a hit.

"At the risk of utterly bonanzal banalistical cliché, where the bleep am I hospital-wise?"

"Cedars," said Milo in a slow, patient way that suggested it wasn't the first time he'd answered the question.

"Didja get to see Rick? You really should, you guys don't spend enough time together."

Pained smiles. Timing, it's all about timing. I said, "Ladies and germs."

Milo edged closer. "Rick says hi. He made sure they did all the necessary crap. No concussion or hematomas and your brain's not swollen—at least not more than it usually is. You do have some bruised disks in your cervical spine and a couple of cracked ribs. Ergo, King Tut."

"Ergo. Pogo. Logo." I touched my side, felt the stiff swaddle of bandages. "Rick didn't get to operate? No unkindest cut?"

"Not this time, pal."

He was blocking my view. I told him so and he retreated to a corner of the room.

I looked at the girls. My girls.

So serious, both of them. Maybe I hadn't said it loud enough. *"No unkindeness cutaroo?"*

Two pretty attempts at sympathy chuckles. I was *dying* up here.

"Just got in from Lost Wages," I said, "and boy, is my vertebral discography tired."

Robin said something to Allison, or maybe it was the other way around, making sense of all this was a pretzel, a pretty girl pretzel, mustard and salt, who the hell could untangle it . . .

"What?" someone who sounded like me shouted. "What's the conversational thread being woven into the warp of the contestants?"

"You need to sleep," said Allison. She looked ready to cry.

Robin, too.

Time for new material . . . "I slept just fine yesterday. *Girls!*"

"They sedated you," said Robin. "You're under sedation right now."

"Demerol," said Allison. "Later, you can take Percocet."

"Why'd they do that?" I said. "I'm no doper, I get low on life."

Robin got up and moved bedside. Allison followed, hanging slightly behind.

All that perfume. *Whoa!*

"You wearing Chanel?" I demanded of Milo. "Come on over, dude, and join the olfactory celebration."

Allison caught my eye. No purse to look for now, she was holding it. "Where were you?" I said. "When I came into the office you weren't."

"He had me in the closet."

Robin said, "Poor thing."

I said, "Her or me?"

"Both of you." Robin took Allison's hand and squeezed.

Allison looked grateful.

Everyone, so sad. Utter waste of energy, time to get dressed and have juice and coffee, maybe an English muffin and be out of here in no time . . . where were my clothes . . . I'd get dressed in front of all of them, we were all chums.

I must've said something to that effect, maybe with a bit of vulgarity, because both of the girls—*my pretty girls*—looked shocked.

Robin inhaled and patted the hand without the I.V. Allison wanted to do the same thing, I could tell she really wanted to, maybe she even still liked me *that* way, but the I.V. stopped her.

I said, "No sweat, you can pat me, too."

She obeyed.

"Hold my hands!" I commanded. "Both of you! *Everyone* join hands."

They complied. Good pretty girls.

I told Milo, "You, on the other hand, can't hold anything."

He said, "Aw, shucks."

I went back to sleep.

Rick wanted me to stay in the hospital another night for observation but I said enough.

He laid on all the medical authority but nothing helps in the face of industrial-strength obstinacy. I called a taxi and checked myself out, carrying a goody bag of painkillers, anti-inflammatories, steroids, and a small-print list of dire side effects.

Robin had been by earlier. Allison had called once but hadn't shown up since the first time.

"I got to know her," said Robin. "She's lovely."

"Female bonding?" I said.

"She's nice, that's all."

"And you talked about the weather."

"Egomaniac." She stroked my hair. "I called you Wednesday because I decided to move back. Still want that?"

"Yes."

"Allison's okay with it."

"Didn't know we needed her permission."

"She adores you," said Robin. "But I *love* you."

I had no idea what that meant. Had regained enough coherence not to ask.

"I told her to feel free to come by to visit you but she wants to give us some time together. She feels horrible about what happened, Alex."

"Why?"

"Leading you to Hauser."

"He had a knife to her throat, she didn't have much choice. I'm sure Hauser asked around, found out we used to . . . hang out. Knowing *me* endangered *her. I* need to apologize."

My eyes brimmed with tears. What was *that* all about?

Robin wiped them. "It's no one's fault, Alex, the guy's obviously unbalanced."

"Now he'll be an unbalanced cripple. Wonder when the police are coming by to interview me."

"Milo's taking care of all that. He says given Hauser's previous arrest, there shouldn't be any problem."

"In a perfect world," I said.

Cool lips braised my forehead. "It'll be all right, honey. You need to rest and keep healing—"

"Allison really blames herself?"

"She feels she should've known better, given what you'd told her about Hauser."

"That's utterly ridiculous."

"I'm sure she'll be thrilled to hear that from you. In those exact words."

I laughed. The bandages around my ribs felt like sashes of ground glass.

"It hurts, honey?"

"Not a bit."

"You poor lying baby." She kissed my eyelids, then my mouth. Too damn delicate, I needed something closer to pain, reached around and pressed her head down. When she finally pulled away, she was breathless.

"More, woman!" I said. "Ugha ugha."

She snaked her hand under the bedcovers, reached down. "One of the parts seems to be in working order."

"Man of steel," I said. "You're really coming back?"

"If you want me to."

"Of course I want you to."

"Maybe after the pain goes away, you'll change your—"

I placed a finger across her lips. "When are you doing it?"

"A few days." Pause. "I'm thinking I'll keep the studio. Like you said, for work."

"And when you want to get away from me," I said.

"No, baby, I've had plenty of that."

CHAPTER
37

I walked out of the hospital trying to look like someone who worked in a hospital. The cab arrived ten minutes later. I was home by seven p.m.

The Seville was parked in front; something else Milo had taken care of.

The taxi driver had hit several potholes in West Hollywood. The city that loves decorating avoids the unglamorous stuff.

Pain on each impact had been reassuring; I could stand it.

I stashed the Percocet in my medicine cabinet, opened a fresh bottle of extra-strength Advil.

I hadn't heard from Milo since yesterday's hospital visit. Maybe that meant progress.

I reached him in his car. "Thanks for getting my wheels home."

"That wasn't me, that was Robin. Are you being a good patient?"

"I'm home."

"Rick okayed that?"

"Rick and I reached a meeting of the minds."

Silence. "Real smart move, Alex."

"If you listened to him, you'd be wearing better ties."

More silence.

"I'm fine," I said. "Thanks for handling Hauser."

"As much as I handled."

"I've got problems ahead?"

"There'll be some shit to deal with, but those in the know say you'll be okay. Meanwhile, the asshole's in the jail ward wearing yellow pajamas and looking at inkblots. What happened, he imploded?"

"He made bad decisions and projected them onto me. How badly did I wound him?"

"He won't be playing soccer any time soon. Allison's little shooter came in handy, huh?"

"Sure did," I said. "Did you find any properties Nora Dowd owns in or near 805?"

"Back in the swing," he said. "Just like that."

"On sound advice."

"Whose?"

"My own."

He laughed. "As a matter of fact, Nora's got three 805 deeds to her name. Condo in Carpinteria, couple of houses in Goleta. All of which have been leased out long term. Her tenants have never met her but they like her because she keeps the rent low."

"BNB manages the buildings?"

"No, a Santa Barbara company does. I spoke to the manager. Nora gets checks in the mail, never visits. That's it, Alex. No tryst-pad, no direct link to Camarillo, no Malibu getaway. Maybe she and Meserve made the calls and took off for that tropical vacation."

I said, "Do the brothers own anything out there?"

"Why would that matter? Billy's a mope and Brad hates Meserve. So far looking for Peaty's hidey-holes has been a big zero. Once I finish with Armando Vasquez, I'll look into private flights."

"What's to do on Vasquez?"

"Second interview. First time was last night, call from Vasquez's D.P.D. at 11 p.m., Armando wanted to talk. Faithful public servant that I am, I trudged over. The agenda was Vasquez embellishing the phone call story. Claiming the night of the murder wasn't the first time, same thing happened a week or so before, he can't remember exactly when or how many times. No hang-ups, just someone whispering that Peaty was a dangerous pervert, could hurt Vasquez's wife and kids. D.A. wants to blunt any justification defense so I've got to stick with it, meanwhile they'll be pulling a month's worth of phone records. While I was there I showed Vasquez my photo collection. He's never seen the Gaidelases, Nora, or Meserve. The thing is, I finally got a shot of Billy, and Vasquez also doesn't recognize him. But I'm sure Billy's been to the apartment with Brad. Meaning Vasquez, not being there during the day, is pretty useless. Like everything else I've come up with."

"Anything you need me to do?"

"I need you to heal up and not be a foolish mummy. One other thing that came up is Peaty's body just got claimed by a cousin from Nevada. She asked to speak to the D in charge, says she left a bunch of messages, thanks again, Idiot Tom. I'm squeezing her in tomorrow afternoon, to see if she can shed some light on Peaty's psyche, D.A.'s orders. With the defense painting him as a psycho-brute, I'm supposed to learn his good points."

"Speaking of Idiot Tom." I recounted Beamish's disgusted expression.

"Wouldn't surprise me. Maybe Beamish remembers more stolen fruit . . . what else . . . oh, yeah, I called some taxidermy supply houses. No record of Nora or Meserve buy-ing creepy accoutrements. Okay, here I am at Le Grande Lockup ready for Mr. Vasquez. Time to add a few more lies to my daily diet."

Daybreak brought the worst headache of my life, stiff limbs, a cottony mouth. A palmful of Advils and three cups of black coffee later, I was moving fine. If I kept my breathing shal-low.

I phoned Allison, thanked her message tape for its mistress's presence of mind, apologized for getting her involved in seri-ous ugliness.

I told Robin's tape I was eager to see *its* mistress.

No listing for Albert Beamish. I tried his law firm. A crisp-voiced receptionist said, "Mr. Beamish rarely comes in. I think the last time I saw him was . . . has to be months."

"Emeritus."

"Some of the partners have professor-ships so we like the term."

"Is Mr. Beamish a professor?"

"No," she said, "he never liked teaching. His thing was litigation."

I reached Beamish's Tudor at eleven a.m. The same Indonesian maid answered.

"Yes!" She beamed. "Mister home!"

Moments later the old man came shuffling out, wearing a saggy white cardigan over a brown knit shirt, pink-striped seersucker pants, and the same house slippers with wolves' heads on the toes.

His sneer was virtuoso. "The prodigal po-liceman arrives. What does it take to *motivate* you people?"

"There've been some problems with the phones," I said.

He cackled with the joy of omniscience, cleared his throat four times, hacked up something wet and swallowed it. "My tax dollars put to good use."

"What did you call about, sir?"

"You don't know?"

"That's why I'm here."

"You still haven't seen the message? Then how did you—"

"I figured it out, Mr. Beamish, from the look of contempt on your face when I drove by."

"The look of . . ." A puckered, lipless mouth curled ambiguously. "A veritable Sherlock."

"What's the message?" I said.

"When you talk you flinch, young man."

"I'm a little sore, Mr. Beamish."

"Carousing on my dollar?"

I unbuttoned my jacket, undid a couple of shirt buttons, and revealed the bandages around my middle.

"Broken ribs?"

"A few."

"Same thing happened to me when I was in the army," he said. "Not combat heroics, I was stationed in Bayonne, New Jersey, and some Irish lout from Brooklyn backed a Jeep right into me. But for the grace of a few inches, I'd have ended up childless, singing soprano, and voting Democrat."

I smiled.

"Don't do that," he said. "Got to hurt like hell."

"Then don't be funny," I said.

He smiled. A real smile, devoid of scorn. "Army doctors couldn't do a damn thing to patch me, just wrapped the ribs and told me to wait. When I mended, they shipped me off to the ETO."

"No medical progress since then."

"When did this happen to you? Not that I really care."

"Two days ago. Not that it's any of your business."

He gave a start. Glared. Plucked brown fabric from his sunken chest. Broke into arid laughter, coughed up more mucus. When the wheezing stopped, he said, "How about a drink? It's almost noon."

As I followed him through dim, dusty, high-ceilinged rooms full of Georgian antiques and Chinese porcelain, he said, "How'd the other guy fare?"

"Worse than me."

"Good."

We sat at a round table in his octagonal breakfast room, just off a kitchen whose stainless steel counters and chipped white cabinets said it hadn't been altered for half a century.

Mullion windows looked out to a shade garden. The table was seasoned mahogany, cigarette burned and water-marked, circled by four Queen Anne chairs. The wall covering was a pale green silk Asian print, crowded with peonies and bluebirds and fictitious vines, faded white in spots. A solitary framed photo hung on the wall. Black and white, also diminished by decades of ultraviolet.

When Beamish left to fetch the drinks, I took a look at the picture. A lanky, light-haired young man in an army captain's uniform stood arm and arm with a pretty young woman. Her cloche hat rested on dark curls. She wore a fitted summer suit and held a bouquet.

Big ship in the background. U.S.S. something. A fountain-penned caption in the lower right border read: *4/7/45, Long Beach: Betty and Al. Back from the war at last!*

Beamish returned with a cut-crystal decanter and a pair of matching old-fashioned glasses, lowered himself to a chair slowly, struggling to hide his own wince. Then changing his mind.

"Eventually," he said, "you don't need to be beat on to ache. Nature does it all by her cruel self." He poured us each two fingers, slid my tumbler across the table.

"Thanks for the encouragement." I held mine up.

He grunted and drank. I imagined Milo in forty years, hacking and swigging and pronouncing about the sorry state the world had gotten itself into. Old and white-haired.

The fantasy ended when I got to heterosexual and rich.

Beamish and I drank. The whiskey was a single malt, peaty, sweetish going down, with a nice after-burn that reminded you it was alcohol.

He licked the spot where his lips used to be, put his glass down. "This is the good stuff, Lord knows why I brought it out."

"Uncharacteristic burst of generosity," I said.

"You're an insolent one—none of the obsequiousness of a public servant."

"I'm not one. I'm a psychologist."

"A what—no, don't answer, I heard you fine. One of those, eh? The fat detective sent you over here to deal with an unbalanced old fossil?"

"All my idea." I gave him a short explanation of my relationship to the police. Expected the worst.

Beamish drank some more and tweaked the tip of his nose. "When Rebecca died I saw no point in living. My children insisted I see a psychiatrist and sent me to a Jewish chap in Beverly Hills. He prescribed pills I never took and referred me to a Jewish woman psychologist in his office. I rejected her out-of-hand as a high-priced babysitter but my children coerced me. Turned out, they were right. She helped me."

"I'm glad."

"Sometimes it's still difficult," he said. "Too much damned space on the bed—ah, enough mawkishness, if we sit here too much longer you'll send me a bill. Here's the message I left the fat detective: A woman came by three days ago, poking around *that* one's pile of logs."

Pointing in the general direction of Nora's house. "I went over and asked her what she was doing and she said she was looking for her cousin, Nora. I told her *Nora* hadn't been seen in a while and that the police may very well suspect *Nora* of nefarious activity. She

didn't seem at all surprised by that possibility—is it 'Doctor'?"

"Alex is fine."

"Did you cheat on your exams?" he
snapped.

"No—"

"Then you earned your *damned degree,*
so *use* it, for God's sake. One thing I *detest*
is the ersatz familiarity the beatniks ushered
in. You and I may be drinking my best single
malt, sir, but if you addressed me by my
Christian name, I'd toss you out on your
ear."

"That would be painful, under the circumstances," I said.

He worked his lips. Conceded a smile.
"What's your family name?"

"Delaware."

"Now, then, Dr. Delaware . . . where was
I . . ."

"The cousin didn't seem surprised."

"On the contrary," said Beamish. "The
possibility that *Nora* was under suspicion
seemed downright *syntonic.*" He grinned. "A
psychological term, I learned it from Dr. Ruth
Goldberg."

"A-plus," I said. "Any reason the cousin
wasn't surprised?"

"I pressed her on that but she was not forthcoming. Quite the contrary, she was eager to leave and I had to prevail upon her to leave her name and phone number."

Another slow rise from the table and a five-minute absence allowed me to finish my scotch. Beamish reappeared holding a piece of white paper folded to a two-inch square. Gnarled fingers labored at unfolding and smoothing.

Half a sheet of heavy-stock letterhead stationery.

Martin, Crutch, and Melvyn
A Legal Corporation

Olive Street address, long list of small-print names, Beamish's near the top.

At the bottom of the page, shaky hand-writing in black fountain pen, smeared around the edges.

Marcia Peaty. A 702 number.

"I looked it up, that's Las Vegas," said Beamish. "Though she didn't seem like the Vegas type."

"She's the *Dowds'* cousin?"

"So she said and it doesn't seem the kind of thing one would pretend. She wasn't particularly well-bred, but not vulgar, and nowadays that's an accomplishment—"

I refolded the paper. "Thanks."

"A little light just switched on in your eyes, Dr. Delaware. Have I been useful?"

"More than you might imagine."

"Would you care to tell me why?"

"I'd like to but I can't."

As I started to rise, Beamish poured me another finger of scotch. "That's fifteen dollars' worth. Don't sip standing up, terribly vulgar."

"Thanks, but I've had enough, sir."

"Temperance is the last refuge of cowards."

I laughed.

He pinged the rim of his glass. "It's absolutely necessary that you bolt like a panicky horse?"

"I'm afraid so, Mr. Beamish."

I waited for him to get to his feet.

He said, "Later, then? Once you've put them all away, would you let me know what I've accomplished?"

"Them?"

"That one, her brothers—nasty lot, just as

I told you the first time you and the fat detective came traipsing around."

"Persimmons," I said.

"That, of course," he said. "But you're after more than purloined fruit."

CHAPTER
38

It took six minutes for the jail deputy to return to the phone.

"Yeah, he's still here."

"Please have him call me when he gets out. It's important."

He asked me for my name and number. Again. Said, "Okay," but his tone said don't count on it.

An hour later, I tried again. A different deputy said, "Let me check—Sturgis? He's gone."

I finally reached him in his car.

He said, "Vasquez wasted my time. All of

a sudden he remembers Peaty threatened him overtly. 'I'll mess you up, dude.' "

"Sounds more like something Vasquez would say."

"Shuldiner's gonna push a chronic bullying defense. Anyway, I'm finished with it, finally able to focus on Nora and Meserve. Still no sign they took any commercial flight but Angeline Wasserman's I.D. of the Range Rover can probably get me some subpoenas for private charter lists. I'm off to file paper. How you feeling?"

"Is the woman the coroner referred to you named Marcia Peaty?"

"Yeah, why?"

"She's the Dowds' cousin, as well." I told him what I learned from Albert Beamish.

"The old man actually had something to say. So much for *my* instincts."

I said, "The Dowd sibs hire their cousin as a minimum-wage janitor and give him a former laundry room to live in. Tells you something about their character. The fact that none of them thinks to mention it says more. Have a chance to look into the brothers' private holdings?"

"Not yet, guess I'd better do it. Marcia

Peaty never told me she was their cousin as well as Peaty's."

"When are you meeting her?"

"An hour. She's staying at the Roosevelt on Hollywood. I set it up for Musso and Frank, figured I'd at least get a good meal out of it."

"Family secrets and sand dabs," I said.

"I was thinking chicken potpie."

"Sand dabs for me," I said.

"You're actually hungry?"

"Starving."

I parked in the gigantic lot behind Musso and Frank. All that land, developers had to be drooling and I imagined the roar of jackhammers. The restaurant was nearly a century old, impervious to progress and regress. So far, so good.

Milo had staked out a corner booth in the southeast corner of Musso's larger room. Twenty-foot ceilings painted a grim beige you don't see anymore, green print hunting scenes on the walls, oak paneling nearly black with age, strong drinks at the bar.

An encyclopedic menu touts what's now called comfort food but used to be just food. Some items take time and the management warns you not to be impatient. Musso might be the last place in L.A. where you can order a slab of spumoni for dessert.

Cheerful green-jacketed busboys circled the cavernous space and filled water glasses for the half dozen parties enjoying a late lunch. Red-jacketed waiters who made Albert Beamish seem amiable waited for a chance to enforce the no-substitution rule.

A few booths featured couples looking happily adulterous. A table in the middle of the room hosted five white-haired men wearing cashmere sweaters and wind-breakers. Familiar but unidentifiable faces; it took a while to figure out why.

A quintet of character actors—men who'd populated my childhood TV shows without ever getting star billing. All of them looked to be pushing a robust eighty. Lots of elbow-bending and laughter. Maybe the bottom of the funnel wasn't necessary for grace.

Milo was working on a beer. "Computer lines are finally back up. I just had Sean run the property search and guess what: Nothing for Brad, but Billy owns ten acres in Latigo Canyon. A short drive above where

Michaela and Meserve pretended to be victims."

"Oh, my," I said. "Just land, no house?"

"That's how it's registered."

"Maybe there are no-code shacks on the property," I said.

"Believe me, I'm gonna find out." He looked at his Timex.

"Brad's the dominant one but he doesn't own any land of his own?"

"Not even the house in Santa Monica Canyon. That's Billy's. So's the duplex in Beverly Hills."

"Three parcels each for Billy and Nora," I said. "Nothing for Brad."

"Could be one of those tax things, Alex. He takes a salary for managing all the shared buildings, has some IRS reason not to own."

"On the contrary, property tax is deductible. So are depreciation and expenses on rentals."

"Spoken like a true land baron."

I'd made serious money buying and selling properties during a couple of booms. Had opted out of the game because I didn't like being a landlord, put the profits in bonds and clipped coupons. Not too smart if net worth was your goal. I used to think my goal was serenity. Now, I had no idea.

I said, "Maybe Cousin Marcia can clue us in."

He tilted his head toward the back of the room. "Yup, being a veteran detective, I'd say that's her."

The woman who stood to the right of the bar was six feet tall, forty or so, with curly dishwater hair and a piercing stare. She wore a black crewneck and slacks, carried a cream leather handbag.

Milo said, "She's checking the premises like a cop," and waved.

She waved back and approached. The purse was printed with a world-map design. A gold crucifix pendant was her only jewelry. Up close, her hair was wiry, combed in a way that obscured half her right eye. The iris and its mate were bright and searching and gray.

Narrow face, sharp nose, outdoor skin. No resemblance I could see to Reynold Peaty. Or to the Dowds.

"Lieutenant? Marcia Peaty."

"Pleased to meet you, ma'am." Milo introduced me, minus my title.

I pictured Al Beamish scowling.

Marcia Peaty shook our hands and sat. "I remember this place as having great martinis."

"You from L.A. originally?"

"Raised in Downey. My father was a chiropractor, had an office there and right here in Hollywood, on Edgemont. A good report card used to earn me lunch with him. We always came here, and when no one was looking, he let me try his martinis. I thought they tasted like swimming pool acid but never let on. Wanting to be mature, you know?" She smiled. "Now I like them all by myself."

A waiter came over and she ordered the cocktail on the rocks, with olives and an onion. "My version of salad."

The waiter said, "Another beer?"

Milo said, "No, thanks."

"You?"

The memory of Beamish's single malt leased space in my palate. "Coke."

The waiter frowned and left.

Milo said, "What can I do for you, Ms. Peaty?"

"I'm trying to find out what happened to Reyn."

"How'd you hear about it?"

"I'm a colleague—used to be."

"Las Vegas PD?"

"Twelve years," she said. "Mostly Vice and Auto and then I did some jail duty. I'm working private security now, big company, we handle some of the casinos."

"No shortage of work in Sin City," said Milo.

"You guys aren't exactly sitting around."

The drinks arrived.

Marcia Peaty tried her martini. "Better than I remembered."

The waiter asked if we were ready to order.

Chicken potpie, sand dabs, sand dabs.

"Another memory," said Marcia Peaty. "Can't get them in Vegas."

Milo said, "Can't get 'em too often in L.A., either. Mostly it's rex sole."

She looked disappointed. "Cheap substitution?"

"Nope, they're basically the same—little flatfish with lots of bones. One lives deeper, no one can tell the difference."

"You into fishing?"

"I'm into eating."

"Virtually the same, huh?" said Marcia Peaty. "More like twins than cousins."

"Cousins can be real different."

She removed an olive from her drink. Chewed, swallowed. "How I found out about Reyn was I'd been trying to call him for days and no one answered. It's not like I call him regularly, but one of our great-aunts died and he inherited some money—no big deal, twelve hundred bucks. When I couldn't get hold of him, I started calling around—hospitals, jails. Finally, I learned what happened from your coroner."

"Calling jails and the crypt," said Milo. "That's a specific curiosity."

Marcia Peaty nodded. "Reyn was high-risk for problems, always had been. I didn't have any fantasies of turning him into a solid citizen, but every so often I'd feel protective. We grew up together in Downey, he was a few years younger, I'm an only child and he was, too, so kin was in short supply. Once upon a time I thought of him as a little brother."

I said, "High-risk brother."

"I'm not going to sugarcoat him but he wasn't a psychopath, just not smart. One of those people who always make bad decisions, you know? Maybe it was genetic. Our fathers were brothers. My dad worked three jobs putting himself through Cleveland Chiropractic, cracked enough backs to go from trailer trash to respectable. Reyn's dad was an alcoholic loser, never held down a steady job, in and out of jail for penny-ante stuff. Reyn's mom wasn't much better." She stopped. "Big sad story, it's nothing you guys haven't heard before."

Milo said, "How'd you both end up in Nevada?"

"Reyn ran away from home when he was fifteen—more like walked out and no one cared. I'm not sure what he did for ten years, I know he tried the marines, ended up in the brig, dishonorable discharge. I moved to Vegas because my dad died and my mom liked playing the slots. When you're an only child, you feel responsible. My husband's from a family of five kids, big old Mormon clan, totally different world."

Milo nodded. "Ten years. Reyn showed up when he was twenty-five."

"At my mother's condo. Tattooed and drunk and he'd put on about sixty pounds. She wouldn't let him in. He didn't argue but he kept hanging around on her street. So Mom called Cop Daughter. When I saw him, I was shocked—believe it or not, he used to be a nice-looking guy. I gave him some cash, set him up at a motel, told him to sober up and move to another city. The last part he kept."

"Reno."

"Next I heard from him was two years later, needing money for bail. I can't tell you where he was in between."

"Bad decisions," I said.

"He's never been violent," said Marcia Peaty. "Just another one of those revolving-door dudes."

Milo said, "His peeper bust could be thought of as scary."

"Maybe I'm rationalizing but that seemed more like drunk and disorderly. He'd never done anything like that before, hasn't since—right?"

"People say he stared a lot. Made 'em uncomfortable."

"Yeah, he tends—tended to space out," said Marcia Peaty. "Like I said, he was no Einstein, couldn't add three-digit sums. I know it sounds like I'm giving a mope a free pass but he didn't deserve to get shot by that banger. Can you fill me in on how it happened?"

Milo gave her the barest details of the

murder, leaving out the whispering phone calls and Vasquez's claim of harassment.

She said, "One of those *stupid* things," and sipped a half inch of martini. "Banger going to pay?"

"He'll get something."

"Meaning?"

"Defense is gonna paint your cousin as a bully."

"Reynold was a booze-soaked loser but he never bullied an ant."

"He have any kind of love life?"

Marcia Peaty's hazel eyes narrowed. Speed-trap gaze. "What does that have to do with anything?"

"D.A. wants a clear picture of what he was like. I can't find evidence of any love life, just a collection of young girl videos."

Marcia Peaty's knuckles whitened around her glass. "How young?"

"Barely legal."

"Why does any of that matter?"

"Reynold worked as a janitor at an acting school. A couple of female students were murdered."

Marcia Peaty blanched. "Uh-uh. No way. I worked Vice long enough to know a sex criminal when I see one and Reynold wasn't—and that ain't family denial. Trust me on this, you'd best be looking elsewhere."

"Speaking of family, let's talk about your other cousins."

"I mean it," she said. "Reyn wasn't wired that way."

"The other cousins," said Milo.

"Who?"

"The Dowds. You were at Nora Dowd's house the other day, told a neighbor you were her cousin."

Marcia Peaty slid her glass toward her left hand. Then back to her right. Lifting the pick skewering the onion, she twirled, put it back. "That wasn't strictly true."

"There's lenient truth?" said Milo.

"She's not my cousin. Brad is."

"He's her brother."

Marcia Peaty sighed. "It's complicated."

"We've got time."

CHAPTER
39

Like I said, I come from trailer trash," said Marcia Peaty. "No shame in that, my father, Dr. James Peaty, pulled himself up, it's even more to his credit."

"Unlike his brother," I said.

"Brothers plural," she said. "And sister. Reyn's dad, Roald, was the youngest, in and out of prison his whole life, later shot himself. Next up was Millard and between him and my dad was Bernadine. She died after being put away."

"Put away for what?" said Milo.

"Alcohol-induced craziness. She was a good-looking woman but she used her looks in not the best way." She pushed her plate away. "I know all this from my mother who hated Dad's family, so she may have heaped it on a bit. But overall I think she was accurate because Dad never denied it. Mom used to hold up Bernadine as a negative example for me—don't do what that 'immoral wench' did."

"What'd Bernadine do?" said Milo.

"Left home at seventeen and went down to Oceanside with a friend, another wild girl named Amelia Stultz. The two of them worked the sailor trade and God knows what else. Bernadine got pregnant by some guy on shore leave who she never saw again. Had a baby boy."

"Brad," I said.

She nodded. "That's how Brad came into this world. When Bernadine got put away he was three or four, got sent to California to live with Amelia Stultz, who'd done a whole lot better, married a navy captain with family money."

Milo said, "Amelia was an immoral wench but she raised someone else's kid?"

"The way my mother told it, my uncle Millard blackmailed her, said he'd tell her rich husband about her past if she didn't 'take the brat.' "

"Conniving fellow, your besotted uncle," I said. "Did he ask anything for himself?"

"Maybe money changed hands, I don't know." Marcia Peaty frowned. "I'm aware that this lays responsibility on everyone but my father. I've wondered about that, could Dad have been that calculated." A cheek muscle jumped. "Even if he'd wanted to help Brad, no way my mother would have agreed to take him in."

"The rich captain was Bill Dowd Junior."

"Hancock Park," she said. "On the surface, Brad lucked out. The problem was Amelia had no interest in raising her own kids, let alone one she'd been stuck with. She'd always fancied herself a dancer and an actress. A *performer,* Mom called it. Which meant stripping in some of those Tijuana clubs and maybe worse."

"How'd Amelia snag Captain Dowd?"

"She was great-looking," said Marcia Peaty. "Blond bombshell, when she was young. Maybe it was like that country song, guys going for women on the trashy side."

Or family tradition. Albert Beamish had

said Bill Dowd Junior married a "woman with no class" just like his mother.

Milo said, "Amelia took Brad in but didn't care to raise him? We talking abuse or just neglect?"

"I never heard about abuse, more like she ignored him completely. But she did that with her own kids, too. Both of whom had problems. Have you met Nora and Billy Three?"

"Yup."

"I haven't seen them since we were kids. What're they like?"

Milo ignored the question. "How'd you happen to see them as kids?"

"Dad must've felt guilty because he tried to make contact with Brad when I was around five. We drove into L.A. and visited. Amelia Dowd liked my dad and started inviting us to birthday parties. Mom griped about it but down deep she didn't mind going to a fancy affair in a big house. She did warn me away from Bill Three. Said he was retarded, couldn't be counted on to control himself."

"He ever act scary?"

She shook her head. "He just seemed quiet and shy. Obviously he wasn't normal but he never bothered me. Nora was a space cadet, walked around talking to herself. Mom said, 'Look at Amelia, marrying rich, living the good life, but she ends up with defective kids.' I don't want to make it sound like Mom was a hateful person, she just had no use for Dad's family and anyone associated with them. His whole life Uncle Millard did nothing but sponge off us, and Roald was no picnic either before he died. Also, when Mom talked like that it was always part of complimenting me. 'Money's nothing, honey. Your children are your legacy and that makes *me* a wealthy woman.' "

Milo said, "Could we talk to your mom?"

"She's gone. Four years ago, cancer. She was one of the ladies you see at the slots. Wheelchair-bound, smoking, and feeding nickels."

I said, "Brad goes by 'Dowd.' Was he adopted legally?"

"Don't know. Maybe Amelia let him use the name to avoid uncomfortable questions."

"Or," said Milo, "she wasn't such a witch."

"I guess," said Marcia Peaty. "Mom *could* be intolerant."

I said, "Captain Dowd didn't mind another child?"

"Captain Dowd wasn't a real tough guy. Just the opposite. Anything Amelia wanted, she got."

"Did your mother ever say anything about how Brad fared psychologically?"

"Her name for him was 'the Troublemaker' and she warned me away from him, too. She said unlike Billy he was smart, but always lying and stealing. Amelia sent him away several times to boarding schools and military academies."

Persimmons and more. Alfred Beamish had pegged Brad's behavior but never uncovered the boy's origins.

Mansions, country clubs, rented elephants at birthday parties. A mother who really wasn't. Who fancied herself a performer.

I said, "How did Amelia Dowd channel her interest in acting?"

"What do you mean?"

"All those performance dreams that never came to pass. Sometimes people live through their kids."

"Was she a stage-door mom? Brad did tell me she tried to get the kids on TV. As a group—singing and dancing. He said he could carry a tune but the others were tone-deaf."

The photo-covered wall of the PlayHouse theater floated into my head. Among the famous faces, a band I hadn't recognized.

Kiddy quartet of mop-haired youngsters . . . the Kolor Krew. "What was the name of the group?"

"He never said."

"When did all this take place?"

"Let's see . . . Brad was about fourteen when he told me, so it must've been right around then. He laughed about it but he sounded bitter. Said Amelia dragged them to talent agents, made them sit for photos, bought them guitars and drums they never learned to play, gave them voice lessons that were useless. Even before that she'd tried to get Nora and Billy Three jobs as actors."

"Not Brad?"

"He told me Amelia only included him in the band because the other two were hopeless."

"He call her that?" I said. "Amelia?"

She thought. "I never heard him call her 'Mom.' "

"Nora and Billy have any success at all, individually?"

"I think Nora got some dinky modeling jobs, department store stuff, kiddy clothing. Bill Three got nothing. He wasn't smart enough."

"Brad told you all this," said Milo. "You and he talk often?"

"Just during those parties."

"What about as adults?"

"Except for one face-to-face twelve years ago, it's been the phone and not often. Maybe once every couple of years."

"Who calls who?"

"He calls me. Christmas greetings, that kind of thing. Mostly showing off how rich he is, telling me about some new car he bought."

"Twelve years ago," I said. "That's pretty precise."

Marcia Peaty fooled with her napkin. "There's a reason for that and it might be important to you guys. Twelve years ago Brad got questioned on a Vegas case. I was doing hot cars, a D from headquarters calls me, says a person of interest is tossing my name around, claiming we're kissing cousins. I find out who it is, call Brad. It's been a while since we've talked but he turns on the charm like it's yesterday, great to hear from you, cuz. He insists on taking me to a big dinner at Caesars. Turns out he'd been living in Vegas for a year, doing some kind of real estate investment, never thought to get in touch. And once he didn't need me I didn't hear from him for seven more years—Christmas, to brag."

"About what?"

"Being back in L.A., living well and running the family real estate business. He invited me to visit, said he'd give me a spin in one of his cars. As in he has a lot of them."

"Platonic invitation?" I said.

"Hard to say with Brad. I chose to take it as platonic."

Milo said, "What kind of case was he questioned on?"

"Missing girl, dancer at the Dunes, never found. Brad had dated her, was the last person to see her."

"He ever go beyond person of interest?"

"Nope. No evidence of a crime was ever uncovered. Brad said she told him she wanted to try for something better and left for L.A. That happens a lot in our town."

I said, "Something better as in breaking into acting?"

Marcia Peaty smiled. "What else is new?"

"Remember this girl's name?" said Milo.

"Julie something, I can get it for you—or you can call yourself. The primary D was Harold Fordebrand, he retired but he's still in Vegas, listed in the book."

"I used to work with an Ed Fordebrand."

"Harold said he had a brother who did L.A. Homicide."

"No evidence of a crime," said Milo, "but what did Harold think about Brad?"

"Didn't like him. Too slick. Called him 'Mr. Hollywood.' Brad wouldn't take a polygraph but there's no crime against that."

"What was his reason?"

"Just didn't want to."

"He get lawyered up?"

"Nope," she said. "Cooperated fully, real relaxed."

"Mr. Hollywood," I said. "Maybe some of Amelia's aspirations rubbed off."

"He actually learned how to act?" she said. "I never thought of it that way, but maybe. Bradley can definitely tell you what you want to hear."

I said, "Those birthday parties Amelia threw. Were any of them for him?"

"Nope, just for Billy Three and Nora. That had to suck but he never showed any anger. They were great parties, rich kid parties, I always looked forward to them. We'd drive up from Downey with my mother complaining about 'those people' being vulgar and my father giving that little smile of his when he knew better than to argue."

"Brad showed no resentment at all?"

"Just the opposite, he was always smiling and joking, would take me around that huge house, show me his hobbies, making wiseass comments about how lame the party was. He is a few years older than me, was cute in that blond surfer way. To be honest, back then I had a crush on him."

"He ridiculed the parties," I said.

"Mostly he poked fun at Amelia, how everything was a big production with her. She was always trying to time stuff precisely, like a stage show. She did tend to go over the top."

"Rented elephant," I said.

"That was something," she said. "How'd you hear about it?"

"A neighbor told us."

"The grumpy old guy?" She laughed. "Yeah, I can see why it would stick in his mind, the smell alone. It was for Billy Three's thirteenth. I remember thinking this is baby stuff, he's way too old for this. Except he was younger mentally and seemed to be digging it. All the kids were digging it, too, because the elephant was messing the street big time, we're whooping and pointing at pounds of stuff coming out, holding our noses, you know? Meanwhile, Amelia's looking ready to faint. Doing the whole Marilyn Monroe platinum-blond thing, tight silk dress, tons of makeup, running after the animal trainer on these gigantic spike heels, everyone's waiting for her to step in elephant doo. *Real* tight dress, busting out of it. She was about twenty pounds past her prime."

Milo took out the photos, showed her Michaela and Tori Giacomo's head-shots.

"Nice-looking girls," she said. "They still that cute or are we talking bad news?"

"Any resemblance to Amelia?"

"Maybe the blondeness. Amelia was

more . . . constructed. Fuller in the face and she looked like she took all morning putting herself together."

"What about Julie the Missing Showgirl, see any similarities?"

She peered closely. "I only saw one picture of her and it was twelve years ago . . . she was blond, too, so there's that. She did make the Dunes stage so we're not talking a toad . . . yeah, I guess, in a general way."

"What about these people?" Flashing the MP shots of Cathy and Andy Gaidelas.

Marcia Peaty's mouth opened and closed. "*This* could be Amelia Dowd, she's heavy around the jaw and the cheeks in the exact same way. The guy's not a dead-ringer for Bill Dowd Junior but he isn't that different, either . . . similar around the eyes— the crags, the whole Gregory Peck thing."

"Dowd looked like Peck?"

"My mom said Amelia bragged about it all the time. I guess there was some truth to it, except Captain Dowd was about five five. Mom used to say, 'He's Gregory Peck on the morning after an earthquake and a tornado and a flood, minus the charisma and sawed off at the knees.'"

I said, "This guy's been compared to Dennis Quaid."

"I can see that . . . not as cute." She studied the pictures some more, returned them. "You guys are dealing with serious bad, aren't you?"

"You said Captain Dowd was no tough guy," I said. "What else can you say about him?"

"Quiet, inoffensive, never seemed to do much."

"Masculine?"

"What do you mean?"

"Manly man?"

"Hardly," she said. "Just the opposite. Mom was convinced he was gay. Or as she put it, a homo. I can't say I saw that, but I was too young to be thinking in those terms."

"Your father have any opinions about it?" said Milo.

"Dad kept his opinions to himself."

"But your mom was definite about it."

"Mom was always definite. Why's it important? Amelia and the captain have been dead for years."

"How many years?"

"It was between the time Brad got called

in for questioning and the next time I heard from him, which was five years later . . . I'm thinking ten years ago."

"They died at the same time?"

"Car crash," said Marcia Peaty. "Driving up to San Francisco. I think the captain fell asleep at the wheel."

"You think," said Milo.

"That's what Mom said, but she was big into blame. Maybe he had a heart attack, I can't say for sure."

"At the birthday parties," I said, "when Brad took you around the house and showed you his hobbies, what kinds of things was he interested in?"

"Typical boy stuff," she said. "Stamp collection, coin collection, sports cards, he had a knife collection—is that what you're getting at?"

"It's just a general question. Anything else?"

"Anything else . . . let's see . . . he flew kites, had some nice ones. Lots of little metal cars—he was always into cars. There was an insect collection—butterflies pinned to a board. Stuffed animals—not the girly kind, trophies he'd stuffed himself."

"Taxidermy?"

"Yeah. Birds, a raccoon, this real weird horned lizard that sat on his desk. He told me he'd learned how to do it at summer camp. Was pretty good at it. Had these boxes—fishing tackle boxes with compartments full of glass eyes, needles and thread, glue, all kinds of tools. I thought it was cool, asked him to show me how he did it. He said, 'Soon as I get something to fix.' He never did. I think I went to maybe one more party and by that time I had a boyfriend, wasn't thinking about much else."

"Let's talk about your other cousin," said Milo. "Any idea how Reynold came to work for the Dowds?"

"That was me," she said. "That bragging call from Brad five years ago. Christmas, there was lots of background noise, like he was doing some heavy partying. This was after Reyn's trouble in Reno. I told Brad, 'Seeing as you're some big real estate honcho, how about helping out a country cousin?' He didn't want to hear about it. He and Reyn didn't know each other, I don't think they'd seen each other since they were kids. But I was in an obnoxious mood and kept working on him—working on his pride, you know? 'Guess your business isn't so big you'd need outside help,' that kind of thing. Finally, he said, 'Have him call me but if he fucks up once, that's it.' Next thing I know Reynold's calling me from L.A., telling me Brad's gonna hire him to manage some apartments."

"Brad hired him to mop and sweep."

"So I've learned," said Marcia Peaty. "Real sweet, huh?"

"Reynold accepted it."

"Reynold didn't have too many options. Brad ever let on to anyone that Reynold was family?"

"Nope," said Milo. "Would Billy and Nora be aware of the connection?"

"Not unless Brad told them. There's no blood tie there."

"Or Reynold told them. We've heard he and Billy hung out."

"That so?" she said. "Hung out how?"

"Reynold dropped by Billy's apartment, allegedly to drop off lost objects."

"Allegedly?"

"Brad denies sending him on errands."

"You believe him?"

Milo smiled. "They're both your cousins but you'd prefer we focus on Brad, not

Reynold. That why you came down to L.A.?"

"I came down because Reynold's dead and no one else is going to bury him. He's all I've got left in terms of family."

"Except Brad."

"Brad's your concern, not mine."

"You don't like him."

"He was raised in another family," she said.

Silence.

Finally, she said, "Julie the dancer. That bothered me big time. Now you're showing me photos of other blond girls. Reynold was dumb and sloppy and a drunk but he was never cruel."

"So far you haven't told us anything Brad did that was cruel."

"No, I haven't," said Marcia Peaty. "And I guess I can't because, like I said, he and I haven't exactly been hanging out."

"But . . ."

"You know, guys," she said, "this is real weird and I don't think I like it."

"Like what?"

"Being on the receiving end of what I used to dish out."

"It's for a good cause, Marcia," said Milo.

"In terms of Julie the Showgirl, did Harold Fordebrand's gut say anything more about Brad than he was slick?"

"You'd have to ask Harold. Once he found out Brad was my cousin he kept me out of the loop."

"How about your gut . . ."

"Brad's demeanor bothered me. Like he was enjoying some private joke. You guys know what I mean."

"Despite that, you got Reyn a job with him."

"And now Reyn's gone," she said. Her face crumpled and she turned to hide it from us. When she faced us again, her voice was small. "You're saying I screwed up big time."

"No," said Milo. "I'm not trying to guilt-trip you, far from it. All this stuff you're telling us is beyond helpful. We're just groping around here."

"No case yet."

"Not hardly."

"I was hoping I was wrong," she said.

"About what?"

"Brad being somehow involved with Reynold's death."

"No indication he is."

"I know, an altercation. You're saying that's all there was to it?"

"So far."

"The old stonewall," said Marcia Peaty. "I've laid a few bricks myself. Let me ask you this: The way Brad treated Reyn, giving him scut work, the Dowds owning all those properties, and they stick Reyn in a hovel. That add up to the milk of human kindness? These people are just what Mom always said they were."

"What's that?"

"Poison palming itself off as perfume."

40

Marcia Peaty switched the subject and Milo didn't stop her.

Procedural questions about how to take possession of her cousin's body. His run-down wasn't much different from the one he'd given Lou Giacomo.

She said, "Paperwork aerobics. Okay, thanks for your time. Am I wasting my time asking you to keep me informed?"

"Something resolves, we'll let you know, Marcia."

"*If,* not when? You have any serious leads?"

He smiled.

She said, "That's why I never did Homicide. Too much effort getting the optimism meter up."

"Vice can get sketchy, too."

"That's why I didn't do Vice for long. Give me a nice boosted set of wheels."

"Chrome don't bleed," said Milo.

"Ain't that the truth." She reached for the check. Milo placed his hand on it.

"Let me pay for my share."

"On the house," said Milo.

"You or the department?"

"The department."

"Right." She put down a twenty, slid out of the booth, shot us a tight smile, and hurried off.

Milo pocketed the cash and pushed crumbs around his plate. "Ol' Brad's been a *baaad* boy."

"Young blondes," I said. "Too bad Tori dyed her hair."

"Amelia, the whole platinum bombshell thing. What, he's killing Stepmommy over and over?"

"His own mother abandoned him, handed him over to someone who didn't even pretend to care. He has lots of reasons to hate women."

534   JONATHAN KELLERMAN

"He was in his thirties when Julie the Showgirl disappeared. Think she was his first?"

"Hard to say. The main thing was he got away with it, built up his confidence for the move back to L.A. After Amelia and the captain died, he managed to take over the family real estate empire. Cared well for Billy and Nora because happy sibs don't complain. Maybe the PlayHouse is a tax dodge and a sop for Nora, but it was good for him, too. Start an acting school, who shows up?"

"Gorgeous mutants," he said. "All those blonde auditions."

"And rejects like the Gaidelases. Normally, Brad would ignore people like Cathy and Andy but they reminded him of Amelia and the captain, down to the captain's effeminate manner. How's this for a scenario: He ran into them leaving an audition. Or waiting for a tryout. Either way, it had to feel like destiny, he played nice guy, promised to help. Told them meanwhile enjoy your vacation. Do some hiking, I know a great spot."

"Billy's acreage in Latigo." He folded and unfolded his napkin. Snatched up his phone, got Harold Fordebrand's number from Vegas 411, called, left a message. "Guy sounds exactly like Ed."

I said, "The Kolor Krew was a quartet."

"Who?"

"The kiddie-pop group Amelia tried to market." I described the publicity shot on the PlayHouse wall. "The Dowd kids plus *one.* Maybe there's someone else who can fill us in about the good old days."

He said, "You feel like researching the history of bubblegum music, be my guest. I need another face-to-face with the sib who really ain't one. Starting with a drop-in at the BNB office. If Brad's not there, it's over to his house. Eventually, a day at the beach will be on the agenda."

I said, "Think Billy even knows he owns the Latigo property?"

"Brad bought it and put it in Billy's name?"

"Brad lives near the ocean, has surfed enough to grow knots on his knees. Meaning he knows Malibu. A nice, secluded oceanview lot on the land-side might appeal to him, especially if it was paid for with Billy's money. Being in charge of family finances, Brad could get Billy to sign on the dotted line. Or just forge Billy's name. Meanwhile, Billy pays the property tax and doesn't have a clue."

"The assessor says there are no structures on the lot. What would Brad use it for?"

"Meditation, planning a dream house, burying bodies."

"Billy pays, Brad plays," he says. "Nora's no business type, either. Meaning Brad can basically do what he wants with all the money." He rubbed his face. "All this time, I've been looking for *Peaty's* stash spots, but *Brad* has access to dozens of buildings and garages all over the county."

"He came right out and told us he stores his cars in some of the properties."

"He did, indeed. What was that, playing mind games?"

"Or bragging about his collection. This is a guy who needs to feel important. I'm wondering if it could've been him watching Angeline Wasserman from that Range Rover."

"Why would it be him?"

"Last time I saw him, he had on a nice linen suit. There were a bunch just like it hanging from a rack at the Barneys outlet."

"Snappy dresser," he said. "Maybe a regular, just like Wasserman. He observes her, knows she's absentminded, lifts her purse."

"The goal was to get her phone, he couldn't've have cared less about the money or the credit cards," I said. "The more I think about that, the better I like it: well-dressed middle-aged guy who shops there all the time, no reason to suspect him. Angeline might know his face but the Rover's tinted windows would've prevented her from realizing it was him. It was his ride she concentrated on, anyway— 'twinsie karma.' "

He retrieved Wasserman's number from his pad and punched it. "Ms. Wasserman? Lieutenant Sturgis, again . . . I know you are but just one more question, okay? There's a gentleman who shops at the outlet regularly, mid-forties, nice-looking, white hair—you do . . . oh . . . no, it's more . . . maybe . . . okay, thanks . . . no, that's it."

He hung up. " 'That's *Brad,* I see him all the *time.* Did he have something stolen, *too*?' "

"Seeing him as a victim, not a suspect," I said, "because he's well-off and stylish."

"You got it. 'Great guy, terrific taste, you should see the gorgeous cars he drives, Lieutenant, each time a different one.' Turns out Angeline and ol' Brad ask each other's opinions about outfits all the time. He's always honest but he does it with 'sensitivity.' "

"Charming fellow."

"You think his driving Nora's wheels means Nora and Meserve are in on it with him? Or tough luck for them."

"Don't know, but either way Brad had something to do with the calls to Vasquez."

"Setting up his own cousin."

"The same cousin he put to work as a janitor and housed in a dump. Given Brad's background, blood ties could twist all sorts of ways. If Vasquez was telling the truth about getting calls the previous week, the setup was extremely well thought out."

"Priming a murder," he said. "How could Brad be sure Vasquez would blow and shoot Peaty?"

"He couldn't, but he knew both parties and Mrs. Stadlbraun, played the odds. He told me he had bad feelings about Vasquez but rented to him anyway because there was no legal out. That's nonsense. A landlord, especially one with Brad's experience, can always find a reason."

"Game of chance," he said.

"Brad lived in Vegas. One table doesn't work out, move to the next one."

"Okay, let's assume he set Peaty up. Why?"

"With Peaty's police record and pattern of creepy behavior, he'd be a perfect scape-goat for Michaela and Tori and any other missing girls who turned up. Look what hap-pened after the shooting: You got to search Peaty's van, discovered the rape-kit stashed conveniently in back—no real effort to con-ceal. And, lo and behold, there was a *snow globe* in the toolbox. Just like the one left on the seat of Meserve's Toyota. Which you knew about in the first place because Brad called you in a panic after finding the car in one of his own parking spaces. If Meserve cut town with Nora, why would he leave his wheels where they were sure to be discov-ered? At the very least, he could've put the Toyota in Nora's garage—which, by the way, is empty—and avoided ticking off Brad."

"By the way," he said.

"Crowbar."

He shook his head, drank.

I said, "Maybe Nora's not the only one with theatrical interests. Only reason we knew about the snow globe in the first place was Brad brought it up when we talked to him at his house."

"Painting Meserve as a gold digger. What was that? Another misdirect?"

"Or it was true and he had good reason to hate Meserve."

He loosened his belt, crushed ice with his molars and swallowed it. Picked up the check.

"On you or the department?" I said.

"For your information, I'm trying out that bumper sticker wisdom, spontaneous acts of kindness blah blah blah. Maybe the Almighty will reward me with a close on this mess."

"Never knew you to be religious."

"There's things that can get me praying."

Walking to the parking lot, I said, "Three personal real estate parcels for Billy and Nora, none for Brad. Just like the birthday parties. His childhood was one big exclusion because the Dowds never stopped seeing him as anything but an imposition. Amelia recruited him for the Kolor Krew only because he could sing. When his behavior grew troublesome, she sent him away."

"Used and discarded," he said. "Persimmons."

"I'd put money on a whole lot more anti-social behavior. The point is, the same pattern's continued into adulthood: As long as Brad serves a purpose—taking care of Nora and Billy—he gets creature comforts. But at the root, he's hired help. Doesn't even own the house he lives in, legally he's just another tenant. In a sense, it's to his advantage, spending other people's money and living large. But still, it has to grate."

"Hired help passing himself off as the boss," he said. "Wonder how he finagled himself into that position."

"Probably by default—Nora and Billy are incapable. He's the caretaker and the payoff is cars, clothes, properties that he palms off as his. Image. He pulls off the aw-shucks big-money thing beautifully. Angeline Wasserman's part of that world and she bought it."

"Good actor."

"Good at impressing women," I said. "Young, naive women would be no challenge. Tori's ex-husband figured she'd been dating someone with money. A starving actress serving fish to make the rent on a North Hollywood dump and a guy with a Porsche? Same for Michaela."

"Michaela never indicated to you that she was seeing anyone?"

"No, but it wouldn't have come up. My consult focused on her legal problems. One thing she did make clear: Dylan was no longer her style. Maybe because she'd found someone better."

"Mr. Hot Wheels," he said. "Still doesn't answer the question of how Brad got to pull the reins. Why would the Dowds hand over all that control?"

"Maybe they didn't but once the parents were dead he wrangled his way in as a trustee of the estate. Cozying up to the lawyers, greasing someone's palm, making the case that he was the best choice—someone with smarts who had Billy's and Nora's best interests at heart. If Nora and Billy agreed, why not? Once he was in, he was set. Trustees don't come up for review unless someone complains about abuse of fiduciary responsibility. Nora and Billy get their needs met, everyone's happy."

"The PlayHouse and the family manse for her, takeout pizza and a wide-screen for Billy."

"Meanwhile Brad collects the monthly rent checks."

"Think he's siphoning off cash?"

"Wouldn't shock me."

He strode to the parking attendant's booth, paid for both our cars.

I said, "Now you're veering into Mother Teresa territory."

He gazed skyward and pressed his palms together. "Hear that? How about some evidentiary manna?"

"God helps those who help themselves," I said. "Time to check the small print on BNB's letters of incorporation."

"First, I want to face Brad one-on-one."

We sat in his unmarked talking about the best approach. The final decision was another chat about Reynold Peaty's shooting, Milo talking, me scoping out the nonverbal cues. Mentioning the phone calls to Armando Vasquez if the timing seemed right.

We took separate cars to the strip mall on Ocean Park. The door to BNB Properties was locked and no one answered. As Milo turned to leave, the door at the end of the second-floor landing caught my eye.

Sunny Sky Travel
We Specialize in Tropical Getaways

Posters in the window. Sapphire ocean, emerald palm trees, bronze people hoisting cocktails.

At the bottom: *BRAZIL!!!*

Milo followed my gaze, had the door open by the time I got there.

A young cat-eyed woman wearing a sleeveless raspberry top sat at a computer station typing. Soft eyes, Rubenesque roundness. A nameplate on the desk said *Lourdes Texeiros.* A hands-free phone headset rested atop a nest of black curls. The walls were papered with more posters. A revolving rack of brochures filled a corner.

She smiled at us, said, "Hold on a sec," to the hands-free mouthpiece. I went over to the rack, found what I was looking for.

Turneffe Island, Belize; Posada La Mandragora, Buzios, Brazil; Hotel Monasterio, Tapir Lodge, Pelican's Pouch. Housed in adjacent compartments.

"Can I help you guys?"

"Your neighbor a few doors down, Mr. Bradley Dowd," said Milo, flashing the badge. "How well do you know him?"

"The real estate guy? Did he do something?"

"His name came up in an investigation."

"White-collar crime?"

"He make you uneasy?"

"No, I don't know him, he's hardly ever at his office. He just seems like a white-collar guy. If he did something."

Dark eyes sharpened with curiosity.

Milo said, "Does he come to his office by himself?"

"Usually with another guy, I think it's his brother 'cause he seems to be looking after him. Even though the other guy looks older. Sometimes he leaves him there by himself. He's kind of . . . you know, not quite right. The other guy."

"Billy."

"Don't know his name." She frowned.

"Has he bothered you?"

"Not really. Once I was here and the air-conditioning wasn't working so I had the door open. He came in, said 'Hi,' and just stood there. I said 'Hi' back and asked if he was thinking of taking a trip. He blushed, said he wished, and left. Only times I saw him after that was downstairs at the Italian place, getting food for his brother. When he saw me he got *real* embarrassed, like he'd been caught doing something naughty. I tried to make a little conversation but it was hard for him. That's when I realized he wasn't normal."

"How so?"

"Kind of retarded? You can't tell by looking, he looks like a regular guy."

"Has Brad ever come in here?"

"Also just once, a couple of weeks ago. He introduced himself, real friendly, maybe too much, you know?"

"Slick?"

"Exactly. He told me he was thinking of taking a vacation in Latin America and wanted information. I offered to sit down with him and discuss choices but he said he'd start with those." Pointing to the rack. "He grabbed a handful but I never heard back. Did he leave the country or something?"

"Why would you ask that?" said Milo.

"The places we book," she said. "In the movies they always have bad guys running to Brazil. Everyone thinks there's no extradition treaty. Trust me, anywhere without a treaty you wouldn't want to vacation."

"I'll bet. Anything else you want to tell us about him?"

"Can't think of any."

"Okay, thanks." He leaned over her desk.

"We'd appreciate it if you didn't mention we were here asking about him."

"Of course not," said Lourdes Texeiros. "Should I be scared of him?"

Milo looked at her. Took in the black curls. "Not at all."

"Another misdirection," I said as we descended the stairs. "Wanting us to think Nora traveled with Meserve. Either because he's protecting her or he made her and Meserve disappear. I'm betting on door number two."

"All these years he takes care of a coupla mopes who just happen to be members of the Lucky Sperm Club. Why change all that now?"

"Nora had always deferred to him. Maybe that changed."

"Meserve shows up," he said.

"And captures her affections," I said. "Another self-styled player, good-looking, ambitious, manipulative. Younger than Brad, but not unlike him. Could be that's what attracted Nora to him in the first place. Whatever the reason, she wasn't giving him up the way she had the others."

"Meserve worms his way into her affections and her pocket-book."

"Deep-pocketbook. Brad's got nominal power but he serves at the discretion of the estate. Nora's a ditz but it would be hard to claim she's not of sound mind, legally. If she demanded control over her own assets, it would pose a major complication for Brad. If she convinced *Billy* to do the same, it would be a disaster."

"Bye-bye, façade."

"Banished when he's of no further use," I said. "Just like when he was a kid."

We walked in silence to the cars.

He said, "Michaela and Tori and the Gaidelases and Lord knows how many others get done for blood-lust and Nora and Meserve get done for money?"

"Or a mixture of blood-lust and money."

He considered that. "Nothing new about that, I guess. Rick's relatives didn't just lose their lives in the Holocaust. Their homes and their businesses and all their other possessions got confiscated."

"Take it all," I said. "The ultimate trophy."

CHAPTER

41

We took the Seville to Santa Monica Canyon.

No Porsche or any other car in Brad Dowd's driveway. Lights out in the redwood house, no reply to Milo's knock.

I joined the traffic crawl on Channel Road, finally made it down to the coast highway, hit moderate flow from Chautauqua to the Colony. Once we got past Pepperdine University, the land yawned and stretched and the road got easy. The ocean was slate. Hungry pelicans dove. I made it to Kanan Dume Road with some sunlight to spare, turned up onto Latigo Canyon.

An assessors' map of Billy Dowd's property rested in Milo's lap. Ten acres, no building permits ever issued.

The Seville's no mountain car and I slowed as the pitch steepened and the turns pinched. Nothing on the road until I neared the spot where Michaela had run across screaming.

An old tan Ford pickup was parked there on the turnoff. An old tan man stood looking into the brush.

Plaid shirt, dusty jeans, beer gut hanging over his buckle. Filmy white hair fluffed in the breeze. A long, hooked nose sliced sky.

Smoke seeped from under the truck's hood.

Milo said, "Pull over."

The old man turned and watched us. His belt buckle was stippled brass, an oversized oval featuring a bas-relief horse head.

"You okay, Mr. Bondurant?"

"Why shouldn't I be, Mr. Detective?"

"Looks like an over-heat."

"It always does that. Pinhole leak in the radiator, long as I feed it faster than it gets hungry, I'm okay."

Bondurant shuffled over to the truck,

reached in the passenger window, and took out a yellow plastic jug of antifreeze.

"Liquid diet," said Milo. "You're sure the block won't crack?"

"You worried about me, Mr. Detective?"

"Protect and serve."

"Find out anything about the girl?"

"Still working on it, sir."

Bondurant's eyes vanished in a mesh of fold and crinkle. "Meaning nothing, huh?"

"Looks like you've been thinking about her."

The old man's chest swelled. "Who says?"

"This is the spot where you saw her."

"It's also a turnoff," said Bondurant. He hefted the antifreeze. Stared at the brush. "Naked girl, it's like one of those stories you tell in the service and everyone thinks you're lyin'." He licked his lips. "Few years back that woulda been something."

Sucking in his belly, he hitched his jeans. The roll of fat shimmered down, covered the horse's eyes.

Milo said, "Know your neighbors?"

"Don't got any real ones."

"No neighborhood spirit around here?"

"Let me tell you how it's like," said

Charley Bondurant. "This used to be horse land. My grandfather raised Arabians and some Tennessee walkers—anything you could sell to rich folk. Some of the Arabians made it to Santa Anita and Hollywood Park, a couple of 'em placed. Everyone who lived here was into horses, you could smell the shit miles away. Now it's just rich folk who don't give a damn about anything. They buy up the land for investment, drive up on Sunday, stare for a coupla minutes, don't know what the hell to do with themselves, and go back home."

"Rich folk like Brad Dowd?"

"Who?"

"White-haired fellow, mid-forties, drives all kinds of fancy cars."

"Oh, yeah, him," said Bondurant. "Guns those things too damn fast coming down the mountain. Exactly what I mean. Wearing those Hawaiian shirts."

"He here often?"

"Once in a while. All I see is the damn cars speeding by. Lots of ragtops, that's how I know about the shirts."

"He ever stop to talk?"

"You didn't hear me?" said Bondurant.

"He *speeds* by." A gnarled hand slashed the air.

"How often is once in a while?" said Milo.

Bondurant half turned. His hawk-nose aimed at us. "You want a count?"

"If you've got charts and graphs, I'll take them, Mr. Bondurant."

The old man completed the turn. "He's the one who killed her?"

"Don't know."

"But you're thinking he could be."

Milo said nothing.

Bondurant said, "You're a quiet guy, except when you want something from me. Let me tell you, government never did much for the Bondurant family. We had problems, no help from the government."

"What kind of problems?"

"Coyote problems, gopher problems, draught problems, prowling hippie problems. Damned mourning cloak butterfly problems—I say 'butterfly,' you think *cute* 'cause you're a city boy. I think *problem.* One summer they swarmed us, laid their eggs in the trees, destroyed half a dozen elms, nearly polished off a sixty-foot weeping willow. Know what we did? We DDT'ed 'em."

He folded his arms across his chest. "That ain't legal. You ask the government can I DDT, nope, against the law. You say what should I do to protect my elm trees, they say figure something out."

"Butterfly homicide's not my thing," said Milo.

"Caterpillars all over the place, pretty fast-moving for what they were," said Bondurant. "I had fun stepping on 'em. The car guy kill the girl?"

"He's what we call a person of interest. That's government double-talk for I'm not gonna tell you more."

Bondurant allowed himself half a smile.

Milo said, "When's the last time you saw him?"

"Maybe a couple of weeks ago. That don't mean nothing. I'm asleep by eight thirty, someone's driving past I ain't gonna see it or hear it."

"Ever notice anyone with him?"

"Nope."

"Ever see anyone else go to that property?"

"Why would I?" said Bondurant. "It's above me a good mile and a half. I don't go prowling around. Even when Walter Mac-

Intyre owned the land I never went up there because everyone knew Walt was nuts and excitable."

"How so?"

"I'm talking years ago, Mr. Detective."

"Always interested in learning."

"Walter MacIntyre didn't kill no girl, he's been dead thirty years. The car guy must've bought the land from Walter's son, who's a dentist. Walter was also a dentist, big practice in Santa Monica, he bought the land back in the fifties. First city folk to buy. My father said, 'Watch and see what happens,' and he was right. Walter started off like he was gonna fit in. Built this huge horse barn but never put no horses in it. Every weekend he'd be up here, driving a truck, but no one could figure out why. Probably staring at the ocean and talking to himself about the Russians."

"What Russians?"

"The ones from Russia," said Bondurant. "Communists. That's what Walter was nuts about. Convinced himself any minute they were gonna come swarming over and make us all potato-eatin' communists. My father had no use for communists but he said Walter took it too far. A little you-know-what." A finger rotated near his left ear.

"Obsessive."

"You want to use that word, fine." Bondurant hitched his jeans again and returned to his truck on bandy legs. He put the antifreeze back on the passenger seat, slapped the palm of his hand on the hood. The smoke had reduced to occasional wisps.

He said, "Ready to go. Hope you find whoever killed that girl. Beautiful thing, damn shame."

The entrance to the property was unmarked. I overshot and had to travel half a mile to find a spot wide enough for a U-turn. As is, my tires were inches from blue space and I could feel Milo's tension.

I coasted back slowly as he squinted at the plot map. Finally, he spotted the opening—ungated and shaded by twisting sycamores. Hard-pack dirt ramping high above the canyon.

Two S-turns and the surface converted to asphalt, continued to climb.

"Keep it slow," said Milo. Doing the cop-laser thing with his eyes. Nothing to see but dense walls of oak and more sycamores, a skimpy triangle of light on the horizon suggesting an end point.

Then, two acres in, the land flattened to a mesa curtained by mountains and canopied by a cumulus-flecked sky. Uncultivated acres had given way to bunchgrass, coastal sage, yellow mustard, a few struggling loner oaks in the distance. The asphalt drive cut through the meadow, straight and black as a draftsman's line. Three-quarters of the way to the back of the property stood a massive barn. Flanks of redwood board silvered by time. Dour slab-face unbroken by windows, shingle roof wind-blunted at the corners. A ludicrously small front door.

Cool air carried some of the mustard tang our way.

Milo said, "No building permits issued."

"Folks round these parts don't truck with no guv-ment."

Nowhere to conceal the Seville completely. I left it parked off the asphalt, partially hidden by tree boughs, and we walked. Milo's hand dangled over his jacket.

When we were fifty feet away, the building's dimensions asserted themselves. Three stories high, a couple hundred feet wide.

He said, "Thing that size but the door's too small to get a car through. Wait here while I check the back."

He took out his gun, sidled around the barn's north side, was gone a few minutes, returned with the weapon reholstered. "Show-and-tell time."

Double rear doors, ten feet high, were wide enough for a flatbed to drive through. Clean, oiled hinges looked freshly installed. A generator large enough to power a trailer park chugged. Behind us some kind of bird trilled but didn't show itself. Tire tracks scored the dirt, a frenzy of tread marks, too many to make sense of.

Near the right-hand door a padlock lay on the dirt.

I said, "You found it that way?"

"That's the official story."

The barn had no hayloft. Just a three-story cavity, cathedral-sized, vaulted by stout, weathered rafters, walls tacked with white drywall. Dust filters like the one we'd seen in the PlayHouse garage whirred every twenty feet or so. An antique gravity gas pump stood to the right of an immaculate worktable. Shiny tools in a punchboard rack, chamois cloths folded into neat squares, tins of paste wax, chrome polish, saddle soap.

A flagstone spine wide enough for a four-horse march ran up the center of the room. Both sides were lined with what Dr. Walter MacIntyre had conceived as horse stalls.

The doors were gone and the concrete floors were swept clean. Each compartment held a gas-eating steed.

Milo and I walked up the flagstone. He looked into each car, placed his hand on the hoods.

A quartet of Corvettes. Two bathtub Porsches, one with a racing number on its door. Brad Dowd's newer silver roadster, a black Jaguar D-Type, lurked like a weapon, unmindful of the cream Packard Clipper towering snobbishly in the next stall.

Slot after slot, filled with lacquered, chromed sculpture. Red Ferrari Daytona, the monstrous baby-blue '59 Caddy Brad had driven to Nora's house, silver AC Cobra, bronze GTO.

Every hood cold.

Milo straightened from the deep bend it

took to inspect a yellow Pantera. Walked to the far wall and surveyed the collection. "A boy and his hobbies."

"The Daytona costs as much as a house," I said. "Either he pays himself a huge salary, or he's been siphoning."

"Unfortunately, chrome *don't* bleed, and it's blood I'm after."

Outside the barn, he replaced the open lock and wiped it clean. "Gazillion dollars' worth of go-carts and he doesn't bother bolting."

I said, "He doesn't expect visitors."

"Confident fellow. No reason not to be." We began the return trip to the car, walked around the south side.

Ten steps later, we stopped, synchronized as a drill team.

A gray circle. Easy to spot; the grass had died two feet from the perimeter, leaving a halo of cold, brown dirt.

Steel disk, nubbed with little metal pimples. A lever folded flat pulled up easily when Milo tried it. An inch of lift evoked a pneumatic hiss. He let it drop back into place.

I said, "Bert the Turtle."

"Who?"

"Cartoon character in these booklets they gave out to schoolkids in the fifties, teaching the basics of civil defense. A bit before my time but I had a cousin who held on to hers. Bert was big on ducking into his shell. Knew proper bomb-shelter etiquette."

"In my school it was drop-drills," he said. "Put your head between your knees and kiss your ass good-bye."

He toed the edge of the shelter lid. "Ol' Walter really was worried about the communists."

"And now Brad reaps the benefits."

CHAPTER

42

Milo walked around looking for a surveil-lance camera.

"None I can see, but who knows . . ."

Returning to the shelter lid, he squatted, lifted the handle a few more inches. Hiss hiss. He let it fall back into place.

"Air lock," I said. "Keep nuclear fallout at bay."

"Play canasta while the bombs drop." Stretching prone, he pressed his ear to steel. "You hear the cries of a damsel in distress like I do?"

Off in the distance, a puny breeze barely ruffled the meadow. The trilling bird had gone mute. If clouds made noise, the silence might've relented.

I said, "Loud and clear. Grounds to search."

He lifted the handle halfway. Peered in. Had to stand and put his weight into completing the arc. The hatch gave way with a final whisper and he stepped back. Waited. Inched over to the opening. Looked down again.

Snaking through a tube of corrugated steel was a spiral staircase, metal treads stripped with friction pads. Bolts secured the flight to the underside of the rim.

"The big question remains," he said.

"Is he down there."

"None of those cars have been driven recently, but that could just mean he's bunked down for a while." Removing his desert boots, he unsnapped his holster but left the gun nestled. Sitting at the edge of the opening, he swung his legs in. "Something happens, you can have my Bert the Turtle lunch box."

He descended. I took off my shoes and followed.

"Stay up there, Alex."

"And be here alone if he shows up?"

He started to argue. Stopped himself. Not because he'd changed his mind.

Staring at something.

At the bottom of the stairs was a door, same gray steel as the hatch. A shiny brass coat hook was screwed to the metal.

From the hook, a white nylon cord hung taut. Its ends were looped around a pair of ears.

Waxy-white ears.

The head they connected to was lean, well-formed, crowned by thick, dark hair.

Well-formed face, but hideous. Dermis more paperlike than corporeal. Lumps distorted the cheekbones where stuffing had settled. Nearly invisible sutures held the mouth shut and pried the eyes open. Blue eyes, wide with surprise.

Glass.

The thing that had once been Dylan Meserve was as lifelike as a milliner's mold.

Milo crawled out. His gullet throbbed. He paced.

I got closer to the opening, smelled the formaldehyde. Saw writing on the door, an inch below the thing's chin.

Shimmied down low enough, I read.

Neat printing, black marker.

PROJECT COMPLETED.

Below that, a date and a time. Two a.m. Four days ago.

Milo walked around for a while, searching for evidence of burial, returned shaking his head, looked into the maw of the bomb shelter. "Lord only knows what else is down there. The moral dilemma is . . ."

"Is there someone down there who can be saved," I said. "If there is, will attempting it make matters worse. You could try calling him, if he's down there, maybe we can hear the ring."

"If we can hear it, he's probably heard us already."

"At least he's not going anywhere." I eyed the dangling head. "Talk about probable cause."

He took out his cell and tried Brad Dowd's number.

No sound from below.

His eyes widened. "Mr. Dowd? Lieutenant Sturgist . . . no, nothing huge but I thought maybe we could chat about Reynold Peatyt . . . just tying up loose ends . . . I was hoping more like tonight, where are you? We stopped by there earlier . . . yeah, we must'vet . . . listen, sir, no, no prob coming back to your house, we're not far. Camarillo . . . actually it is related, but I'm not at liberty to sayt . . . sorryt . . . so can we—you're sure? Today would be a lot easier, Mr. Dowdt . . . Click.

He said, "Hard day out in Pasadena, plumbing leaks, blah blah blah. Mr. Cool and Charming until I mentioned Camarillo. Got this little catch in his voice. Happy to cooperate, Lieutenant, but I just can't today."

"You shook him up, he needs to regroup. Maybe he'll revert to what calmed him down when he was a kid."

"What's that?"

"Arts and crafts."

Milo went down in the hole again, pounded the door while keeping his distance from the thing on the coat hook.

Sidled away from it and found a spot on the door where he could press his ear without touching dead flesh. He knocked on the metal door, then pounded.

Climbing back out, he brushed away

nonexistent dirt. "If anyone's in there, I can't hear it and the door's bolted solid."

Lowering the hatch, he wiped it clean, scuffed out the footsteps we'd left in the dirt halo.

We put our shoes on and retraced our steps back to the car, worked hard at obscuring our tracks.

I drove off the property and repeated the climb I'd taken when I'd overshot. When we found nowhere to hide the Seville within walking distance, I turned around and descended.

A mailbox two properties down from Billy Dowd's land was lettered with gold stick-ons: The Osgoods. A sagging plank-and-chicken-wire fence blocked a gravel drive.

Flag up on the box. Milo got out and checked. "Least a week's worth, let's trespass."

Unlatching the gate, he stood back as I drove through, swung it closed, hopped back in.

The Osgoods owned a much smaller spread than Billy Dowd. Same oak-sycamore combo, a flat brown lawn in place of a meadow. In the center, a pale green fifties ranch house with a white-pebble roof squatted behind an empty corral. No animals, no animal smell. Half a dozen empty trash cans stood against one side. A cheap prefab swing set tilted nearby and a child's plastic trike blocked the front door.

The sky had started to darken. No light spat from any windows.

Milo reached over the tricycle and knocked on the front door anyway. Left his card wedged between the door and jamb and a note under one of the Seville's wiper blades.

As we walked back to the road, I said, "What'd you write?"

" 'Oh, lucky citizens,' " he said, " 'you are doing your bit for God and country.' "

We reentered Billy's property on foot, found a watch spot just shy of where the trees met the meadow.

Thirty feet back from the drive. The ground was spongy with dead leaves and dust. We sat against the stout trunk of a low-branching oak, nicely concealed.

Milo and me, bugs and lizards and unseen scampering things.

Nothing to talk about. Neither of us wanted to talk. The sky was bruised deep blue, then black. I thought of Michaela and Dylan, camping down the road.

Led to the hoax spot by Brad Dowd.

Had he harbored plans of ending the game with a bloody surprise, only to be stymied by Michaela's escape?

Was that reason to kill her?

Or did she just fit some kind of role?

Same for Dylan. I struggled to remember him from his photos, not the *thing.*

Time passed. Squeaks sounded above us, leaves shivered, then a delicate flutter of wings as a bat zipped out of the oak and circled high above the meadow.

Then another. Then four.

"Great," said Milo. "When does the ominous soundtrack start?"

"Da dum da dum."

He laughed. I did, too. Why not?

We took turns napping. His second snooze lasted five minutes and when he shook himself awake, he said, "Shoulda brought water."

"Who knew we'd be camping?"

"A Boy Scout's always prepared. You scouted, right?"

"Yup."

"Me, too. If BSA only knew, huh? Think anyone's down in that hole?"

"Hopefully not someone like Dylan," I said.

He rested his face in one hand.

A moment later: "If he doesn't show up tonight, Alex, you know how it'll have to go."

"Task force."

"Can't wait to write that warrant application. 'Yes, your honor, taxidermy.' "

Night had settled in so completely it seemed permanent.

Neither of us spoke for the next half hour. When headlights yellowed the asphalt, we were both wide awake.

Fog lights. Engine purr. The vehicle's squarish bulk passed us fast and sped toward the barn.

We got to our feet, stayed in the tree cover, advanced.

The Range Rover came to a stop just to the left of the barn's undersized front door, then silenced. A man got out the driver's side, switched on a bug light above the door.

The bulb had a yellow-green tint and it turned Brad Dowd's white hair chartreuse.

He went around to the passenger side, opened the door.

Held a hand out to someone.

Female, petite. A blousy jacket over trousers obscured her contours.

The two of them walked to the door and the woman waited as Brad opened it. Moved into the yellow beam. Profile limned.

Firm chin, nubby little nose. Bobbed gray hair tinted olive by the light.

Nora Dowd said something that sounded perky. Brad Dowd turned toward her. Spread his arms wide.

She rushed into the hug.

Nothing sisterly about the gesture as her hands began caressing the back of his neck.

His hands cupped her rear. She giggled.

Her face tilted up as their mouths met.

Long, grinding kiss. She reached down for his groin. He laughed. She laughed.

They went inside.

They were back moments later, walking hand-in-hand around the south side of the barn.

Nora skipping.

Brad said, "Gorgeous night, isn't this just the best?"

Nora said, "Party time."

They reached the bomb-shelter hatch. Nora stood by, fluffing her pageboy as Brad worked the lever. Putting weight into it, just as Milo had.

"Ooh," she said. "My big strong *ma*-yan."

"Got something *beaucoup* strong for you, babe."

"Got something soft and sweet for you, babe."

The lid popped open. Brad pulled out a small penlight and aimed it into the opening. "You were right. I like him there."

"Talk about a welcome," said Nora. "Knock knock knock."

"He always did like to hang out."

Nora laughed.

Brad laughed.

She walked over and goosed him. "Is that a nuclear missile in your pocket or are you just happy to see me?"

Atrocious Mae West rendition.

Brad kissed her and touched her and switched off the penlight.

"Let's get your stuff out of there. I'm sure you're tired of mole life."

"I'm ready," she said. "But it was fun."

Brad sat on the rim of the entry. As he prepared to descend, Milo rushed him, threw a choke hold around his neck, yanked him back hard onto his back. Flipped him onto his belly just as quickly, did the arm twist and cuffed him.

Nora gave no struggle when I grabbed her and yanked her arms behind her.

Milo's knee bore down on the center of Brad's back. Brad gasped. "Can't breathe."

"If you can talk, you can breathe."

I felt Nora tense up, was ready when she tried to break free. Soft arms, not much muscle tone and her wrists were so small I could grip both with one hand. I used two anyway, pulled her hard enough to arch her torso.

"You're *hurting* me."

"Leave her alone," said Brad.

"Leave *him* alone," said Nora.

"Family togetherness," said Milo. "Touching."

"It's not what you think," said Nora. "He's not really my brother."

"What is he?"

She laughed. Not a pretty sound.

Brad said, "Wait until you hear from our lawyer."

"What's the beef?" said Milo. "Taxidermus interruptus?"

The two of them shut up.

CHAPTER
43

We marched them into the barn. Brad kept looking at Nora. She didn't look back.

Milo said, "Hold on to her, Alex," as he propelled Brad up the center path.

Choosing the '59 Caddy, he stashed Brad in the front passenger seat.

"Looky here, an after-market seat belt." The sash was drawn over Brad's abdomen. The skin on the back of his neck had gone as white as his hair. He looked like a piece of marble statuary.

Nora focused straight ahead. Her wrists felt soft, as if bones had begun to melt. She smelled of French perfume and cannabis.

Milo made sure Brad was secured, then closed the Caddy's door. As metal hit metal, I felt a shock of tension course from Nora's shoulder to her hip. She said nothing but her breathing quickened.

Then she lifted her right foot and tried to drive a spike heel into my instep.

As I danced away she began twisting and spitting. I probably hurt her maintaining control, because she cried out. Or maybe that was acting.

Milo strode over and took her. "Check the workbench and see if you can find suitable bindings for Ms. Funnel here."

Nora Dowd said, "Brad raped me, it was nonconsensual."

"That's redundant," said Milo.

"Huh?"

"Nonconsensual rape."

Confusion in the dope-ruddy eyes.

Milo said, "That's some art project hanging from the door."

Nora began sobbing tearlessly. "Dylan! I loved him *so* much, Brad got jealous and did that *horrible* thing! I tried to *stop* it, you've got to *believe* me!"

"How'd you try to stop it?"

"By reasoning with him."

"Intellectual debate?" said Milo. "The merits of organic kapok versus polyurethane foam?"

Nora wailed. "Oh, my *God*! This is *terrible*!"

Still dry-eyed. An onion would've helped. She sniffed. Looked up at Milo.

He said, "Your show's closing due to bad reviews."

In a workbench drawer, I found a roll of duct tape and two spools of heavy, white rope. Milo said, "Do it."

He had Nora's arms bent behind her back and she'd switched from crying to cursing. She swore louder as I bound her wrists, tried to head-butt Milo's arm. By the time he managed to drag her across the barn from the Caddy and get her in the passenger seat of a white '55 Thunderbird, she'd gone mute.

He said, "Fun, fun, fun, when Milo takes it away," and belted her in, too.

The two of us stood there. Panting. His face was sweaty and I felt moisture trickle down the side of my head. My ribs hurt. The back of my neck felt as if I'd encountered a blunt guillotine.

Milo used his phone.

The sirens began as distant moans, enlarged to nuclear trombone slides.

I was working hard at not thinking and the noise was sweet music.

Eight sheriff's squad cars, strobe-fest of blinking lights.

Milo had his badge out right away.

A slit-eyed, sunburned sergeant in body-conscious tans got out of the lead car.

"LAPD," said Milo.

"Keep your hands where I can see 'em."

Multiple weapons trained on us. We complied. The sergeant swaggered toward us with that mixture of fear and aggression cops display when they're faced with uncertainty. His mustache was orange and bristly, big enough to nest hummingbirds. *M. Pedersohn* on his tag. Tight neck muscles. A squint at the small print on Milo's shield didn't warm the atmosphere.

Freckled hands slapped on tan hips. "Okay . . . you came up here for what?"

"Job-related," said Milo. "Lemme show you—"

"The dispatcher said something about a body," said Pedersohn.

"That's partially accurate," said Milo.
"What?"

Milo motioned round the south side of the barn. Pedersohn stood in place, showing his men he couldn't be bossed around. Milo disappeared from view. Pedersohn went after him.

A peek inside the hatch turned the sergeant's sunburn to chalk.

"Jesus . . ." He grabbed his mustache, rubbed his teeth with the side of his index finger. "Is that . . ."

"It ain't plastic," said Milo.

"Jesus . . . oh, man . . . how long's it *been* there?"

"One question of many rearing their nasty little heads, Sarge. Have you called your lab guys?"

"Um . . . not yet . . ." Another look down. "Our downtown guys are obviously going to need to deal with this."

"Then you should call them, too."

Pedersohn yanked his radio off his belt. Stopped. Squinted. "Where are the suspects?"

"Pretending to be taking a road trip."

"What?" said Pedersohn.

Milo walked away from him again.

Pedersohn looked at me.

I said, "Multiple murder makes him cranky."

A deputy coroner named Al Morden who lived in the Palisades was called to the scene. He descended the stairs, looked at the head, refused to go farther until the shelter was declared safe.

Lots of who-me? looks from the deputies. Sergeant Mitchell Pedersohn said, "Our downtown guys should be here soon."

Milo said, "My offer vis-à-vis the lunch box stands, Alex."

Pedersohn said, *"What?"*

Milo climbed down in the hole.

He was back moments later. "Look, Ma, no booby traps."

"What's down there?" Pedersohn demanded.

"Three separate shelters linked by tunnels. Think of it as your basic paranoid triplex. One of them's got women's clothes and toiletries and a comfy bed, pictures of our suspects on the walls, kinda homey. The others aren't homey at all."

"I meant in terms of evidence."

"That's kinda complicated," Milo said, addressing Dr. Morden.

Morden's smile was grim. "My type of complicated?"

"Oh, yeah."

CHAPTER

44

Homicide Investigation Progress Report

DR#S 04-592 346-56

VICTIMS: BRAND, MICHAELA
                        ALLY
                        GAIDELAS, ANDREW
                        WILLIAM
                        GAIDELAS, CATHER-
                        INE ANTONIA
                        GIACOMO, VICTORIA
                        MARY
                        MESERVE, DYLAN
                        ROGER

PEATY, REYNOLD
MILLARD
WHITE FEMALE JANE
DOE #1
WHITE FEMALE JANE
DOE #2
WHITE FEMALE JANE
DOE #3
WHITE FEMALE JANE
DOE #4

LAS VEGAS,   DUTCHEY, JULIET
NV VICTIM   LEE

SECTION VIII: EVIDENCE
I. FROM STORAGE BUILDING OWNED BY BNB PROPERTIES, 942½ WEST WOODBURY ROAD, ALTADENA, CA, 91001:

1. 3 CARDBOARD CARTONS CONTAINING CLOTHING, SOME IDENTIFIED AS BELONGING TO VICTIMS BRAND, M, GAIDELAS, A, GAIDELAS, C, MESERVE, D, GIACOMO, V. VARIOUS FEMALE ATTIRE, IDENTIFICATION UNKNOWN.

2. 2 "MADE IN MEXICO" ONYX BOXES CONTAINING VARIOUS GOLD, SIL-

VER, AND COSTUME JEWELRY, 3 PRS. EYEGLASSES, 1 BELONGING TO VICTIM GIACOMO, V, 2 UNAT-TRIBUTED, 1 SET SOFT CONTACT LENSES BELONGING TO VICTIM BRAND, M, 1 PARTIAL DENTAL BRIDGE BELONGING TO VICTIM GAIDELAS, A.

3. 3 POLYETHYLENE GARBAGE BAGS CONTAINING 53 BLEACHED HUMAN BONES, IDENTIFICATION IN PRO-GRESS PER THE CORONER'S OF-FICE. (REF: PROFESSOR JESSICA SAMPLE, FORENSIC ANTHROPOLO-GIST.)

4. 1 CARDBOARD CARTON MARKED SEARS-KENMORE CONTAINING 10 JUMBO ZIPLOC SANDWICH BAGS EACH CONTAINING A CLUMP OF HU-MAN HAIR BOUND BY TWO RUBBER BANDS. (REF: PROF. J. SAMPLE.)

II. FROM TRUNK OF 1989 LINCOLN TOWN CAR VIN 33893566, REGIS-TERED TO BRADLEY MILLARD DOWD, GARAGED BEHIND STORAGE BUILD-ING AT 942½ WEST WOODBURY ROAD:

1. 1 SONY DIGITAL CAMERA MODEL DSC 588.

2. 1 EXCISED SECTION OF BLACK CAR-PETING FROM LTC.

3. FRONT AND REAR BLACK LEATHER SEATS FROM LTC.

III. FROM TRIPLEX SUBTERRANEAN BOMB SHELTERS, 43885 LATIGO CANYON ROAD, MALIBU, CA, 90265:

FROM UNIT "A" (NORTHERNMOST, SEE DIAGRAM):

1. CLOTHING, COSMETICS, PERSONAL EFFECTS BELONGING TO SUSPECT DOWD, N.

2. COLLAPSIBLE TWIN BED AND BED-DING.

3. PHOTOGRAPHS OF SUSPECTS DOWD, B, AND DOWD, N.

4. 5 TEETH BELONGING TO VICTIM MESERVE, D. PIERCED AND STRUNG ON A SILVER CHAIN.

5. 1 TAXIDERMICALLY PRESERVED HU-MAN HEAD BELONGING TO VICTIM MESERVE, D.

6. 2 SIMILAR PRESERVATIONS, VIC-
TIMS GAIDELAS, A, GAIDELAS, C.

7. 1 COMPACT DISK CONTAINING
DIGITAL PHOTOGRAPHIC IMAGES,
MARKED "PARTY-TIME" CONTAIN-
ING PORNOGRAPHIC IMAGES OF:

A. SUSPECT DOWD, B, HAVING SEX-
UAL INTERCOURSE WITH V'S
BRAND, M, GIACOMO, V, GAIDE-
LAS, C, GAIDELAS, A, JANE DOES
1, 2, 3, 4. LAS VEGAS VICTIM,
DUTCHEY, J.

B. SUSPECT DOWD, B, HAVING
SEXUAL INTERCOURSE WITH
SUSPECT DOWD, N.

C. SUSPECT DOWD, N, HAVING
SEXUAL INTERCOURSE WITH
VICTIM MESERVE, D.

D. SUSPECT DOWD, B, HAVING SEX-
UAL INTERCOURSE WITH VICTIM
MESERVE, D.

8. 4 DIGITAL VIDEO DISKS CONTAINING
MOTION PICTURES, CONTENT SIMI-
LAR TO 3.

FROM UNITS "B" AND "C":
1. 2 250 MB COMPUTER ZIP DISKS

MARKED "PT CLIMAX," CONTENTS
SCRAMBLED, POSSIBLY DAMAGED.
(REF: LAPD TECHNICAL DIVISION,
SGT. S. FUJIKAWA.)

2. 1 IBM CLONE PERSONAL COM-
PUTER, 1 APC BATTERY BACKUP, 1
MICROTEK 19" MONITOR, 1 HEWLETT-
PACKARD LASERJET 4050 PRIN-
TER.

3. 1 42" SONY FLAT-SCREEN TELEVI-
SION.

4. 1 BRASS COAT HOOK.

5. 1 213 SQ. FT. EXCISED SECTION,
BEIGE NYLON CARPETING. 1 215.5
SQ. FT. EXCISED SECTION, BEIGE
NYLON CARPETING.

6. 12 BOXES OF DISASSEMBLED
ACOUSTICAL CEILING TILES.

7. 2 SETS SMITH & WESSON DOUBLE
LOCK POLICE-ISSUE HANDCUFFS
AND KEYS.

8. 1 SET ANTIQUE "E.D. BEAN" LEG
IRON RESTRAINTS, C. 1885. (REF:
PROFESSOR ANDRE WASHINGTON,
HISTORIAN.)

9. 3 WOODEN BOXES CONTAINING VARIOUS SURGICAL KNIVES, NEEDLES, SAWS, SCRAPERS, SHEARS, CANNULAS, FUNNELS.

10. 1 "TI-DEE" HEAVY-DUTY SUCTION PUMP, MODEL A-334C.

11. 1 KINGSLEY SECRETION ASPIRATOR, MODEL CSI-PG005.

12. 4 SPOOLS MEDIBOND NYLON MONOFILAMENT SURGICAL SUTURE MATERIAL, TWO 20 MM, TWO 24 MM.

13. 2 UNMARKED CARDBOARD CARTONS CONTAINING SEALED CLEAR PLASTIC BAGS OF COTTON STUFFING.

14. 4 PLASTIC GALLON CONTAINERS, HYDROGEN PEROXIDE.

15. 1 BOX "PLEASURE-RIB" LATEX CONDOMS.

16. 1 5-GAL. PLASTIC CONTAINER, FORMIC ACID PICKLING SOLUTION.

17. 5 SETS "SNUG-FIT" LATEX GLOVES.

18. 1 EPOXY "TAXI-FORM SCULPTING KIT."

19. 1 QUART BOTTLE EATON SKIN DE-
GREASER AND PRESERVATIVE.

20. 1 5-LB. BAG "READI-TAN" DRY
PRESERVATIVE.

21. 1 OAKES G-235C "MINOR SURGICAL
PROCEDURE" TABLE WITH HEAD-
REST AND DETACHABLE DRAIN . . .

Milo returned to his office and took the
murder book from me.

"I wasn't finished."

He dropped the file in a drawer.
"Michaela's Honda finally showed up.
Parking garage of a BNB building in Sierra
Madre, towed to the motor lab as we
speak."

"Congratulations. As I was saying—"

"How's my prose?"

"Eloquent," I said. "Please don't tell me
you want to have lunch."

"It's way past lunchtime, have your people call my people and we'll do dinner."

He sank down hard enough to make the
desk chair groan. "Enough with the glib macho posturing. I'm thrashed and not
ashamed to admit it."

"Get any sleep?"

"Around five hours," he said. "Over five days."

"Time for a break," I said.

"It ain't the workload that's keeping me up, boy-o, it's the reality. As long as you've perused, care to add any insights?"

"The PlayHouse was a talent pool in a much worse way than we imagined. For Nora, it served double duty. She got to feel omnipotent and she and Brad both enjoyed selecting victims."

"Cold bitch," he said. "Arrogant, too. That time we came to her house, she didn't even pretend to care about Tori or Michaela."

"I'm not sure she's capable of pretending."

"No acting chops? How'd she get so many people to believe in her?"

"By attracting a hungry crowd who thought they were getting a bargain. Emotionally needy people will swallow poisoned Kool-Aid."

He sighed. "All those pretty folk auditioning, having no idea what the part really was."

"Any luck identifying the other girls?"

"Not yet. No other male bodies show up yet, but I'm not counting on this being the

end of it. There's still a dozen BNB properties we haven't looked at and the backhoes
have only dug up a corner of the property.
How do you see the hoax figuring in?"

"Theater of the cruel. Nora and Brad
hatched it up for fun, convinced Dylan
Meserve he was a coconspirator. But he
was a human chess piece."

"Think he knew what was in store for
Michaela?"

"Have you found any indication that he
was aware of the other victims?"

"Not so far," he said. "But the way he had
Michaela pretend to choke him, that coulda
been foreshadowing her fate, right?"

"Or he had his own kinks," I said. "We'll
probably never find out unless some kind of
diary shows up. Or Brad or Nora start talking."

"So far, they're both dummying up," he
said. "I got Brad on suicide watch, like you
suggested. Jail guard said Brad thought
that was funny."

"Maintaining the facade," I said. "Once it
crumbles, he'll have nothing left."

"You're the shrink . . . back to the hoax.
Nora wink-winks at Meserve, pretends to be

outraged and kicks Michaela out of class. Why?"

"My bet's still on setting Michaela up for Brad's 'rescue.' She was broke, unemployed, hungry for attention, frustrated career-wise. If Brad just happened to drive by in one of his shiny cars and struck up a conversation, it could've seemed like providence. She already knew his face from the PlayHouse so there wouldn't be any stranger anxiety. And Brad's connection to Nora would've made Michaela eager to hook up with him."

"Trying to get back in Nora's good graces."

"Or he might've told her he had his own connections, could help her career. Same for Tori. Same for all of them."

"Seduction instead of abduction," he said. "Nice dinner, good wine, come up and enjoy the sunset at my Malibu place. Wonder how Michaela felt when she saw he was taking her back to Latigo Canyon."

"If he'd built up trust by wining and dining her, it could've kept her anxiety in check. Or he took her somewhere else first and restrained her."

"If he's got another chamber of horrors, it hasn't turned up yet. One thing's for sure:

Nothing went on at his house or Nora's. Not a speck of nasty at either."

I said, "Why sully the home front when you've got a special place set aside for your hobbies. These people are all about splitting."

"Speaking of hobbies, any theory about why Meserve and the Gaidelases were the only specimens they preserved?"

"The neck wound says they thought of preserving Michaela," I said. "Went so far as to insert a cannula in her neck then changed their minds. No way to get inside their heads, but the Gaidelases and Meserve fit some kind of fantasy. If I could finish the file—"

"There's nothing in there about the past, Alex. Just more ugly. I'm stuck with this, but you're not. Go home and forget about all of it."

I said, "Any luck decoding the scrambled disk?"

He ran his tongue over cracked, dry lips, scratched his scalp, rubbed his face. He'd shaved carelessly and a patch of white fur ran along his jaw. His eyes were hooded and weary. "You've developed a hearing problem?"

I repeated the question.

"You never let go," he said.

"That's why you pay me the big bucks."

"The disk is decoded and loaded in Room Four. I've been watching it for the last hour. Hence, my sage advice about going home."

"No sense postponing the inevitable," I said.

"What's inevitable?"

"I was at the scene when you found the shelter. Someone's going to subpoena me. Either the D.A. or Stavros Menas."

"Both Dowds *tried* to hire Menas but Nora got him and she wasn't feeling sisterly. Brad's looking for new representation."

"Money talks and she's got the mike."

"Minus the millions Brad skimmed," he said. "Most of which seems to have gone into the car collection and a little island he bought off the coast of Belize two months ago. And one more luxury purchase, three weeks ago: jet card for a Gulfstream V, twenty-five hours. That's three hundred fifty grand for a plane with international range. Wanna take bets on there being an offshore bank account somewhere south of the equator? The estate lawyers who appointed him trustee are gobbling Prilosec and the new court-appointed lawyers are licking their chops. We're talking years of litigation, there goes the rest of the estate."

I said, "Planning his escape, those brochures were for real. Then he got clever and planted them in Nora's nightstand."

"Too clever," he said. "Sitting in that Range Rover, using Billy's land. Dutiful caretaker of his sibs, meanwhile he's screwing them, literally and financially. Think he was planning to take Nora with him or go it alone?"

"Unless she knew about the island I'd say alone. Is anyone protecting Billy's interests?"

"The court-appointed lawyers claim to be."

"I finally got permission to see him yesterday, drove out to Riverside."

"How's the place they put him in?"

"Grim," I said. "Assisted care facility, a hundred Alzheimer's patients and Billy."

"Learn anything?"

"He's in shock and disoriented. I got about three minutes before the attorney-on-premises ended it."

"Why?"

"Billy started crying."

"Because of you?"

"That was learned counsel's opinion," I said. "Mine was that Billy has lots to cry about and not letting him express it will only make matters worse. I told learned counsel Billy needs a full-time therapist, I wasn't volunteering for the job, only suggesting he find someone. He begged to differ. When I got back, I phoned the judge who wrote the placement order. Haven't heard from her yet but I'm thinking of other judges who might be willing to help."

"You see Billy as totally clean?" he said.

"Unless you find something more ominous at his duplex than *Star Wars* action figures and Disney videos."

He shook his head. "Like a kid's place. Boxes of sugar cereal, bottles of chocolate milk."

I said. "Being a kid's hard enough. Being neither boy nor man is something else. Any sign of Billy's allowance money?"

"Nope, just coins in a piggy bank. Some of the pennies date back to the sixties."

"Fifteen hundred a month and all he spent on was pizza and Thai food and rental movies. It explains Reynold Peaty's drop-ins. He pretended to be Billy's friend, had his way with the cash."

"Makes sense," he said. "Except no money showed up in Peaty's dive."

"A guy like Peaty would have ways to spend it," I said. "Or, if his relationship with Brad went beyond janitor and boss, maybe the money found its way back to Cuz. Then Cuz set him up to die."

He frowned. A muscle just below his left eye jumped.

I said, "What?"

"What a family." He found a stale cigar in a drawer, rolled it, and bit off the end. Spat it into his wastebasket.

"Two points." I stood and walked to the door. "Time to view the disk."

He stayed put. "It's really a bad idea, Alex."

"I want to get it over with."

"Even if someone does subpoena you, it could be months away," he said.

"No sense harboring fantasies all that time."

"Trust me, your fantasies can't be worse than reality."

"Trust *me*," I said. "They can."

CHAPTER

45

Cold, yellow room.

The interview table had been pushed to one side. Metal table, same battleship gray as the bomb shelter.

The things you notice.

Two chairs faced a thirty-inch plasma TV on a wheeled table. A DVD player sat on the bottom shelf. Lots of snarled cables. A sticker affixed to the bottom of the monitor warned against anyone outside the D.A.'s office touching the equipment.

I said, "Suddenly the prosecutors turn generous?"

"They've sniffed the air," said Milo.

"Smelled Court TV, screenplays, book deals. The warning from on-high is no O.J. on this one." He drew a remote control module from his jacket pocket and flicked on the monitor.

Sat down next to me, slumped and closed his eyes and stayed that way.

Blue screen, video menu printout. Time, date, D.A's evidence code.

I took the remote from Milo's hands. His eyes remained shut but his breathing quickened.

I flicked.

A face filled the screen.

Big blue eyes, tan skin, symmetrical features, shaggy blond hair.

Jane Doe Number One.

Milo had asked if I wanted to start out of sequence with Michaela. I'd considered that, said let's do it in order.

Hoping lack of personal contact would help.

It didn't.

The camera stayed close.

An off-screen voice, male, smooth, amiable, said, "Okay, audition time. Digging it so far?"

Zoom shot of the girl's smile. Moist, white teeth, perfectly aligned. "Sure am."

"Sure am, *Brad*. When you're presenting yourself to a casting agent or anyone else, it's important to be direct and specific and *personal*."

The girl's smile altered course, became an ambiguous crescent. "Um, okay." The camera moved back. Nervous blue eyes. Giggle.

"Take two," said Brad Dowd.

"Huh?"

"Sure am . . ."

"Sure, Brad."

"Sure. Am. Brad."

The girl's eyes shifted to the left. "Sure. Am. Brad."

"Perfect. Okay, go on."

"With what?"

"Say something."

"Like what?"

"Improvise."

"Umm . . ." Lip-lick. A glance back at battleship-gray walls. "It's kind of different. Down here."

"Dig it?"

"Umm . . . I guess."

"I. Guess . . ."

"I guess, Brad."

"It *is* different," said Brad Dowd. "Hermetic. Know what that means?"

Giggle. "Umm, not really."

"It means isolated and quiet. Away from all the hassle. The Sturm und Drang."

No response from the girl.

"Know why we're auditioning you in a hermetic place?"

"Nora said it was serene."

"Serene," said Brad. "Sure, that's a good word. Like one of those meditation things, ohmmmm, Shakti, bodhi vandana, cabalabaloo. Ever do any meditation?"

"I did Pilates."

"I. Did. Pilates . . ."

"Brad."

Off-screen sigh. "A hermetic place means less distraction. Right?"

"Right—Brad."

"A hermetic, serene place strips away superfluous elements so it's easier to find your center. Not like back in class where everyone's looking and judging. No one will judge you here. Never."

The girl smiled again.

"What do you think of that?" said Brad.

"It's good."

"It's good?"

"It's real good."

"Brad!"

Blue eyes jumped. "Brad."

"It's. Good—"

"It'sgoodBrad. I'm sorry I'm kinda nervous."

"Now, you *interrupted* me."

"Sorry. Brad."

Ten-second silence. The girl fidgeted.

Brad Dowd said, "Totally forgiven."

"Thanks. Brad."

Ten more seconds. The girl worked at relaxing her posture.

"Okay, we're serene and hermetic and ready to do some serious work. Do you like Sondheim?"

"Um, don't know him—Brad."

"Doesn't matter, we're not going musical, this is a drama day. Lower your left shoulder strap—make sure it's the left one because that's your good side, your right side's a little weak. Be sure not to take off your whole top, this isn't porno, we just need to see your undraped posture à la classical sculpture."

The camera pulled back, showed the girl sitting primly on a folding chair, wearing a skimpy red top held in place by spaghetti straps. Bare, tan, slender legs, advertised by a short, denim skirt. Sandaled feet planted on the ground. High-heeled brown sandals.

"Go ahead," said Brad.

Looking confused, she reached up and loosened the right strap.

"Left!"

"Sorry, sorry, always had trouble with— sorry, Brad, always had trouble . . ." She switched to the left, fumbled, lowered.

The camera moved in on smooth, golden shoulder. Drew back to a full-body view.

Fifteen seconds passed.

"You've got a beautiful torso."

"Thanks, Brad."

"Know what a torso is?"

"The body—Brad."

"The upper body. Yours is classical. You're very lucky."

"Thanks, Brad."

"Think you've also got talent?"

"Umm, I hope so—*Brad.*"

"Oh, c'mon, let's hear some insouciance,

some confidence, some superstar can-do *attitude*."

Blue eyes batted. The girl sat up straight, tossed her hair. Pumped a fist and shouted. "I'm the best! Brad!"

"Up for anything?"

"Sure. Brad."

"Well, that's good."

Five seconds. Then: clang clang. Thud thud thud thud thud.

Noise from behind made the girl turn.

"Don't move," barked Brad.

The girl froze.

"Here's your costar."

"I—umm—oh—didn't know there was going to be—"

"A star's got to be up for anything."

The girl's head began to swivel again. Froze, once more, responding to a command that never came.

"Good," soothed Brad. "You're learning."

The girl licked her lips and smiled.

The gray behind her turned flesh-colored.

Hirsute expanse of chest and belly. Tattooed arms.

The camera trailed lower to a bearish clump of pubic hair. A limp penis dangled inches from the girl's cheek.

The girl's shoulders stiffened.

"I—uh—"

"Relax," said Brad Dowd. "Remember what Nora taught you about improv."

"But—sure. Brad."

"Remain perfectly still—think body control . . . *that's* a good girl."

The hairy bulk pulsated. Tattoos jumped.

The camera panned up to a sweat-glossed dinner-plate face. Frizzy mutton-chops. Clipped mustache.

Reynold Peaty's hands lowered onto the girl's shoulders. His right thumb slipped under the right spaghetti strap. Toyed with the string. Slid it off.

The girl jumped and twisted, craned to see him. His left hand gripped the top of her head and held her in place.

"He's hurting—"

"Mouth shut!" said Brad Dowd. "Don't want to catch flies."

Peaty's right hand reached around and clamped over the girl's mouth.

She made frantic little muffled noises. Peaty's hand slapped her so hard, her eyes rolled back. With one hand, Peaty pulled her up by her hair. The other edged closer to her throat.

"Yeah," he said.

"Perfect," said Brad. "This is Reynold. The two of you are going to improvise a little skit."

I flicked off the picture.

Milo was wide awake, looking sadder than I'd ever seen him.

I said, "You told me so," and walked out of the room.

CHAPTER

46

The next week was emotional bouilla-baisse.

Trying, with no success, to get Billy Dowd more appropriate lodgings and regular therapy.

Fending off Erica Weiss's requests for another deposition, so she could "slam the final nail in Hauser's coffin."

Ignoring increasingly strident calls from Hauser's defense attorney.

I hadn't been to the station since viewing the DVD. Six minutes watching a girl I'd never met.

The day I moved Robin in, I pretended my

head was clear. After I schlepped the last carton of her clothes into the bedroom, she sat me down on the edge of the mattress, rubbed my temples, and kissed the back of my neck. "Still thinking about it, huh?"

"Using unfamiliar muscles. The ribs don't help."

"Don't waste energy trying to convince me," she said. "This time I know what I'm getting myself into."

My contact with Milo was limited to one eleven p.m. phone call. His voice, thick with fatigue, wondering if I could take care of some "ancillary stuff" while he coped with the mountain of evidence on what the papers were calling the "Bomb Shelter Murders."

One nitwit columnist in the *Times* trying to connect it to "Cold War paranoia."

I said, "Sure. What's ancillary stuff?"

"Anything you can do better than me."

That came down to being a grief sponge.

A forty-five-minute session with Lou and Arlene Giacomo lasted two hours. He'd lost weight since I'd seen him and his eyes were dead. She was a quiet, dignified woman, hunched over like someone twice her age.

I sat there as his rage alternated with her anguished accounts of Life With Tori, the two of them trading off with a rhythm so precise it could've been scripted. As the time ground on, their chairs edged farther and farther apart. Arlene was talking about Tori's confirmation dress when Lou shot to his feet, snarling, and left my office. She started to apologize, changed her mind. We found him down by the pond, feeding the fish. They left silently and neither answered my calls that night. The clerk at their hotel said they'd checked out.

The widowed mother of Brad Dowd's Las Vegas victim, Juliet Dutchey, turned out to be a former showgirl herself, a veteran of the old Flamingo Hotel. Mid-fifties and still toned, Andrea Dutchey blamed herself for not discouraging her daughter from moving to Vegas, then switched to squeezing my hand and thanking me for all I'd done. I felt I'd done nothing and her gratitude made me sad.

Dr. Susan Palmer came in with her husband, Dr. Barry Palmer, a tall, quiet, well-coiffed man who wanted to be anywhere else. She started off all business, crumpled fast. He kept his mouth shut and studied the prints on my wall.

Michaela Brand's mother was too ill to travel from Arizona so I spoke with her over the phone. Her air machine hissed in the background and if she cried, I didn't hear it. Maybe tears required too much oxygen. I stayed on the line until she hung up without warning.

No relative of Dylan Meserve surfaced.

I phoned Robin at her studio and said, "I'm finished, you can come back."

"I wasn't escaping," she said. "Just doing my job."

"Busy?"

"Pretty much."

"Come home anyway."

Silence. "Sure."

I called Albert Beamish.

He said, "I've been reading about it. Apparently, I can still be shocked."

"It's shocking stuff."

"They were spoiled and indolent but I had no idea they were fiends."

"Beyond persimmons," I said.

"Good God, yes! Alex—may I call you that—"

"Sure. *Mister* Beamish."

He chortled. "First off, thanks for inform-ing me, that was uncharacteristically cour-teous. Especially coming from a member of the me-generation."

"You're welcome. I think."

He cleared his throat. "Second, do you golf?"

"No, sir."

"Why not?"

"Never got into it."

"Damn shame. At least you drink . . . per-haps one day, should you have time . . ."

"If you bring out the good stuff."

"I only stock the good stuff, young man. What do you *take* me for?"

Two weeks after his arrest, Brad Dowd was found dead in his cell. The noose he'd used to hang himself had been fashioned from a pair of pajama pants he'd ripped into strips after lights-out. He'd been on suicide watch, housed in the High Power ward where things like that weren't supposed to happen. The guards had been diverted by a neighboring inmate pretending to go crazy and smearing his cell with feces. That prisoner, a gang leader and murder suspect named Theofolis Moomah, underwent a miraculous recovery the moment Brad's body was cut down. A search of Moomah's cell uncovered a stash of extra commissary cigarettes and a roll of fifty-dollar bills. Brad's attorney, a downtown court regular who'd defended several gang leaders, express-mailed his bill to the arraignment judge.

Stavros Menas, Esq. called a press conference and bellowed that the suicide supported his claim that Brad had been a "mad Svengali," and his client an unwitting dupe.

The D.A. offered a contradictory analysis.

Get ready for a circus the animal-rights people wouldn't mind.

I vowed to forget about all of it, figured the whydunit would stop eating at me eventually.

When it didn't, I got on the computer.

CHAPTER

47

The woman said, "I still can't believe you tracked me down that way."

Her name was Elise Van Syoc and she was a Realtor working out of the Coldwell Banker Encino office. It had taken a long time but I'd found her using her maiden name, Ryan, and a decades-old nickname.

Ginger.

Groovy bass player for the Kolor Krew!

Her identity and a print of the photo I'd seen at the PlayHouse finally surfaced courtesy www.noshotwonders.com, a cruelly mocking compendium of failed pop bands flung by the gargantuan slingshot that was the Internet.

When I called her, she said, "I'm not getting involved in any court stuff."

"It's not about court stuff."

"What, then?"

"Curiosity," I said. "Professional and personal. At this point, I'm not sure I can separate the two."

"That sounds complicated."

"It's a complicated situation."

"You're not writing a book or doing a movie?"

"Absolutely not."

"A psychologist . . . whose therapist are you, exactly?"

I tried to explain my role.

She cut me off. "Where do you live?"

"Beverly Glen."

"Own or rent?"

"Own."

"Did you buy in a long time ago?"

"Years ago."

"Have any equity?"

"Total equity."

"Good for *you,* Dr. Delaware. A person in your situation might find it a good time to trade up. Ever think about the Valley? You could get a much bigger place with more land *and* some cash back. If you're open-minded about the other side of the hill."

"I pride myself on being open-minded," I said. "I'm also big on remembering people who've extended themselves for me."

"Some negotiator—you absolutely promise I won't end up in court?"

"Swear on my trust deed."

She laughed.

I said, "Do you still play bass?"

"Oh, please." More laughter. "I got asked to join because I had red hair. She thought it was some kind of omen—the Kolor Krew, get it?"

"Amelia Dowd."

"Crazy Mrs. D . . . this is sure taking me back. I don't know what you think I can tell you."

"Anything you remember about the family would help."

"For your psychological insights?"

"For my peace of mind."

"I don't understand."

"It's a horrendous case. I'm pretty close to haunted."

"Hmm," she said. "I guess I can sum it up in one sentence: They were nuts."

"Could we discuss it, anyway?" I said. "Time and place of your choosing."

"Would you seriously consider a trade-up?"

"I hadn't thought about it, but—"

"Good time to start thinking. Okay, I need lunch anyway, what the heck. Meet me at Lucretia on Ventura near Balboa, hour and a half, I need you to be prompt. Maybe I can show you life on the other side of the hill can be tasty."

The restaurant was big, pale, airy, nearly empty.

I arrived on time. Elise Van Syoc was already there, bantering with a young male waiter as she nursed a cosmopolitan and chewed on a single Brazil nut. "Ginger" was no longer a redhead. Her coif was puffy, collar-length, ash-blond. Tailored black pantsuit, tailored face, wide amber eyes. A deal-closing smile accompanied a firm, dry handshake.

"You're younger than you sound, Dr. Delaware."

"You, too."

"How sweet."

I sat down and thanked her for her time.

She glanced at a diamond Movado. "Did Brad and Nora really do what everyone's saying?"

I nodded.

"How about some juicy tidbits?"

"You don't want to know."

"But I do."

"You really don't," I said.

"What, it's disgusting?"

"That's an understatement."

"Yuck." She sipped her cosmopolitan. "Tell me anyway."

I parceled out a few details.

Elise Van Syoc said, "How'd you get all that equity working with the police? It can't pay very well."

"I've done other things."

"Such as?"

"Investments, private practice, consults."

"Very interesting . . . you don't write?"

"Just reports, why?"

"It sounds like a good book . . . I'm afraid this isn't going to be lunch, just a drink. I've got an escrow to close, huge place south of the boulevard. And there's really nothing I can tell you about the Dowds other than they were all weirdos."

"That's a good place to start."

The waiter came over, lean, dark, hungry-eyed. I asked for a Grolsch and he said, "For sure."

When he brought the beer, Elise Van Syoc clinked her glass against mine. "Are you in a relationship? I'm asking in terms of your space needs."

"I am."

She grinned. "Do you cheat?"

I laughed.

She said, "Nothing ventured," and finished the last bit of Brazil nut.

I said, "The Kolor Krew—"

"The Kolor Krew was a joke."

"How'd you get involved?" I said. "The other three members were sibs."

"Like I told you over the phone, I was recruited by Crazy Mrs. D."

"Because of your hair color."

"That and she thought I had talent. I was in the same class as Nora at Essex Academy. My dad was a surgeon and we lived on June Street. Back then I thought I liked music. Took violin lessons, switched to the cello, then I conned my dad into getting me an electric guitar. I sang like a goose on downers, wrote ridiculous songs. But try telling me, I thought I was Grace Slick. Brad and Nora *really* killed all those people?"

"Every one of them."

"Why?"

"That's what I'm trying to figure out."

"It's so bizarre," she said. "Knowing someone who did that. Maybe *I* should write a book."

Something new in her eyes. Now I understood why she'd agreed to meet with me.

"I've heard it's tough," I said.

"Writing?" She laughed. "I wouldn't do it myself, I'd hire someone, put my name on it. There are some big best sellers who do that."

"Guess so."

"You don't approve."

I said, "So Amelia Dowd thought you had talent—"

"Maybe I *shouldn't* give you my story."

"I have no interest in writing it up. In fact, if you do write a book, you can quote me."

"Promise?"

"Swear."

She laughed.

I said, "Amelia Dowd—"

"She heard me play cello in the Essex Academy orchestra and thought I was some kind of Casals, which tells you about *her* ear. Immediately, she calls my mother, they knew each other from school affairs, teas at the Wilshire Country Club, acquaintances more than friends. Amelia tells Mother she's putting together a band—a wholesome family thing, like the Partridge Family, the Cowsills, the Carpenters. My hair makes me perfect, I obviously have a gift, and bass is just another form of cello, right?"

"Your mother bought that?"

"My mother's a conservative DAR lady but she's always loved anything to do with showbiz. The 'secret' she tells everyone once she knows them long enough is that she dreamed of becoming an actress, looked exactly like Grace Kelly, but nice girls from San Marino didn't do that even if nice girls from the Philadelphia Main Line did. She was always on me to join drama club but I refused. Ripe for Mrs. D's picking. Plus, Mrs. D made it sound like a done deal—big record contract pending, interviews, TV appearances."

"Did you believe it?"

"I thought it sounded idiotic. And lame. The *Cowsills*? My taste was Big Brother and the Holding Company. I went along with it on the off chance something would happen and I'd be able to miss school."

"Did the Dowd kids have any musical experience?"

"Brad played a little guitar. Nothing fancy, a few chords. Billy held a guitar like a spaz, Amelia was always adjusting it. If he could carry a tune, I never heard it. Nora could but she couldn't harmonize and she was always bored and spaced out. She'd never shown interest in anything other than drama club and clothes."

"Fashion plate," I said.

"Not really, she always dressed wrong. Way too fancy. Even at Essex things had gotten casual."

"Was joining drama club her idea or her mother's?"

"Hers, I always thought. She always pushed for the big parts, never got them because she couldn't memorize lines very well. A lot of people thought she was semi-retarded. Everyone *knew* Billy was, I guess the assumption was it was hereditary."

"What about Brad?"

"Smarter than those two. Anyone would be."

"How'd he adjust socially?"

"Girls liked him," she said. "He was cute. But he wasn't what I'd call popular. Maybe because he wasn't around much."

"Why not?"

"One year he'd be there, the next year he'd be gone—at some out-of-state school—because of trouble he'd gotten into. But Mrs. D sure wanted him around the year she tried to start the band."

"How far did you guys get?" I said.

"Halfway to nowhere. When I showed up at their house for the first rehearsal and saw what utter bullshit it was going to be, I went home and told Mother, 'Forget it.' She said, 'We Ryans don't have quitting in our blood,' and notified me that if I wanted my own car I'd better buckle down."

She slapped one palm against the table, then the other, sounded a slow, ponderous four-four beat. "That was Nora's idea of playing drums. Billy was supposed to play rhythm guitar and he'd managed to learn two screechy chords—C and G, I think. But it sounded like a pig being strangled." She screwed up her lips. "As if that wasn't bad enough, we tried to sing. Pathetic. That didn't stop Crazy Amelia."

"From what?"

"Dragging us to have promo pictures taken. She found a discount photographer on Highland near Sunset, some old fart who slurred his words and had forty-year-old black-and-whites of people you've never heard of taped to the walls of his studio." She wrinkled her nose. "The place smelled like cat pee. The *costumes* smelled like an old-age home. I'm talking boxes of stuff, all jumbled together. We had to pose as Indians, pilgrims, hippies, you name it. Everyone in a different color. 'Varied garb and hue,' as Mrs. D phrased it, was going to be our 'signature.' "

"It worked for the Village People."

"So where are *they*? Once the photos were done, it was agent-time, one blow-dried sleaze after another. Amelia flirted with every one of them. I'm talking hip rub, deep cleavage flash, calculated eyelash flutter, the works. She had this blond bombshell thing going on, played it to the hilt."

"That doesn't sound like someone a conservative DAR lady would trust," I said.

"Funny about that, isn't it? I guess showbiz trumps everything. You ask people in this city if they'd give up a vital organ for a walk-on in a movie, I guarantee you most would ask where's the scalpel. Half the people in *my* business have had some connection to the industry. Come over to the office and you'll see faces you vaguely recognize but can't place. I'm talking the girl who served coffee to the banker lady on *The Beverly Hillbillies* during the second act of one episode. She's still got that SAG card in her purse, works it into every conversation. The smart ones learn that even if they make it, it lasts as long as warm milk. The others are like Amelia Dowd."

"Living in fantasyland."

"Twenty-four seven. Anyway, that's the history of the Kolor Krew."

"The project never got anywhere."

"We must've done two dozen auditions. None lasted longer than fifteen seconds because the moment the agents heard us sing they winced. *We* knew we were horrendous. But Amelia would be standing there, snapping her fingers, beaming. When I got home I'd light up a doobie, call my friends, get all hysterical-giggly."

"How'd the Dowd kids handle it?"

"Billy was an obedient robot, might as well have come with wheels. Nora spaced out, just like always, did the whole Mona

Lisa thing. Brad was always hiding a smirk. He's the one who finally spoke up. Not disrespectfully, more like, 'C'mon, we're not getting anywhere.' Amelia ignored him. I mean, literally, just pretended he wasn't there and went on talking. Which was a switch."

"In what way?"

"Generally she paid *plenty* of attention to Brad."

"Abusive?"

"Not exactly."

"Special attention?"

Elise Van Syoc tried to impale a lime wedge on her stirrer. "This could be the important part of my book."

"She seduced him?"

"Or maybe it was the other way around. I can't even say for sure something happened. But the way those two related wasn't exactly mother-son. I never noticed until I started spending all that time with them. It took a while to notice Mrs. D being odder than usual."

"What'd she do?"

"She was no great shakes as a mom. With Billy and Nora she was distant. But with Brad—maybe she figured, technically, because Brad was an adopted cousin and not her son . . . still, he was fourteen and she was a grown woman."

"Hip rubs and cleavage?" I said.

"Some of that but usually it was more subtle. Private smiles, little looks that she'd sneak in when she thought no one was watching. Occasionally I'd catch her brushing his arm and he'd touch her back. Nora and Billy didn't seem to notice. I wondered if I was imagining it, felt like an alien dropped on Planet Strange."

"How did Brad react?"

"Sometimes he'd pretend not to be aware of what she was doing. Other times he'd clearly be liking it. There was definitely some kind of chemistry going on. How far it went, I don't know. I never told anyone, not even my friends. Who thought in those terms, back then?"

"But you were grossed out."

"I was," she said, "but when Amelia's own kids didn't seem bothered I started to wonder if I was seeing things." Small smile. "Being fortified by puffs of an illegal herb fed my doubts."

"Amelia was seductive," I said, "but she sent Brad out of state."

"Several times. Maybe she wanted him out of the picture so she could deal with her own impulses? Would you call that a psychological insight?"

"Sure would."

She smiled. "Maybe I should be an analyst."

"How many times is 'several'?"

"I'd say three, four."

"Because he'd gotten into trouble."

"Those were the rumors."

"Did the rumors get specific?" I said.

"Your basic juvenile deliquency," she said. "Do they use that term anymore?"

"I do. What're we talking about, theft, truancy?"

"All that." She frowned. "Also, some people in the neighborhood had pets that went missing and there was talk Brad was involved."

"Why?"

"I honestly don't know, that's just what was said. That's important, isn't it? Cruelty to animals is related to being a serial killer, right?"

"It's a risk factor," I said. "When was the last time Brad was sent away?"

"After Amelia gave up on the band. Not right after, maybe a month, five weeks."

"What convinced her to quit?"

"Who knows? One day she just called up Mother and announced that there was no future for popular music. As if *she'd* made the choice. What a loon."

"And soon after that, Brad was gone."

"Guess she no longer needed him . . . now that we're talking about it, I realize how bad it must've been for him. Used and discarded. If he was bothered, he didn't show it. Just the opposite, he was always calm, nothing got to him. That's not normal, either, is it? Would you be my psychological consultant?"

"Get a contract and we'll talk. What about Captain Dowd?"

"What about him?"

"Was he involved in the band?"

"He wasn't involved in anything I ever saw. Which wasn't that different from most fathers in the neighborhood. But they were gone because of work. Captain Dowd lived off inheritance, never held down a job."

"How'd he spend his time?"

"Golf, tennis, collecting cars and wine and whatever. Lots of vacations abroad. Or, as my mother called them, 'grand tours.' "

"Where?"

"Europe, I guess."

"Did he travel with his wife?"

"Sometimes," she said, "but mostly it was by himself. That was the official story."

"Unofficially?"

She played with her glass. "Let's put it this way: once I overheard Father joking to a golf buddy about how the captain had joined the navy to be close to boys in tight blue uniforms."

"He traveled with young men?"

"More like traveled to *find* young men."

"The rumor mill," I said.

"Keeps the grass green," she said.

"Captain Dowd being gay was public knowledge?"

"If my father knew, everyone did. He seemed like a nice enough man—the captain. But not much of a presence. Maybe that's why Amelia flirted with everyone."

"Including Brad," I said.

"I guess they were all crazy," she said. "Does that explain what happened?"

"It's a start."

"That's not much of an answer."

"I'm still figuring out the questions."

Amber eyes hardened and I thought

she'd come back with a sharp retort. Instead, she stood and smoothed the front of her trousers. "Gotta run."

I thanked her again for her time.

She said, "I know you were snowing me about keeping an open mind, but I'd like to call you if a hot property comes up. Something really worth your while, it's a terrific time in the market for someone in your position. How about a phone number?"

I gave her a card, paid for the drinks, and walked her to her silver Mercedes roadster.

She got in, started up the car, lowered the top. "I'll probably never do a book, hate writing. Maybe a cable movie."

"Good luck."

"It's strange," she said, "after you called, I tried to make sense of it—looking back for something that could've predicted it."

"Come up with anything?"

"This is probably irrelevant—I'm sure I'm reading all kinds of crazy things into insignificant stuff. But if what they're saying about what happened to those people is true . . . the gory details, I mean . . ."

"They're true."

She drew a compact from her purse, checked her face in the mirror, tamped her hair, put on a pair of sunglasses. "Mrs. D had this routine she'd go through. When we goofed off during rehearsal, which was often, and she lost her patience but was trying not to show it because she wanted to be one of the gang. Like Mama Cowsill or Shirley Jones."

"Cool mom," I said.

"As if that's ever possible . . . anyway, what she'd do is start clapping her hands to quiet us down, then she'd make like she was the Red Queen—from *Alice in Wonderland.* The first few times she announced it. 'I am the Red Queen and I will be obeyed!' Eventually we caught on. Whenever she clapped it was going to be a Red Queen routine. Which consisted of her spouting lines like 'I'm five times richer and cleverer than you,' or 'What use is a child with no meaning?' I took it for just another of her eccentricities, but maybe . . ."

She went silent.

"Maybe what?"

"This will probably sound literal to you. After spouting all this Lewis Carroll stuff, she'd scrunch up her eyebrows and cackle and raise a finger in the air and start waving it around. Like she was testing the wind. If we *still* weren't paying attention—which we usually weren't—she'd let out this honking noise, could've been a man's it was so deep. Then she'd make goofy eyes and shake her chest like a stripper gone berserk. She was big up there, it was ridiculous."

Running her hands over her own narrow torso.

"Finally, if we still weren't toeing the line, then she'd lower her hand like this, and run it across her throat and place both hands on her hips and scream, 'Off with your heads!' It was silly but creepy, I hated when she did it. Nora and Billy didn't seem to care."

"And Brad?"

"That's the thing," she said. "Brad used to smile. One of those private smiles. Like it was a private joke between him and Amelia. You know about his hobby, right? He was really into it back then. Had all kinds of knives, used to carry knives around. I never saw him hurt anyone and he was never threatening. At least not to me. So it proba- bly means nothing—Amelia with her hand over her throat."

I said nothing.

Elise Van Syoc said, *"Right?"*

CHAPTER

48

I drove over the hill thinking about what family had meant to the Dowd kids.

Boundaries were to be blurred, people were to be used, performance was all.

Brad had been abandoned, taken in reluctantly, exploited, expelled. Brought back to be pressed into service by a woman who resented him and lusted for him.

Years later, after her death, he'd wormed his way back into the family and attained the power role. Knowing he'd never belonged, never would.

By that time, he'd murdered Juliet

Dutchey. Maybe other women yet to be discovered.

Reserving his boyhood hobby for three victims.

Back when Milo and I had been theorizing, he'd wondered out loud about Cathy and Andy Gaidelas being parental symbols.

You guys still believe in the Oedipal thing?

More than I did a few weeks ago.

Why Meserve?

The only time I'd seen Brad express overt anger was when he talked about Meserve.

Young, slick manipulator.

Brad seeing himself two decades younger?

Despite the smooth manner, the clothes, the cars—the image—did it all boil down to self-hatred?

A body hanging in a jail cell said maybe.

Used and discarded . . . it didn't explain the extent of the horror. It never does. I wondered why I kept trying.

I reached Mulholland, coasted down past dream houses and other encumbrances, unable to let go.

Brad had been the ultimate actor. Protecting Billy and Nora, bedding her, stealing from both of them.

Pressing his own cousin into murderous service, then setting him up to be executed.

Coming on to another cousin—a female cop—at the same time he was being investigated by her colleagues in a showgirl's disappearance.

Why not? Why would blood ties mean anything to him?

Marcia Peaty had no problem seeing Brad as evil but she was certain Cousin Reynold had just been a penny-ante loser.

Ex-cop, but way off. She'd be dealing with that for a long time. If she were my patient, I'd work at getting her to see she was human, nothing less, nothing more.

When you got down to it, rules and exceptions were hard to separate.

Church deacons sneak into dark houses and strangle families. Diplomats and CEOs and other respectable types embark on sex tours of Thailand.

Anyone can be fooled.

But for arrogance, Brad and Nora might've plied their hobby for years.

How long would it have taken before he

looted the trust fund completely and decided Nora was no longer useful?

The jet card and the island off Belize said not long.

Did Nora—numbed, callous, perpetually stoned—have any idea her life had been saved?

What kind of life lay ahead for her? Initial severe depression, for sure, once the reality of prison life set in. If she was deep enough to suffer. If she coped and set up a prison theater, things could get rosier. Casting, directing. Experiencing. A few years down the line, she might even merit one of those rehab-miracle puff-pieces in the *Times.*

Or maybe I had too much faith in the system and Nora would never see the inside of a penitentiary cell.

Back on McCadden Place, walking her stuffed dog.

Stavros Menas was wasting no opportunity to shout that she was just another of Brad's victims.

Milo and I had heard her joking about Meserve's head but both of us could be made to look foolish on the stand and L.A. juries distrusted cops and shrinks. The disks showed her having consensual sex with Brad and Meserve but nothing more. No forensic evidence tied her directly to the killings and nowadays juries expected nifty science.

Menas would rack up billable hours trying to get everything ruled inadmissible. Maybe he'd put Nora on the stand and she'd finally get a starring role.

One way or the other, he'd earn his million.

The lawyers vying for stewardship of Billy Dowd's diminished life would also do fine.

Still no callback from the judge who'd warehoused Billy and sentenced him to eating soft food with plastic utensils.

The time I'd visited, he'd called me his friend, put his his head on my shoulder, and wet my shirt with his tears.

What use is a child with no meaning?

Amelia Dowd had no idea what crop she'd cultivated.

I wondered what Captain William Dowd Junior had known as he'd ambled abroad on grand tours.

Both of them perishing in a car crash. Big Cadillac veering off the road and over a cliff on Route 1, on the way to the Pebble Beach auto show.

No suspicion it hadn't been an accident.

But Brad had been in town the week they'd set out and Brad knew cars. Milo had raised that with the D.A. The prosecutors agreed it was interesting theoretically but the evidence was long gone, Brad was dead, time to concentrate on building a case against a living defendant.

Time for me to . . . ?

Robin's truck was parked in front of the house. I expected to find her in a back room, drawing or reading or napping. She was waiting for me in the living room, sitting on the big couch with her legs tucked under her. A sleeveless, sky-colored dress set off her hair. Her eyes were clear and her feet were bare.

"Learn anything?" she said.

"That maybe I should've taken up accounting."

She got up, took me by the hand, led me toward the kitchen.

"Sorry, not hungry," I said.

"I wouldn't expect you to be." We continued into the service porch.

A plastic pet crate sat in front of the washer-dryer. Not Spike's crate, she'd junked that. Not in the spot Spike's crate had occupied. Off slightly to the left.

Robin kneeled, unlatched the grate, drew out a wrinkly fawn-colored thing.

Flat face, rabbit ears, moist black nose. Huge brown eyes met Robin's, then aimed at me.

"You can name her," she said.

"Her?"

"I figure you deserved that. No more macho competition. She's from a championship line with great disposition."

She rubbed the puppy's belly, handed her over.

Warm as toast, almost small enough to fit in one hand. I tickled a fuzzy, blunt chin. A pink tongue shot out and the puppy craned the way bulldogs do. One of the rabbit ears flopped over.

"It'll take a couple of weeks before they stay up," said Robin.

Spike had been a lead-boned package of muscle and grit. This one was buttery-soft.

"How old?" I said.

"Ten weeks."

"Runt of the litter?"

"The breeder promises she'll fill in."

The puppy began licking my fingers. I brought her closer to my face and she tongue-bathed my chin. She smelled of dog shampoo and that innate perfume that helps puppies get nurtured.

I scratched her chin again. She jutted her mandible in response. Licked my fingers some more, made a throaty sound closer to feline than canine.

"Love at first sight," said Robin. She petted the puppy but the puppy pressed closer to me.

Robin laughed. "I'm really in for it."

"That so?" I asked the puppy. "Or is it just infatuation?"

The puppy stared at me, followed every syllable with those huge brown eyes.

Lowering her head, she nuzzled my cheek, purred some more, butted until her knobby little cranium was buried under my chin. Squirming, she finally found a position she liked.

Closed her eyes, fell asleep. Snored softly.

"Mellow," I said.

"We could use a bit of that, don't you think?"

"We could," I said. "Thanks."

"Sure," she said, tousling my hair. "Now, who's getting up tonight for housebreaking?"

ABOUT THE AUTHOR

Jonathan Kellerman is one of the world's most popular authors. He has brought his expertise as a clinical psychologist to two dozen bestselling crime novels, including the Alex Delaware series, *The Butcher's Theater, Billy Straight, The Conspiracy Club,* and *Twisted.* With his wife, the novelist Faye Kellerman, he co-authored the bestseller *Double Homicide.* He is the author of numerous essays, short stories, scientific articles, two children's books, and three volumes of psychology, including *Savage Spawn: Reflections on Violent Children.* He has won the Goldwyn, Edgar, and Anthony awards, and has been nominated for a Shamus Award. Jonathan and Faye Kellerman live in California and New Mexico. Their four children include the novelist Jesse Kellerman. Visit the author's website at www.jonathankellerman.com.

Books by Jonathan Kellerman

FICTION

ALEX DELAWARE NOVELS

Gone (2006)
Rage (2005)
Therapy (2004)
A Cold Heart (2003)
The Murder Book (2002)
Flesh and Blood (2001)
Dr. Death (2000)
Monster (1999)
Survival of the Fittest (1997)
The Clinic (1997)
The Web (1996)
Self-Defense (1995)
Bad Love (1994)
Devil's Waltz (1993)
Private Eyes (1992)
Time Bomb (1990)
Silent Partner (1989)
Over the Edge (1987)
Blood Test (1986)
When the Bough Breaks (1985)

OTHER NOVELS

Twisted (2004)
Double Homicide (with Faye Kellerman, 2004)
The Conspiracy Club (2003)
Billy Straight (1998)
The Butcher's Theater (1988)

NONFICTION

Savage Spawn: Reflections on Violent Children (1999)
Helping the Fearful Child (1981)
Psychological Aspects of Childhood Cancer (1980)

FOR CHILDREN, WRITTEN AND ILLUSTRATED

Jonathan Kellerman's ABC of Weird Creatures (1995)
Daddy, Daddy, Can You Touch the Sky? (1994)